In the privacy of the bedroom,
she turned to him. . .

Drew removed her hat, its once saucy plume askew. Next he removed the pins from her hair until it swirled around her face and spilled down her shoulders in a glorious mass. With an urgency underlying their deliberate movements, they undressed each other. Naked, they came together. Late afternoon sunlight filled the room with diffused light that added to the dreamlike quality of their lovemaking . . .

Fortune's Captive

Elizabeth Turner

DIAMOND BOOKS, NEW YORK

FORTUNE'S CAPTIVE

A Diamond Book / published by arrangement with
the author

PRINTING HISTORY
Diamond edition / April 1991

ISBN: 1-55773-487-9

Diamond Books are published by The Berkley Publishing
Group, 200 Madison Avenue, New York, New York 10016.
The name "DIAMOND" and its logo are trademarks
belonging to Charter Communications, Inc.

PRINTED IN THE UNITED STATES OF AMERICA

10 9 8 7 6 5 4 3 2 1

To my family because I love you.
To my friends for sharing and caring—
I love you, too.

Fortune's Captive

CHAPTER 1

June 1887

THE CONVENT GATE CLANGED SHUT WITH THE FINALITY OF a closing prison door. Juliana Butterfield stared at Sister Esther's retreating back through wrought-iron pickets of the seven-foot fence that enclosed Queen of Angels Convent School for Girls. She continued watching until the nun disappeared through a side door; then, squaring her shoulders, she turned and resolutely trudged down the dusty road that led into Philadelphia and the train depot. Behind her a bell pealed, the sound clear and sweet in the quiet June evening, summoning the nuns to evening worship. To Juliana, it was a poignant reminder of a way of life she had been forced to leave—in disgrace.

Her steps faltered, then resumed.

It wasn't fair, Juliana told herself miserably. Mother Superior never even gave her a chance to explain. How could the nun believe her guilty of such disgustingly wanton behavior? Things would have been different if Mother Margaret Ann were still alive. . . . It just wasn't fair.

* * *

What more could possibly go wrong? Juliana wondered late the following afternoon as she sank wearily onto a bench in New York's Central Park. Was it only yesterday that she had been a novice contemplating final vows? Yesterday. It seemed years away.

The insistent gurgling of her stomach disrupted her thoughts. Juliana pressed her hand against her midsection to smother the unladylike rumble. She darted her gaze left and right, afraid someone had heard. A nursemaid wheeled a baby carriage while a tot with blond ringlets trotted alongside. A couple strolled by, the young man obviously flirting while the girl twirled a pink parasol and acted coy. No one spared Juliana a passing glance.

She leaned back and pretended interest in a ball game a group of boys were playing nearby. But her problems refused to be easily diverted. She had been optimistic— overly so, it would seem—when her train had pulled into the railway terminal in the early morning hours. She had convinced herself that it would be a simple matter to find a position and lodgings. After all, she was well educated, reasonably intelligent, and not averse to hard work. Surely someone would be willing to overlook her lack of references.

"Hey, lady, watch out!" a boy yelled.

Juliana ducked just as a baseball whizzed past her ear. The close call forced her thoughts back to the present, and she glanced around with renewed interest. The pathways suddenly seemed congested with people, and the atmosphere was charged with expectancy.

"What's going on?" she asked the youth who came to fetch the ball.

"Big rally down at the bandstand."

"What kind of rally?"

"Why, a suffragette rally, miss. Heard Susan B. herself is going to speak." The boy ran off to rejoin his friends.

Juliana rose to her feet, picked up the worn carpetbag containing her only possessions, and trailed after the crowd. Even the good sisters at Queen of Angels had heard of Miss Susan B. Anthony and her crusade to gain women the right to vote. Having been brought up in a convent society governed by women, Juliana found it difficult to comprehend a world where women were regarded as inferior citizens with few privileges. Setting her immediate problems aside, she joined the onlookers gathered around a white-latticed structure shaded by lofty elms.

A tall, spare woman with wire-rimmed spectacles and gray hair coiled into a bun, was trying to make herself heard above a group of hecklers. "I assure you, ladies, we will never be free from men's tyranny until women are allowed to cast their ballots. Then and only then will we truly govern our destinies." Susan Anthony's voice rang with conviction.

"You loony old spinster!" a florid-faced man shouted. "What would you know about a man's tyranny?"

Ribald laughter greeted his remark. Juliana noted that although Miss Anthony's mouth compressed into a thin line she maintained her composure.

"We must unite and raise our voices until they are heard throughout the land. Our outcry will echo from the Atlantic to the Pacific," the aged suffragette declared. "Eighteen years ago, the territory of Wyoming granted women the privilege of voting. Let Wyoming serve as a shining example for the rest of the nation."

"And where will it end?" a man jeered. "Read there's even talk in Wyoming of women serving on juries!"

His remark stirred up a flurry of controversy among the men who, Juliana noticed with a sinking sensation, now far outnumbered the women. She was somewhat relieved to observe a handful of uniformed police among the audience. As though sensing trouble, the more timid of the women edged toward the fringes of the group. Juliana took advantage of their departure and pressed forward until she stood near the front of the bandstand.

"Ladies," Susan Anthony beseeched her dwindling audience, "I call upon each and every one of you to make your demands known. We are not totally without influence. We are not without power—"

"First thing you women'd do is close the bars."

"And build a church on every corner," another shouted.

"You're nothing but a bunch of bullies," a sweet-faced, elderly woman next to Juliana scolded. "Let Miss Anthony speak."

"You oughta be home knittin' booties fer yer grandkids," the man retorted.

Juliana's eyes widened in disbelief as she watched him rudely jostle the woman aside, causing her to totter and nearly lose her balance.

"And you, sir, someone ought to take a hickory stick to your backside!" Juliana fired at him while grasping the woman's arm to steady her.

The heckler's attention shifted, and Juliana felt herself subjected to his blatantly lusty regard. The man's dark eyes fastened on her shapeless cotton frock as if trying to discern the form beneath. "You gonna be the one to try, girlie?" He leered, displaying large tobacco-stained teeth.

Before Juliana could frame a reply, the elderly woman came to her defense. "Mind your manners, you rabble-rouser." She brandished her parasol.

The man grinned broadly before he spat a stream of tobacco juice out of the side of his mouth. The spittle landed on

Juliana's dress. Appalled, she stared at the offensive liquid trickling down the side of her skirt. Then, coming to her senses, she dug into a pocket for a handkerchief and scrubbed at the stain.

"Send 'em back to their kitchens where they belong!" someone hollered.

Others picked up the chant.

Juliana shot a hopeful glance over her shoulder, expecting to see policemen removing the troublemakers. Instead, they stood to one side and idly watched the scene. Turning toward the bandstand once again, she saw Miss Anthony engaged in a whispered conversation with two associates. At that precise moment a tomato sailed over Juliana's head, narrowly missing Miss Anthony.

The act heralded a full-scale riot. Garbage rained through the air. Juliana gaped as a bunch of wilted radishes landed on the woman next to her, looking like an obscene corsage against the white of her dress. Juliana dodged a grapefruit hurled in her direction and nearly slipped on a banana peel. To her right, a woman screeched in outrage as a plum smacked her forehead and burst, its juice dripping down her nose. It was time to flee. Juliana tried to push her way out of the crowd, but she was hemmed in by a shoving swarm of humanity.

Though she had managed to avoid the first barrage of refuse, she was pelted by the second. An overripe tomato splattered against her shoulder. Seeds and pulp soaked the bodice of her dress. A rotten egg struck a post of the bandstand and spewed its vile-smelling contents over everyone close by, Juliana included. Frantically, she looked for a way to escape this mayhem.

A kaleidoscope of frenetic activity revolved around her. Suddenly blue uniforms were everywhere. Policemen no longer hugged the sidelines but were in the thick of the fray, blowing shrill blasts on their whistles, yelling, and swinging clubs. There was no place to which the women could retreat.

Juliana's arm was caught in a bruising grasp, causing her to drop her valise. When she tried to tug free, the grip tightened painfully.

She had had enough. All her convent teachings, admonitions to turn the other cheek, vanished in that brief instant, overcome by the primal instinct for self-defense. Balling her free hand into a fist, she swung her arm in a wide arc. Her unaimed punch landed a solid blow that was immediately followed by a loud whoosh of air. Her arm was released; she had won her freedom. When she half turned, her eyes widened in dismay. A policeman was doubled over, groaning and clutching the lower portion of his torso.

"I'm terribly sorry—" Her apology was cut short. Juliana was seized on either side by a pair of burly men in blue.

"Got 'er, Delaney. She'll pay dearly for this."

The grim expressions beneath the visored helmets were anything but reassuring. Juliana swallowed the lump of fear lodged in her throat and licked lips that felt parched. "I never—"

"Save yer story fer the judge," the heftier one snarled.

In numb horror, Juliana watched the second officer remove a pair of handcuffs from his belt and snap them around her wrists. "Takin' no chances on havin' you slip away before you get yer day in court."

Amid clanging bells and the clatter of horses, precinct reinforcements arrived in paddy wagons to quell the rebellion. Juliana was unceremoniously escorted to one of the empty vans, hurled inside, and sent sprawling on the floor. The door, its small window heavily fortified by steel bars, closed behind her. The bolt slid home.

Juliana, holding panic at bay, blinked to adjust her eyesight to the gloom, then slowly picked herself up from the floor. Two wooden benches were suspended along the sides of the narrow enclosure. Not trusting her knees to support her, she sank down on one and scooted along its length until she huddled in a far corner. The door opened again and the Black Maria filled with women passengers.

"Please, sir," a young woman begged tearfully. "I've babies at home who need me."

"Shoulda thought of that sooner."

"What are we being charged with?"

"That's up to the judge. Could be disturbing the peace, might be inciting a riot. Ain't up to me."

After being subjected to a long, uncomfortable ride downtown, a calm but subdued group of prisoners were unloaded from the paddy wagon at the Ludlow Street jail, herded through a back entrance, then led up three steep flights of stairs and down a long corridor lined with cells. Women inmates shuffled to their barred doors to view the newcomers.

Juliana found herself staring back. Some of the women reminded her of bedraggled exotic birds with garishly painted faces and brightly colored gowns. She couldn't help but wonder about what type of work they engaged in.

The women from the suffrage rally were pushed into cells in groups of two and three until only Juliana and the elderly woman who had been shoved during the melee remained. Juliana was painfully aware that she was the only one handcuffed, but wise enough to acknowledge that she was probably the only one who had struck a police officer.

"Your new home, ladies," a buxom prison matron with a pockmarked face announced. Her key grated in the lock of an end cell; its door creaked open. The elderly lady entered hesitantly. The matron placed her hand between Juliana's shoulder blades, urged her inside, and after pulling the door closed, locked it securely.

The woman interceded in Juliana's behalf. "Can't you take those beastly handcuffs off the girl?"

"Ain't my job, Granny. Goldilocks here must be a pretty dangerous character. Whatcha do, girlie, hit a copper?"

Juliana paled. "I-I didn't mean to. I didn't strike the policeman intentionally. Someone was pulling my arm. I merely tried to defend myself."

"Strikin' an officer of the law could get ya sent to Blackwells Island. Better say yer prayers, girlie, that Judge Spears ain't feelin' indisposed when he hears yer case." Laughing, the matron turned and ambled off.

"What's Blackwells Island?" Juliana couldn't control the tremor in her voice.

"Don't mind what she said, dear. That creature was only trying to frighten you."

"What is it?" Juliana repeated, her voice firmer.

The older woman sighed. "It's an island in the East River. There's a prison there reserved for the most incorrigible criminals. It's been likened to Newgate in London. But surely you have friends or family who will come to your aid."

A sad smile curved Juliana's mouth. "I've neither. I just arrived in New York this morning and don't know a soul."

Compassion crossed her companion's wrinkled features. "Perhaps the judge will take that into account and only levy a small fine."

"Then I'll surely be shipped to Blackwells Island, for I haven't a cent to my name." Juliana's shoulders slumped with defeat. Even the carpetbag containing her meager personal belongings had disappeared during the fracas. She realized with a gnawing sensation in the pit of her stomach that she was completely without resources.

"Since we're forced to share these quarters for the time being, let me introduce myself. I'm Emma Lattimer." She offered a gloved hand.

The pair awkwardly shook hands. "I'm pleased to meet you, Mrs. Lattimer. I'm Juliana Butterfield."

"It's Miss Lattimer, dear, but this isn't the time for formalities. Call me Emma." She patted Juliana's shoulder. "Don't fret; it'll make lines on your pretty face. I'll speak to my brother and ask him to use his influence on your behalf. He has friends in high places."

Juliana managed a weak smile at her benefactress. "Thank you, Miss Lattimer . . . er, Emma. That's very kind of you."

Emma dismissed Juliana's gratitude with a wave of her hand. "Bertie will be absolutely livid to hear I've been arrested again."

"Again?"

"Suffrage is not a popular cause, Juliana. This isn't the first time the police have been summoned to disperse our rallies. It wasn't accidental that we were brought to the Ludlow Street jail instead of one much closer to Central Park. The authorities will do anything to make our ordeal as unpleasant and as difficult as possible in order to discourage us. They are trying to break our spirit, but they will not succeed. We will continue to fight until the war is won."

Police, jails, wars, riots. The world outside the convent walls was a violent place, Juliana thought dismally as she inspected her surroundings. The cell was small, not more than five by eight, its cement walls smelling of dampness, mold, and human despair. Late afternoon sunlight slanted into the cell from a single window set high in the wall. The stench from a slop jar, half full from previous occupants, pervaded the tight confines.

Emma pressed a hand to her chest. "Oh, dear, I'm afraid I'm going to have one of my attacks."

Juliana's attention quickly returned to her cell mate. The woman's round face had lost its rosy hue and had become alarmingly pale. "Come lie down and rest." Juliana guided her new friend toward one of the narrow cots and pressed her to the straw mattress.

"Please don't look so worried, Juliana. I'm subject to palpitations."

Juliana wasn't convinced. "Perhaps a glass of water will help," she said, spotting a pitcher in one corner. She quickly crossed the cell and, the manacles on her wrists making her movements clumsy, picked up the pitcher before noticing the water's surface was covered with a scummy film. A wave of nausea washed over her.

"Never fear, I'll be fine." Emma Lattimer's protest was feeble as she lay with her eyes shut, a bluish tinge to her lips.

Juliana ran to the cell door. "Matron!" she called.

There was no response.

"Matron!" she tried again. "My friend is ill and needs a doctor!"

"You fibbin' or tellin' the truth, honey?" a harsh voice asked from the neighboring cell.

"I swear I'm telling the truth. I think it's her heart."

"All right, girls," the disembodied female voice instructed. "Let's show these newcomers how we get the matron's attention."

The prisoners sent up such a clamor of strident voices and tin cups clanking against iron bars that the disturbance reverberated through the thick walls.

"Quiet! Keep it down or you'll have no supper tonight."
The matron stormed down the corridor with jingling keys
and swishing skirts. Two male officers followed in her
wake, billy clubs drawn, ready to lend assistance. "What's
the fuss about?"

"Matron, here, quick," Juliana called, her hands wrapped
around the bars, her body straining forward. "Miss Lattimer
needs a doctor."

The matron stood outside the cell, hands on her ample
hips, and squinted toward the figure on the cot. Satisfied that the elderly lady was indeed ill, she unlocked
the door. "Stand aside, Goldilocks." She shook a wood
cudgel at Juliana. The policemen hoisted Emma Lattimer
and, shouldering their way past Juliana, carried her out of
the cell.

Before the prison door closed, Emma managed to give
Juliana a wan smile. "Thank you, dear. I won't forget your
kindness."

Juliana sank down on the cot, drew both legs up and, circling them with her bound wrists, rested her forehead against
her knees. All concept of time vanished. Lengthening shadows crept across the floor. Never had she felt so utterably
alone . . . or so close to despair. Would anyone believe she
hadn't deliberately struck the policeman, that she had lashed
out only in self-defense? As minutes stretched into hours,
her anxiety increased. What was to become of her? There
was no one to care. No one at all.

Steeped in misery, Juliana failed to hear the matron
approach. "Get a move on, Goldilocks," the woman announced. "Judge Spears don't like to be kept waitin'."

Juliana's head snapped up. "What is he going to do with
me?" The tremor in her voice betrayed her nervousness.
Slowly she got to her feet, her muscles stiff and cramped.

"Do I look like a goddam Gypsy?" The matron unlocked the door and entered the cell. "Keep yer mouth shut and step lively if you know what's good fer you."

With the woman's impatient shove, the toe of Juliana's shoe caught in the hem of her dress. She tripped, her arms flying up in an automatic attempt to regain her balance. But with her wrists handcuffed she was unable to right herself in time. She fell to the cold cement floor. Her outstretched arms took the brunt of the fall, and her tender palms were abraded by the harsh contact, the steel restraints biting into her wrists and drawing blood. Juliana felt tears sting her eyelids and determinedly blinked them back.

"Now look whatcha done," the matron accused as she hauled Juliana to her feet. Juliana followed the woman's gaze to the four-inch tear where the skirt of her dress had separated from its bodice. "Ain't you a sight? I use better fer cleanin' rags than that dress yer wearin'."

Juliana's glance reflected her dismay as she realized the woman's statement wasn't exaggerated. She was, quite simply, a fright. Her dress, an item from the good sisters' used clothing bin, had been laundered repeatedly to the unbecoming shade of dirty dishwater. In addition to its assorted rips, the garment was stained with refuse thrown at her during the riot, and it reeked unpleasantly.

"Please, could you give me some wash water and allow me to make myself presentable?" Juliana ventured hopefully.

"Ain't you hoity-toity. Where you think yer goin', girl, the Met? Jest make sure you stand downwind of the judge." The matron chuckled at her own wit. Taking Juliana's arm, she escorted her from the cell and, once again, down the long corridor.

Juliana's departure was observed by the women inmates

of the Ludlow Street jail. Fascinated against her will, Juliana stared back. The gaslight lent a jaundiced look to the faces peeking through the iron grilles. Blowsy faces. Thin faces. Pathetic faces. Some reflected bravado, others despondency. But the ones that frightened Juliana the most were those that mirrored a calm acceptance of their fate. How could anyone be reconciled to life in a cage? That wasn't living: it was merely existing. To Juliana, being locked away in a place without sunshine, a place without hope, would be sentencing her spirit to death.

Juliana was led through twisting hallways and down winding flights of stairs until the matron motioned her toward a dingy, windowless room where a uniformed policeman stood guard. After appraising Juliana, he winked at the matron. "So here's the culprit who laid Delaney a low blow."

The matron gave him a sly look. "To hear Delaney tell it, Goldilocks here almost ended his days as a Bowery Romeo."

"Almost worth it to end his braggin'." The policeman opened the door and waved the women inside. "You won't have long to wait. Judge Spears is anxious to get home. Heard he ain't happy these fool women are up to their shenanigans again. Beats me why they can't be content mindin' their menfolk."

No sooner had Juliana sat down on a hard straight-backed chair when her name was called.

Half of her hairpins had been lost during the course of the riot. Her spinsterish bun had come loose of its moorings, and her hair straggled untidily down her back. She stood and smoothed back a dark gold strand. Painfully aware of her disheveled state, Juliana took a tentative step into the courtroom.

The room was impressive, with dark wood paneling and

a high judge's bench flanked by an oversize American flag. Just as imposing was a tall, broad-shouldered man who was deep in discussion with the black-robed judge. This man was dressed in black as well with his coat cut away from a trim waist to fall into tails at the back, a brocade waistcoat, and an intricately pleated white shirt with a bow tie. As though feeling her gaze, he turned.

Arrogance was plainly stamped across austerely handsome features. Arrogance—and power. The man's thickly lashed eyes were the same blue-gray as a winter's sky with an identical coldness. His chilling gaze swept over her, assessing and cataloging, then dismissing.

Resentment bubbled inside Juliana. He hadn't so much looked at her as he had looked through her, making her feel small and insignificant. She drew herself up to her full five feet five inches and glared back. Her effort went unnoticed. The stranger had already resumed his conversation with the judge.

"The prisoner will approach the bench," the bailiff instructed.

The matron nudged the small of Juliana's back. With her heart thumping so loudly against her ribs that she feared everyone would hear, Juliana stepped before the judge.

Judge Spears, a balding, heavy set man with side-whiskers and a mustache peered down at her. "For the court records, please state your name."

Juliana started to speak, but no sound came out. She cleared her throat and tried again. "Juliana Butterfield, sir."

"In the future, address me as Your Honor," he corrected sternly. "You are entitled to benefit of counsel. Since it is my understanding you are of limited means, Mr. Andrew MacAllister has graciously consented to represent you. Is that agreeable?"

Juliana's gaze slid to the infuriating stranger next to her. She saw him pull a gold watch from the pocket of his waistcoat, frown, then replace the timepiece. For a fleeting moment, Juliana was tempted to refuse the man's help, but practicality asserted itself. This was not the time for rash acts. "Yes, Your Honor," she answered through gritted teeth. "It's agreeable."

The judge picked up a sheaf of papers and began to read. "The charges against you are inciting a riot, disturbing the peace, and striking an officer of the law. How do you plead?"

Her mouth suddenly parched, Juliana swallowed.

"My client pleads not guilty."

"Very well, Mr. MacAllister. A date will be set for a hearing. Your client will need to post bond."

Andrew MacAllister nodded and was beginning to turn away when Juliana spoke. "Your Honor, I have no money with which to post a bond."

"In that case, the cost of bond will be subtracted from your earnings." He stacked the papers in a neat pile and picked up a pen.

"Your Honor, I haven't yet found employment." Her words stayed the judge's hand as he was about to dip his pen in the ink pot.

"In that case, you will be released on personal recognizance. Just give the bailiff your permanent address."

Juliana dropped her gaze to the floor, her fingers nervously pleating the folds of her dress. "I don't have a permanent address, Your Honor."

"Do you have a temporary address, Miss Butterfield?" Judge Spear's scowl grew darker. "Or do you plan to sleep in Central Park?"

"Surely there must be kin who are willing to assume

responsibility for the girl," Andrew MacAllister interceded.

The judge pounced on the idea. "I find that suggestion acceptable. Kindly notify the bailiff of your nearest kin, Miss Butterfield, and be sure you appear for your hearing, or the law will not look favorably on you." For the second time, he reached toward the inkwell.

"I have no relatives, Your Honor," Juliana informed him in a dwindling voice. "Or friends either, for that matter. I just arrived in New York this morning." Beside her, she heard her court-appointed attorney heave a sigh of exasperation.

"Then I have no choice but to return you to jail until your hearing." The stalemate broken, he banged his gavel. "Bailiff, return the prisoner to her cell."

Juliana felt a rush of anxiety, making her chest tighten until it was difficult to breathe. For a fraction of a second, a distant childhood merged with the present. She envisioned herself bereft and abandoned behind a barred gate. The prospect of once again being locked away and forgotten filled her with blind terror. Reaching out, she clutched the sleeve of Andrew MacAllister's impeccably tailored evening jacket. "Please," she gasped. Under the fine black cloth, she felt the muscles in his arm tense. "Please help me."

Drew bent his dark head and stared at the ugly manacles circling the girl's fragile wrists, the delicate skin lacerated and blood-smeared. Slowly he raised his gaze to hers and met eyes the hue of shimmering gold. "I'll accept full responsibility for my client," he said at long last.

The gavel sounded again. "Let it be noted, the prisoner is remanded into the custody of her attorney, Andrew MacAllister."

CHAPTER 2

DREW MACALLISTER WAITED IMPATIENTLY ON THE CURB outside the Ludlow Street jail with his client in tow. Tugging on the gold chain swagged across his waistcoat, he pulled out his pocket watch and frowned at the Roman numerals. Gwendolyn would be furious; Arthur Gardner, her father, would be livid. "Damn," he muttered, slipping the watch back into his pocket.

When Arthur had discovered Drew was planning to escort his daughter to tonight's concert, he had graciously asked Drew to share his private box. Drew's friend and mentor, Daniel Tennant, had been elated by the invitation. "Gwendolyn's from one of the best families. Heed my advice, Andrew," Daniel had counseled. "Propose to the girl. If you hope to win an assembly seat in next year's election, a wife will prove a valuable asset. Voters don't hold much trust in a man who's unattached. They favor those who are settled down—family men."

It was a long-standing dispute between them. While Drew recognized the wisdom of his friend's advice, he balked at the notion of marriage for the sake of a political career. Such meetings always ended on a note of bitter discord.

Narrowing his eyes, Drew peered through the twilight.

What was keeping Jack Burrows? Drew had specifically instructed his driver to meet him outside Ludlow
Street jail after delivering flowers and a note of apology to
Gwendolyn. Still no sign of Jack. Drew shoved his hands
in his pockets.

A brisk breeze whipped down the narrow street. It curled
around a crumpled newspaper resting in the gutter, sending
it pinwheeling across the cobblestones. The wind caught a
honey-colored strand of the girl's hair and whipped it across
her cheek. Drew watched her absently raise a hand and tuck
the errant lock behind her ear. Another gust of wind promptly caught it again and teased it free. She made no further
attempt to subdue the wayward tress. As though too tired to
care, she hugged her arms tight to her body and shivered.

Drew felt an unexpected stab of pity. Memories flooded
back. He recalled growing up in the slums of Glasgow,
remembered how it felt to be hungry and dirty and cold.
But unlike Juliana Butterfield, he hadn't been alone and
friendless. Governed by impulse, Drew draped his satin-
lined evening cape over her shoulders.

For a moment Juliana stared at him wide-eyed, then
started to remove the cape. "It's much too fine. It'll get
soiled."

"Nonsense," he said brusquely. "You're chilled."

She hesitated, uncertainty etched on her delicate features.
"How very kind of you, Mr. MacAllister."

"My pleasure, Miss Butterfield." Drew studied the client
foisted on him. Lord, but she was a mess. Her bun was
askew and loose strands of hair straggled down her back.
The pungent scent of overripe produce exuded from her torn
dress, causing Drew to wrinkle his nose in disgust. Though
she looked like a ragamuffin, her diction was precise, her

voice clear and pleasing to listen to, and in variance with her appearance. Irritated by the girl's intrusion into his orderly life, he shrugged aside the puzzle and turned to search the traffic for sight of his driver. Where the devil was Jack?

Juliana felt compelled to express her gratitude. "I appreciate your intercession on my behalf, Mr. MacAllister. Without it, I would still be in that horrid place." She shivered, more violently this time in spite of the cape's warmth.

"You're quite welcome." Drew continued to scan the street.

Juliana pulled the cape tighter, and for the first time in her life experienced the luxurious smoothness of satin. A faint scent of sandalwood clung to the fine fabric. "Why did you help me, Mr. MacAllister? I can't afford to pay for your services."

"Perhaps I make a practice of defending young women charged with inciting riots and striking police officers."

"You're avoiding my question. What made you decide to represent me?"

Drew shot her a glance that was part irritation, part admiration. Who was this girl who dressed like a vagabond but spoke like a lawyer? "I did it as a favor to a friend."

His explanation didn't satisfy her. "Why would your friend ask you to defend me? I don't know anyone in New York."

When Bertram Lattimer had asked him to defend the girl as a personal favor, Drew had considered it a small price in view of Lattimer's help when he was establishing a law practice. What else could he have done under the circumstances? "Does the name Lattimer sound familiar?"

"Lattimer?" Juliana repeated.

Drew watched her reaction. It had occurred to him that this young woman might very well be an opportunist who had seized the chance to ingratiate her way into the graces of a wealthy eccentric. Emma Lattimer with her crazy allegiance to woman suffrage was a well-known eccentric.

Juliana's expression cleared. Now everything made sense. As ill as she was, Emma Lattimer hadn't forgotten her promise. "Will she be all right?"

"I have no idea. The lady has a weak heart; yet she persists in these foolish causes. Today's episode may have proved too much."

Remembering the bluish tinge to the elderly woman's mouth and the pastiness of her complexion, Juliana fell silent. While she stood here wallowing in self-pity, the dear lady could be fighting for her life. She had much to be grateful for. Thanks to Emma's intervention, she had her freedom. The numbing indecision that had blanketed her since she left the courtroom vanished.

Shrugging off Andrew MacAllister's evening cape, she handed it back. "Thank you for all you've done. I must be going."

"And just where do you plan to go?" He made no move to accept the wrap. "If memory serves, Miss Butterfield, twenty minutes ago you informed Judge Spears you were totally without hearth, kin, or coin. In simple terms, you implied you were destitute. Is that not the case?"

"Yes, but—"

"Then exactly what do you plan to do, Miss Butterfield? Wander the streets? Perhaps sell your favors in the Washington Market?"

Juliana had no idea what he was referring to, but took offense at his tone. "My plans are no concern of yours." Shoving his cape into his hands, she turned and started down the street.

Drew was at her side before she had gone more than half

a dozen steps. "Oh, but you're wrong," he said, catching her arm and turning her to face him. "You seem to have had a convenient lapse of memory, Miss Butterfield. Have you forgotten Judge Spears placed you in my custody?" In the unflattering glare of a gaslight, her face looked alarmingly pale. Dark smudges of fatigue were evident beneath her eyes. Again he felt an unwanted stirring of compassion. "When did you last eat?"

Surprised by the sudden change in his manner, Juliana blinked. "This morning . . . at the railroad station."

He shook his head. "And I suppose that's where you also spent the night?" Her quickly averted gaze told Drew his guess was accurate. "The railway terminal notwithstanding, where have you been living?"

"In a convent not far from Philadelphia."

"You? A nun?" Disbelief was evident in his tone.

She nodded, a mutinous set to her mouth. "I was a novice."

A carriage pulled by matching bays rolled down the cobblestones and reined to a halt at the curb. Jack Burrows, a grizzled man wearing a slouch cap set low on his forehead, leaned down from the driver's seat. "Sorry, guv, ran into a nasty accident along the way. Traffic was snarled for miles."

Maintaining a firm hold on Juliana's arm, Drew ignored her protests, guided her toward the carriage, and assisted her inside. "Did you deliver my message to Miss Gardner?" he asked his driver.

Jack looked offended. "'Course I did, guv. And if you want my opinion, the lady looked plenty miffed."

Drew climbed into the carriage beside Juliana. "If we hurry, I can still make it to the theater by intermission. First, though, drop Miss Butterfield at my place."

"Your place?" Juliana exclaimed as the carriage lurched forward.

"You heard me." Drew sat back and crossed his legs. "Tomorrow will be time enough to decide what to do with you. My manservant will see to your comfort. Frankly, you look in need of a decent night's rest and a good meal, not to mention a bath."

The insult stung; Juliana recoiled. Acknowledging the underlying truth of Andrew MacAllister's words failed to make the slur more palatable. She might be tired, hungry, and in dire need of bathing, but she wasn't stupid. She didn't need Andrew MacAllister to remind her of the obvious. Fighting back tears spawned by weariness and frustration, she huddled in the seat and watched New York City roll past.

Unsightly rail tracks extended up the street. The driver skillfully controlled the team as a noisy train chugged past, spewing cinders and belching smoke. At last the carriage turned down a side street and drew up before a four-story residence standing among a row of similar brownstone houses. A stoop flanked by cast-iron railings wound from the sidewalk to the main entrance.

"Wait here." Drew jumped from the carriage and helped Juliana alight. Taking her arm once more, he hustled her across the walk and up the stairs. "Gilbert!" he shouted, flinging open the door and thrusting Juliana inside a narrow entryway.

"Coming, Mr. MacAllister." A thin elderly gentleman with rigid posture appeared from the back of the house. "What can I do for you, sir?"

"Miss Butterfield will be our guest tonight. Please see to her supper and draw her a bath."

"Very good, sir. Will that be all?"

"Yes, thank you, Gilbert." Drew directed his attention to Juliana. "If there's anything else you need, just ask. Now, if you'll excuse me, I'm already late for an engagement." Not waiting for a response, he turned and disappeared out the door.

From behind wire-rimmed glasses, Gilbert inspected Juliana, beginning with her untidy hair and proceeding down to the scuffed toes of her shoes. "Follow me," he directed with a sniff.

Picking up her skirts, Juliana trailed after him. The servant led her up two flights of stairs to a Spartan guest room with a narrow bed, a straight-backed chair, and a pine dresser. "I'll bring your dinner. The bathroom is at the end of the hall."

"I can see to my own bath," Juliana said hastily.

"Very well, miss. If you'll leave your clothing outside the door, I'll see that it's laundered."

As soon as the sound of his footsteps faded, Juliana headed for the bathroom. She sighed in pure pleasure at the sight of the claw-footed porcelain tub. When she twisted the taps, hot water gushed through the pipes. She had half the buttons of her dress unfastened before she remembered her valise had been lost during the scuffle in Central Park. She had nothing else to wear. A large linen bath towel hanging above the tub temporarily solved her dilemma. Stripping off her clothes, she stepped into the tub and sank up to her neck. Eyes closed, she let the steamy water soak away the day's problems.

When Gilbert returned to the guest room to collect the dinner tray he had taken up earlier, he found Juliana curled up in bed, sound asleep. She didn't even stir as he picked her soiled garments from the chair. Holding them at arm's length, he carried them downstairs.

* * *

"See what you've done."

"What I've done!"

"It was your idea to order another bottle of wine."

"How was I to know Nick would pass out cold?"

"Well, what are we going to do now?" Billy Craddock's voice took on a whiny note. "We can't very well show up at Lucinda's with him in this condition. They wouldn't let us past the front door."

"Damned if I'm going back to Cambridge without getting laid." Clarence Rogers aimed a look at his classmate that defied challenge.

For a long moment, the two classmates stared at Nick Kincaid. The object of their dispute sat slumped in a chair, chin on his chest, arms dangling limply, blissfully unaware of being a problem.

"Sure would like to spend an hour or two with that new girl at Lucinda's," Billy spoke at last. "So help me, her breasts are as big as cantaloupes. She has nipples like ripe plums, and—"

"Crissake, you make her sound like a damn fruit salad. Think, man!" Suddenly Clarence leaned forward and snapped his fingers. "Why not drop Nick at his big brother's and let him sleep it off?"

"But we don't know where his brother lives."

"Don't be such a dimwit. All the way from Harvard Nick did nothing but brag about the brownstone house his brother just bought. He even read a description of it from a letter. I saw him tuck the envelope in his pocket. We take one peek at the return address and our problem's solved. That leaves us free." He chuckled.

"Seems a mean trick after promising him the time of his life, but . . . " Billy's protest faded as the idea took root.

"Poor Nick. When he finds out, he'll be fit to be tied."

"He'll get over it." Clarence signaled a waiter to bring the check while Billy hoisted Nick to his feet.

Nick opened his eyes, a loose smile spreading across his youthful features. "On to Lucinda's." His words were slurred.

Clarence darted a glance around the Knickerbocker, his father's exclusive club, to see if anyone had overheard, then caught Nick's arm. Billy took the other. Together the pair escorted their friend from the dining room. Wealthy diners watched with indulgent smiles, no doubt recalling how they, too, had once sowed their wild oats.

Hansom cabs lined the curb outside the club. Clarence hailed the one closest. The night air had little sobering effect on Nick. With the driver's help, they half lifted, half dragged him inside where he lolled across an entire seat. The schoolmates scrambled in after him. Nick never stirred as Billy rifled his pockets. Grinning, Billy held up the letter as a key fell to the floor. Clarence snatched the key and read off the address on the envelope.

At last the carriage turned off Fourth Avenue onto a side street lined with rows of brownstones. They stopped before a house bearing a discreet brass nameplate inscribed MacAllister.

Clarence gave Nick a shake. "Wake up." When the youth mumbled incoherently, he shook him again. "Wake up, Kincaid."

Nick's eyes opened, drooped shut, then slowly reopened. He pushed himself to a sitting position and tried to focus. "Where are we?"

"This is your—"

"Lucinda's," Clarence interrupted.

Nick craned his neck. "Doesn't look like a whorehouse."

"Christ, man, what do you expect? A flaming sign out front? This is a high-class place. They don't need to advertise."

The explanation seemed to satisfy Nick. "Lead me to that gal you talked about on the train. The one with the big bosom." He started to climb out of the carriage, but his long legs tangled like a newly foaled colt's. If Billy hadn't latched on to his coattail, he would have fallen flat on his face.

The driver shook his head in disgust, then ignored the trio as they made their way across the walk. Nick clumsily negotiated the stoop to the parlor-floor entrance. Clarence fitted the key into the lock, and the front door swung open. A single light from a wall sconce dimly illuminated the foyer. Nick squinted at the unfamiliar surroundings, a befuddled expression on his face. "Sure this is the right address?"

"This is it, buddy." Clarence prodded Nick toward the stairway. "Go on. Not bashful, are you?"

Nick climbed three steps and glanced back over his shoulder. "Hey, aren't you fellas coming?"

"We'll be up soon as we pay the driver. Go ahead. That pretty little blonde is already warming those sheets. Don't want her to get tired of waiting, do you?"

"Big as melons, right, Billy?" Making a lewd gesture, Nick teetered precariously.

Guilt flickered across Billy Craddock's round face. The sharp jab of Clarence's elbow reminded him of practical considerations. This was the only solution. With Nick in his present state, they wouldn't be invited beyond Lucinda's stoop. Besides, he wanted to get laid every bit as much as Clarence. "Melons," he repeated with false jocularity.

Nick clutched the banister with his left hand and used his right to guide himself up the stairway. The simple task required total concentration; he never heard his friends depart. After climbing two flights, he leaned against the wall in the upstairs landing. So far he hadn't seen a soul, much less a shapely blonde. Or his friends. There was no sign of them. Clarence and Billy had disappeared. His brow puckered. Was this a trick of some kind? Stumbling, he lurched down the hallway and pushed a door open.

Except for moonlight filtering through a window shade, the room was dark. Nick stood in the doorway, straining to see through the gloom. When his eyes adjusted to the dim light, he discerned a feminine form reclining on a bed, and he grinned. His frustration was washed away in a flood of anticipation. His friends hadn't lied. A woman with her back to him was pretending to be asleep. Hell, no one loved games better than he did.

With exaggerated care, Nick tiptoed across the bedroom and, assuming a wide-legged stance for better balance, methodically emptied the contents of his pockets onto the dresser. Lastly he took out a slim silver flask and set it next to a crumpled twenty dollar bill, some loose change, a pocketknife, a comb, and his good luck charm. After peeling off his clothes, he picked up the flask and sank down on the edge of the mattress. He needed another drink.

He unscrewed the cap, raised the flask to his mouth, and took a long swallow before remembering he wasn't alone. Not wanting his companion to think him less than a gentleman, he clumsily extended the liquor in her direction. "Have some?"

Bourbon dribbled across the sheets and spilled down Juliana's bare shoulders. When she didn't respond, he shrugged, took another swig, and after several fumbled attempts managed to screw the cap on the container.

Nick slipped between the sheets. The woman was already undressed and waiting for him. Drunk as he was, he realized he wasn't in any shape to contend with the tiny fastenings of a woman's undergarments. "Good," he mumbled, snuggling closer.

His head began to whirl like a carousel. To rid himself of the sensation, he drew in a deep breath and smelled the faintly antiseptic aroma of soap. His brow puckered. Even with his limited knowledge, he knew whores were supposed to smell like expensive French perfume, not college infirmaries.

Undeterred by the girl's lack of interest, Nick slid his arms around her, cupping a firm breast in each hand. He gauged their fullness. Bigger than baseballs, he calculated, but definitely smaller than melons.

Juliana stirred.

"No offense, honey." He squeezed playfully. "They're awfully nice, even if they are on the small side." He withdrew his hands and pressed them to his head to still the spinning.

Juliana's eyes flew wide. In the space of a heartbeat, she crossed the barrier between sleep and wakefulness. Something was dreadfully amiss. She remained still, trying to assemble her wits.

A wet sloppy kiss landed on the nape of her neck. She squirmed and, to her horror, felt a smooth, muscled chest hard against her back. Holy Mother of God! There was a naked man in her bed.

"Heard you liked fun and games." Nick wrapped his arms around her midsection and hugged with so much enthusiasm he forced the air from her lungs.

"Mr. MacAllister!" Juliana gasped.

The mistaken identity failed to register in Nick's befuddled brain. "Don't have to be so formal, honey." He continued to fondle her.

How dare he! Just because she was penniless didn't give Andrew MacAllister the right to steal her virtue. She counted to five and gathered her courage. Bringing back her elbow, she drove it into his rib cage.

His hold loosened. "Aw, honey, what did you do that for?"

"Take your hands off me!" Juliana's voice shook with outrage.

"The fellows said you were frisky as a kitten." Undaunted, he pulled her tighter and ran one hand down the smooth expanse of her thigh.

"Stop it!" Juliana grabbed his wrist and tried to pry it from her waist.

Nick chuckled in delight. "I love a good romp." He flipped her over on her back.

Hair streaming across her face, Juliana raised her arms, curled her fingers into talons, and raked them down her tormentor's hairless chest. Nick caught them easily and pinned them above her head. His body trapped her flailing legs. "I win the first round."

She was about to be ravished by a lunatic. Though she couldn't make out his features through the curtain of hair that covered her face, she was certain he was smiling. Squeezing her eyes closed, she forced herself to go limp until she felt his grip relax. In a final, frantic surge of strength, she arched her body and bucked.

"You little vixen," he said, trying to regain his balance. In a desperate attempt to right himself, he caught her shoulders just before he toppled over, his weight carrying her with him.

The momentum sent her head cracking against the bed's iron headboard with a sickening thud. A million fireflies danced in front of Juliana's eyelids before she sank into peaceful oblivion.

"Hey, honey." Nick stared at his inert companion who lay sprawled across the sheets. He poked her twice, then gave up. "Women," he grumbled. "First she wants to play; now she wants to sleep." He yawned and made a space for himself on the mattress. Maybe a little nap wasn't such a bad idea. Women, would he ever understand them? he wondered, pulling the sheet over both of them.

"No telling about a woman like that," Gilbert said reprovingly.

Andrew MacAllister silently concurred. He never should have brought Juliana Butterfield into his home. Dammit, why had he? Because he felt sorry for her? Because she said she had nowhere to go, no one to turn to? And he had believed her. "You say you found them together, asleep in her bed?"

"Yes, sir." Gilbert's mouth was set in a prim line. "Both naked as the day they were born. The room fairly reeked of alcohol." He hesitated. "There's something else, sir."

Andrew MacAllister quit his restless pacing and spun to face his servant. "Out with it, man."

"I found twenty dollars on the dresser."

His expression grim, Drew took a moment to digest the implication. Had she lied to him about being in a convent? Was she simply a young woman of easy virtue who plied her trade on street corners? "The lady can no longer claim she's penniless. Though one can hardly call her type a lady."

Gilbert nervously scrutinized an arrangement of family portraits on the mantel in the study. "You don't suppose, sir . . . " From beneath a starched shirt collar, a bright flush crept upward, staining his sallow cheeks a dull red.

He cleared his throat. "You don't suppose the young woman is diseased? After all, we know nothing about her."

Drew's expression hardened. "Should she harm Nick in any way, she'll rue the day we met."

Gilbert wisely kept silent. He recognized the pugnacious thrust of his employer's jaw, the stiff set of his shoulders, the steely glint in his eyes. He had seen that look of determination hundreds of times since that cold February day twenty-one years ago when he had found Drew MacAllister, a thin, ragged lad of thirteen, on the doorstep holding his baby brother in a fiercely protective grip and demanding to speak with an uncle he had never met. As a result of that confrontation, Angus MacAllister had become the legal guardian of the two parentless boys.

During the ensuing years, the older boy's determination to succeed, combined with his unswerving loyalty to his younger brother, had won Angus MacAllister's respect. Angus had finally forgiven his only sister for disgracing the MacAllister name by bearing, Drew, an illegitimate child. If he were alive today, Angus MacAllister would have good cause to be proud of his nephew. Shrewd and canny in business, the boy had grown into a wealthy, powerful man in his own right.

One thing had remained constant—Drew MacAllister's passionate loyalty to those he loved. His younger half brother, Nick Kincaid, topped the list.

Gilbert watched Drew stalk to the window and stare at the garden swathed in predawn darkness.

"Wake Miss Butterfield and bring her to me." A soft Scottish burr, reserved for times of deep emotion, had crept into his speech. "That woman willna harm Nick."

CHAPTER
3

"WAKE UP, MISS."

Juliana clung to the anesthetizing effects of sleep, yet part of her struggled toward awareness.

Gilbert shook her, more insistently this time. "Mr. Mac-Allister wishes to see you."

Mention of that hated name cut through her sleep-fogged mind. In one continuous motion, Juliana tugged the coverlet up to her neck and scooted to the far edge of the mattress. She darted a fearful look around. There was no trace of him. "Well, I don't wish to see him." A tremor underlay her brave words.

"Mr. MacAllister doesn't like to be kept waiting."

"No." Juliana clutched the bedding tighter.

"No, miss?" Gilbert blinked nearsighted eyes and stared at the young woman who blatantly refused to budge. What was wrong with the girl? Now what was he to do? Deciding a firmer approach was called for, he drew himself up straighter and peered down his rather long, narrow nose. "He said immediately, miss."

Juliana's golden gaze swept the room. "My clothes . . . ? What have you done with them?"

Gilbert shuddered delicately. No telling what disagreeable creatures her garments had harbored. "Your clothing, if you can call it such, has been laundered. Cook took the liberty of mending the tears." He indicated the well-worn dress draped over the back of a chair. "Mr. MacAllister is not in the best of moods, miss. Five minutes." With this, he turned and marched out.

Juliana let out a shaky breath. Dear Lord, would this nightmare ever end? She wished she never had to set eyes on Andrew MacAllister again. He was a monster. Satan incarnate. She despised the man. Besides, he terrified her. She had never viewed herself as a coward . . . until now.

Perhaps, once dressed, she could slip unnoticed down the stairs and out the front door. Bolstered by the thought, she pushed aside the covers and climbed out of bed. The second her feet touched the floor, she grabbed her head with both hands, her palms pressed against her temples to quiet the drumming. Her skull felt ready to explode. Andrew MacAllister musn't be kept waiting, she reminded herself bitterly as she reached for her dress.

Glancing downward, she frowned at her bare toes sticking out beneath the hem. Getting on her hands and knees, she searched under the bed for her footwear, the action renewing the pounding in her head. Cautiously she straightened, then slid her feet into the disreputable shoes. Arranging her hair was the next hurdle.

Feeling like a thief, she rummaged through the drawers until she found a hairbrush. Her gaze rested on a small mirror hung from a hook above the dresser. Mirrors had been forbidden at the convent. Vanity was sinful, she had been taught. Juliana stared at her reflection as though memorizing the features of a stranger. Brush in hand, she studied the fine-boned oval face with its high cheekbones, small straight nose, and rosy pink mouth. The eyes staring back at her were an unusual color, not blue, green, or brown, but a deep golden hue. Hair nearly the same shade as her eyes fell thick and curling midway to her waist.

Her mind spun back to the shameful incident two days ago. "Beautiful," Freddie Westhaven had pronounced after pulling the veil from her head. "Much too beautiful to hide beneath veils and habits." Giving herself a mental shake, Juliana banished the unpleasant memory. Holding the brush in a fierce grip, she tugged it through the tangled mass, scraping it away from her face. She winced as the bristles came in contact with a sensitive spot near the base of her scalp. Putting the brush down, she explored the area with her fingers. Hair, stiff and matted with dried blood, surrounded a lump the size of a goose egg. A sharp knock on the door startled her, sending the hairbrush clattering to the floor.

"Mr. MacAllister said that if you're not down in two minutes, he's coming up." Gilbert's warning sounded through the wood.

Juliana retrieved the brush and quickly secured her hair in a prim bun. Squaring her shoulders, she left the room.

Gilbert waited in the hallway. Wordlessly he escorted her downstairs to a study that opened off the entryway. The door stood ajar. Apparently Andrew MacAllister wished to monitor all comings and goings. Juliana cast a lingering glance at the heavy outer door leading to freedom. But there was no escape. Her heart pounding with dread, she stepped over the threshold.

Drew MacAllister stood behind a massive mahogany desk, hands clasped behind him, gazing out a window beyond which dawn was only a pink glow. He rocked back on his heels. He was furious with Juliana Butterfield and even more so with himself. He prided himself on his common sense, his sound judgment. Yet both had failed him. He should have known better than to invite a strange young woman into his home. If only he hadn't been in such a damned hurry to join Gwendolyn at the opera house. How could he have guessed that Nick would pick last night of all nights to pay him an unscheduled visit?

Nick. When would he grow up? Instead of preparing for a summer session of classes, he was in town carousing with friends. Drew's expression turned bleak. Maybe he was at fault for spoiling the lad. Ever since that cold February day when his mother and stepfather had been killed, leaving him responsible for a brother barely a year old, he had tried to make the loss up to Nick. "Promise you'll take care of the bairn. Promise, Andrew," his mother had pleaded with her dying breath. For Nick's sake, Drew had buried his fierce Scottish pride. Unannounced, he had arrived on his uncle's doorstep prepared to grovel if necessary for the man's charity. It was for Nick, only for Nick. Drew could have managed on his own. He knew how to survive in the streets. After all, he had done it in Glasgow. He could survive in New York.

Juliana waited in painful uncertainty. A single lamp burning on a small table lent a stingy light. Andrew MacAllister, standing with his back to her, gave no indication that he was aware of her presence. She noted that he was still dressed as he had been last evening in the courtroom. The mantel clock sounded overly loud in the still room. Her nerves coiled tighter as it ticked off the seconds; she was barely able to restrain the urge to bolt.

A slight movement drew his attention. "Come in and close the door."

Accustomed to obeying orders, Juliana did as she was told.

Turning, Drew crossed the study with measured tread until he stood before her and surveyed her critically.

Juliana forced herself not to retreat and to meet his gaze without flinching.

"My, my, you look terrible," he said. "I hope you aren't ill."

Her spine stiffened at his caustic tone. "My health is fine, sir, except for an abominable headache."

"No doubt." A mirthless smile curved Drew's mouth. Gilbert had mentioned that the guest room smelled like a cheap saloon. He made a note to check his supply of bourbon. It wouldn't surprise him if the young woman had been well into her cups even before Nick arrived on the scene. A headache was better than she deserved. "Now that the amenities are dispensed with, what do you have to say in your behalf?"

Juliana was at a loss. This barbarian acted as if she, rather than he, was guilty of some heinous offense.

He arched one dark brow. "Nothing to say?"

Her head jerked up, the motion making the demons inside pound with renewed vigor. "What do you mean?" she retorted angrily.

"Women like you have a knack for . . . how shall I phrase it?" He folded his arms over his chest and stared down at her, his expression hard. "Persuasive conversation?"

Juliana's apprehension increased. He wasn't making the slightest bit of sense. How did one deal with someone who was irrational? Aggravating him further might ignite his violent temper. She sought to placate him while inching toward the door. "While it was kind of you to offer shelter last night, I feel it's best if I find another place to stay."

He shifted position and blocked her exit. "We both know this sudden reversal in plans isn't because of your concern for propriety, don't we?"

Panic burst into full bloom. "I-I'm afraid I don't understand."

"Don't play the innocent. I know your kind, Miss Butterfield. Men are easy prey to your wiles. Women like you disgust me." He gave her a look of pure loathing before turning and stalking across the room. He sat down at his desk, dipped a pen in ink, and furiously scribbled in a leatherbound ledger.

"*I* disgust *you?*" Juliana's voice rose. She no longer worried that she might anger him. All that mattered was that she put an end to this silly charade once and for all. "If the truth be known, Mr. MacAllister, *you* disgust *me*. Your behavior last night was vile and reprehensible."

He ceased writing. "*My* behavior?"

"You heard me. Surely there must be laws against that type of behavior. I could have you arrested."

Now it was Drew's turn to stare in disbelief. The young woman was obviously confused. She couldn't possibly believe that he was the one she had offered her favors to— for a price. Or could she?

Had she been so drunk that she had propositioned Nick, all the while believing it was Drew? Well, he decided, let her think that. Better to keep Nick out of this.

He tore out a sheet of paper, shoved away from his desk, and got to his feet. "It would be your word against mine. Come, Miss Butterfield, you look like an intelligent woman. Which of us do you think the police are more likely to believe?"

Juliana opened her mouth, then closed it. Her experience yesterday provided the answer.

"I can see by your expression that I've made my point. Here's a check to tide you over until you make other . . . arrangements." He held out a bank draft.

Juliana stepped back as he advanced. Reaching out, Drew caught her arm and pressed the check into her hand. She looked at it for a moment, not seeing the large sum scrawled in bold strokes, but viewing it as a ticket out of the room, away from him. An escape.

"What's wrong, Miss Butterfield? Do you think you deserve more?"

He might as well have been speaking a foreign tongue, for his words made little sense to Juliana. But his insulting tone was unmistakable. Her fingers curled around the slip of paper. "This is . . . adequate."

She groped behind her for the doorknob. Giving it a twist, she whirled and fled, not caring that the study door banged shut after her. She paused in the hallway to draw a calming breath. Her gaze dropped to the check still clutched in her hand. Evidently Andrew MacAllister was a man who believed money could compensate for a deplorable lack of morals. She folded the check, then ripped it into small, even pieces and let them flutter to the floor as she moved toward the door.

Standing on the walk outside the house, she glanced around. The city was just beginning to stir. A milk wagon plodded past; on the corner, a boy hawked the morning edition of a newspaper. Her spirits began to lift. It was a new day, a new beginning. As she turned down Fourth Avenue, she failed to notice a man disengage himself from the shadows of a building and start to follow her.

Long after Juliana's departure, Drew sat brooding at his

desk. Thus far, his ability to judge a person's character had played an important role in his success. In the case of Juliana Butterfield, it had deserted him completely. Emotion had blinded his better judgment. Instead of the destitute innocent the woman had appeared to be, she was a scheming opportunist, quick to take advantage of a young man's baser instincts and bilk him out of an entire month's allowance in the bargain.

Poor Nick, Drew thought with a scowl. He must have been desperate for a woman. But choosing the likes of Juliana Butterfield was beyond his ken. With her dowdy clothes and hairstyle, she resembled a nun more than a whore. Further ruminations were interrupted by Gilbert's timid knock.

The elderly retainer entered, looking shamefaced and decidedly uncomfortable. "Mr. MacAllister, there's something you ought to know."

"You needn't look as if I'm going to bite your head off. What is it?"

"It's about Master Nick." Gilbert's usually pale face flushed rosy pink. "And Miss Butterfield, sir."

Drew leaned back in his chair and tossed his pen aside. "What about them?"

"I . . . I, ah . . . " Gilbert shifted his weight from one foot to the other.

"Go on," Drew encouraged.

"I went upstairs to change the linens in the guest room, the room Miss Butterfield used."

"And . . . "

"I found bloodstains."

"Bloodstains!" Drew leapt to his feet and rounded the corner of his desk. He towered over the elderly servant. "Where?"

Gilbert's Adam's apple bobbed noisily. "On the sheets, sir."

Drew felt as though he had been punched in the stomach. It couldn't be. Impossible! Or was it? The ramifications of the servant's words began to dawn on him.

"I've given the matter considerable thought, sir," Gilbert continued. "Loud voices woke me out of a sound sleep last night. At first I thought it was the two of them having a gay old time, but now I'm not so sure. I remember hearing Miss Butterfield tell Master Nick not to touch her."

Drew winced as his worst fears crystallized: Juliana Butterfield, not Nick, had been the victim. It sickened him to think that in all probability his brother had raped a virgin. His own behavior had also been less than exemplary. He had written a check and tossed the poor girl into the street.

Gilbert cleared his throat. "I found these in the hallway, sir." He dropped bits of torn paper in Drew's upturned palm.

Like a slumbering tiger awakened from a lengthy nap, New York City came slowly to life. Prodded toward wakefulness by the noise of pushcarts and drays, it seemed to rise on its haunches and lazily flex its muscles. Juliana stood outside a café and regarded the city warily, trying to assess its mood. Already she had experienced the city's cunning and strength.

The smell of sizzling bacon and freshly brewed coffee drifted out to her, making her stomach rumble. Hunger pangs were becoming a familiar sensation, Juliana acknowledged to herself. As she began to walk away, a man exited the restaurant and carelessly tossed a newspaper in the gutter before adjusting his straw boater. She watched him stroll off, then impulsively bent to retrieve the discarded paper.

"Hey, girlie, whatcha tryin' to do? Lose yer hand?"

Juliana's eyes rounded in terror. Mere inches from her outstretched fingers were horse's hooves easily the size of dinner platters. Her gaze traveled up over the huge animal hitched to a bakery wagon.

"Quit yer gawkin'," the red-faced driver snarled.

Juliana grasped the newspaper and clutched it tightly to her chest.

"What are ya, a halfwit?" He shook his arm menacingly. "Off with ya!"

Juliana fled. It wasn't until several blocks later that her pulse slowed to normal. Spotting an apothecary, she sat down on the doorsill and spread her prized newspaper across her knees. Quickly she thumbed through the pages until she found the classified section. She trailed a fingertip down the columns, stopping at an ad for a tutor. Her spirits rose. The position seemed perfect for someone with her scholastic background.

After asking directions from a milkman, Juliana found the address on West Fifty-fourth Street. She offered up a quick prayer, then climbed the stoop of a stately brick and stone residence and pulled the bell cord.

A maid in a neat uniform and starched white apron answered the ring. A swift encompassing glance registered Juliana's shabby appearance. "Deliveries are made in the rear." The door slammed in her face.

Juliana rang the bell a second time. "I told you, miss, deliveries are made in the rear," the maid insisted through a crack in the door.

Wedging the toe of her shoe in the narrow opening, Juliana hastened to explain. "I'm here in response to the advertisement in this morning's paper. The one for a tutor," she added when the maid continued to look skeptical.

"Do you have an appointment?"

"No, I don't. But my qualifications are excellent."

"I'll check with Mrs. Vincent. If you'll kindly remove your foot . . . "

Juliana complied, and the door closed on her once more. She was left to wait on the stoop while the maid consulted her mistress. In a state of nervous anticipation, she smoothed her hair and brushed a wrinkle from her skirt. She hoped she wouldn't appear as desperate as she felt. If she failed to find a position . . . well, she hated to think of that possibility.

Twenty minutes later the maid returned. "Mrs. Vincent will see you." She led the way to a small parlor off the entrance hall. "She'll be down shortly."

After the simple way of life in the convent, Juliana was overwhelmed by the room's decor. Every available space was crowded with ponderous furniture upholstered in tufted red velvet. Family portraits set in ornate gilt frames vied for prominence on the walls. Bric-a-brac sprouted in epidemic proportions from tabletops and mantel. Juliana perched on the edge of a chair, hands primly folded to still their tremor, and wondered about the type of woman who preferred such ornate furnishings.

Beyond the parlor door, she glimpsed the maid patrolling the hallway, feather duster in hand, as though ready to wage battle should Juliana try to abscond with a porcelain figurine. Finally, Juliana heard the rustle of taffeta. A moment later a short blond woman, whose plump figure strained the seams of her gown, entered the parlor.

"Edith said you came in answer to the ad, Miss . . . "

"Butterfield," Juliana supplied, rising to her feet. "Juliana Butterfield."

Mrs. Vincent eyed Juliana's dress in distaste and drew back slightly. "I assume you have references, Miss Butterfield?"

Juliana's palms grew moist. "Well, actually, Mrs. Vincent, I don't. You see—"

"How unfortunate," the woman replied without a trace of sympathy. "Under the circumstances further discussion would be a waste of time. Good day, Miss Butterfield."

"I taught at a private school near Philadelphia. I left rather suddenly . . . for personal reasons. If you'll give me a chance, I'm certain you won't be disappointed."

"Impossible." Mrs. Vincent stood aside and indicated the interview was over. "My husband would never consider hiring someone without impeccable references to instruct little Winthrop. Besides, a man would be much better qualified to teach math and the sciences."

"Thank you for your time." Her spine stiff, her eyes straight ahead, Juliana left. Her final impression of the interview was the smirk on the face of the housemaid.

The remainder of the day's encounters yielded similar results. By late afternoon Juliana was no closer to finding a job than she had been that morning. She was footsore, hungry, and discouraged, and her headache had returned with a vengeance.

Stores were beginning to close for the day when she leaned wearily against a milliner's shop and scanned the crumpled newspaper a final time. She glanced up as a carriage rolled past. Sucking in her breath, she stared at its male occupant: Andrew MacAllister.

He was smiling at his attractive, fashionably dressed female companion, his dark hair gleaming in the sunlight. His head was cocked as he listened attentively while the woman spoke.

Fury coursed through Juliana. How dare he play the gentleman? He was a brute. A defiler of women. Her grip on the newspaper tightened until her knuckles whitened.

How could the woman with him be so gullible? She ought to be warned. Before Juliana could act, the carriage moved forward, converged with other vehicles, then disappeared around a corner.

Shaken, Juliana slumped against the brick storefront. Nausea washed over her. Closing her eyes, she feared she might be sick right there on the sidewalk.

"You all right, miss?" Juliana heard someone ask in a lilting Irish brogue. She opened her eyes to find a pretty girl of seventeen or eighteen with auburn curls, green eyes, and a dusting of pale gold freckles watching her with concern.

Juliana nodded. "I'll be fine."

"Blarney. You don't look fine to me." The girl took Juliana's arm, led her inside the shop, and gently pushed her down on a straight-backed chair. "If you feel faint, stick your head between your knees. That's what my mum would say. I'll be back in a jiff."

She vanished through a curtain separating the shop from a back room. When she returned, she carried a cup of tea and a tin of cookies. "You look a bit peaked. I thought a spot of tea might help." She smiled, handing the cup to Juliana. "My name's Maura O'Toole."

"I'm Juliana Butterfield." Juliana returned the smile. "Thank you for your kindness."

" 'Tis nothing." Maura dismissed the gratitude with a wave of her hand. "Take your tea while I finish closing the shop; then perhaps we can chat. I'm the milliner's assistant. My employer, Mrs. Blum, left early today."

Juliana sipped the hot brew and nibbled a cookie, all the while observing Maura. The girl's dark blue skirt swayed as she moved about the shop with crisp efficiency. "I'm looking for work," Juliana ventured hopefully. "Would you, by chance, happen to know of any?"

"Not at the moment, I'm afraid." Maura shrugged. "But don't fret. Something will turn up. It always does."

Without warning, tears sprang to Juliana's eyes and spilled down her cheeks. Setting the cup aside, she buried her face in her hands and sobbed.

Maura was at her side in an instant. "There, there now, it'll be all right," she crooned softly, patting Juliana's shoulder.

"No, it won't." Juliana shook her head. "E-Everything's such a mess. I have no money, no job, no place to stay, and n-no r-r-references."

Maura waited patiently for Juliana's crying to subside, then gave her a handkerchief. "Wipe your eyes and blow your nose. I'm taking you home to my mum."

CHAPTER
4

HOME TO MAURA WAS A SIX-STORY TENEMENT WEDGED back to back and side by side with similar buildings. It had the pervasive odor of too many bodies in too little space, of boiled cabbage and dirty diapers. It had the look of hope, despair, and determination. Sounds of angry voices and crying babies filtered through the walls.

Juliana quickly discovered that Maura O'Toole was a sympathetic listener. By the time they reached the apartment the girl shared with her family, Maura had ferreted out a great deal about Juliana's background, and her imagination had supplied the rest. In exchange, Maura explained that the O'Toole family had immigrated to the United States two years earlier.

Juliana followed Maura up five flights of stairs and, following a brief introduction to Mrs. O'Toole, waited uncertainly while Maura conferred with her mother in a bedroom. This afforded Juliana the opportunity to look around the cramped living quarters. Maura had already explained the sleeping arrangements. The smallest of the rooms, belonging to Mr. and Mrs. O'Toole, allowed space for little else than a bed with a sagging mattress. The second bedroom was not much larger. This was occupied by Maura, her fifteen-year-old sister, Mary Bridget, and until her marriage, her older sister Katie. The largest of the three rooms served as a combination kitchen and parlor, as well as sleeping space for the two boys, twelve-year-old Mickey and twenty-two-year-old Dennis. Juliana hated the idea of being an additional burden to the family.

"But, Mum," Juliana overheard Maura coax through the thin partition, "she has no friends, no family, not a dime to her name. How can we turn her out . . . and her just fresh from the convent?"

"The convent, you say?"

"Aye, the poor girl was on the brink of taking her final vows when doubts set in. She needs time."

Mrs. O'Toole clucked her tongue sympathetically. "And prayer. I'll light a vigil candle tomorrow morning after mass." She bustled out and warmly welcomed Juliana into the family.

That night, over a supper of boiled potatoes and ham, the O'Toole clan was eager to help Juliana find employment.

"Try the shops along Ladies' Mile," Mary Bridget suggested, her black curls bouncing in her enthusiasm. "That's where I'm going to work someday."

"Mrs. Grady's oldest girl, Molly, is an upstairs maid in one of the fine new mansions along Fifth Avenue," Mrs. O'Toole said while spooning another serving onto Dennis's plate. "She gets room and board and every other Sunday off. You might try there."

"A foreman at Baker Textile is a friend of mine. I could put in a word for you—that is, if you're not above factory work," Dennis offered.

His bright green eyes challenged her to refuse. Juliana

returned his look. "I'm not averse to hard work. Tell your friend I'm not only interested but I can start immediately."

"Don't be hasty, Juliana," Maura counseled. "Work in a sweatshop means long hours bent over a sewing machine in a dusty, airless room. Pure drudgery. With an education such as yours, surely you can do better."

"Marry her if you must! Do anything short of cold-blooded murder, but stop this scandal." Daniel Tennant's outburst started another fit of coughing.

Drew MacAllister shifted in the plush leather seat of a wingback chair, his gaze resting on the newspaper spread across Daniel's cluttered desk. Bold print posed a question: "Who Is the Mystery Woman in Andrew MacAllister's Life?" Below the headline was a smudged likeness of Juliana Butterfield. But not the tired, frightened girl he remembered. Gone were the high-necked dress and the matronly bun. This woman's hair swirled thick and curling around bare shoulders. The expression on her face, far from innocent, was rather the knowing one of a woman who had learned how to give and receive pleasure. It was the kind of sensual look that knotted a man's gut, the type that stuck in a man's memory and haunted his late night hours.

The article that accompanied the sketch was anything but complimentary. It implied that Juliana and Drew were carrying on a clandestine affair and, furthermore, that Drew was not the sterling character he pretended to be.

"Marriage? It's not that simple," Drew replied at length.

"Suppose you tell me why not."

"Because the lady in question would prefer my head on a platter to my hand in marriage."

"You're a good catch by any standards. The girl doesn't look like an imbecile. She must have reason to want to toss you back in the pond."

"She has. She thinks I raped her."

"Rape!" Daniel Tennant's face flushed a blotchy purple as he reached for a tumbler of scotch. "Did you?"

Drew slammed his fist on the desk. "What do you take me for?"

"Steady, boy." Daniel slumped back in the chair, took a swig of scotch, and regarded Drew over the rim of his glass.

Drew rose and paced the width of his mentor's first-floor office. "I swear I didn't lay a hand on the girl."

"Then who did?"

Jamming his hands in his pockets, Drew paused to look out the window. He felt himself the object of the old man's shrewd gaze. He debated whether or not to protect Nick with a lie, but the truth won out. "Nick," he admitted grudgingly.

"That young scamp! Does he have any notion of the trouble he's in?"

"The lady isn't even aware that Nick exists. She thinks I'm the culprit."

"And of course you let her go on thinking that." Sighing, Daniel wagged his head. "Andrew, you're the most sensible, level-headed man I know—except when it comes to your brother."

"Don't blame Nick. We had a long talk the next morning, and he explained everything. He confessed to being drunk. Never having been to my new place, he was under the impression that his classmates had dropped him at a whorehouse." Drew left the window and sat opposite Daniel. "When he found Miss Butterfield in the guest room, he assumed she was one of the girls. He thought she was being coy when she resisted his advances. How was he to know she was my client? He feels terrible about the whole affair."

"As he damn well should. He put your political future at risk before it even got under way. Everything could be ruined. Everything." He slapped the newspaper for emphasis. "When I announce my retirement next spring, I don't want any blight on the man I handpicked to be my successor."

Drew reached for the scotch and poured a stiff drink. He couldn't fault Daniel's logic. Drew had had this same conversation with himself on numerous occasions over the past thirty-six hours.

"Have you thought what might happen if the girl decides to press charges? Or worse yet, if she takes her story to the papers? Think of the sensation this would create. The press would have a circus."

"You're the master planner. What do you propose I do?"

"Find the girl. Hire a private investigator if you must. Have Nick apologize and offer to make it up to her."

"I want Nick kept out of this. He's young and just on the brink of manhood. I'm better able to cope with a situation like this."

"When it comes to Nick, you're like a mother hen. It's time he learned to stand on his own two feet."

"I've been all he has since he was a babe."

"If memory serves, you were hardly more than that yourself when your mother died. And as stubborn and feisty as they come." Daniel's dry chuckle ended in a wheeze.

Concerned, Drew studied the aged assemblyman, noting the wrinkled countenance, the pallor, the flame that burned brighter than ever in his dark eyes. "I'll do what's necessary to avoid a scandal, short of dragging Nick's name into this mess."

"Very well." Daniel nodded his approval, then splashed more scotch into his glass. "Everyone has a price. Buy her off. Jewels, furs, a trip to Europe, whatever it takes to guarantee her silence."

Drew's gaze fell to the newspaper image of Juliana Butterfield, and he recalled the torn-up check. "She won't be bought." He raised his glass and took a long swallow. "I already tried."

Daniel Tennant leveled a cold stare at his young protégé. "Then I'm afraid that leaves only one solution. A wife can't testify against her husband."

Maura O'Toole's optimism proved ill-founded. Three days later Juliana was still unsuccessful in finding work. It was late afternoon as she slowly approached the O'Tooles' building. Once again she tasted the bitter draft of failure. How would she ever repay the O'Tooles for their hospitality? She had been almost certain the bookshop owner would hire her. Preoccupied, she rounded a corner and walked headlong into a man. He grasped her elbows to steady her.

"Excuse me, I wasn't . . . " The apology died unspoken. Juliana's golden eyes widened in dismay at seeing Drew MacAllister. He looked much too attractive in his light gray jacket, matching vest, and dark trousers—and very much out of place in a working-class neighborhood.

A hard smile curved his mouth. "You should be more careful where you're walking, Miss Butterfield. New York can be a hazardous place."

"You!" Juliana pulled out of his grasp and took a half a step backward.

The single word was injected with such undiluted loathing that Drew winced. Juliana Butterfield obviously despised him—and for good reason. While entrusted into his care, her virtue had been brutally stolen; then he had tried to pay her off like a common whore and send her back to the streets. Small wonder she reacted as she did. "I'm sorry if I startled you."

"How did you find me?"

"That isn't important."

Juliana ignored his words. "How did you find me?" she demanded.

Drew sighed in exasperation. He should have remembered she could be more tenacious than an attorney with a reluctant witness. Would she believe him if he told the truth? That he had received an unsigned note telling him where she was staying? How could he explain something he didn't understand himself? "The important thing is that I did find you. We need to talk."

She raised her chin defiantly. "We have nothing more to say to each other."

"I disagree," he insisted, his expression somber. "After thinking matters through, I feel a certain responsibility for your welfare."

"This sudden display of conscience is a bit late, don't you think?" Her slender body ramrod straight, Juliana swept past him.

For a moment Drew stared at her retreating back, noting her proud carriage and the gentle sway of her hips. Unexpectedly, he felt a glimmer of admiration for her undaunted spirit. Then, recalling the purpose of his mission, he closed the distance between them with long strides, caught her arm, and turned her around. "Not so fast, Miss Butterfield. Our business isn't finished."

"Let go of my arm!"

"Not until we talk."

"Release me. Immediately!" Juliana looked around, expecting someone to come to her rescue. Incredible. It was broad daylight, the dinner hour. All around her a sea of people plodded homeward. Yet she felt as though she were on an isolated isle. No one paid the slightest attention to them arguing in the middle of the sidewalk.

"No need to get hysterical. Surely you can spare five minutes."

"Hysterical?" With effort she brought her voice under control. "Must I spell it out? I don't want to talk to you. I don't want to look at you. I don't want to be anywhere near you."

"You're conveniently overlooking one salient point, Miss Butterfield," Drew stated calmly.

"Which is . . . ?"

"In case you've forgotten, Judge Spears placed you in my custody. The charges against you are quite serious and as yet unresolved. Unless I'm kept apprised of your whereabouts, he could issue a bench warrant for your arrest."

Juliana grew very still as she realized the full implications of his threat. *Prison.* In her attempt to cope with such basic concerns as food and lodging, she had forgotten her precarious legal predicament. "What do you want of me?" she asked, her voice a husky whisper.

"Just hear me out."

She nodded.

He released her arm. "I meant it when I said I was concerned for your welfare. Whether you choose to believe me or not, I deeply regret what happened the other night. You just said you wished to be far away from me. Well, I want to make that possible." Drew reached inside his jacket and pulled out a wad of bills fastened with a gold money clip. "Here." He peeled off a liberal number and held them out.

Juliana stared in disbelief.

"Go ahead, take it," he urged. "Now you can afford to get away from New York, to go back home."

God help her, the offer was tempting. Except for her friendship with Maura, Juliana had experienced nothing but misfortune since arriving in New York. The city was filled with pandemonium, barbarians, and buildings that blotted out the sun. She longed to return to Pennsylvania. But her ties to the convent had been severed. She had no place to return to.

Besides, she recognized the money for what it was. A bribe. Means to salve a guilty conscience. "Keep your money, Mr. MacAllister. It's time you learned there are some things your money can't buy."

Drew clenched his jaw angrily. She had seen through his ruse. He was trying to buy her off, to ensure her silence—to get her the hell out of town. Without her presence, the newspapers would soon look elsewhere for grist for their scandal mills.

Frowning, he regarded the indignant young woman in front of him. She was still dressed in the same ugly garment she had worn in court, her hair in a severe bun, but he found himself intrigued. Delicate hollows accentuated her high cheekbones and patrician features. But her eyes were truly remarkable. Framed by thick sable lashes, their unusual color was the rich shade of honey.

The image in the illustrated newspaper became superimposed over that of the flesh-and-blood woman. However, there was one major difference. In the sketch, the golden eyes weren't wide and accusing. Rather the lids were lowered beguilingly, so one could easily imagine their lambent glow.

"Please reconsider," he said impulsively, uneasy with his thoughts. "Consider this a loan until you get situated." He thrust the money at her.

"Thank you, no. I don't want to be beholden to someone of your ilk."

"Your scruples are commendable, Miss Butterfield, but they can't fill your stomach or keep you warm." His tone became mellow with a faint Scottish burr. "They won't buy medicine if you're ill. Money can. Don't be a bloody fool. Take it."

Juliana felt herself respond to the persuasive timbre of his voice. She shook her head to negate the effect. "No," she whispered. "No!" she repeated more firmly.

"You do me a grave injustice, Juliana. My only hope is that you never reach that level of desperation where money is so vital you'd do anything to get it. Lie, steal, cheat—anything."

Now it was Juliana's turn to stare. What had he been forced to do? For a rare instant, she had glimpsed raw pain hidden behind an urbane surface. Instead of being intimidated, she felt sympathy for the man.

Drew stuffed the bills into his pocket. "Should you change your mind you know where to reach me. If you're wise, you'll heed my advice and leave town."

Not content to let him have the last word, Juliana forged ahead. "You accused me of forgetting a salient point, Mr. MacAllister. Well, in that respect you're also guilty."

He raised one dark brow inquiringly. "How is that, Miss Butterfield?"

"You're conveniently overlooking your own criminal act. If you continue to harass me, I shall inform Judge Spears that you're a lecherous drunk, preying on innocent females placed in your protection. Good day, sir, and good-bye."

She skirted him and hurried toward the O'Tooles' building midway down the block.

Drew turned and stalked down the street. Seeing his expression, people wisely gave him a wide berth. Because of Juliana Butterfield, he was on the brink of political ruin, and he shuddered to think of what could befall his unsuspecting young brother should she ever divine the truth about that fateful night. Daniel was absolutely right, Drew thought bitterly: she held the power to bring him to his knees.

At the time, Daniel's suggestion that he marry the girl to guarantee her silence had seemed ludicrous, but now . . .

CHAPTER 5

WHY COULDN'T ANDREW MACALLISTER JUST LEAVE HER alone? Why wouldn't he stay out of her life? Filled with righteous indignation, Juliana sailed down the block. Did he think her gullible enough to believe he was concerned with her well-being? Who was he trying to fool? His ruse had been so transparent she had seen through it immediately. The man didn't possess a conscience. The only well-being he was concerned about was his own.

She approached the building housing the O'Toole family. In a city teeming with people, how had the man discovered her whereabouts? Juliana stopped so abruptly the woman walking behind her slammed into her back.

"Fer cryin' out loud, yer lucky I didn't knock ya down." With a scowl of disgust, the woman shifted her parcels and hurried off.

Uneasy, Juliana stood in the middle of the sidewalk. Several times during the last two days she had felt the hair prickle at the nape of her neck. She had told herself she was silly to think she was being watched, yet the sensation had persisted. Feigning a nonchalance she didn't feel, she glanced around, half expecting to see Andrew MacAllister.

There was no sign of him. She resumed walking. Had he been following her? He had deliberately evaded the question when she asked how he had found her. After all he had done, she was certain he was capable of anything.

"The devil take the man," she muttered, borrowing one of Mrs. O'Toole's phrases. She shoved open the tenement door and started up the stairs.

On the second-floor landing, she recalled MacAllister's reminder of her legal predicament. The idea of a prison sentence turned her anger into fear. Whether she liked it or not, he held power over her. The thought of being locked away and forgotten, a prisoner behind iron bars, turned her knees to water. She looked up the stairwell and wondered how her legs would support her for the remaining flights of stairs. Clutching a banister sticky from the grime of countless hands, Juliana dragged herself up another flight.

"Hey, Juliana! Wait for me."

Footsteps pounded on the stairs below. Juliana looked down and saw Dennis O'Toole, a package under one arm, his jacket draped over the other, his shirt collar unbuttoned. He closed the remaining gap by taking the steps two at a time. The newspaper-wrapped parcel he carried reeked strongly of fish.

"Typical Friday-night supper." He grinned as she wrinkled her nose. "Mum makes a terrific fish stew."

"I don't believe I've ever tasted that. The sisters usually served fish baked or fried."

"So, do you miss convent ways?" Crooking a finger, he slung his coat over his shoulder and matched his gait to hers.

"Sometimes," she replied truthfully.

"Can't understand why any girl would want to take the veil and spend the rest of her life praying the beads—unless she's so ugly no man would want her." He eyed Juliana. "If you got gussied up, let your hair down, and put on a pretty dress, you'd have suitors standing in line."

Unused to compliments, Juliana felt only embarrassment. She changed the subject. "I still haven't found work. Did you speak to your friend at the shirtwaist factory?"

"Not yet, but I will tomorrow."

Juliana hugged the wall to let another tenant pass. A cockroach ran across the landing and disappeared beneath an apartment door.

"Say, I've got an idea," Dennis continued. "Peggy Flynn's getting married tomorrow, and the whole family's invited. How about going with me? Nothing like good Irish whiskey and dancing the jig to cheer a person."

"That's very kind of you, Dennis, but I don't think so."

"Why not? If you don't know how to dance, I'll teach you."

"It isn't that."

"C'mon." He took her arm, stopping on the landing between the fifth and sixth floors, and backed her into the corner. His palm flattened against the cracked plaster wall, his arm braced, he grinned at her. "No girl who's been out with Dennis O'Toole has ever complained she hasn't had a good time."

His face was so close to hers that for the first time Juliana noticed his chipped front tooth. Red hair, several shades darker than Maura's, fell in a thick shock over his forehead. Green eyes flecked with gold sparkled with deviltry. She could understand why girls found him attractive. Under different circumstances, she might have, too. But her experience with Freddie Westhaven, and then Andrew MacAllister, had spoiled that. Men, all men, seemed repugnant.

"Don't be bashful."

"The answer is no," she stated firmly. "Now let me pass."

The teasing glint in his eyes disappeared. His engaging grin hardened into a sneer. "What's the real reason you're turning me down? Does it have anything to do with the man you were talking to out on the street?"

Juliana's mouth opened, then closed in shock.

"Don't bother to lie," he snapped. "I saw the pair of you."

"It's not what you're thinking."

"I thought you didn't know anyone here in New York. At least that's the story you've been telling while sponging off Mum and Dad. Why did your friend offer you money?"

Color stung her cheeks. She had been quick to learn why men offered women money in this decadent city. Ducking under Dennis's arm, she picked up her skirts and tried to flee. He grabbed her roughly and whirled her around, shoving a crumpled dollar bill at her. "How much will this buy me, Juliana? A kiss or two? A quick feel?"

She slapped him. The sharp crack of her hand against his smoothly shaven jaw seemed to reverberate through the stairwell. The skin on his cheek blanched, showing the imprint of her fingers, then pinkened. They stood eye to eye, glaring at each other. "You deserved that," she told him, her voice unsteady.

He rubbed his face. "Mum treats you like some kind of plaster saint, but we both know better, don't we, now? Your friend's money is the same color as mine."

His insult ringing in her ears, Juliana turned and ran up the remaining flight of stairs.

By the time she reached the O'Toole flat, she was breathless.

Mrs. O'Toole was peeling potatoes at the kitchen table. "Any luck today, dear?" she asked, not glancing up from her task.

"One shopkeeper said he'd hire me if no one more suitable applied for the job. He seemed to think a man might be better qualified."

"Tsk, tsk," Mary O'Toole clucked. "'Tis a man's world, love."

The matter-of-fact statement rankled. Why couldn't it be a woman's world, too? Juliana wondered resentfully. She was just as qualified to be a clerk as any male applicant. Being a woman didn't mean being less intelligent. Why did so many believe differently? She found a knife in a drawer, pulled up a chair next to Mrs. O'Toole, and reached for a potato.

Dennis and Maura were quarreling as they entered the flat together. "I'm telling you, Dennis, you're pixilated," Maura told her brother.

"The hell I am."

"Dennis Patrick O'Toole." Mrs. O'Toole waggled the paring knife in her son's direction. "Shame on you for that kind of language. What will our guest be thinkin'? Now, apologize."

Dennis looked as though he was about to refuse, but the expression on his mother's face made him reconsider. "Sorry." He threw the package of fish on the table and shot Juliana a dark look, then took a beer from the icebox and stomped off to fling himself onto the sofa at the far end of the room.

Mrs. O'Toole shook her head. "Somethin's put the poor boy in a foul mood." She rose from her chair, unwrapped the fish, and began chopping it into small pieces.

"Let me change out of my working clothes; then I'll help

with dinner," Maura volunteered before disappearing into the bedroom.

Juliana peeled the last of the potatoes. She picked up the newspaper that the cod had been wrapped in and was about to discard it when she froze in the act. Staring back at her was a bold black banner that shouted the question: "Who is the Mystery Woman in Andrew MacAllister's Life?" Below the headline was her own likeness. Horrified, she began to read the article. But before she had gone beyond the first paragraph, she heard someone approaching. Bunching the paper in her hands, she quickly stuffed it into the trash can under the table. Straightening, she turned. Dennis stood, beer bottle in hand, watching her speculatively.

"Juliana, you look as though you've seen a ghost." Maura came to stand behind her brother.

"I'm fine, really." Juliana forced a smile. "It must be the heat."

"If you think June is hot, wait until August." Mrs. O'Toole scooped up the potatoes and added them to the stew pot.

"Aye," Maura agreed. "People sleep anywhere they can find a little air." She began setting the table. "Up on the roof, out on the curb, even down on the docks."

Patrick O'Toole arrived home from his job on a construction crew. The two youngest, Mary Bridget and Mickey, arrived five minutes later, and the family sat down to the evening meal. Juliana's appetite had vanished. She took only a small portion of stew. She had to find a way to finish reading that damning article linking her with Andrew MacAllister. Holy Mother of God, what more could happen to her?

"Heard there was a fire this afternoon down at yer pal's factory." Patrick directed the comment to his oldest son.

Mrs. O'Toole crossed herself. "Oh, dear Jesus."

"It's all right, love." Patrick patted his wife's hand. "Not a soul was hurt, but it means a lot of girls are out of work until they can get the plant running again. Too bad, with all those experienced girls to pick from, I fear Juliana is going to have a hard time finding herself a factory job."

"Juliana doesn't belong in a sweatshop," Maura spoke up.

"At this point, I'd be happy with any job. I don't know how I would have managed if you hadn't been so kind." Juliana's heartfelt gratitude encompassed all of them, even the sullen Dennis.

"I won't be hearin' that kind of talk. We're happy to help a young woman as fine as yourself and fresh from the convent. Aren't we, now?" Mary's elbow unerringly found her husband's rib cage.

"Yes, yes, of course we are." He tore off a chunk of soda bread and sopped up the last of his stew.

Talk turned to other topics, and Juliana fell silent. As soon as supper was over and the dishes washed, she pleaded fatigue and retreated to her room. Her lack of success in securing a position was overshadowed by her newest worry—the newspaper story. She pretended to be asleep while Mary Bridget, then Maura, prepared for bed and crawled in next to her. She lay tense, waiting. One by one, Juliana heard the others also retire for the night. The flat grew quiet. Mr. O'Toole's snoring was the only sound.

Slowly Juliana inched out of bed. After crossing the room, she eased open the door and peered into the living room. Both Mickey and Dennis appeared to be fast asleep on the couch. Moving stealthily so as not to awaken them, she crept toward the kitchen. The trash bin was in its usual place, waiting for Mickey to empty it in the morning. Though she tried to be quiet while picking her way through the garbage, papers rustled and a can rattled as it fell to the floor and rolled into a corner. Juliana darted an anxious glance at the sofa, then breathed a sigh of relief. Mickey and Dennis slept undisturbed.

She found the newspaper covered with potato peels and smelling of cod near the bottom of the bin. Unable to risk turning on a lamp, she crossed to an open window where silvery moonlight streamed through. Kneeling, she spread the newspaper on the floor and smoothed the wrinkles as best she could. Juliana sat back on her heels and regarded the picture. The woman smiling up at her looked like a stranger. The artist had portrayed her as beautiful, not plain, sophisticated, not naive—and void of innocence. Yet it was Juliana. Unmistakably.

Tearing her gaze away, she forced herself to concentrate on the text. Drew MacAllister, as he was called, was a man with political aspirations to the state assembly. He had earned the backing of the extremely influential incumbent, Daniel Tennant. The article cast doubt on Drew's character. It was less kind to hers. It implied she was a woman of loose morals, a woman of the night, a woman who sold her favors to the highest bidder. Is MacAllister the sort of man, the article concluded, who deserves your vote for public office?

"Juliana, what in blazes are you up to?"

Juliana started at the sound of Dennis's voice. She picked up the paper and scrambled to her feet just as he came toward her. Like a youngster caught swiping cookies, she hid her booty behind her back.

He stopped in front of her clad only in trousers. "What are you hiding?" he asked.

"N-nothing." She shrugged, averting her gaze from his

bare chest. "I couldn't sleep. I thought maybe if I had something to read."

"So that's why you were rummaging through the garbage, looking for something to read?" He looked skeptical.

Juliana sidled toward the bedroom. "I happened to remember the newspaper you brought home."

"Now that you woke me up, I could use something to read, too. How about sharing the paper?" He held out his hand.

"It's the society pages," she lied, promising to confess the sin. "It wouldn't interest you. Good night."

Far from sleepy, Dennis went back to his bed and stared at the ceiling. What did Juliana Butterfield find so interesting in an old newspaper? It had to be something out of the ordinary if it caused her to rifle through the trash in the middle of the night. He had always loved puzzles; he'd find the solution to this one. And if it meant knocking the plaster saint off her pedestal, well, so much the better.

Most of Saturday was spent helping Mrs. O'Toole with the cleaning and baking. The entire family planned to attend Peggy Flynn's wedding celebration that evening. Even young Mickey was excited at the prospect.

Juliana sat on the edge of the bed and watched Maura fuss with her hair. "What have you done to Dennis?" Maura asked. "His eyes shoot daggers whenever he looks at you."

Juliana contemplated the scuffed toe of her shoe. "He asked me to go to the wedding with him and got angry when I refused."

Maura laughed. "Poor lad. You're probably the first girl to turn him down since Eileen O'Malley when we were in school." Her expression grew serious. "Oh, Juliana, change your mind and come with us. It'll be fun."

"I have nothing to wear. Besides, I promised Sister Esther I'd write her a letter."

"If only we were the same size, I'd be more than happy to share my wardrobe with you."

Juliana came off the bed and hugged Maura. "I know you would, but on me your skirts would show a disgraceful amount of leg."

"And as for the bodice, the buttons would pop. God saw fit to make me flat-chested instead of well endowed like you." Maura clapped her hand over her mouth and giggled. "That's a fine way to be talking to a nun."

Mary Bridget popped her head into the room. "Maura, c'mon. We'll be late."

"Coming, pet." Giving her red curls a final pat, Maura hurried to join her family.

For a time, Juliana enjoyed having the flat to herself. She wrote a short note to Sister Esther, omitting the tawdry details and assuring the kindly nun that she had been befriended by an Irish Catholic family. She stuffed the sheets of paper into an envelope and addressed it.

Consumed by a restless energy she was at a loss to contain, she prowled the apartment's small confines. Perhaps she had been hasty in refusing the O'Tooles' invitation. Noises filtered in to her: voices raised in anger, laughter, sounds of a baby crying and of children at play. Juliana felt alienated. For much of her life she had been segregated from the rest of society. So eager had she been to emulate her idol, Mother Margaret Ann, she would gladly have embraced convent life. But circumstances had intervened. It was time to put the past behind her. Time to stop being a spectator in life and become a participant. After a glance in the mirror, she picked up the letter and hurried out of the apartment.

There was still time to join the O'Toole family. How difficult could it be to find Saint Brendan's Hall? she asked herself. After listening to Maura and Mary Bridget talk, she had a good idea where it was located. She turned down Worth Street and headed toward Broadway, where she stopped at a mailbox and slipped her letter through the slot. She glimpsed a man darting into a doorway. A quiver of uneasiness shot through her, but she ignored it and continued on her way.

A light fog was rolling in off the harbor, shrouding the city. Juliana quickened her pace. She passed few people. Her apprehension grew. She began to doubt the wisdom of trying to find the wedding reception alone. Behind her, she heard something or someone bang into a trash barrel. When she turned to look, there was no one in sight. Once again she experienced the unsettling sensation that she was being followed.

To test her theory, Juliana decided to change course. She ducked down Mulberry, a side street scarcely wider than an alley. Hardly had she gone more than a dozen steps before she realized her error. By then it was too late.

Men, some in shirtsleeves, others in derbies, a few with walking sticks, lined the narrow passageway. They loitered in doorways, hung from windows, perched on wooden stoops. In the eerie mist, they appeared to be figures in a smudged pen and ink drawing. They fell silent, watchful, as Juliana stumbled to a halt. Danger was in the very air she breathed. Her chest felt tight and starved for oxygen, while her heart raced like a hummingbird's.

Two men wordlessly positioned themselves behind her, effectively cutting off any hope of retreat. The rest remained motionless. Juliana tamped down her panic. If only she could reach the end of the block . . . Once there, she could run; she could seek help. Willing herself to be courageous, she forced herself to place one foot ahead of the other. Slowly she began to walk the gauntlet. She could feel the dark heat of the men's stares. Just a little farther, she tried to bolster her resolve.

She was nearly there.

So close she could taste her victory.

She gasped.

A giant of a man separated from the shadows and blocked her path. "Welcome to Bandits' Roost."

CHAPTER
6

"BANDITS' ROOST?" JULIANA REPEATED, UNAWARE THAT she had uttered the name aloud. Dear Lord, what had she blundered into?

"You lost, girlie?" The giant hooked his thumbs in his suspenders and rocked back on his heels.

"I must have taken a wrong turn." She took a tentative step forward. "If you'll let me pass . . . "

The man didn't budge. Juliana's feet dragged to a halt. She cast a nervous glance around. The situation was as bad as she had feared. She was surrounded by a group of sinister-looking men.

"Yer mama shoulda warned you about this part of town," another man threatened, his hat brim pulled low as he lounged against a building. A cigarette dangled from his fingertips, its tendril of smoke rising to mingle with the fog.

Juliana's heart raced, but she tried to control her mounting panic.

"Nice girls don't come to Bandits' Roost," the giant spoke again.

The second man took a drag from his cigarette. "Maybe she ain't so nice."

71

The rest of the audience remained silent. As silent and watchful as a pack of wolves, Juliana thought. Or a flock of vultures. She was more frightened than she had ever been in her life. These men were lawless, evil. It would be impossible to defend herself against so many. Would her body be discovered in the morning, broken and lifeless, flung on a garbage heap? Her mouth felt so dry she couldn't swallow.

"Let her pass!" The quiet command rang with authority.

Heads turned in surprise. A newcomer stood in the street at the end of the block directly behind the giant, his black cape billowing in the ghostly mist. Though his face was shadowed, Juliana recognized the voice instantly. Andrew MacAllister. He had appeared dramatically, seemingly out of nowhere, and come to her rescue like a knight of old. At that precise moment, she could have forgiven him anything.

"If you value your life, you won't touch that young woman."

The giant tossed back a laugh. "That right? You and who else gonna stop me?" He made a show of looking around for imaginary allies. His antics drew guffaws.

"I don't need a bunch of thugs to back me up. I can fight my own battles. What about you?" Drew challenged.

"Name's Bull. Friend's don't call me that for nothing. Time comes I can't take on the likes of you, it's time to change my moniker."

Drew unfastened his cape. "Then it's just the two of us, Bull. We'll go a few rounds and see who's still standing. Winner takes the girl."

"Don't seem like much of a contest to me. You'll be dog meat when I get through."

Juliana's glance slid back and forth between the two men. Drew MacAllister was out of his mind if he thought he could best this bully in a street fight. He belonged in a courtroom or dressed in evening clothes, not brawling in some back alley like a common ruffian.

Drew motioned Juliana to one side, then tossed her his cape. His jacket followed. He loosened his collar and rolled up his sleeves, his eyes never leaving his opponent.

Pulling his suspenders down, Bull unbuttoned his shirt and shrugged out of it. The muscles in his massive chest rippled with each movement, and he proudly flexed his biceps for the appreciative crowd.

Juliana heard the low rumble of male voices placing wagers on the outcome of the fight. She shuddered. There was no question who would win the contest, only how long it would last. Without realizing she was doing so, she hugged Drew's garments tighter to her breast.

"Show 'em, Bull," shouted a scrawny man in a cloth cap. "Show 'em how we treat strangers in Bandits' Roost."

"I plan to, Jimmy. Yer in for a treat."

Bull dropped into a low crouch. Drew did likewise. The combatants began to circle each other warily. Bull threw the first punch, but Drew anticipated the move and dodged, the blow glancing off his shoulder. Drew's arm shot out and connected solidly with his opponent's chin. Though his head jerked backward, Bull didn't go down.

"Well, well, sonny boy had some boxing lessons," Bull snarled. Lowering his head like the animal that was his namesake, he rammed it into Drew's midsection while both fists viciously pummeled Drew's rib cage.

Juliana stifled a gasp.

"Give 'em hell!" someone shouted.

Drew let out a grunt of pain as jabs connected with

cracked ribs. Balling his left hand, he drove it into the giant's stomach. Breath left Bull's lungs in a loud whoosh. Drew didn't pause in his attack. He hurled a powerful right-handed punch that sent blood spurting from Bull's nose.

"Why, you son of a bitch!" Bull swiped at his bleeding nose with the back of his hand.

"Quit whining. Let's get on with it."

"You'll pay for this." Like dancers in a carefully re-hearsed routine, they circled each other, feinting and jab-bing, dodging and weaving.

Juliana held her breath and watched. Out of the corner of her eye, she saw the man in the cloth cap extend his walking stick. "Drew, watch out!"

Her cry came too late. Drew's legs tangled with the walk-ing stick, and he tumbled to the fog-slicked pavement.

Bull aimed a kick at his opponent's head. Instinctively, Drew rolled away, but not before the toe of a boot slammed into the side of his face.

Pressing back against a wall, Juliana turned her head, unable to watch the beating any longer.

Injured but tenacious, Drew reached out, grabbed Bull's pant leg, and pulled. Bull lost his footing. Reeling back-ward, he crashed into a rain barrel. Juliana ventured a look at the sound of staves splintering. An iron hoop from the rain barrel rolled drunkenly down the street and wobbled around the corner.

The two men lunged for each other. Locked together, they rolled over and over, fists flailing and blows landing with sickening thuds, until they were brought up short at the foot of a flight of stairs.

Bull groped through a trash heap for something to use as a weapon. His fingers curled around the neck of an empty whiskey bottle. Raising it, he smashed it against the nosing of one of the steps. "Now, you bastard, you'd better say your prayers!"

Drew scrambled to his feet, his gaze fixed on the jagged glass pointed menacingly at him. With a confident grin, Bull got to his feet, clutching the broken bottle. In a move that was surprisingly agile for a man of his size, he brought the glass slashing upward. Drew leapt away barely in time to avoid being ripped in half.

A murmur rippled through the audience.

Juliana bit down on her lower lip and forced herself to watch. Drew MacAllister had come to her rescue, but instead, it appeared, he would lose his life as well. She prayed for the nightmare to end.

As though already savoring the taste of victory, Bull inched forward. "They say a stab wound in the belly hurts like hell. It's a slow, painful way for a man to die." He rotated the lethal piece of glass in a narrow arc.

Drew's gaze never wavered from his opponent's. When Bull sprang forward to strike the fatal blow, Drew was ready. Neatly sidestepping his attacker, he caught Bull's wrist and squeezed. "Drop it," he ordered through clenched teeth.

"You son of a bitch," Bull panted, not relinquishing his grip.

Drew raised his knee and brought Bull's arm slamming down against it. The bottle shattered on the pavement; bones snapped.

With a howl of pain, Bull sank to the ground, his arm cradled against him. "You broke it, you broke my arm," he whimpered.

Drew stood above him, legs planted apart, chest heaving. Dark and disheveled, his hair hung over his forehead. His once immaculate white shirt was soiled, torn, and drenched with sweat. But to Juliana, he was brave and strong, the fabric heroes were made of.

Their eyes met, and Drew held out his hand. She caught it and stepped to his side. Fingers entwined, they faced the crowd. One by one, the once jeering audience melted into the shadows and silently slunk away.

"Let's go." Drew led Juliana away from Bandits' Roost.

At the end of the block, Juliana hazarded a final glance over her shoulder. Bull, still sniveling, laboriously staggered to his feet and lurched in the opposite direction.

"My carriage is just ahead," Drew said.

Juliana discerned its vague outline in the thickening fog. After their ordeal, it seemed a haven of safety. They had both survived. They were alive. The anxiety that had kept her nerves highly charged disappeared in a rush, leaving her drained. She stumbled. Drew's grip on her hand tightened protectively.

"Steady, lass."

The overwhelming need to be comforted rolled over her like a giant breaker, washing away reservations and misgivings. She turned toward the man who had rescued her and buried her face in his shoulder. Drew hesitated, then wrapped both arms around her and pulled her close.

"There, there, lass, it's all right." His voice deepened, the Scots burr pronounced. "No one is going to hurt you. I willna let them."

She grabbed onto his shirt and clung fast. "I was so scared. I thought we'd both be murdered."

"It's over now. Put it behind you." He continued to hold her until her trembling ceased and she pushed away.

She stared up at him, her expression sober. Blood trickled from the corner of his mouth, and the skin around his eye was turning an ugly purple. "You're hurt."

"Nothing time won't cure." He dug in his pocket for a handkerchief.

"Here, please, let me." She took the handkerchief from him and gently dabbed at his cut lip. He jerked back when she touched a particularly tender area. "Hold still," she chided. "Until tonight I was under the impression that lawyers used words, not their fists, to defend themselves.

"I was a boxing champ in college."

"A boxer? You?"

"Aye, lass." He grinned at her disbelief. "And when still a lad, I used my fists in the streets of Glasgow."

His smile was disarming and brought forth a smile in return. She stepped back, feeling suddenly shy. "Thank you for rescuing me. What you did took a lot of courage."

He shrugged off her gratitude. "Now I'm going to see you safely home." He took her elbow and helped her into the carriage, then climbed in himself. A slap of the reins sent the bays trotting down the street.

Juliana sat as close to Drew as she dared, scenes from the fight vivid in her memory. When the carriage approached an intersection, she noticed a lone man leaning against a street lamp. He raised a bottle and took a swig. She continued to watch as a gaudily painted woman, like the ones she had seen at the Ludlow Street jail, sauntered up and spoke to the man. He offered her a drink from his bottle; then the pair strolled off, laughing at some private joke.

Drew had also observed the exchange. His jaw clenched angrily. Juliana had very nearly gotten herself killed—or worse. Didn't she have any common sense at all? Perhaps she had been telling the truth all along. Didn't the convent teach young women about the ways of the world? He turned on her. "Whatever possessed you to venture down Mulberry Street? Good heavens, it isn't safe in broad daylight."

She debated how to respond. Should she confide that she suspected someone was following her? That she had darted into Mulberry Bend to test her suspicions?

Before she could decide on an answer, he went on, "Didn't those people you're staying with warn you of the dangers of the Five Points? The Bowery, the Tenderloin, Bottle Alley. These areas spawn thieves and holdup men. The criminal population is so great that even the police avoid certain sections."

She regarded him warily. The dashing hero who had sprung to her defense had disappeared. In his place was a fierce, dangerous man who could more than hold his own among the roughest elements. Could Drew have been the one following her? Moistening her lips, she asked the question foremost in her mind. "How did you happen to find me tonight?"

"I came looking for you. No one was home. When I asked the neighbors, one of them remembered that the O'Tooles were going to a wedding celebration tonight. For a five dollar gold piece, a boy said he saw you leave a short time ago and head across Worth—alone."

"So you were following me!"

Puzzled, he glanced at her briefly, then turned his attention to the street. "Hardly. I was about to return home when I saw an unescorted woman ahead of me. The fog was too dense and the distance too great for me to see who it was. When she veered down Mulberry Street, of all places, I decided to circle around the block just to make certain she was safe. Fortunate for you that I did."

Juliana laced her fingers together. His explanation sounded convincing. In spite of niggling doubts, she found herself wanting to believe him. Still, a small part of her was rankled that he would have come to the defense of a total stranger as easily as he had come to hers. "Assuming you're telling the truth, why did you seek me out? I thought I had made it perfectly clear I wanted no more to do with you."

He cast a fulminating look in her direction. "What a dour disposition you have, Miss Butterfield. How quickly you forget that I risked life and limb to save you."

She stared at her folded hands in embarrassment. He made her ashamed of her callous disregard of his heroics. "I didn't mean to sound ungrateful."

"Whether you choose to believe me or not, I've earned a reputation for honesty."

"And do you also have a reputation for ravishing clients charged to your care?" The accusation popped out of its own volition.

Slapping the reins, he urged the horses to a faster clip. He swallowed the truth that surged to his lips. No, Nick had to be kept out of this. It would never do to reveal his jealously guarded secret in a moment of anger. Yet it galled him to have Juliana question his moral character, brand him a defiler of helpless young women.

"To get back to your question as to why I called on you tonight: I came to warn you."

"Warn me? Of what?"

He guided the carriage to a halt near the O'Tooles' building, then turned to face her. Strands of dark gold hair had come loose from her prim bun, moisture in the air shaping them into ringlets around her face. She looked young, vulnerable—and very attractive. Drew shifted position, the pain in his bruised ribs making him grimace. "You and I, it seems, have become the target of a scandal-monger."

"The newspaper article," she breathed.

"Then you're aware of the situation." At her nod, he went

on. "I'd hoped that, with time, interest would fade. My hopes were premature."

"What do you mean?" She forced the query from lips that felt stiff.

"I came tonight to let you know that a second article appeared in this afternoon's edition, along with another picture."

"Holy Mother of God!" she exclaimed. "What kind of lies did they print this time?"

"It was a sketch of us. Together." He hesitated, weighing how much to tell her.

"Exactly how *together* were we in this picture?"

Her reputation was as much at stake as his. She had every right to know what was being printed. "To be precise, it was a picture of us locked in a passionate embrace, under the headline 'Lovers Reunite.' "

Her face paled. "But I don't understand. Who would report such a thing, and why?"

"Why? The answer is obvious. I plan to seek nomination to the state legislature when Daniel Tennant announces his retirement this fall. Someone is trying to discredit me by casting aspersions on my integrity. I need to find out who."

"You have no idea? Surely you know your enemies."

"Not necessarily. That's the reason I came to see you tonight. I planned to ask your help in tracking down the culprit."

"I'd like to help you, but I don't know how I can be of any use to you. I found out about the first article quite by accident."

"Have you noticed anything out of the ordinary? Anyone suspicious hanging about?"

"No," she said slowly. "But . . . "

"But?" he prodded. "Don't hold back on me, lass."

"Well, I've never actually seen anyone." She couldn't stop herself from anxiously scanning the street. "However, several times I've felt that I was being followed. I had the same feeling earlier tonight."

He leaned closer, his face intent, and placed a hand over her clenched ones. "Did you see anyone?"

Her thoughts took flight like startled birds. While his touch made her stomach quiver, the sight of his battered face made her want to soothe his bruises with a gentle touch.

"Think, Juliana. Did you see anyone at all?"

Juliana shook her head vigorously, the action more a denial of the disturbing sensations he stirred within her than a response to his question. She scooted along the seat until she was wedged in a corner of the carriage, well out of his reach.

He watched her for a moment; then his expression hardened, and he fixed his stare on the row of dingy tenements. "Sorry my touch is repugnant. I won't forget again."

Juliana flinched. That wasn't it at all, but how could she explain her reaction when she didn't understand it herself?

"I take it that your friends are unaware of the situation," he said.

"Dennis—" she began, her voice sounding small. She cleared her throat and tried again. "Maura's brother brought home a paper, but I don't think he saw the picture."

Favoring his injured rib cage, Drew stiffly climbed down from the carriage and came around to her side. "It's best they don't. This way they're not swayed by vicious slander."

He held out his hand to assist her, but she preferred instead to clamber from the carriage unaided. He walked with her to the door of the building. They stood facing each other, separated by more than distance.

"Can't we simply deny the lies they've printed?" she asked. "Demand the newspaper retract the stories?"

He smiled at her naïveté. "It would only be our word against theirs—and another story to distort. This sort of malicious gossip sells newspapers. Our best chance of stopping it is finding the person responsible."

One hand on the doorknob, she paused. "As long as I live, I'll never forget what you did for me this evening." Her eyes were troubled. "But under the circumstances, I think it would be wise if we never see each other again. Good night, Mr. MacAllister."

She left him standing there. A profound weariness came over her as she trudged up the five flights of stairs. Contradictory impressions bombarded her. Was Drew MacAllister a valiant hero or a mad rapist? Good or evil? Opposite sides of a coin. He had her totally confused.

In a Fifth Avenue mansion, two men regarded each other over a wide mahogany desk. It was near midnight; the brocade drapes were drawn.

"No one saw you come here?" the bearded, heavyset man asked.

The smaller man chuckled dryly. "Sure enough to bet my last nickel. Bein' invisible is what I get paid for. It's my God-given talent."

"Along with being the best sketch artist in the city." The heavier one drummed his fingers impatiently on the desktop. The gold crest on his onyx signet ring gleamed in the lamplight. "You said you followed the Butterfield woman tonight? What have you got for me?"

"I stayed with her until she turned down Mulberry Street.

No way I was goin' in after her. Lucky for her, MacAllister showed up when he did."

"MacAllister!"

"He musta come callin' after she left and been lookin' for her."

"What happened?"

"He beat the livin' daylights outta this thug named Bull. Afterward, I saw MacAllister huggin' the Butterfield woman. Only this time it was for real," he added.

"Hmm." The heavyset man puffed thoughtfully on a thick cigar. "Lovers embrace in back alley. Maybe we can use this to imply he's set her up in a love nest in some secluded section of town." He blew out smoke. "Dig into her background. See what you can find."

"Whatever you say, boss." The slight, balding, nondescript man rose to his feet. "Why the grudge against MacAllister?"

The man referred to as boss settled back in his oxblood leather chair. "MacAllister is handpicked to be Tennant's replacement. Tennant's a tired old man. He's let things slide. But with MacAllister, it'll be different. He's already talking about investigating certain contracts awarded to my company. He could ruin me."

"With Willie the Mole at your service, the only vote he'll get is his own."

Long after William Smith, alias Willie the Mole, had departed, the heavyset man sat at his desk, smoking. No need for Willie to know everything. It was time to settle an old account with MacAllister. Government contracts aside, there was still the matter of Victoria. He stubbed out his cigar.

Even after all these years, revenge would be sweet.

CHAPTER
7

AFTER TWO FRUITLESS WEEKS OF SEARCHING FOR WORK, her efforts were about to be rewarded. Elated, Juliana reread the note. "Maura, this is it. I can feel it."

Maura stopped primping and squeezed Juliana's shoulders. "I knew you would do better than a job in a sweatshop."

"A clerk in a bookstore," Juliana said enthusiastically. "What could be more perfect?" She set the note aside to finish repairing a torn seam. "The first thing I'm going to do is buy a new dress. This one has been laundered so many times it's falling apart."

Maura studied her friend with a shrewd eye. "Nothing personal, love, but in the future try to avoid wearing that horrid color."

"What?" Juliana feigned outrage. "Are you trying to tell me that I don't look good in dishwater gray? That it makes my skin look muddy and dull? Why, I think you're jealous."

"Dishwater gray," Maura sniffed. "That's too polite a term. I could think of better."

"Maura O'Toole," her mother scolded, coming into the

bedroom with a pile of folded laundry. "Keep a civil tongue in your head."

"Sorry, Mum." Maura's impish smile held no remorse.

"Here, dearie, best you take this just in case." Mrs. O'Toole handed Juliana the hat pin from her Sunday bonnet. "A woman's not safe walking the streets alone." Depositing the stack of clothing on the bed, she bustled out before Juliana could thank her.

"That's my mum," Maura laughed. "Just what does your note say?"

"The proprietor wants to talk to me after he closes his shop tonight. I'm to come around the back to his office. If all goes well, perhaps I can start tomorrow."

"What's he like?"

Juliana shrugged and snipped a piece of thread. "To be honest, I don't remember him. I must have applied for at least a hundred different jobs."

"Do you want me to come with you? I can spend some other evening with Jamie Flynn."

"Nonsense." Juliana slid off the bed and slipped on her dress. "Ever since I've known you, it's been Jamie this, and Jamie that. How can you even think of canceling?"

"This bookstore of yours is a good distance. I don't want anything happening to you."

Juliana was touched by her friend's concern. She also felt a little deceitful. She hadn't told anyone, not even Maura, about the incident at Bandits' Roost. It would have been impossible to do so without mentioning Drew MacAllister's name. She was thankful that no more pictures had appeared since then.

Mary Bridget opened the door and stuck her head in. "Maura, your beau's here."

"Hush!" Maura held a warning finger to her lips. "He'll hear you."

"He's got his hair all slicked down and smells like rose water." The young girl giggled, ignoring her sister's censorious look.

"Here, take this." Maura pressed a shiny penny in Juliana's hand. "It's my lucky charm. Maybe it'll work for you tonight." With a wave, she left to greet her newest admirer.

Ten minutes later, the good wishes of the O'Toole clan ringing in her ears, Juliana was on her way uptown. The family had been more than kind, giving her food, lodging, and unconditional friendship. But each day she felt more and more like a burden on their limited resources. And each day she felt Dennis's animosity grow. Although he never said a word, Juliana's instincts told her that he had seen at least one of the newspaper articles and was biding his time.

Buildings cast long shadows in the gathering twilight. A ragpicker, his dogcart heaped with castoffs, plodded homeward. Lights flickered in windows like fireflies on a summer evening. Couples strolled arm and arm, smiling and laughing. Juliana passed an ice cream parlor and wondered if Maura and her beau were enjoying each other's company. What would it feel like, she wondered, to be half of a couple? To have someone to share her life with—the laughter and the tears? To have someone special to talk with on the front stoop? What would it be like to be loved?

Juliana had known precious little love in her lifetime. Her mother had died when she was hardly more than a baby. Her father had abandoned her when she was ten to seek his fortune in the Nevada silver mines. At the convent, Sister Margaret Ann had taken her under her wing and, later, carefully prepared Juliana to follow in her footsteps. But her father and Sister Margaret Ann were both gone now. Juliana had no one.

Enough memories! she admonished herself. She winced as she stepped on something sharp. Bracing her arm against a storefront, she eased off her shoe and shook out a pebble. She frowned at the hole in the leather. After buying a dress, her next purchase would be a new pair of shoes, perhaps kid boots that buttoned above the ankle. And she would go to the ice cream parlor and treat herself to a big dish of chocolate, or maybe strawberry, ice cream. Feeling somewhat better, she continued her long walk.

As she neared Twenty-third Street, she checked the address under a gaslight. It was completely dark now. She looked around, but didn't feel frightened. The area appeared safe enough. Just the same, she slid her hand into her skirt pocket for the reassuring touch of Mrs. O'Toole's hat pin. Halfway down the block, she spotted the sign: Prose & Poetry, New and Used Books.

Juliana went around the back of the store as the note instructed. The alley appeared deserted. She made her way down the narrow passageway lined with trash cans and located the rear entrance of the shop. After rubbing Maura's penny for good luck, she knocked on the door. She waited patiently. When there was no answer, she tried again. Still no response. She stood, debating what to do next.

A loud crash exploded the stillness. Letting out a cry, Juliana whirled around as a tin can rolled to her feet. A tiger-striped tomcat meowed at her from atop a trash barrel, then leapt down, and slunk away.

"Either you have a lot of courage or you desperately need a job."

Startled, she clasped her hand to her chest. Distracted by

the stray cat, Juliana had been unaware of Drew's approach. "What are *you* doing here?" she breathed.

He sauntered closer, hands shoved in his pockets. "Sorry to disappoint you, but there's no job. I'm the one who sent the note."

"Disappointment" was too mild a word for the crushing sense of defeat that weighed on her. Tears stung her eyes. She blinked them back. Drew MacAllister could not have played a crueler prank. What a mean, spiteful thing to do. Her dashed hopes were transformed into rage. "You tricked me," she accused, unable to keep the angry quaver from her voice.

He shrugged. "I knew you'd never agree to meet me otherwise, so I was forced to resort to trickery."

"You're absolutely right." Her hands balled into fists at her sides. "I meant it when I said I never wanted to see you again."

"Not so fast!" His words lashed out, halting her as she turned to leave. "It's important that we talk."

"No," she shouted, her eyes blazing.

She reminded him of a tawny jungle cat, sleek, tense, and, if cornered, ready to scratch and claw. He had to make her realize the gravity of the situation. He needed her cooperation, not her enmity. However, what he was about to propose was not intended to be said in some back alley. He reached for her. "Let's go somewhere private."

She jerked away from his touch. "I'm not going anywhere with you."

"Stop acting childish," he said, impatience creeping into his tone.

"Me? Childish?" She tossed her head. "You're the one who refuses to take no for an answer."

"My carriage is waiting. You're coming with me."

"Who do you think you are to order me about?"

"Trying to reason with a woman is impossible." His supply of patience exhausted, Drew adopted a firmer approach. "You're coming, Juliana, if I have to pick you up and toss you over my shoulder."

"You can't bully me." She turned on her heel.

His hand snaked out and latched on to her arm.

She looked at the strong, tapered fingers digging into her upper arm. The heat of their touch seared through the thin sleeve of her dress and seemed to brand her flesh. As she met his fierce gaze, her anger nearly faltered. "If you don't let go of me this instant, I'll scream."

"Stop behaving like a hysterical female," he said through gritted teeth. "Come along like a good girl."

Juliana opened her mouth to carry out her threat. The sound, scarcely more than a peep, was cut off when his hand clamped over her mouth. She pried at his hand.

He hauled her backward against him. "I hate to use force—" He yelped as the sharp point of a hat pin jabbed into his thigh.

Gaining her freedom, Juliana clutched her skirt in both hands and sprinted away. Drew recovered quickly and caught hold of her arm. "Damn you," he swore. "You're creating a scene." He glanced around anxiously, relieved to find that except for Jack Burrows patiently waiting in the carriage, no one was in sight. His and Juliana's purported relationship had already generated enough unwanted publicity. He propelled her back into the alley.

The situation was spiraling out of control. Juliana felt close to panic. "Help!" she cried.

The last vestiges of his restraint snapped. Drew had had enough. "Think what you will, lady, but you're going to hear what I have to say."

He stuffed a handkerchief into her mouth and secured it in place. Capturing both of her wrists in one hand, he removed his tie. Juliana struggled. Eyes wide with terror, she watched as Drew twisted an end of his silk tie around one of her wrists and then, forcing both of her arms behind her back, bound her wrists together. Without another word he picked her up and slung her like a sack of grain over his shoulder, jolting the air from her lungs.

At the end of the alley, he looked up and down the street. He waited for a lone buggy to drive past, then called to his driver, "Jack, pull closer."

"Sure thing, guv." Jack stuck his pipe in his mouth. He deftly maneuvered the carriage over the sidewalk, close to the entrance of the alley. "How 'bout this?"

Yanking open the carriage door, Drew deposited Juliana on a leather-covered seat, climbed in, and sat opposite her. "The Wentworth place," he barked.

"Anywhere you say." Jack slapped the reins, and the carriage moved forward. "Don't know why you didn't try flowers," the driver muttered, shaking his head. "Worked on the rest of your ladies."

His mouth a hard line, Drew stared out the carriage window. The young woman hadn't given him any choice. He had only wanted to talk. All she had to do was come along peaceably. Was that too much to ask? Apparently it was. She had proved as obstinate as a mule and thickheaded in the bargain. This situation was entirely her fault.

He shifted his brooding gaze to Juliana. Just when he was close to realizing his lifelong goal, he stood to lose everything. All because of her. If she wasn't stopped, Juliana Butterfield would destroy his dreams before they had a chance to become reality. "Ever since you came into my life, you've brought me nothing but trouble. It's time we put an end to this."

Each word struck Juliana like a steel blade, the implied threat embedding itself as deeply in her heart as the blade of a sword. He was a madman, and she had foolishly pushed him beyond his endurance. His expression was black. She remembered belatedly the volatile temper cunningly hidden beneath a veneer of polished sophistication. Hadn't Drew MacAllister brutally raped her, then attempted to buy her silence? Then there was the fight with Bull at Bandits' Roost. Drew had come away the victor. Dear Lord, when provoked the man was capable of anything—even murder.

The ride seemed interminable, taking her farther and farther from civilization. This fact only seemed to confirm her worst suspicions. He was going to kill her—and wanted no witnesses.

Her stomach churned with nausea. She felt light-headed and dizzy. She knew she needed her wits about her if she hoped to come away alive. She concentrated on taking slow, deep breaths, but the air felt unusually heavy and difficult to inhale. Juliana received no reassurance as she watched the man across from her. He looked dangerous.

The wheels crunched on loose gravel, slowed, and came to a stop. Drew flung the carriage door open and scooped Juliana off the seat. He stepped out onto a winding drive, but before Juliana could shake the hair from her eyes, he flung her over his shoulder once again. Her hair, loosened in the struggle, obscured her vision as effectively as a blindfold.

"Wait here," Drew instructed his driver as he climbed a short flight of stairs. He paused to rummage through his pockets, and Juliana heard the jingle of silver, followed by the scrape of a key in a lock. He strode inside a building, slamming the door behind him. Abruptly, he stood Juliana on her feet.

A buzzing, like a swarm of locusts, started in her head. A gray fog descended, making objects hazy. Juliana tried to focus on Drew, but he seemed to be standing at the far end of a tunnel. Suddenly her knees buckled, and she sank to the floor.

When her eyelids fluttered open, Drew's face swam into focus.

"Are you all right, lass?" He knelt at her side, alternately fanning her face and rubbing her wrists. "You gave me quite a scare."

She licked dry lips. "What happened?"

"You fainted dead away. Here, take a sip." He held a bottle to her mouth and tipped it so that she was forced to take a swallow. The liquid burned a path down her throat and pooled in her stomach. Coughing, she pushed the bottle aside.

"Enough of Jack's whiskey?"

"Where have you brought me?"

"This place is being built for friends of mine. They're in Italy for the summer. They asked me to check its progress while they're away."

Juliana braced herself on both elbows and looked around. They appeared to be in the drawing room of a mansion still under construction. In the darkened room, the light from a single candle cast ghostly shadows. She could distinguish the shapes of assorted wooden crates shoved to one side, buckets of paint stacked nearby, and plasterer's scaffolding erected against a long wall. A few pieces of furniture were draped with sheets, including the sofa she was lying on.

The house was obviously vacant, and probably so isolated

that no passerby would hear a scream for help. "What are you going to do with me?" she whispered, her earlier fears returning.

"You try me sorely, lass." Drew sighed impatiently. "At times I'm tempted to strangle you."

Bent on escape, Juliana jumped to her feet and raced across the room.

"What the hell . . . " Drew swore, and chased after her.

Juliana darted behind a row of tall shipping crates, which blocked out the meager candlelight, and found herself in total darkness. Her hands groped the walls, hoping to find a doorway, encountering instead the smooth, cool plaster of a mitered corner. A sob tore from her throat at the realization that she was trapped with nowhere to run.

"Juliana, come out. Stop playing silly games."

Pressing her hand to her mouth to smother another cry, she wedged herself into the corner, hoping . . . praying. Drew's footsteps echoed on the uncarpeted wood floors. Over the tops of the crates, she saw the candlelight grow brighter as he neared her hiding place. Her heart hammered in her ears.

"There you are!" He loomed in front of her, candlestick in hand.

Tears shimmered in her eyes, making them look like liquid gold. "Please don't hurt me."

"Hurt you?" He frowned. "Where did you get a fool notion like that?"

"You said it's time to put an end to the trouble I've caused, that you want to strangle me. Why else would you bring me here?"

"Good grief. You really think I mean you harm?"

She nodded. A tear slipped down her cheek.

"What kind of monster do you take me for?" Drew already knew the answer. She believed him to be a man capable of rape—and even murder. The knowledge brought a sharp stab of pain. "All I wanted to do tonight was talk to you. I tried to make that clear at the bookstore. What I have to say demands privacy. Now, lass, are you willing to listen?"

Juliana searched his face. He seemed sincere. If he was telling the truth, her behavior had been abominable, the result of an overactive imagination, a fault the good sisters had often lectured her on. "All right," she finally agreed.

Drew held out a hand to assist her, but she shied away. Understanding her reluctance, he stood back as she moved past the crates. He motioned toward the sofa. "You have my word, I won't touch you again. Just sit and listen to what I have to say. Afterward, I'll see you home."

She perched on the edge of the sofa, hands folded primly. Drew set the candlestick on a box and walked to a curtainless window at the end of the room. "Another, even more damaging newspaper article has appeared," he began. "The reporter found out that you were a client released in my custody. They're claiming that I corrupted an innocent young girl. My ethics and my professional reputation are being questioned."

"You expect me to deny the truth? You're forgetting how you came home drunk, forced yourself on me, then tried to buy me off like a common strumpet." Juliana clenched her hands tightly, afraid she had gone too far.

Drew realized his error. Raking a hand through his hair, he cursed his stupidity. "It gets worse," he said. "Your reputation is being destroyed as well. The article goes on to charge that you, no longer the innocent, have become my plaything. That we're carrying on a sordid affair in some secluded love nest." He paused, hands behind his back, regarding her as though she were on the witness stand. "How will the O'Tooles react when they hear these allegations? Will they still want you under their roof?"

Juliana tensed. One lesson she had learned over the last weeks was that people were quick to jump to conclusions without considering all the facts. Not even Mother Superior had given her a chance to explain what had happened with Freddie Westhaven. Instead she had summarily dismissed Juliana from the convent. Would the O'Tooles be any different if they read the newspaper's lies? She doubted it. It was a chance she couldn't take. "What do you suggest we do?"

"I have a business proposition. I spoke with my friend, Assemblyman Tennant. We've decided the best course of action is for you to marry me. A wedding will put an end to the gossip once and for all."

"Married!" Juliana gasped, feeling as though she was about to faint again. "Surely you aren't serious?"

"I've never been more serious. As Daniel pointed out, it's the perfect solution for both of us."

"Your logic escapes me. Kindly explain how you came up with such a ludicrous idea."

"We both stand to benefit from the arrangement. I plan to seek public office, and a wife will make me appear more stable and mature to the voters. They prefer someone settled, a family man. As for your part, you have everything to gain. You'll have a certain social standing as my wife and will never want for anything."

Juliana shot to her feet. "The thought of marriage to you sickens me."

"Well, you're not the woman I've dreamed of marrying either," he retaliated, looking her up and down.

His insolent perusal brought a flush of color to her pale cheeks. She knew she must look bedraggled, and she restrained the urge to smooth the tangle of hair cascading over her shoulders.

"Sorry," he relented. "I didn't mean to be insulting. Where you're concerned, I always seem to do or say the wrong thing." He began to pace. "My political future is dangling by a thread. Your reputation is in tatters. A bold move now and we can salvage both. Daniel is influential. He's certain we could convince the public that ours is the romance of the decade."

"But I don't love you. And you certainly don't love me." She raised her hand in supplication, then let it fall. "Don't you see that it's all wrong?"

"I'm speaking of a marriage in name only, complete with separate bedrooms. Ours won't be the first. This kind of partnership has advantages. We'll be expected to make occasional appearances together, of course, but the rest of the time we'll be free to pursue our own interests."

"The answer is no. Absolutely, unequivocably, no." She drew herself up to her full height. "As I see it, the problem is not so much that I don't love you—but, Mr. MacAllister, that I don't even like you."

CHAPTER
8

UPON REACHING THE FOURTH-FLOOR LANDING OF THE TEN-
ement, Juliana heard a heated argument in progress. On
the fifth-floor landing, she identified the angry voices as
belonging to members of the O'Toole family. Starting up
the remaining flight of stairs, she realized that she was the
cause of their quarrel. A sinking feeling started in the pit
of her stomach.

Clutching the stair rail with one hand, she gnawed her
lower lip and wondered what to do. Barge into their midst?
Or leave unnoticed? While she debated, the fight continued.

"How many times do I have to tell you? It's right here in
black in white!" Dennis shouted. "She's been making fools
of us. Telling us how she almost took the vows. Hah! She
and her rich uptown boyfriend probably laugh themselves
silly at how gullible we are."

"I don't believe a word of it! There has to be a simple
explanation." Maura came to Juliana's defense.

"I think it's romantic," Mary Bridget piped up. "He's so
handsome."

"Hush, child," Mrs. O'Toole chided. "Juliana's a God-
fearing girl. She could never do what that story claims."

"I'm telling you, Mum," Dennis insisted, "she's a slut."

"Dennis Patrick O'Toole, how many times do you have to be told to keep a civil tongue?"

"Mum," twelve-year-old Mickey wailed, "you don't have to put your hands over my ears. I'm no baby."

"None of your sass, Michael. You're my baby and always will be."

Mr. O'Toole, the family patriarch, spoke next. "Dennis has a point, Mary. The newspapers wouldn't be printin' a pack of lies. There must be some truth to the story. Don't be forgettin' we have children to protect. We don't want the likes of her influencin' our youngsters. The Butterfield woman has to go."

"But, Patrick," Mary O'Toole pleaded, "can't we at least ask her to explain before we turn our backs on her?"

"Mum's right, Pa," Maura interjected. "What if Juliana's telling the truth?"

"Sometimes I don't know if you womenfolk are soft-hearted or just plain softheaded," Patrick grumbled. "All right, I'll listen. But her explanation better be good."

The battle lines in the O'Toole household were clearly drawn, women on one side, men on the other. But men wielded the power. Juliana fished in her skirt pocket for the lucky penny Maura had loaned her. It was no longer there; neither was Mrs. O'Toole's hat pin, both lost in her scuffle with Drew MacAllister. A bad omen, she thought as she opened the apartment door.

A tableau greeted her. The family, gathered in the kitchen, stared back. Mr. O'Toole sat at the table, a mug of tea cradled in his large callused hands. Mrs. O'Toole, still wearing her apron, sat opposite. Mary Bridget, chin propped on her fists, occupied the seat between her parents, while Mickey slumped on a low stool, a bored look on his young face. Dennis lounged against the sink, arms folded across his chest in a belligerent pose. At Juliana's entrance, Maura had stopped pacing the floor.

"I couldn't help but overhear." Juliana stepped inside and closed the door.

Dennis broke the strained silence. "So, the little tramp returns. Where have you been? Meeting your lover?"

A telltale flush spread over Juliana's cheekbones.

Maura gave her brother a menacing look. "Did you get the job?" she asked Juliana.

"No." Juliana shook her head. "There was no job. It was a cruel trick."

Mrs. O'Toole looked puzzled. "Then who sent the note?"

"Probably her rich boyfriend," Dennis answered. "Tell me, Miss Butterfield, isn't he the one I saw you talking to, the one who offered you money?"

"Enough shilly-shally!" Patrick O'Toole slammed his mug on the table and shoved himself to his feet, his chair scraping the floor. "Let's set matters straight. Miss Butterfield . . . Juliana . . . Dennis brought home this here newspaper with your picture all over the front page." He poked at the incriminating evidence, which lay on the kitchen table.

Her gaze followed his stubby finger. The newspaper carried a sketch of Drew and one of herself.

"It claims," Mr. O'Toole continued, "you've been carryin' on with this lawyer fellow. Do you know the gent?"

Juliana found a rapt audience waiting for her next words. Nervously she cleared her throat. "Yes, I know Mr. Mac-Allister. But not the way the newspaper makes it appear."

"See, dear." Mrs. O'Toole reached out and patted her husband's arm. "I told you Juliana was innocent."

Dennis snorted. "You're the one who's innocent, Mum."

He crossed the room to stand so close to Juliana they were almost toe to toe. His gaze bored into her. "Have you spent the night at MacAllister's for a price? Have you been seeing him regularly?"

Juliana fought the urge to back away.

"No glib answers?" he taunted. "Cat got your tongue?"

"Dennis, quit badgering the girl." Maura went to Juliana's side. "Go ahead, Juliana," she encouraged. "Tell everyone none of this is true."

Juliana glanced at the expectant faces, willing them to believe her. "What Dennis said is all true, but—"

Mr. O'Toole, his face florid, slapped his hand on the table. "That settles it. The woman goes."

"But, Pa—" Maura turned to her father.

"I won't have a loose woman corruptin' the morals of my children. That's final."

Stunned by the edict, Juliana stared into Patrick O'Toole's set face. The shocked gasps of Maura and Mrs. O'Toole barely registered in her befuddled mind. Finally, turning her gaze to Dennis, she saw his satisfied smirk.

"Patrick, it's nearly midnight. At least let Juliana stay the night," Mary O'Toole coaxed her obdurate husband.

"Very well," he relented. "But don't expect me to go changin' my mind come mornin'. It's late, let's get some sleep." He ambled toward the bedroom followed by Mrs. O'Toole, who gave Juliana a tentative smile before disappearing after him.

"I'm going to bed. I'm tired." Yawning widely, Mickey wandered toward his bed on the sofa.

Mary Bridget hid a yawn behind her hand and after a last curious glance at her sister and Juliana, went to the girls' bedroom. Dennis gave the two a jaunty salute and left them alone.

Maura put her arm around Juliana's shoulder. She lowered her voice. "You can't believe half of what you read in the newspapers. Nothing people love more than juicy gossip. Mum will try to talk Pa into changing his mind. Things will look brighter in the morning."

Juliana's shoulders slumped in defeat. "Oh, Maura, I hope you're right. If not, I don't know what I'm going to do."

"Come sit. I'll make you a cup of tea and we can chat just like the first time we met."

Juliana gratefully sank onto a kitchen chair and let Maura pamper her. Maura knew only that she had spent her first night in New York at Andrew MacAllister's brownstone and that at first light he had requested she leave. Juliana hadn't confided how Drew had forced himself on her. The subject, too embarrassing and humiliating to mention, was best left unspoken. Now she wished she had confessed everything to her new friend. She desperately needed someone to understand her predicament. But her life had become so terribly complicated that she didn't know where to begin.

Maura placed a cup of tea in front of Juliana and joined her at the table. "Someone must have seen you leave Mr. MacAllister's place that morning. Why do you suppose the paper would print stories like that?"

Juliana wrapped icy fingers around the cup. "Someone is set on ruining Drew MacAllister's chances of being elected to the state assembly."

Maura's brows drew together. "Who?"

"Drew has no idea. But he said that if this scandal doesn't end soon, his reputation will be tarnished beyond repair— and mine along with it."

A pounding on the door ended their whispered conversation.

"Mum, Pa, let me in," a tearful voice pleaded.

Maura was the first to reach the door. "Katie!" she cried in surprise upon finding her older sister.

Juliana got to her feet and craned to see the figure standing on the threshold. She found a young woman of perhaps twenty-four with dark curly hair and eyes red-rimmed and puffy from tears. Her most outstanding feature, however, was a huge belly. The woman, holding a sleeping toddler in one arm and a large parcel in the other, was obviously in the final stages of pregnancy.

"Katie darlin'." Mrs. O'Toole flew out of the bedroom, tying her wrapper as she hurried to greet her firstborn. "What are you doing here this time of night?"

"Oh, Mum, Sean up and left me." Sobbing, Katie flung herself in her mother's arms.

"There, there, darlin'," Mrs. O'Toole crooned. "It's all right. You've come home."

Juliana stood to one side and watched the O'Tooles file past to gather around Katie. Maura took the baby from her sister's arms and settled him on her parents' bed, then rejoined the others.

"Tell us what happened, darlin'." Mrs. O'Toole guided Katie into the kitchen and gently pushed her down on a chair.

Juliana slid her teacup, still full, toward the distraught woman. Patrick O'Toole went to the cupboard, took out a bottle, and added a generous amount of Irish whiskey to the cup. Before recapping the bottle, he took a healthy swallow and handed it to Dennis.

"He left me, Mum." Katie sniffed back tears. "His letter came an hour ago. It said by the time I read it his ship would have set sail for Dublin. Sean said he hated America, hated New York, and hated being m-married."

"The dirty low-down scum!" Patrick's massive hands curled into fists. He looked as though he longed to throttle his errant son-in-law.

"That no-good . . . " Dennis was about to elaborate but a warning look from his mother cut short his tirade.

Katie's chin quivered, and tears rolled down her cheeks. "He even took the rent money. I had nowhere else to go."

Mary O'Toole planted a kiss on her daughter's brow. "Hush, darlin', don't you worry. You always have a home with us. We O'Tooles stick together."

Long after the household quieted, Juliana lay sandwiched between Maura and Katie, staring into the darkness. Even if Mr. O'Toole chose to reverse his decision, Katie's return had made it impossible for her to remain with the family. The cramped quarters were strained to their limits with Katie and her small son. And soon there would be another baby.

Juliana enumerated the problems she faced, but found no solutions. No job, no money, no place to stay. A vicious circle. Though she had looked for work, the prospect of finding it, especially by tomorrow, appeared bleak. She was only one among New York City's many jobless.

Emma Lattimer's kindly face surfaced in her memory. Besides the O'Tooles, Emma had been the only one to befriend her. But in view of the dear lady's fragile health, Juliana wouldn't think of imposing on her—providing she knew how to contact her, which she didn't.

You'll never want for anything. Like a litany at vespers, Drew MacAllister's promise repeated itself in her head. Juliana wrestled with her conscience. His marriage proposal didn't seem nearly as ludicrous now as it had earlier. Would it be so wrong to accept his offer? Her needs were simple— food, clothing, shelter. Security. Drew's needs, on the other hand, were more complex. He was an ambitious man who dreamed of being an assemblyman. As his wife, she could help him attain his goal.

Each had something the other wanted.

In the hours before dawn, she reached a decision. A business proposition, he had deemed it; a business proposition it would be.

The legal jargon wasn't making sense. Drew gave up all pretense of reading the contract and flung it aside. Rising, he crossed his office and stood before the window, scowling down at the street.

He had accomplished little. Throughout the day thoughts of Juliana Butterfield had intruded into his orderly routine. He recalled her stricken expression when she discovered that the note was a hoax and there was no job. And he remembered all too well her stark terror when she believed he intended to kill her. His treatment of her had been unforgivable. He had behaved like a barbarian.

His scowl deepened. Why couldn't the girl simply bend to his sound judgment and advice? Instead, she constantly challenged both. She irritated the hell out of him. Weren't nuns supposed to be submissive creatures, devoted to serving others? With Juliana's headstrong disposition, it was no wonder she hadn't remained in the convent. Yet he couldn't help but feel a reluctant admiration. The young woman had spirit.

Further ruminations were halted by a timid knock. "What is it?" he growled.

Drew's secretary, Norman Wilcox, a man in his midtwenties, his hair parted in the middle and slicked down with Macassar oil, opened the door. "Assemblyman Tennant would like to see you, sir."

Daniel Tennant burst into the room. "Goddammit! Can't you lease an office on the first floor instead of making an old man climb two flights of stairs?"

At a look from his employer, the secretary withdrew. "What brings you here, Daniel?" Drew asked.

Winded, Daniel leaned heavily on his walking stick as he crossed the room. Tossing his black derby on the desk, he sank into a chair. "You know damn well what brings me here," he wheezed. Taking out a starched linen handkerchief, he blotted beads of perspiration from his brow. "Did you see the girl?"

Drew walked to a sideboard and, after taking out a bottle of scotch and two glasses, poured drinks. "Yes, I saw her."

"Well?" Daniel sounded impatient. "How did it go? Did you make her see reason?"

"The lady turned down the chance to become Mrs. Andrew MacAllister." Drew handed Daniel a drink.

"Turned you down, did she? I don't think you're making much of an effort to convince the young woman." Daniel leaned forward. "What's the real problem? Doesn't she look as good in person as she does in her pictures? Want a fancier wife?"

Uncomfortable under his mentor's unrelenting stare, Drew sat down again and rearranged a stack of papers. "She's passable."

"Passable!" Daniel's voice rose. "What the hell is that supposed to mean? Boy, you're sounding more and more like a politician every day. Does that mean she hasn't got buck teeth? That her face won't scare young children?"

"She's quite ordinary-looking, actually. The type you'd pass on the street and never glance at twice. The word 'plain' might best describe her." Except for her eyes, Drew added silently. Her amber eyes were truly remarkable. And in all fairness, her features were delicate, almost patrician, considerably finer than average.

Sipping his scotch, Daniel observed his protégé. "Is she fat?"

"No, Juliana's quite slender. If anything, she's even slimmer now than when I first saw her." Drew's expression turned introspective. "I doubt that she's eating properly, living in that tenement."

"If she's not fat or ugly, what's the problem? Is she holding on to some silly schoolgirl notion about marrying for love?"

"She claims that isn't the problem." Drew's mouth twisted into a humorless smile. "It seems she doesn't like me."

"What the devil does that have to do with getting married?"

Drew raised his glass and took a swallow. "Everything, it seems." Her dislike bothered him more than he cared to admit. He could have accepted, even respected, the fact that she might not want to marry him because she didn't love him. But it was difficult to reconcile himself to the low esteem in which she held him. Her loathing had been unmistakable.

"Doesn't like you, eh? In my experience, women want to be cosseted, want to be courted. Candy and flowers work miracles."

"She's not like most," Drew said. "She's one of a kind."

Daniel finished his drink and set the glass down. Using his walking stick, he levered himself to his feet. "The election is just a year away. If you don't take control of this situation soon, we stand to lose all we've worked for. Something like this tests a man's mettle. Separates the doers from the dreamers." He picked up his hat. "You disappoint me, boy. I thought you were made of sterner stuff than to be bested by a mere slip of a girl."

After Daniel left, Drew leaned back in his chair, massaging stiff muscles in his neck. Daniel was right. His chances of winning the nomination were rapidly dwindling. The assembly seat meant more to him than just power. It symbolized two very important elements he had lacked as a bastard in the streets of Glasgow: respectability and acceptance.

From the very beginning, he had mishandled the situation with Juliana Butterfield. But how could he have done differently without jeopardizing Nick's future? If protecting his brother cost him a seat in the assembly, so be it. He wouldn't ruin Nick's life to save his own.

Juliana waited patiently in the outer office. Like Drew's home, the office was Spartanly furnished. Two identical brown leather chairs were arranged side by side along one wall, secretary's desk and file cabinet on another. A coat rack stood near the door. Everything was serviceable, practical.

Trying to ignore the butterflies that flitted in her stomach, Juliana glanced at Drew's secretary. Upon her arrival, the man had made it clear that he regarded her as a nuisance for barging in and insisting she be allowed to see Drew without an appointment. Now he sat hunched over his typewriter, seemingly engrossed in his work.

Surreptitiously, she wiped her sweaty palms on her skirt. She looked up as the door to the inner office opened and closed. An elderly gentleman carrying an ivory handled walking stick and wearing a black derby left without a glance in her direction.

The secretary stopped typing and turned to Juliana. "I'll

see if Mr. MacAllister can fit you into his schedule. He rarely sees people without an appointment."

He disappeared into the inner office and reappeared moments later. "Follow me." He led her to Drew's private sanctuary, opened the door, and stepped aside.

Juliana took a deep breath and crossed the threshold. Drew sat facing her behind a large desk, looking every bit as formidable as he had the first time they met. A saying of Mrs. O'Toole's sprang to mind: *"It's like makin' a bargain with the devil."* It took all Juliana's willpower to stay when she wanted to run.

Drew stood. "That'll be all, Wilcox," he told his secretary. "See that we're not disturbed."

"Yes, sir." The secretary closed the door, leaving them alone.

"If you're too busy . . . " Juliana's voice trailed off.

"No," he said. "I'm glad you came."

She hated herself for what she was about to do. Coming here was an admission of her defeat—and his triumph. Her pride in tatters, she was left with precious little dignity. Conflict and doubt played across her mobile features.

"Please, have a seat." He motioned toward the chair recently vacated by the assemblyman.

A wide gulf seemed to separate them. Swallowing her misgivings, Juliana took the first tentative step to narrow the gap. It was an odd sensation, that short walk across the room. In doing so, she was aware that she was leaving the past behind to step into a future fraught with uncertainties. The journey once made, there could be no return. Nothing would ever be the same.

Drew watched, tense and unsmiling, as Juliana sat with rigid posture on the edge of the chair.

On her way uptown, Juliana had rehearsed exactly what

she would say to him. But now, as she sat in his office, her mind went blank. She groped for something to break the awkward silence. Her gaze fastened on a picture in a silver frame sitting on his desk. Two boys grinned back at her, the youngest about five, the older perhaps eighteen. Even with the wide age difference, they bore a striking family resemblance. "Is that you and your brother?"

"Yes, that's Nick. He's away at school." Drew turned the frame so she could no longer see the photograph, then focused his attention on her. "You look as though you haven't had much sleep. Is everything all right?"

She felt uncomfortable under his critical regard. "I'm fine."

"Funny," he mused. "You don't look fine. Care to tell me about it?"

He seemed sincere. The temptation to unburden herself became too great to resist. "The O'Tooles read the story in the newspaper." The admission came out haltingly. "They were arguing about what to do when I went home last night."

"Did they believe the newspaper's lies?"

"I think Maura and her mother believed me, or were at least willing to listen to my side, but . . . "

"But . . . ?" he prompted.

"Dennis, Maura's brother, called me all sorts of vile names. He persuaded his father that the story was true."

Drew studied her for a long moment. "If the opinion of these people is so important to you, I'll go to them and explain what really happened."

Juliana was touched by his offer. "You'd do that for me?"

"Yes, if that's what you want. I never meant you harm, although I know you find that difficult to understand."

"You might convince them, but I'm afraid I can no longer continue to live there. You see, Katie's husband left her destitute, with a little boy and another baby on the way. She had to come home."

"And who is Katie?"

"Maura's older sister. Even if the O'Tooles wanted me to stay, they have no room for me now."

"I see." Drew sat behind his desk and reached out absently to trace with his thumb the filigree on the picture frame.

Juliana lowered her eyes, then raised them slowly to meet the gray-blue ones studying her so intently. "I came here this afternoon to tell you I accept your proposal. I'm willing to marry you, providing you agree to one stipulation."

He raised a brow. What did she have in mind? Had she suddenly turned mercenary? Whatever the cost, he was willing to pay it. "Name your price."

"A bolt on the inside of my bedroom door."

He digested her demand in silence. "And that's all?"

"You already agreed to separate bedrooms, but there is one more thing." She took a deep breath and let it out in a rush. "I want your promise that you'll never lay a hand on me again."

Drew had won. He should have felt victorious. But a look at her unhappy face, a glimpse of her lingering fears, stole the joy from his victory. "Word of honor." He raised his right hand in a pledge. "I'll never touch you again—unless you want me to."

Her eyes searched his, seeking and finding the reassurance she needed. Nodding, she said, "Then it's settled. I accept your proposal."

"You shall have your bolt and a sturdy lock as well. If it will relieve your mind, I'll buy a guard dog to sleep at the foot of your bed."

He sounded bitter, though Juliana didn't understand why. "I'd like that. I've never had a pet."

He rose and came to stand in front of her. "You will have a good life, Juliana." He hesitated, then took her cold hand in his. "I vow you won't regret your decision. I'm a generous man. You'll never want for anything. I'll buy you everything . . . everything your heart desires."

CHAPTER
9

"Miss, miss, I brung your breakfast."

Juliana burrowed deeper into luxurious softness. "Just five more minutes," she pleaded drowsily.

"But, miss, that's what you said the last two times I tried to wake you," the little housemaid pointed out. "Miss Lattimer's been up for hours, what with planning the wedding and all. Don't know when I seen 'er so excited."

Wedding! Juliana woke with a start and sat up in bed. It was *her* wedding that the maid referred to. The date and time were set; the ceremony would take place the day after tomorrow.

The maid fluffed the pillows and propped them up against the headboard. She waited until Juliana reclined against them, then placed a wicker breakfast tray over her lap. "If there's anything else you need, miss, just ring."

After the maid left, Juliana gazed around the guest room in bemusement. Until yesterday, she had thought having Maura fix her a cup of tea was being pampered. This morning she occupied a room nearly the size of the O'Tooles' entire apartment. Dainty blue and white flowered paper covered the walls; white lace curtains fluttered in the gentle breeze. Her tray held a crystal bud vase with a single red rose and the morning edition of a newspaper. She dipped a spoon into a dish of strawberries and cream.

She had to admit Drew MacAllister knew how to expedite matters. He had simply reached for the telephone and called Emma Lattimer, explaining that Juliana had consented to be his wife and asking her to recommend a suitable ladies' hotel. Without hesitation, Emma had invited Juliana to be her houseguest. Emma was also adamant that the wedding take place in her front parlor rather than in a musty office at City Hall.

Emma bustled into the room just as Juliana was finishing a flaky breakfast roll. "Good, you're finally awake. I told Harriet to prepare your bath. We have so much to do today; there's not a minute to spare."

"Miss Lattimer—I mean, Emma," Juliana quickly corrected herself, having already been chided good-naturedly for forgetting, "I don't want you taxing yourself. I thought we agreed the wedding was to be kept simple."

"You're such a sweet thing." Emma patted Juliana's hand. "I can see why Drew is so taken with you. But the truth is, I never felt better. The doctor said that the attack I experienced in jail was brought on by despair. And planning your wedding, dear, gives me nothing but joy. I never married, you know. So please humor me and let me pretend you're the daughter I never had."

Juliana blinked back the moisture that sprang to her eyes. In that instant she vowed she would go along with Emma's plans no matter how elaborate. "What do you have planned for today?"

"Shopping." Emma walked over to the chair where Juliana's dress was draped. Picking up a fold of the skirt, she regarded it with disgust. "We're going to buy you a complete wardrobe, one befitting the wife of a wealthy attorney and businessman. Drew said he never wanted to see this horrid dress again. He told me to give it to a ragpicker."

Juliana knew she should be grateful for her good fortune, but she couldn't overcome a surge of resentment. She knew the frock was stained and ugly. She also knew that only her neat stitches kept the seams together. But it was all she owned. She didn't need Drew MacAllister to remind her of its shabbiness. Did he think she'd wear such a dress to elicit pity? Because pity was what she had glimpsed in Drew's expression the day before.

Yesterday he had offered to send his driver to the O'Tooles' apartment to collect her belongings. Juliana had confessed there was nothing to send for. She owned only the clothes on her back, the shoes on her feet. Her singular dowry was her willingness to become his wife.

Juliana's gloomy thoughts were interrupted when Harriet returned for the breakfast tray and to assist with her toilette. Thirty minutes later, Juliana and Emma rode in a carriage to Ladies' Mile, the center of New York City's retail trade. It extended up and around Broadway roughly from Union Square to Madison Square. Merchandise tantalized shoppers from behind glimmering display windows, some overflowing with ruffles, ribbons, and lace, others dazzling with ropes of pearls, still others featuring boots of fine French kid. Shops offered everything and anything a woman could dream of.

"Mrs. Ulysses S. Grant and Mrs. Grover Cleveland shop here," Emma informed Juliana. "Also the Vanderbilts and the Whitneys."

The driver pulled the carriage alongside the curb and helped the women alight. Emma led the way up the street.

"We'll start with the basics, then proceed from there.

You'll need chemises, petticoats, drawers, negligees, an assortment of bustles, and naturally, corsets. Not that you need one, mind you, but no fashionable lady would dare appear in public improperly dressed. A lady," she instructed, while heading toward a lingerie store, "must wear her corset and bustle, no matter how strenuous the activity, even on the tennis court. Bathing costumes are the only exception."

Shopkeepers addressed Emma by name and were eager to assist her. Juliana was measured, laced, poked, and prodded. Cash registers jangled as they left the store. Juliana felt corseted to within an inch of her life. A deep breath seemed impossible. She feared a sneeze might prove fatal. For a kindhearted woman, Emma proved merciless when it came to stays.

"It'll be simpler to have our purchases delivered," Emma explained as they approached the milliner's where Maura was employed.

"Please, could we stop here for just a moment? My friend, Maura O'Toole, the one I told you about last evening, works here. I'd like to say hello."

"Of course, dear." Emma beamed. "I'd like to meet this wonderful young lady myself."

Maura was arranging merchandise in a display case when they entered the store. She stopped and rushed to greet Juliana. Not caring who watched, she threw her arms around her. "Juliana, love, I was so thrilled when I received your note yesterday. You must feel like the luckiest woman on earth." She stepped back, smiling. "You never once let on how deeply you cared for Mr. MacAllister. Poor Mary Bridget," Maura said, laughing, "the girl was quite beside herself. This is all so romantic."

Juliana refused to perpetuate the lie. Instead she introduced Maura to Emma Lattimer.

"I'm so pleased to meet you, Miss O'Toole." Emma smiled warmly at the girl. "Juliana has done nothing but rave about how kind your family has been to her. I hope you'll all be able to attend the wedding. It would be so nice for Juliana to have her friends present on such an important occasion."

"I'm not sure if—"

"Perhaps if I dropped your mother a note I could persuade her that we'd very much like her to attend."

Maura's green eyes sparkled with anticipation. "What a thoughtful person you are, Miss Lattimer."

"Call me Emma. All my friends do. You strike me as a young woman of good taste. It just occurred to me how much fun it would be if the three of us could go shopping together. Juliana needs a complete trousseau, and making all these decisions is quite tiring for me."

Excited at the prospect, Juliana touched Maura's sleeve. "Oh, Maura, do you think . . . ?"

Maura glanced at her employer, who was speaking with a customer. "I'm afraid not, love. Even with Mrs. Blum's permission, I can't afford to lose a day's wages."

"Let me speak privately with Mrs. Blum," Emma offered. "Perhaps we can work out an arrangement."

Juliana and Maura watched Emma approach the shopkeeper. Emma was smiling when she rejoined them. "Mrs. Blum wants you to take the rest of the day off with her blessing, and Friday afternoon as well."

"But I can't afford—"

"Tsk, tsk," Emma clucked. "You needn't look so worried. You'll notice no difference in your pay envelope."

A squeal of delight greeted Emma as both young women embraced her at once.

Maura's fashion expertise proved invaluable. Her discerning eye for color and style was quickly evident as they selected morning gowns, tea dresses, and walking dresses as well as several dinner and evening gowns at a fashionable department store. Juliana was grateful for Maura's advice. The young woman's taste mirrored her own more closely than did that of Emma, who had a penchant for frillier styles weighted with flounces and embellished with bows.

"Thank goodness for ready-made clothing," Emma sighed. "We were fortunate to purchase some essentials, but a woman in your position will need the services of a good dressmaker. I'll send Madame LaCroix to call on you when you're back from your honeymoon."

Honeymoon. Juliana blushed at the thought. To cover her embarrassment, she looked at the profusion of expensive gowns they had just purchased. Guilt pricked her conscience. "I really don't need all of these. I had no idea how expensive they'd be."

"Of course you didn't, dear," Emma replied. "Drew worried you might be conservative when it came to spending his money. That's why he put me in charge of the purse strings."

"While I was in the convent, I wore nothing but a simple white habit. After that, all I had was that unsightly gray dress you asked the salesgirl to dispose of. Now I have so many things. I'm afraid I'll stand for hours in front of my closet trying to decide what to wear."

Emma smiled, but Maura looked thoughtful. She got up abruptly from a small settee in the spacious fitting room. "What you need is a lady's maid. Someone to help you with those decisions, to help you dress and to do your hair."

"An excellent idea," Emma chimed in. "I should have thought of that myself."

"A maid? Me?" Juliana found the notion entertaining. Twenty-four hours ago she had been penniless. Now she was expected to have a maid? What a strange twist her life had taken.

Maura snapped her fingers. "I know just the person."

"Who?" Emma and Juliana asked in unison.

"Mary Bridget," Maura said with a broad grin. "My sister would be perfect. She's eager to please, and if you provided room and board, she'd be willing to work for a pittance."

"But she's so young," Juliana protested.

"She turns sixteen next month."

"She should still be in school."

"Pa says education is wasted on women," Maura countered. "Besides she detests schoolwork."

The saleswoman brought an itemized bill. "If she's young, she's trainable," Emma said, signing her name with a flowing script.

"Mary Bridget's got a knack with hair, and no one loves pretty things better than she." Maura gave Juliana a steady look. "With Katie at home, sleeping space is cramped. An extra income would ease things for the family."

"Very well," Juliana capitulated. "If she's interested, have her come by early next week."

Emma stood and adjusted her bonnet. "Speaking of hair, dear," she addressed Juliana, "you need to do something about yours. It's such a lovely color, but that tight bun is not very flattering. I know just the hairdresser. Women from the best families frequent his salon. With everyone away for the summer, I'm sure Monsieur Philippe will have time for you."

The Frenchman, at Emma's request, saw Juliana immediately. She was seated before a large mirror, a cape draped over her shoulders to protect her new dress. The diminutive hairdresser shook his head from side to side. "Ah, mademoiselle, why do you make yourself so plain? That hairstyle is more suitable for a nun or one of those aging suffragettes. With your eyes, your bone structure, you have the makings of a rare beauty. Let Philippe show you." He removed the hairpins, then picked up his scissors.

"*Magnifique!*" he exclaimed an hour later. With a flourish, he offered Juliana a hand mirror.

She scarcely recognized the woman staring out at her. The hairdresser was an artist. The style he had chosen was extremely flattering. Instead of tightly drawn back, her hair was left fuller and softer about her face, with tendrils at her temples and the nape of her neck. He had coiled the rest of her thick tresses into a chignon.

Emma and Maura, who had been shopping for accessories while Juliana was with Monsieur Philippe, were also amazed at the change. "Oh, my." Emma clapped her hands together. "What a beauty you turned out to be!"

"Wait until your beau sees you." Maura smiled.

"Oh, my," Emma repeated. "It's getting late. I promised Drew we'd meet him at a tearoom I know of."

"I wish I could linger, but I really must get back to the shop. I'll see you both on Friday." Maura gave Juliana's hand a squeeze, then turned to Emma. "Thank you again for this special day and for the wedding invitation."

The women parted company, going in opposite directions. Juliana didn't feel like the same person she had been that morning. Not only was she aware of her altered physical appearance, but she felt different inside. She was no longer embarrassed or ashamed by her shabbiness. Self-confidence made her hold her head proudly.

Once seated in the tearoom, Emma checked the ornamental watch pinned to her bodice. "Dear, would you mind terribly if I left you to wait for Drew alone? My brother and I are dining with friends tonight. I told Bertie I'd come by his office when we finished. It's already late, and he's apt to think I've had another of my spells."

"By all means, go. I'll be fine."

Emma looked relieved. "Thank you, dear, for being so understanding. Enjoy the evening with your young man. Give Drew my love."

Juliana watched Emma leave, and then, after ordering tea and a small plate of cakes, she prepared to wait for Drew. At first she didn't pay attention to the gentleman at the next table. It wasn't until she glanced over her teacup that she noticed him watching her. He smiled and tipped his hat. She acknowledged his smile with a nod, then tried to ignore him. Hoping Drew would hurry, she looked toward the doorway.

Her view of the entrance was suddenly blocked. Startled, she looked up and found the man from the adjoining table standing in front of her. "Excuse me," he said, doffing his derby. "I didn't mean to stare, but you look familiar. Have we met?"

She studied him for a moment. He was dark-haired, of average height, with full sideburns and a mustache. "No," she replied, shaking her head, "I don't think so. I'm certain I'd remember."

"And I'm just as certain I know you from somewhere," he insisted. "A woman as lovely as you is sure to make an impression. Newport, perhaps?"

"You must have me confused with someone else."

"What a shame. I was hoping we could renew an old acquaintance over dinner. I don't suppose you're free this evening?"

"That's out of the question. I'm meeting someone."

"Another night, then?"

Juliana had no experience with persistent men. She searched for a way to discourage his unwanted attention without sounding rude. Glancing across the tearoom, she was relieved to see Drew. Mary Bridget was right, she thought; he was quite dashing. His tall, muscular figure combined with handsome features gave him a commanding presence. Before he had a chance to spot her, he was detained by a fleshy man who appeared to be in his fifties.

Juliana's admirer followed her glance. His brows drew together. "Aha!" he said as comprehension dawned. "Now I know why you look familiar. You're MacAllister's doxy." Pulling a calling card from a gold case, he presented it to her. "When he tires of you, drop me a note. I'll be happy to show you a good time." He turned and sauntered away.

Dumbfounded by the man's audacity, Juliana stared at the card. "Doxy," the man had called her. Though she was unfamiliar with the term, she recognized the tone. It had the same degrading ring as Dennis's insults. The word implied she was a loose woman, one who sold herself to men. With a hand that trembled, she smoothed the pleats of her gown, a toast-colored silk finely striped with brown. She thought of the dozens of new dresses, shoes, accessories, and pretty undergarments she had purchased that day. Doxy, she repeated silently. That's exactly what she was! She had sold herself to Drew MacAllister!

Juliana glanced back to the doorway. The conversation with his acquaintance completed, Drew scanned the tables. She held her breath and waited for him to notice her.

His gaze snagged hers, lingered for a moment, then moved on. Recognition had been absent from that brief look. Juliana wasn't offended. Intuitively, she perceived the glance for what it was—the appreciation of a man for an attractive woman. The ultimate compliment. Her transformation was complete. Undiluted exhilaration bubbled through her veins.

Drew's eyes widened in disbelief, and his gaze swung back. Juliana! My God, how could he have been so blind? He hadn't seen through the guise of a tight bun and a shapeless dress. What loveliness had been hidden there! He wasn't sure how he felt. She was a pleasure to look upon, but knowing he could not touch her was another matter entirely. As it was, there had been odd moments when he'd felt the urge to hold her in his arms—or had caught himself wanting to test the softness of her mouth.

As he strode toward her, Juliana let out pent-up breath. She greeted him with a tentative smile.

He returned the smile. "My little wren has turned into a swan. You're beautiful."

Warmth spread across her cheeks, giving them the delicate appeal of sun-kissed apricots. She was more adept at sparring with him than at accepting his compliments. "Thank you," she said shyly.

He held out his arm. "Sorry I'm late. A matter came up at the last moment that needed my attention."

"I didn't mind." She rose, her movements graceful despite the encumbrance of corset and bustle and, imitating what she had seen other women do, tucked her hand into the crook of his arm.

When they turned to leave the tearoom, Drew spied the calling card on the table and picked it up. "What's this?"

"It's nothing, really."

He pocketed the card. "Juliana, don't evade the issue. When there's a problem, I want you to discuss it with me."

As they made their way across the tearoom, people stopped talking to watch the lovely young woman and the dashing man listening so attentively to her every word. Diners quizzed one another about the identity of the striking couple. Both Juliana and Drew were unaware of the stir they created. Once on the street, Drew hailed his carriage. He helped Juliana alight, then climbed in and sat beside her.

"Now," he said, leaning back, "to return to the matter of the calling card. Have you ever seen the man before?"

"Not that I can recall, but he thought I looked familiar." She shifted her gaze to the hopeless snarl of horse-drawn vehicles. "When he observed you in the doorway, he immediately connected me with the newspaper articles. He called me your doxy."

"That filthy—" Drew bit back the epithet and lapsed into silence. From time to time he caught himself stealing glances at the young woman seated beside him. The transformation was truly extraordinary. She was breathtakingly lovely. An aura of innocence merged with an exotic, tawny beauty to form a provocative combination. One that would leave few men unaffected, himself included.

Jack Burrows pulled the carriage to a stop in front of a five-story edifice on Union Square. "Tiffany and Company," he announced grandly.

"Charles Tiffany happens to be the finest jeweler in the country," Drew explained, noting Juliana's startled look at the cast-iron facade painted in no-nonsense drab.

The explanation was unnecessary. Juliana had heard Mary Bridget rhapsodize over the name during her stay with the O'Tooles. In addition to being the finest jewelry store in New York, she surmised it was also the most expensive. "I thought you were taking me to dine," she blurted.

"Later. First I intend to buy you an engagement ring."

He helped Juliana down from the carriage and escorted her inside.

The interior was every bit as plush and elegant as the exterior suggested. Juliana gazed about in awed wonder at the treasures housed in glass cases.

"I want to purchase an engagement ring," Drew informed the neatly attired clerk who hurried to assist them.

"Follow me, sir." The clerk led them to the diamond salesroom where a dazzling array of merchandise was displayed in the firm's specially designed airtight cases. With a flourish, he pulled out a tray of sparkling gems.

Drew dismissed the entire array with a shake of his head. "Since my bride-to-be is unique, I'd like something a bit out of the ordinary. What have you, for instance, in yellow diamonds?"

"Excellent choice, sir." The clerk unlocked a drawer and brought out a second tray.

Intrigued, Juliana watched Drew inspect, then reject, several gems. His fingers hovered above the display for a long moment. "That one." He pointed to a tear-shaped stone nearly the size of a ten-cent piece set in a narrow platinum band with two baguettes on either side.

"Mr. Tiffany personally designed the setting." The clerk spread a black velvet cloth on the counter and set the ring on it. "The diamond is of a superior quality. A sound investment. Something you'll bequeath your heirs."

Drew picked up the ring and studied it critically, then nodded in satisfaction. "Its golden beauty and hers are well suited." Addressing Juliana, he asked, "Is it to your liking?"

Words caught, and she had to clear her throat. "It's exquisite."

"Then it's yours." He reached for her left hand. "Let's see if it's the right size."

The ring slipped over her knuckle and onto the third finger as though crafted with Juliana in mind.

"Perfect," the clerk pronounced. "If you'll excuse me, I'll take care of the formalities." He left to fill out the purchase agreement.

Drew continued to hold Juliana's hand, looking deep into her amber eyes. "The day after tomorrow, you'll become my wife. Never again will you have to bear poverty and injustice alone. Your honor will be my honor. Let this ring be my pledge."

CHAPTER 10

IT RAINED ALL FRIDAY MORNING. HOW APPROPRIATE Juliana thought as she stared out the window. The dismal weather matched her mood perfectly. By midafternoon, however, the skies had cleared and the sun had broken through. Outside her bedroom window, in the small garden, raindrops glistened on rose petals. The lovely July day only made her feel sad. In an hour she would become Mrs. Andrew MacAllister.

"Happy the bride the sun shines on, or so I've heard said," Emma chirped as she hurried into the guest room, her plump figure swathed in yards of lavender taffeta. She clucked her tongue when she saw Juliana, still in her dressing gown, standing by the window. "My dear, you haven't even started dressing. I brought Harriet to arrange your hair." Harriet followed, carrying a large box, which she placed on the bed.

Juliana let the lacy curtain drop. After crossing the room, she sat on a bench before a rosewood vanity and allowed herself to be fussed over by the two women. Harriet pinned Juliana's thick tresses atop her head in a coronet, leaving wispy curls at her forehead and temples. Next, Juliana stepped into an elegantly simple gown of oyster-white linen. Pleated inserts trimmed in cotton lace adorned the bodice and long sleeves. The skirt was swagged snugly across her hips to form a modest bustle.

"I knew from the minute I saw it that dress would be perfect for you," Emma exclaimed, handing a small velvet box to Juliana. "Go ahead, dear, open it."

Juliana pressed the catch, and the lid sprang open. An ivory cameo brooch in a gold filigree setting rested inside. It was fastened on a blue ribbon and meant to be worn as a choker. "Emma, I don't know what to say. It's lovely."

"It belonged to my mother, but I want you to have it." She waved away Juliana's protest. Taking the brooch from its box, she fastened it around the high collar of Juliana's gown. "Every bride needs something old."

Harriet stood aside and surveyed Juliana. "Let's see. Your dress is new; Miss Lattimer gave you something old and something blue." She ticked off the items on her fingers. "All that leaves is something borrowed." She plucked a small tortoiseshell comb from her hair and secured it in Juliana's. "There," she said with a wink. "Make sure you give it back."

Juliana's conscience troubled her. She felt like a fraud. These two women were so sincere in their good wishes that she wanted to confess this entire wedding was a sham, no more than a pageant being enacted before a roomful of guests. Her deception formed a painful lump in her throat. She swallowed hard and tried to speak.

Emma threw her arms around her and kissed her cheek. "Just be happy, dear." Her pale blue eyes were misty when she drew back.

"It's nearly time, miss," Harriet reminded her. "Now for the final touch." She went to the box she had brought with her and lifted out an intricate wreath fashioned from baby's breath and orange blossoms.

Juliana sat before the mirror while the maid adjusted the flowery wreath so it circled the coronet of curls. The wreath had been a compromise. Juliana had adamantly refused to wear the traditional veil. It would only have served as a poignant reminder of the convent, of the unspoken vows of chastity and poverty.

Emma sighed with pleasure. "You're absolutely breathtaking. Wait until your bridegroom sees you."

"Miss Lattimer's right, miss," Harriet concurred. "Don't know when I've seen a lovelier bride. But"—she frowned— "you're pale as a sheet. What you need is a bit of color." Reaching out, she pinched Juliana's cheeks, then stepped back in satisfaction. "That's better."

The doorbell chimed repeatedly. "Oh, dear." Emma looked flustered. "Guests have started to arrive. Come, Harriet, we had better see to them." Before sailing out of the guest room, she turned to Juliana. "I'll send Bertie to escort you downstairs when it's time for the ceremony to begin."

Juliana alternately paced and wrung her hands. She wanted to vanish or run away. She fervently wished the incident with Freddie Westhaven had never happened. Oh, for the uncomplicated routine of convent life.

Why had she consented to this madness? Perhaps the O'Tooles wouldn't have asked her to leave. Maybe, if she had tried harder, she could have found employment. But "perhaps" and "maybe" didn't fill an empty stomach or provide a roof over her head. Without resources, one couldn't survive. And quite simply, she had none. Drew MacAllister had tossed her a lifeline, and, foundering in a sea of despair, she had grasped it with both hands.

"Miss Butterfield, it's time."

The voice of Emma's brother brought Juliana up short. Drawing a shaky breath, she opened the door.

Bertram Lattimer was a masculine replica of his sister. Fraternal twins, they were both short and plump with silvery hair and pale blue eyes. Devoted to each other, they possessed sunny dispositions and were unfailingly generous. "My sister wasn't exaggerating when she said you were a vision. Your husband-to-be is a lucky man."

Husband! Juliana blanched. She tried to summon a smile, but failed.

Alarmed at her pallor, Bertie took Juliana's icy hand and placed it on his arm. "You have a bad case of nerves, my dear, but everything will work out." He led her down the hallway toward the stairs. "Drew will make a fine husband. A woman needs a man's protection. The world can be cruel to a woman all alone."

Midway down the stairs, Juliana felt the force of Drew's stare. Her golden eyes mirrored trepidation; his silver-blue eyes were filled with steely resolve. She walked down the rest of the stairs as though in a trance.

"I'll give you a few moments' privacy." Bertie tactfully withdrew.

A soft babble of voices filtered through the double doors of the front parlor, but the entry hall was deserted. Drew tried to lessen Juliana's apprehension. "Smile, lass. You're not going to a hanging."

Juliana nervously twisted her engagement ring. "We're getting married for the wrong reasons. I can't go through with this." The words tumbled out in their haste to be said.

His expression hardened. "You not only can but will."

"Surely there must be someone you'd rather wed, someone who cares for you enough to disregard the vicious lies printed in the paper."

"We made a bargain. I won't allow you to renege." His tone was frigid. "How like a woman to go back on her word."

A rush of color stained Juliana's pale cheeks. Her head came up with a snap. "I merely thought you might be as eager as I to extricate yourself from a mutually detestable bargain. If not"—she shrugged—"the agreement stands."

Emma slipped out of the parlor, followed by Bertie. She handed Juliana a bouquet of yellow roses. "Take your places everyone. Drew, you're to stand next to the judge. Wait until you hear the pianist begin the wedding march, Bertie; then escort Juliana into the parlor."

Minutes later the opening chords resonated throughout the house. Bertie reassuringly covered Juliana's hand with his own, then stepped forward, drawing her with him. The double doors swung wide, revealing a dozen or so people gathered in the parlor. Ferns and potted palms formed a bank of green before the marble fireplace. A profusion of yellow roses perfumed the air. Juliana picked out Maura O'Toole and was encouraged by her friend's wide smile. Then she was immediately dismayed. Judge Spears from the Ludlow Street jail, a black leather-bound book open in his hands, stood next to Drew ready to perform the ceremony. Giving Juliana a kind smile, he opened the book and began to read.

Love. Honor. Obey.

In a strained voice, Juliana exchanged vows with a man she scarcely knew.

The judge's voice boomed with authority. "By the power vested in me by the state of New York, I hereby pronounce you man and wife." He addressed Drew: "You may kiss the bride."

Juliana's eyes widened. Never having so much as witnessed a wedding before, she'd had no idea what to expect. She hadn't stopped to consider that kissing might be involved. An air of expectancy enveloped the gathering, as though all of the guests were holding their breath, waiting, and watching. She instinctively looked to Drew for guidance. He made no attempt to kiss her. He, too, seemed to be waiting and watching.

The reason for his hesitancy dawned on her. Drew had promised never to touch her without her consent. He was honoring that pledge. She couldn't subject him to humiliation in front of all these witnesses. Closing her eyes, she lifted her face to his.

The initial brush of his lips against hers was so slight she wondered fleetingly if it was real or imagined. The pressure increased subtly as his mouth moved over hers in gentle exploration. An unfamiliar but pleasant tingling started in her midsection, then spread outward. Her mind emptied. All that existed was this wonderful magical spell he was weaving.

Beguiled by his tenderness, she slowly moved her hand upward over the dark lapel of his jacket, past the starched collar of his shirt, until it rested along the sturdy column of his neck. Not caring where Drew was taking her, she wanted only to follow his lead. Her lips parted, and leaning into him, she returned the kiss. Beneath her fingertips, she felt his pulse bound. It was thrilling to know he, too, was affected by the contact.

Drew was the one who finally ended the kiss. Juliana's eyelids fluttered open. Stunned, she gazed at him. His usual self-assurance had vanished.

A deluge of congratulations swept over them.

Judge Spears slapped Drew on the back, then pumped his hand. "Good luck, young man. Mind if I kiss your lovely bride?" He planted a wet kiss on Juliana's cheek. "Put your worries aside, my dear," he said in a low voice. "All charges against you have been dropped. Delaney apologizes for causing you distress."

Blinking in astonishment, Juliana couldn't believe her good fortune. She managed to stammer her thanks before Emma, clutching a damp hankie, came to offer her best wishes. Bertie was next, followed by the women of the O'Tooles.

Juliana smiled at each of the guests and made the appropriate responses, all the while aware of Drew's hand riding lightly at her waist. He looked so very attractive, so distinguished. He brought to mind Prince Charming. For an unguarded moment, she yearned to be Sleeping Beauty or Cinderella. Suddenly sadness welled inside her. Circumstance had determined that she and Drew could never be friends—and certainly never lovers.

If only things were different . . .

If only they could start anew . . .

Daniel Tennant was the last of the well-wishers. He brushed parchment-dry lips across Juliana's cheek. "At last we meet. You led Drew a merry chase, but I'm glad you finally saw reason. This marriage will be mutually beneficial. Your husband has a brilliant future ahead of him." His dark gaze bored into her. "I trust you will do your utmost to enhance Drew's career. Make his goals yours."

Instant dislike of the aging politician swept through Juliana. Daniel Tennant's aggressiveness marked him as a master of intimidation. "Should my demeanor be a source of embarrassment, I trust you won't hesitate to bring it to my attention." She smiled thinly.

"Of course." The assemblyman nodded. "Stick to fashions and recipes. Topics that appeal to women. Leave the real issues for men to solve."

Juliana was spared the need to reply by the arrival of the wedding cake. Harriet wheeled in the three-tiered confection festooned with pink-winged cherubs and topped with plaster figures of a bride and groom. In the ensuing confusion, Juliana forgot her irritation with Daniel Tennant. Bertie popped the cork from a chilled bottle of French champagne. Glasses of the sparkling wine were poured and distributed.

When everyone held a glass, Bertie raised his aloft in a toast. "To the MacAllisters, Andrew and Juliana. May today be the beginning of a lifetime of happiness."

Drew touched his glass to Juliana's. "To new beginnings," he said quietly, his gaze holding hers.

As their glasses chinked in a toast, Juliana was heartened to know that Drew, also, wished for an auspicious start of their life together.

As the train passed through Greenwich, Juliana studied her new husband covertly. From the seat opposite hers, he pored through a sheave of documents he had brought along in a leather carrying case. Turning her head, she watched the Connecticut countryside slide past her window. To a casual observer, she thought, they might pass for an ordinary married couple escaping the city for a weekend—or perhaps two strangers—but definitely not newlyweds on a honeymoon.

The conductor strolled down the aisle. "Next stop Westport," he called out.

Drew collected his papers and stuffed them into his folder. "We'll be getting off at Westport. I've reserved a buggy at the livery station. The inn we'll be staying at is another six miles from here." Drew led Juliana off the train and helped her into a hired carriage, then set the vehicle in motion.

Once they had left Westport behind, Juliana was uncertain how to bridge the awkward gap between them. She sat clutching her handbag and observed the rolling terrain. Drew concentrated on the road ahead.

It was the time of day Juliana loved best—when the earth seemed to hover between day and night. It was the time when diffused light softened harsh textures and the earth blended with the sky in a mélange of pastel hues. Above, shades of mauve and rose competed for prominence amid gilt-edged clouds. Misty blue veiled the landscape, tinting fields and forests dusty green. Peace and tranquillity reigned.

Forty minutes later, they arrived at a quaint village. A whitewashed church with a tall steeple stood sentinel at the far end of the village green. Directly across from the church was a town hall. Stately colonial homes lined another side, small shops the last. "What a pretty place," Juliana exclaimed. "It's hard to believe a town like this exists so close to New York City. They seem worlds apart."

"They are," Drew said, flicking a glance over her. "Different ways of life, different values. Poles apart."

"Have you always lived in a city?" she ventured.

"Always. I don't feel comfortable anywhere else."

"And I don't feel at ease in a place where concrete and skyscrapers replace grass and trees."

"I have a hard time sleeping in the country with its chirping crickets and noisy tree frogs." A trace of a smile curved his mouth at the confession.

Leaving the town behind, they continued down the road and lapsed into silence once again. Juliana was struck anew by the disparity between herself and her husband. They were poles apart in tastes and values. Would they ever span the chasm? Or would their differences be magnified with the passage of years?

A carved wooden sign adorned with pink blossoms and bearing the name Mountain Laurel Lodge hung from a post at the edge of the road. Drew urged the buggy past the sign and down a narrow dirt road, little more than a country lane.

"Where are we going?" Juliana asked.

"You'll see." Drew's reply was noncommittal.

Ten minutes later the road curved and an inn came into view. The hostelry, lovingly preserved from a bygone era, crowned a small rise. In the front, it boasted a lawn sloping down to the road and, in the rear, terraced gardens, which descended to a gurgling stream. Beyond the gardens, as far as the eye could see, were dense woods. Fashionably attired couples strolled over the manicured grounds.

Drew handed the reins to a youth who hurried forward. He climbed out of the buggy, then came around to assist Juliana, swinging her down to the gravel drive. His hands tarried at her slender waist.

She rested her palms lightly on his chest and gazed up at him. Like Drew, she was in no rush to terminate the closeness. Astonishingly, she liked the feel of his hard muscles beneath her fingers. The contact did odd things to her heartbeat, accelerating it to an alarming degree. "This place is absolutely charming!" she said, smiling shyly. "How did you ever find such a spot?"

"Daniel knew of it."

His admission soured Juliana's pleasure, and her smile faded. "The assemblyman seems to have an undue amount of influence over your life."

Releasing her, Drew stepped back. "What are you implying?" His voice hardened. "Be advised, Juliana, that any decisions I make are my own, not Daniel Tennant's. I'm the one accountable for my actions."

Chastened, Juliana accepted his arm and allowed him to escort her into the inn.

Upon their entering the lobby, the innkeeper greeted them cordially and ushered them to separate but adjoining rooms. "I hope you enjoy your stay. If there's anything you need, please let us know." The innkeeper smilingly excused himself.

Juliana stood in the center of a large bedroom filled with ornate Queen Anne furniture. Her gaze immediately darted to the door between her room and Drew's. A sturdy brass lock was affixed to the portal. She glanced away to find Drew watching her, his look bitter. Afraid I'll attack you? it seemed to taunt. A guilty flush spread over Juliana's cheeks.

"I'll leave you to freshen up before meeting me downstairs for dinner." He turned and was gone.

Juliana wanted to call him back and apologize—but apologize for what? she wondered. For demanding a lock on her bedroom door? After what he had done, why shouldn't she? She bit her bottom lip. What was wrong with her? Why should she be concerned that she might have offended him?

When she joined Drew in the dining room half an hour later, her appearance gave no indication of inner turmoil. She had changed from her traveling dress into one of deep periwinkle blue trimmed with black grosgrain. When the maître d'hôtel lead her toward the table, Drew rose, approval evident in his eyes.

The maître d'hôtel held out a chair for her, then retreated.

"I hope you don't mind, but I took the liberty of ordering for both of us. The tenderloin of beef is said to be superb."

A waiter arrived with a bottle of champagne in a silver ice bucket and two stemmed glasses. "Courtesy of Assemblyman Tennant." He uncorked the bottle and poured each of them a glass.

Drew raised his champagne in a silent toast; Juliana followed suit.

The wine had a relaxing effect on her. After taking another sip, she leaned back in her chair and looked around. The room was nearly deserted, most of the guests having dined earlier. Candlelight imparted a feeling of intimacy. They were seated next to a window overlooking what Juliana thought must be the garden, though it was too dark now to be certain. Only their reflections were visible in the small panes of glass. Waiters stayed discreetly in the background; the occasional chink of china or crystal the only reminder that they weren't alone.

Juliana was determined to make conversation. Talk was preferable to lengthy silences, which made her uncomfortable. "I expected your brother to be at the wedding."

"Nick is in the middle of the summer term at Harvard. He needs to devote all his time to his studies."

"I'm eager to meet him. Is he anything like you?"

Drew weighed his response before answering her question. "There's a strong family resemblance. But Nick is just a boy. He seems much younger than I was at that age."

"There are times I detect a burr in your speech. Were you born in Scotland?"

"In Glasgow."

Juliana rested her elbow on the table, propped her chin on her fist, and leaned forward in her eagerness to learn more about this enigmatic man. "How old were you when you came to America?"

"Eleven. My mother had just married Jamie Kincaid, who

had heard fantastic tales of New York. Mother and I were not sorry to leave Scotland."

"Do your mother and stepfather still live in New York?" she asked softly, already suspecting the answer.

"No." Drew stared out at the darkened garden. "They were killed when a boiler on the Staten Island ferry exploded. Nick was a baby."

"But who took care of you afterward? You were just a boy yourself."

"Nick became my responsibility. I took care of him then—and still do." He shifted his gaze to Juliana, his eyes the deadly blue of a polished gun barrel. "Where Nick's welfare is concerned, I'll do whatever is necessary to protect him."

Later that evening, as Juliana lay alone in the four-poster bed, she recalled their dinner conversation. Drew had sounded so fierce when he spoke of his younger brother. It had frightened her. It had also elicited her respect. How fortunate Nick was to have the devotion and protection of a wiser, stronger brother.

From the adjoining room, she heard the floor creak as Drew moved around. A thin pencil of light showed beneath his door. Juliana's thoughts spun back to earlier that day. Though she barely remembered the wedding ceremony, she was unable to forget what had happened afterward. She pressed her fingertips to her mouth, thinking of Drew's kiss. Gentle, sweet, cajoling. It had been everything a first kiss should be—everything and more, so much more.

Smiling, she fell asleep to the steady hum of crickets outside her bedroom window.

CHAPTER
11

THE FIRST THING JULIANA NOTICED UPON RISING THE NEXT morning was an envelope that had been slipped under her door. Bending, she picked it up and saw her name written in bold strokes. She opened the envelope and read the message: "Here is some money to amuse yourself with. We'll dine at seven. Drew."

Brief and to the point, typical of him. Juliana counted the bills. She couldn't fault Drew's generosity. The amount was probably more than Mr. O'Toole earned in a week. Finally she could repay her debt to the family. She knew their pride wouldn't permit them to take the entire sum, but she would persuade them to accept part of it.

"Pity he's not as generous with his time," Juliana muttered with annoyance. Drew seemed eager to be free of her company. She should be relieved she didn't have to spend the whole day with him, but . . .

The day loomed ahead of her. How odd, she mused, to have hours to spend doing exactly as she pleased. She could fill them in any way she chose, or she could simply do nothing at all. In the convent, life had been regimented; every hour had to be accounted for to Mother Superior. Later, in New York City, she had spent every waking moment looking for work or helping Mrs. O'Toole with chores. The final days before the wedding had been the most hectic of all. Emma Lattimer could put Mother Superior to shame as a taskmaster. Having nothing to do until dinnertime was a novelty.

After dressing, Juliana ventured downstairs. A buffet of breakfast foods was arranged on a linen-covered table in the dining room; she was hard pressed to identify many of the dishes. Feeling adventurous, she heaped a plate with delicacies, then sat at a table overlooking the rose garden and enjoyed a leisurely meal.

Geometrical beds of roses were arranged in a rainbow of colors. A blush of champagne and ivory blended delicately with peach, apricot, and lemon. In the northern sector of the garden, roses ran the gamut of vivid hues from coral to crimson. Guests wandered along the flagstone walks. One couple, probably newlyweds, held hands and stopped to steal a kiss when they thought no one was looking.

Juliana daintily licked icing off her index finger from a cinnamon cake. The whalebone stays of her corset reminded her none too subtly that she had overindulged. Deciding a good, long walk was just the thing, she left the dining room. By her calculations, the quaint village they had passed through last evening was probably no more than two miles distant. Nodding politely to guests she passed along the way, Juliana strolled down the drive and headed toward town.

The village was every bit as charming as Juliana had remembered. She poked around the shops, purchasing a pillbox hand-painted with mountain laurel for Emma and a pretty enameled brooch for Maura. But the place in which Juliana spent most of her time was the bookshop.

She browsed the aisles, selecting titles at random and leafing through pages. Feeling absolutely wicked, she settled on several romance novels, the type she often overheard the older students at the convent school talking and giggling over. Mother Superior had expressly forbidden the girls to read these books, claiming they were sinful and destroyed the moral fiber of young women.

"These are two of my favorites. All my women customers have read them," the proprietress confided, slipping the books into a plain brown bag. "I've never seen you in here before. Are you staying at the inn?"

"Yes," Juliana replied. "My husband and I are there for the weekend."

"It's a shame you won't be here next week. We're having a rally supporting woman suffrage. I'll give you the information anyway. Maybe you pass it along." She slipped a pamphlet into Juliana's bag.

"Thank you," Juliana murmured as the woman turned to wait on another customer.

Before leaving town, Juliana stopped for lemonade at a tearoom. After she had been served, she opened the bag and pulled out her books. The pamphlet rested on top. She stared at the title: "Women: Citizens or Slaves?"

Two men passed her table. One happened to glance at the pamphlet and nudged the other. "Garbage!"

"Trash," the other agreed. "That sort of thing only stirs up trouble. A real man should control his wife." They moved on.

Juliana shoved her purchases back into the bag and left the tearoom. Was that how all men viewed women? she wondered angrily. As something to control? Why were they so antagonistic toward the idea of women being able to think for themselves?

The walk to the inn seemed longer than she remembered. A hot July sun beat down on her. Wisps of hair clung damply to her temples. The weight of bustle and petticoats made her footsteps drag. An occasional carriage rumbled by, its passage dusting her with grit. Juliana stopped to dab at her flushed face with a handkerchief. A bright orange butterfly flitted in front of her. As she watched it swoop down and land on a nearby branch, she noticed a path that angled into the woods, following the course of a meandering creek.

On impulse, she followed it. She soon found that the air was cooler here in the woods. Golden sunlight slanted through the boughs. Continuing along, Juliana found that the creek widened into a shallow basin. A tree grew close to the water's edge, a lower branch extending over the water to form a natural seat. The sight was too tempting to resist.

Juliana plunked herself down, stretched her legs, and flexed her ankles. Her brand-new shoes pinched her toes. Slipping out of them, she peeled off her silk stockings and dipped her bare feet into the water. She shifted, trying to find a more comfortable position. Despite her efforts, the cumbersome bustle wouldn't accommodate her movements. Without another thought, Juliana reached under her skirts, untied the hated contraption, removed it, and propped it up against the trunk of the tree. She resumed her seat on the limb, a slim foot trailing in the water, and began to read one of her romantic novels. After a while, she yawned and dozed off.

Drew needed a reprieve from hours of reading financial reports. He left his room and wandered through the gardens, then strolled down to the creek. He was about to turn back when he saw an overgrown path that veered into the woods and decided to investigate it.

Jamming his hands into his pockets, he glanced around curiously. What was it about the country that Juliana found so appealing? Drew felt like a tourist in a strange land. He was city-bred, totally ignorant when it came to Mother Nature. He couldn't tell an azalea bush from poison ivy, a pine from a spruce, or a woodchuck from a muskrat. And as for the quiet— Well, it was just too damn quiet.

He soon came to a spot where the creek widened into a pool and a tree grew close to the bank. Taking a step, he stopped and sucked in a sharp breath. Juliana reclined against a sloping branch, sound asleep. Her head rested against the bark, her face tipped to one side. An open book lay across her lap, and—Drew smothered a chuckle—her bustle was propped up against the tree.

Until Juliana disrupted his life, he had liked to think he was very observant. Now he wondered again why he had been so slow to detect her uncommon beauty. Hair and eyes the shade of old gold were a striking combination. And her mouth, with its full lower lip, had a seductive appeal. Asleep, she looked vulnerable. But appearances could be deceiving. The lady had an indomitable spirit and the resiliency of India rubber.

Careful not to waken her, Drew moved forward, his glance unwavering. Incredibly long eyelashes, like sable fans, rested against her peaches-and-cream complexion. Her slightly parted lips were soft and pink, ripe for kissing. Drew bent down and sampled another taste of her unforgettable sweetness.

A mistake. The brief encounter only whetted Drew's appetite. His craving unappeased, he deepened the kiss. Juliana sighed, her breath a gentle zephyr. Drew tensed, expecting her to resist. To his amazement, Juliana's arms crept up and twined around his neck, drawing him closer. Her book slid to the ground.

Drew's arms tightened around her, and his tongue sought urgent entry into the honeyed cavern of her mouth. Desire to lay her on a bed of tall grass and wildflowers and make love to her raged through him like a flash fire.

Through a haze of mindless pleasure, Juliana sensed the change and pulled back. Her eyes became shadowed with the first stirrings of passion as she stared into the face of Drew MacAllister. She hadn't been dreaming. This was real. Drew was actually here, holding her, kissing her, making her respond to forbidden delights. Was she truly wanton, as Mother Superior had charged? Confused and embarrassed by her reaction, she pushed him away.

"You should have pushed me away sooner," he grated and stalked to the edge of the small clearing. With his back turned, he attempted to bring his carnal urges under control.

"I was asleep," she said defensively. "You took unfair advantage of me."

He raked a hand through his hair. "I'd advise you to exert more caution as to where you choose to nap. You offered an open invitation to any red-blooded man. Not many would have been content with a single kiss."

But she hadn't responded to just any man, Juliana acknowledged privately, only to Drew. Somehow he had merged with the intrepid hero of the novel she had been reading. Drew had been the last thought in her mind before dozing off; he had been the vague lover of her dreams. The discovery was disquieting.

Turning, Drew advanced toward her. His grim expression almost made her quail. He glanced around, then with a frown bent to pick up her silk stockings and soft kid shoes. "Here." He handed them to her. "Unless you plan on returning to the inn barefoot, you'll need these."

She snatched them from him. Swinging her legs so that she sat sideways, Juliana carefully eased on the delicate silk hose.

Drew stifled a groan. Her innocently provocative action was wreaking havoc on his honorable intentions. He could imagine his hand, not hers, smoothing the stocking over a slender foot, a shapely calf, and a silky thigh. Grinding his teeth, he forced himself to look elsewhere. His eyes rested on the book lying open on the grass.

Stooping, he picked it up and read the title aloud: *"The Misadventures of an English Miss.* Your choice of reading material astounds me. Hardly the type of book I'd expect a nun to read."

Juliana colored and tugged on the remaining stocking, nearly tearing it in her agitation. "I wasn't a nun. I was a novice."

Her reaction amused him. "What's the difference?"

"A nun is someone who has taken vows of poverty, chastity, and obedience. A novice is merely contemplating them."

"Obedience, you say? Somehow I have a difficult time imagining you as a meek, docile creature scurrying to obey orders. You're much too outspoken and headstrong."

His comment prompted a small smile. "Before her death, Mother Margaret Ann voiced the same opinion. She called me a maverick." Juliana slipped on a shoe.

"And are you?"

She shrugged. "If that's what you call a person who's independent and has definite opinions, then that's what I am." She put on her other shoe and stood. Snatching her novel out of his hands, she dropped it into her bag. "I'm ready," she announced.

Drew raised a brow askance. "Are you certain?"

"Of course," she retorted impatiently.

"Positive?"

What was he driving at? Juliana glanced around to see if she had forgotten something. "Oh, no," she groaned as her gaze fastened on the bustle leaning against the tree. The omission sent her beyond embarrassment; she was mortified.

Drew threw back his head and roared. At the sound of his merriment, her embarrassment faded. How different he seemed when he laughed, how human, even likable. Suddenly the situation struck Juliana as funny, too, and she joined in the laughter.

"I'll turn my back while you make yourself presentable," Drew volunteered, still chuckling.

Juliana wasted no time hiking up her skirts and fastening the bustle around her waist.

He shook his head in bafflement. "I can't understand why women wear such contraptions."

"They were probably an invention of the Grand Inquisitor." She tugged at her dress and smoothed the pleats. "Now I'm ready."

Drew presented his arm like a proper gentleman. Juliana silently debated whether or not to accept. It seemed impossible to avoid his touch without acting churlish. But she was finding excuses to touch him all too frequently—and the contact was too enjoyable. Reluctantly, she placed her hand on his arm.

He guided her along the path in a new direction. "This path leads directly to the inn," he said in the way of explanation when doubt crossed her features. When she made no reply, he abruptly changed the subject. "I was raised Presbyterian and have little knowledge of religious life. Tell me more about convent ways."

"There's not much to tell, really." She gave a deprecating shrug. "Life there is simple, our time divided between prayer and work. Contrary to what many think"—she shot him an accusatory glance—"the convent is not filled with weak, docile females. Nuns live in a self-governing community composed solely of women. It's quite a democratic society. Much more so than the world outside convent walls where women are treated like second-rate citizens," she stated with conviction.

"Democratic, eh?"

She detested his condescending tone. "All of us were assigned certain tasks and responsibilities compatible with our abilities. As a group, nuns are well educated in the classics and the sciences." She paused to pick a wildflower growing alongside the path.

"I thought nuns did nothing but pray."

"Some orders are cloistered, but most, including the teaching order I belonged to, are not. Others are devoted to nursing, while some work among the poor or the aged. Women who join a convent leave behind their families and loved ones and renounce the ways of the world. Only the strong and determined succeed."

"You're both strong and determined. Why did you leave the convent?"

She stumbled to a halt. The wildflower fell from her nerveless fingers.

"Why, Juliana?"

Shame wouldn't allow her to meet his gaze. "The new mother superior was convinced I didn't have a vocation. She gave me no choice but to leave."

They resumed walking. "Your talk of the religious life has enlightened me," Drew said. "Until now I always thought finding a rich husband was the goal of all young women."

"I couldn't say." She studiously followed the antics of a squirrel scampering up a tree, its cheeks stuffed with nuts. "Anyway," she added, "I don't consider myself truly wed."

The woods thinned and the inn came into view. Drew swung her to face him. "What do you mean, not truly wed?"

"Our marriage is legally binding, just as any business agreement would be. But in my church, banns have to be published, and the couple must be married by a priest in front of witnesses. For a wedding to be real, it must take place before both God and man."

Juliana's logic irritated him. She had very conveniently found a way to rationalize her refusal to sleep with him, to salve any uncomfortable twinges of conscience. She was a cold-hearted, unemotional woman. Then he recalled the kisses they had shared. No, she was far from unemotional. Logic aside, she was a woman of fire and passion.

They ascended the flagstone steps of the tiered garden, stopping on the terrace. Drew trailed a fingertip down her nose, which was pinkened by the sun. "Next time you go for a stroll, don't forget your parasol."

As he sauntered off, he wondered if she'd heed his advice or ignore it. She was a maverick all right. He smiled to himself, thinking of her bustle propped up against the tree.

CHAPTER
12

THE FOLLOWING DAY WAS SUNDAY. JULIANA HADN'T SEEN
Drew since dinner the night before. The hours had seemed
unusually long. Bored, she had wandered through the gardens of the inn, admiring the carefully pruned roses. When
that no longer held her attention, she had tried to nap, but
instead had tossed restlessly. She was grateful when it was
finally time to bathe and dress for dinner. She chose a gown
of buttercup yellow and tucked a spray of silk flowers into
her hair.

Drew was waiting for her when she came downstairs.
"Yellow becomes you. You look as lovely as a summer
garden."

His compliment created a warm glow of pleasure deep
inside her. "Thank you," she said, suddenly shy.

The maître d'hôtel escorted them to the table they had
occupied on the two previous nights. "Our chef recom-
mends the loin of mutton." He made a short bow and
left.

Drew gave the waiter their order. When the wine was set
in front of them and the waiter had gone, he leaned forward
slightly, his expression intent. "There are some things we

should discuss before we return to New York tomorrow."

"By all means."

"I want you to feel at ease in my home. I bought the brownstone as an investment. Since I spend more time at the office than I do there, it seemed more than adequate."

Juliana nodded, not sure where the conversation was leading.

"Women, I'm told, view the matter differently. They like a larger place, something that will impress friends and acquaintances. I happen to own a substantial bit of property along Fifth Avenue." He was watching her closely, as though waiting for a reaction. "Besides my law practice, I dabble in real estate. What started as a lark succeeded beyond my wildest dreams. I'm a wealthy man, Juliana. If you want, I'll build you a mansion to rival those of the Vanderbilts."

Needing time to adjust to his surprising offer, she took a sip of wine. "That's very generous, Drew, but the brownstone will be quite satisfactory."

"The offer stands." He leveled his gaze on her. "Should you reconsider, don't hesitate to bring the subject up. You may feel differently in a few months' time."

The first of a succession of dishes arrived. Juliana was just finishing her soup when he broached the subject again. "Since you wish to remain in the present residence, feel free to decorate and furnish it to your liking. I've been much too busy to pay attention to such things. Have Emma help, if you wish."

"You've already given me so many things," she demurred, overwhelmed by the offer.

"Anything, just ask."

She lowered her eyes. "There is one thing . . . "

"Don't act coy. I find your directness refreshing."

"I'd like to hire Mary Bridget O'Toole as my lady's maid. Maura assured me that she'll work for room and board and a pittance of a salary. What with Katie and the babies living at home now, her family could use the extra income."

Drew steepled his fingertips together and appeared to ponder the request. "I hope the girl isn't easily intimidated. I fear Gilbert envisions himself as a field marshal when it comes to domestic concerns. He's used to an all-male household. If the truth be known, I think he's uncomfortable around women."

"Mary Bridget doesn't strike me as a timid girl. I'll instruct her not to disrupt Gilbert's routine."

"All right," Drew agreed. "Consider the matter settled."

Juliana was enjoying the last bite of chocolate soufflé, and Drew his brandy, when the maître d'hôtel appeared in the doorway of the dining room and clapped his hands. "Ladies and gentlemen, may I have your attention?" When the room quieted, he announced, "The inn has a special treat for you this evening. In honor of Independence Day there will be a band concert in town, followed by a fireworks display. Carriages will be waiting in the drive to take you and bring you back."

"Would you like to go?" Drew asked.

Juliana's eyes sparkled with anticipation. "Oh, yes, I'd love to. I've never been to a band concert or seen fireworks. I've heard they're marvelous."

Drew grinned at her childlike enthusiasm. "Then run upstairs and get a wrap. Evenings can turn cool."

Laughing, chattering couples squeezed into a coach and four for the short ride into town. As they approached the green, Juliana drank it all in. Apparently, there was nothing the citizens loved more than a promenade and a band concert.

The village green was crowded with families holding small children, couples walking arm in arm, boys playing tag, young girls in their Sunday best giggling and whispering among themselves. Residents watched the goings-on from wicker rockers on front porches that faced the green. Vendors hawked ice cream. The smell of freshly popped corn filled the air. The band, decked out in bright red and blue uniforms, warmed up shiny brass instruments on a makeshift platform constructed in the center of the green, their discordant notes adding to the cacophony.

"Would you like some ice cream?" Drew had to repeat the question twice.

Juliana nodded vigorously. "Chocolate. No, strawberry. Wait," she placed a delaying hand on his arm—"maybe vanilla."

"Don't wander away. I'll be right back." He left her standing near the bookshop while he went off. He returned with a dish containing a scoop each of chocolate, strawberry, and vanilla. "This should solve your dilemma."

Juliana's mouth dropped open; then she burst into laughter. "You're the most extravagant person I've ever met," she said, taking the dish.

Drew looked pleased. "That's a first. I've been accused of being a thrifty Scot but never an extravagant one. You'll ruin my carefully cultivated reputation."

She accepted a spoon. "Thank you for the ice cream."

"My pleasure." He would have handed her the moon on a silver platter if he could have. What was there about this woman? He had offered her anything her heart desired, and she asked nothing of him beyond a lock on her bedroom door. Was he trying to buy her good opinion?

"You didn't get any for yourself," Juliana said.

"No, maybe later." Drew found himself distracted by the

way she savored each spoonful of the creamy confection. She ate slowly, as though allowing herself to fully appreciate the distinct flavors. He loved watching the way her mouth opened and her lips closed around the spoon. When her tongue darted out to lick a drop of chocolate from the corner of her mouth, he jammed his hands in his pockets and fought for control.

"The concert is about to start. Why don't we find a good place from which to listen?" he suggested.

Together they edged their way toward the center of the green. The conductor sporting wire-rimmed glasses, an impeccably trimmed mustache, and spotless white gloves, stepped onto the podium. He nodded to the audience, turned, and raised his baton. The band immediately launched into a rousing march.

Juliana's toe tapped in time to the lively tempo. One piece followed another. Happy and smiling, she looked around. To her right was a cherubic toddler scarcely two years old, clinging to his father's hand and bouncing to the beat of the music. She caught Drew's attention. "Look."

Drew's gaze followed the direction she pointed in. "He's enjoying the concert almost as much as you are," he teased.

The warmth in his smile lent her hope. Maybe they could be friends after all. She swallowed hard, remembering their passionate kisses. Could she live with him and be content with just his friendship? She frowned. If she wanted more than friendship from a man who had raped her, perhaps there was a serious flaw in her character. Yet it was becoming increasingly difficult to reconcile the drunken brute who had stolen her virtue with her controlled, thoughtful husband.

The concert ended to a round of applause. Juliana clapped until her palms stung. Afterward she and Drew merged with the crowd as it headed for the fireworks display to be held at a clearing on the edge of town.

"If you enjoyed this, wait until we visit Emma and Bertram in Saratoga Springs next month," Drew said.

"That sounds wonderful. Emma talks of little else."

"During August there's a ball every other night. You do waltz?"

Her excitement at the prospect of visiting Saratoga quickly diminished. "You forget, I was raised in a convent. Gregorian chant doesn't lend itself to dancing."

Drew chuckled. "Then we'll hire a dance master to teach you. I guarantee that in a month you'll be ready for a cotillion."

It was dark when the crowd arrived at the site selected for the pyrotechnics. Juliana and Drew stood side by side, close but not touching. The night cloaked them in intimacy. Juliana shivered.

"Are you cold?" Drew asked.

He had no way of knowing her reaction had nothing to do with the temperature. "A little," she lied, draping her cashmere shawl over her shoulders.

A firecracker exploded nearby, startling her. It was followed by a loud hissing as a long tail of smoke soared heavenward, erupting in a colorful shower of stars that slowly wafted to earth. The display met with oohs and aahs from the spectators. For the next thirty minutes, Juliana watched spellbound.

The best was saved for the grand finale. Half a dozen Roman candles and rockets were shot off simultaneously. The ground reverberated, and the sky was alight with red, white, and blue star bursts. Juliana turned to Drew, her face aglow with happiness. "Isn't this the most beautiful sight you've ever seen?"

He looked into her upturned face. "Absolutely beautiful," he agreed.

When the fireworks ended, the coach was waiting to take the guests back to the inn. Juliana was wedged tightly against Drew in a corner. The steady plodding of horses' hooves had a lulling effect, and the group was much more subdued on the return trip. Juliana's eyelids felt heavy and slid shut. With a yawn, she fell asleep, her head resting on Drew's shoulder.

Drew studied his wife for long moments before he reluctantly slipped his arm around her shoulders and eased her head to his chest. He had to distance himself from her, had to resist these urges to touch and watch. Feelings were growing inside him that he adamantly refused to nourish. He had cared deeply for a woman once. That love had nearly destroyed him. Never again. His marriage to Juliana was a business arrangement, a marriage in name only, and would remain so.

His jaw grimly set, he stared straight ahead. Tomorrow at noon they would return to the city. The honeymoon was over.

One week lengthened into two; then two dragged into three. Since returning from Connecticut, Juliana had seen little of Drew. He either stayed late at the office or came home and went directly to his study. It was almost as if he was deliberately avoiding her. Although why he would do that she simply couldn't fathom.

Shopping forays and visits to the dressmaker filled Juliana's mornings until her closets and drawers bulged with new acquisitions. She spent her afternoons with the dance master. Each evening after dinner she would compose thank-you notes for wedding gifts, which still continued to arrive.

This task finished, she would retire to her room, bolt the door, and read until she fell asleep.

Tonight's outing to the theater was an unexpected treat. Anticipation had made the day pass slowly until it was finally time to dress. Juliana sat at her dressing table while Mary Bridget fussed with her hair. Her gaze settled on the mirrored reflection of the bedroom door. Human beings, she had discovered, erected barriers between one another, invisible walls that were as effective as those made of wood or stone. True, she was the one who had insisted on a stout lock, but logic aside, she sometimes wished she hadn't.

Mary Bridget pulled the brush through Juliana's thick tresses. "Is anything wrong? You're looking at that lock on your door ever so strangely."

Juliana roused herself with a shake of her head. "I was just woolgathering."

"One can't help but wonder why Mr. MacAllister had such a sturdy lock installed," Mary Bridget mused. Before Juliana could frame a reply, she continued. "Bet it belonged to the people who first lived here. Maybe the husband traveled about, and his wife didn't feel safe."

"Perhaps," Juliana answered noncommittally. Mary Bridget was never at a loss for questions. After living under the same roof with Juliana and sleeping in the same bed, the girl found it difficult to keep the relationship impersonal. Many times, the boundary between mistress and servant became blurred. But Mary Bridget proved adept at her new responsibilities, and her lively chatter helped to pass the lonely hours. Juliana didn't have the heart to reproach her.

"There's something I've been meaning to ask." Mary Bridget concentrated on twisting Juliana's hair into an elaborate coil. "I don't understand why you and Mr. MacAllister don't sleep in the same bedroom."

Juliana's head snapped around, and she stared at the girl. This time she had gone too far. "Mary Bridget! That simply is none of your business!"

Mary Bridget paused, brush poised in midair, her large blue eyes filled with remorse. "I'm sorry, Juliana. Maura keeps telling me I have to learn to mind my tongue."

"And I'm sorry I lost my temper."

"I wasn't being nosy. It's just that I don't understand why rich folks do things different from us working people." Mary Bridget resumed fussing with Juliana's hair. "Why, Mum and Dad have been married for twenty-five years and have never slept apart a single night."

"From what Emma has told me, it's not uncommon for married couples to have separate bedrooms. Though how she gathered her information, I was afraid to ask."

"I thought my dad worked long hours. But his are nothing compared to the time Mr. MacAllister puts in. I rarely see him at all."

Juliana was tempted to confess that she could echo that statement, but to do so would only have renewed Mary Bridget's volley of questions. "Nearly finished? Emma should be here soon. I'd like to show her the wedding gifts before we leave for the theater."

"Just let me fasten this egret feather in your hair." She picked up a black plume, secured it with a comb, then stepped back to view her handiwork. "You and Mr. MacAllister make such a striking pair that photographers will swarm to take your picture. The newspapers call it a fairy-tale romance—handsome, wealthy attorney marries his beautiful but penniless client." She held the hairbrush to her breast, a dreamy smile wreathing her face. "A case of love at first sight."

The doorbell chimed downstairs, saving Juliana a reply.

Gilbert was showing Emma into the parlor as she came downstairs. "Would you like me to serve tea, miss?" he asked, his face impassive.

Juliana noted with exasperation how he still avoided calling her Mrs. MacAllister. "Yes, please, Gilbert."

"What a sour pickle!" Emma commented when Gilbert was out of earshot.

The phrase was apt. Juliana giggled, then felt a twinge of guilt. "Poor Gilbert, he's been quite out of sorts ever since his domain was invaded by females."

"Well, I definitely won't ask him to sign my petition." Emma plunked herself down on the sofa.

"What is the petition for? Can I sign?"

"Oh, dear, you still have much to learn about the battle for women's rights. The petition asks the United States Congress to grant the National Woman Suffrage Association a chance to speak when it reconvenes. Only men can affix their signatures."

Juliana sat on an adjacent chair. "I've never heard of such a group."

"I've been a member for years. It was formed by Susan Anthony and Lizzie Stanton. Bertie claims they're a pair of radicals." She tugged off her gloves. "There's also another group, American Woman Suffrage Association. It's headed by Lucy Stone. She, along with her husband, Dr. Henry Blackwell, publish *The Woman's Journal,* a woman's suffrage weekly. Naturally I subscribe." She opened her handbag and pulled out a copy. "Here, keep this. I've already read it."

"Ahem." Gilbert stood in the doorway. He carried a silver tea tray into the parlor and set it on a low table in front of the sofa. His jaw slackened as he spied the folded newspaper. He glanced from Juliana to Emma, then back to the paper.

"If that's all, miss . . . " His voice was faint.

"You look a bit pale, Gilbert," Juliana said. "Are you all right?"

"Quite. Ring if you need anything." Lips clamped together with disapproval, he left the parlor.

Mary Bridget came into the room shaking her head. "What's wrong with Gilbert? I heard him mutter something about women plotting a revolution."

Emma's plump cheeks creased in a grin. "Absolutely not a prospect to ask to sign our petition."

"What's that?" Mary Bridget pointed to *The Woman's Journal*.

Juliana poured tea into fragile porcelain cups. "It's a weekly newspaper supporting women's right to vote."

"Pa found Mum's copy once. He made her burn it." Mary Bridget imparted the news matter-of-factly. "Pa said all a woman needs is a good man to look after her."

Emma accepted a cup of tea from Juliana and, patting the sofa, invited Mary Bridget to sit next to her. "Is that what you think, too, dear?"

"Well, I did until I saw what happened to Katie." A frown marred the girl's smooth brow. "Seeing how Sean up and ran off, now I'm not so sure. If Katie didn't have family, she and her babies would be in the streets. A woman needs to be able to look after herself, to be able to find a job, and earn her own way."

The story of Katie's plight had a sobering effect on the women. Juliana tried to lighten the mood by changing the subject. "Let me show you some of the wedding presents, Emma."

They spent the next half hour inspecting gifts arranged on a library table: a cut-crystal compote, a pair of porcelain vases, a sterling silver teapot in a rococo flower pattern from Tiffany's, a Swiss olivewood card box inlaid with two dancing couples on the cover.

Juliana held up an item for Emma to see. "Neither Mary Bridget nor I could quite figure out what this was meant to be used for."

"It's an English Sheffield domed bacon dish," Emma replied with a smile. "Alice Kent believes it's what every new bride needs in her kitchen."

From the doorway, Gilbert cleared his throat. "Excuse me, ladies. The carriage has arrived to take you to the theater."

After promising to tell Mary Bridget all about the play, Juliana picked up her beaded handbag and left with Emma. Once the carriage was under way, Emma turned to Juliana. "I've been invited to address several women's groups on the suffrage movement. It would please me greatly if you would be in the audience. Unless, of course, you fear Drew might object."

"Drew says I'm free to do as I choose. You can count on me to be there cheering you on."

"Thank you, dear." Emma patted Juliana's knee with a gloved hand. "I'm glad Drew's so open-minded on the subject. Once he's elected, he could do our cause much good."

The talk turned to the upcoming visit to Saratoga Springs, and almost before they knew it they had arrived at the theater. Emma spotted Drew near the marquee and waved at him as he moved forward.

A man toting a camera noted their arrival and pushed his way toward them. "Henry Mitchell, from the *Globe*." He doffed his derby. "Mind if I take a picture of you and your bride for the morning edition?"

"Not at all." Drew assisted Juliana to alight, then turned to help Emma.

"'Preciate it, Mr. MacAllister. Newlyweds make great copy. Folks can't seem to get enough of you. Just give me a minute." He fussed with the settings on his camera.

"He's right, you know. You do make a handsome couple." Emma's benign smile included them both. "I was just about to tell Juliana about the lovely room I've set aside for you to share during your visit to Saratoga."

Share?

The single word zinged between Juliana and Drew like an electric current. Simultaneously, they turned to look at each other. A flash of light exploded. The photographer captured the moment.

CHAPTER
13

DREW AND JULIANA STEPPED FROM THE PULLMAN CAR onto the platform, and she gazed around in awe at Saratoga Springs, New York, playground of the privileged.

Juliana had been told that thousands of people made the annual summer pilgrimage to this spa. After taking up residence in one of the lavish hotels, they would partake of medicinal waters, promenade under shady elms, cheer the thoroughbreds at the racetrack, and gamble in the casinos. Emma had said that nouveau riche and society bluebloods, Wall Street titans and Broadway actors, politicians and writers, all wished to take part in the renowned gaiety that was Saratoga.

From the depot cupola, a bell clanged, heralding the arrival of yet another trainload of vacationers as Juliana followed Drew across the platform. Equipages of every sort surrounded the station, and a line of porters stood under various hotel signs waiting to claim guests' baggage. Both residents and visitors crowded the platform to greet newcomers. It was a scene of cheerful bedlam.

"Emma regrets that she can't meet us personally." Drew signaled a porter. After getting his instructions, the man hurried off to collect their luggage and hail a buggy. "But her cousins and their married daughter were scheduled to arrive by steamboat, and she wanted to be at home to greet them."

"Maybe this isn't a good time for our visit," Juliana said. "I don't want to impose."

"Emma would have been insulted if we'd refused. There's nothing she loves more than a houseful of people."

"I worry about Emma's heart condition."

"So does Bertie." Drew checked his watch. "That's why he insisted they purchase a house here rather than take up residence in one of the hotels. Those places are a circus. He feared the commotion would prove fatal to Emma."

The porter returned and led them to a waiting carriage. Drew tipped the man and climbed in beside Juliana. The driver eased into the flow of traffic. Fascinated by the carnivallike atmosphere, Juliana looked up and down the street. Lavish hotels occupied both sides of Broadway, a triple width of dirt road, shaded by giant elms.

A mammoth five-story building caught her attention. It sported two wings that, Juliana quickly estimated, must have measured an eighth of a mile each. Flags flew from high turrets. The most distinguishing feature, however, was a wide veranda—called a piazza, Drew informed her—that swept across the facade of the hotel, with ornamented pillars that soared fifty feet to flower into a jumble of scrollwork. Wicker rocking chairs occupied by well-dressed guests crowded the piazza. Unthinkingly, Juliana laid a hand on Drew's arm. "What is that place?"

"The United States Hotel."

"I've never seen anything quite like it."

"Well, you're about to." Drew pointed to the opposite side of the street.

Juliana's gaze followed the direction of his. She gasped as another magnificent building, even larger than the first, came into view.

"That's the Grand Union Hotel," Drew explained. "It boasts it can serve fourteen hundred guests at a single seating. I've been told it has more than eight hundred guest rooms, many of them suites large enough to accommodate entire families." He smiled at her amazement. "Both hotels have extensive landscaped gardens that are quite pretty. If we have time, I'll take you to see them."

"I'd like that," Juliana murmured. She retreated into silence. The idea of so much wealth amassed in one small area was difficult to assimilate. Just a short time ago, her only possessions were the clothes she wore. Now she was in a land inhabited by the rich and famous. She felt like a foreigner, an outsider.

Drew frowned at her downcast expression. "What's wrong? I thought you were enjoying yourself."

"I don't feel as though I belong here." She gave him a covert glance, expecting him to be angered at her admission.

"I'd forgotten Saratoga can be a bit overwhelming," he confessed. "In Glasgow, I stole bread to keep my mother and myself from starving. Nothing prepared me for such an extravagant life. On my first visit here, I didn't feel that I belonged either."

His confession tugged at Juliana's heart. She wanted to probe deeper, discover more about the desperate young boy who had become a self-assured, wealthy attorney. Unfortunately this wasn't the time, but someday . . .

They turned onto a side street of stately houses built in the French and Italian styles. The carriage stopped before a three-story home encircled by a wrought-iron fence.

While the driver removed the luggage, Drew helped Juliana down. He placed her hand in the crook of his arm, then covered it with his own and squeezed gently. "Relax and enjoy Saratoga. Your natural charm and grace would make you welcome anywhere."

She felt so buoyed by his praise that her feet seemed to skim over the front walk.

Emma and Bertie welcomed them effusively. One arm linked in Juliana's, the other in Drew's, Emma introduced them to her other guests, who were enjoying coffee and conversation in the parlor. Emma's cousin Lydia Morton and her husband, Roger, were in their early fifties. Their daughter, Suzanne, and son-in-law, Lawrence VanDorn, had recently returned from a month abroad. They seemed like a cordial group, and they immediately included the new arrivals in their plans.

"We're going to the racetrack tomorrow. You'll come, of course." Suzanne took their acceptance for granted as she rushed on. "Lawrence is ever so clever when it comes to betting on the horses."

Lawrence beamed proudly. "The Travers Stakes is being run tomorrow. Cassius is favored to win." He gave Juliana a conspiratorial wink.

"Is this your first visit to Saratoga?" Lydia inquired.

"Yes, it is." Juliana perched on the edge of a settee and accepted a cup of tea from a servant. Drew stood behind her, an arm casually braced against the mantel.

"You'll love it," Lydia assured her. "Roger and I come every year. We find it ever so much livelier than Newport."

"The casinos alone make it worthwhile," her husband agreed.

A discussion of favorite activities followed. Juliana wondered how they would cram everything into a short period of time. Tired after the long train ride from New York City, she tried to hide a yawn.

Emma noticed. "How thoughtless of me. You must be exhausted. Besides you'll want to be fresh for tomorrow. I'll have one of the servants show you to your room."

Drew intercepted Juliana's look of panic. "Go ahead," he encouraged. "I'm going to play some bridge before coming up."

Grateful for his consideration, Juliana bade good night to the others and went upstairs to the bedroom where she quickly donned a high-necked, long-sleeved muslin nightdress, crawled between the sheets, and pulled the bedclothes up to her chin. She hugged the edge of the mattress, wide awake.

An hour ticked by. One by one she heard the guests retire for the night. When the bedroom door opened, she stiffened and pretended to be asleep. Drew undressed in the dark and climbed into bed. He, too, clung to the far side of the mattress.

"Good night, Juliana," he said quietly, sensing that she wasn't asleep.

"Good night," she whispered into the darkness.

The next day was bright and sunny. Fluffy white clouds drifted aimlessly across a cobalt sky. A gentle breeze sifted through the leaves of majestic oaks. The air was spiced with the scent of pine.

"Perfect afternoon for the racetrack," Emma proclaimed.

No one disagreed.

Following what Emma described as a light lunch—in actuality, it was a hearty meal—they piled into two carriages, the Lattimers and Mortons in one, the younger couples in the other. Rounding the corner onto Broadway, they joined a cavalcade of coaches and carriages headed for the track. Juliana surveyed the passengers. All the women were extravagantly costumed, wearing hats that mimicked miniature gardens or aviaries and carrying lacy parasols. The men, too, were resplendent in summer finery.

A surrey pulled by high-stepping bays passed along the right side of their carriage. Juliana turned to admire the perfectly matched horses and caught her breath. A male occupant bore a disturbing resemblance to someone she had hoped never to see again.

Freddie Westhaven?

Her heart skipped a beat, then tripped to an accelerated rhythm. Juliana couldn't be sure. She leaned forward for a better look, but the surrey had outdistanced them and she could see only the back of a pale blond head.

"Did you spot a friend?" Suzanne asked. She craned her neck to see what Juliana found so interesting.

Juliana shook her head in vigorous denial. "No. Just a person who reminded me of someone I once met." She settled back into the upholstery and determinedly stared the other way.

The carriage passed the Club House, a popular casino built by John Morrissey, former prizefighter and congressman, and twenty minutes later deposited its occupants at the entrance to the grandstand. The scene was colorful, the atmosphere festive. Friends regrouped, chattering and laughing, and began to make their way to the stands. It was soon apparent to Juliana that everyone possessed an opinion on which horse would win one of the most prestigious races of the season.

Smiling down at her, Drew took her arm. "Well, Juliana, which horse will you wager on? Cassius?"

"Me? Place a bet?" Until now she had regarded herself as an observer. The idea of testing her luck, however, intrigued her.

"Of course." Drew's smile broadened into a grin. "That's what one does at the track."

"Well . . . " Juliana twirled her parasol, torn between her natural inclinations and the good sisters' admonitions against gambling.

Emma concluded her conversation with Lydia and Roger and turned to Juliana. "Isn't this fun, dear?"

Bertie reappeared, carrying racing forms, which he distributed among them. "Choose your favorites, ladies. We gentlemen will place your bets at the windows."

"See! What did I tell you?" Lawrence VanDorn stabbed the paper with a forefinger. "Cassius is expected to win by a length."

"I'll bet on Cassius," Suzanne declared loyally.

Once they were seated in the grandstand, Juliana studied the sheet listing each contestant's attributes.

Drew leaned close. "Made your decision, lass?"

Juliana loved the way his voice deepened with a Scottish burr. She liked having him at her side. And she was beginning to miss him when he wasn't there. She didn't want to soften toward him, but couldn't seem to resist. "Yes, I've made my choice."

"Cassius?"

She shook her head. "D'Artagnan."

"You select a rogue instead of a Roman conspirator, eh?" His mouth quirked in amusement. "Once again my wife proves to be a maverick."

Lawrence grumbled that Juliana disregarded his sound advice. Roger and Bertie, long resigned to the follies of women, exchanged anecdotes illustrating the deplorable lack of logic exhibited by females. Drew quietly resisted Lawrence's urgings to dissuade his wife.

The bets were placed. As the big race neared, the crowd became charged with excitement. Tension mounted until it hummed in the air. Sleek thoroughbreds mounted by jockeys garbed in bright silks trotted to the post. A panoply of colorful tradition was arrayed before the spectators.

"Your jockey is the one wearing green and white striped silks," Drew told Juliana. "Cassius's jockey is in red."

The starting gate opened; horses flew down the track. The spectators leapt to their feet, yelling and cheering, the roar deafening. Juliana wasn't aware that she was standing also, her voice raised with the others. Two horses galloped to the head of the pack, then broke away. The remainder of the field ate their dust.

Cassius commanded a slight lead, D'Artagnan at his neck. Soon after passing the quarter pole, D'Artagnan appeared to break stride. A collective gasp went up. The horse faltered momentarily, but rallied when his jockey applied the quirt to his mount's rear quarters. Juliana's fingers bit into Drew's arm.

On the turn, running on the inside, Cassius kept the lead. Midway through the mile-and-a-quarter race, it was obvious that something was seriously wrong with D'Artagnan. The powerful horse spread his forelegs, widening his gait. His rider pulled him together and applied the whip a second time. Juliana was torn between the desire to bury her face in Drew's chest and the need to watch the valiant drama being enacted on the racetrack. Sensing her anxiety, Drew placed his arm around her shoulders and held her to his side.

Coming down the homestretch, D'Artagnan gallantly lengthened his stride. Turf spewed from the hooves of the two swift animals speeding toward the judges' stand. As though summoning his last reserves of energy, D'Artagnan outdistanced Cassius by a length. Cheers rent the air.

"He won, he won," Juliana cried. She flung herself into Drew's arms, half laughing, half crying in her exuberance. Lifting her off her feet, he hugged her close. Their expressions sobered. Her color high, Juliana dropped her gaze and pulled back. She wondered if she had imagined Drew's reluctance to release her. Or was the fleeting impression merely a projection of her own desire to be held in his arms?

Everyone watched D'Artagnan limp to the judges' stand where he was examined by his trainer. Applause greeted the announcement that the injury to the great horse wasn't serious.

"I'll go collect our money," Drew volunteered.

His choice of words wasn't lost on Juliana. "*Our* money?"

He held up two winning tickets. "I decided to cast my vote for a dashing rogue rather than a wily Roman."

"Looks as if Juliana has more horse sense than the rest of us," Bertie observed when the pandemonium faded.

Lawrence snorted in disgust. "Roger and I lost a bundle on that one. Maybe we'll have better luck on the next race. C'mon, let's go place our bets."

Emma gave Juliana an indulgent smile. "Don't let the men bother you, dear. My horse didn't even place."

"My word!" Lydia exclaimed. "There's Adele Westhaven." She waved her lace handkerchief, frantically trying to draw the attention of a large-boned brunette several rows down. "We met in France a year ago. You remember Adele, don't you, darling?" she asked her daughter.

Suzanne waved, too. "Of course, Mother, though I can't for the life of me understand how such a painfully plain woman could catch such an attractive husband."

"Money, darling. She inherited millions."

Emma squinted at the couple under discussion. "He must be years younger than she is," she observed snidely.

"Adele watches Freddie like a hawk," Lydia confided. "It's rumored he has an eye for the ladies. I pity the poor thing who catches his fancy should Adele get wind of it."

Juliana wanted to slump down in her seat and hide. The pleasant afternoon had turned into a nightmare. Adele Westhaven was a vicious, spiteful woman—one who hated her with a passion.

"Adele. Yoo-hoo," Lydia singsonged.

Adele Westhaven glanced over her shoulder. Recognizing Lydia and Suzanne, she smiled and waved back, then nudged her husband, who also turned. Freddie nodded a perfunctory greeting to the matron before he looked more closely at the women accompanying her. His pale blue eyes rested on Juliana in silent admiration. His brow furrowed briefly before he forced his attention back to the track.

Throughout the remainder of the afternoon Juliana felt the force of that questioning gaze. Freddie hadn't recognized her—yet. The thought gave her small comfort.

Juliana wore black that evening. Considering her mood, it seemed appropriate. The Club House was the unanimous choice of Emma and Bertie Lattimer's houseguests. As they approached the impressive redbrick building, set amid a terraced lawn, Juliana hoped that in the crush of visitors to Saratoga she could avoid another meeting with the Westhavens.

The small party was ushered inside a richly appointed casino. The public gaming room on the first floor invited modest bettors to try their luck at faro or roulette. Heavier gamblers were invited to private rooms upstairs where they could play uninterrupted for escalating stakes. Women were barred from the gaming rooms, but were made welcome in a chandeliered dining salon, where they were treated to pastries, ice cream, punch, and iced tea.

The men promptly disappeared into the gaming rooms, leaving the women to chat.

"Emma, are you still out crusading for woman suffrage?" Lydia asked her cousin as she bit into a small cake. "I daresay it has taken a toll on your health."

"I do what I can." Emma helped herself to a pecan tart from a dessert tray. "This fall I've been asked to address several women's groups on the subject."

Suzanne fluffed her fringe of curly red-brown bangs. "Lawrence can't understand why all women aren't more like me. He says no good will come from women who aren't content with their lot."

"Next they'll want to wear pants like Amelia Bloomer." Lydia looked aghast at the notion.

With an almost imperceptible shake of her head, Emma warned Juliana it would be useless to argue.

Lydia continued, "Speaking of fashions, wait until I tell you what they're showing in Europe. . . . "

After a time, Juliana excused herself. She was bored with idle chatter of fashion and gossip about strangers. Besides, the unexpected appearance of the Westhavens had made her edgy. She slowly made her way across the crowded salon toward the ladies' parlor.

"Juliana! It really *is* you." Freddie Westhaven stepped directly into her path.

She stared at him in dismay.

"You look absolutely stunning. I thought I saw you at the racetrack."

"Please, just pretend we've never met. I don't need any more trouble on your account."

"My dear Juliana, you should thank me, not vilify me." He smiled good-naturedly. "I see you've done quite well for yourself since we last met. You wasted no time finding yourself a wealthy benefactor."

Juliana's chin jutted out defiantly. "How dare you!"

Freddie threw back his head and laughed. "I always knew beneath that modest nun's habit a real woman waited to be set free. A shame my wife discovered us when she did."

Juliana spun away and nearly collided with Drew.

His eyes took on the turbulent blue-gray of a wintry sea. "Did you run into someone you know?"

"N-no," she stammered.

A guilty flush betrayed her lie.

CHAPTER
14

JULIANA SLEPT FITFULLY. FRAGMENTED MEMORIES SNATCH-
ed restful moments and stole her peace. Freddie. Adele.
Mother Superior. Even though she was asleep, the mi-
asma of shame poisoned the air she breathed. She tossed
and turned, trying to escape the odor. It was her fault that
Freddie Westhaven had tried to take liberties. She should
have guessed his intent, should have discouraged him sooner.

"I'm sorry, so sorry," Juliana mumbled in her sleep. She
tried to make Mother Superior understand. "Please, please,
let me stay." Juliana's voice throbbed with contrition, but
the nun's glacial gaze failed to thaw under her pleading.

"Hush, lass," a gentle voice soothed.

"Don't send me away."

"Shh, you've nothing to fear. I'll protect you."

Comforted by the sound of a Scottish burr and the feel
of someone stroking her hair, Juliana snuggled closer.

The next morning she drifted awake on a fluffy cloud of
contentment. The demons that haunted her dreams had been
vanquished; peacefulness prevailed. Her sleep-heavy eyelids slid open. Drew's countenance filled her vision. They
were lying, facing each other, so close their breath mingled.

179

She tried to ease away, but discovered that a lock of her hair was trapped beneath his cheek. Debating how to extricate herself, she used the moment to study him.

In repose, he looked younger, more approachable, and, if possible, even more handsome. Stubble shadowed his jaw. Juliana felt the desire to lightly rub her knuckles over his cheek and feel its rough texture. She caught her lower lip between her teeth.

Shameless hussy! her conscience chastised.

Just this once, an inner voice wheedled.

Deep within her a battle raged as woman struggled to break free from innocent girl. Don't be afraid to touch. Don't be afraid to feel, an insidious voice urged. Be a woman, a wife, just this once.

Reaching out, she tentatively brushed her knuckles across the dark bristle. A fierce thrill of forbidden pleasure surged through her, a feeling so intense she couldn't resist a second touch.

She inhaled sharply as Drew's hand moved up to capture hers. With eyes as round as gold doubloons, she awaited his reaction. Though his eyes remained shut, he pressed her hand to his lips and brushed a kiss along its back. Still not relinquishing her hand, he placed it against his chest. Beneath his cotton nightshirt, Juliana could feel the steady thud of his heart.

Then he opened his eyes and smiled. "Good morning."

"Good morning." She smiled back, happy and shy at the same time. Waking up beside him, warm and protected, had been a heady experience. For the first time she felt truly married.

"I think we've slept away half the morning." He idly picked up a honey-gold curl and began to play with it.

"Emma will wonder about us."

Another smile tugged at his mouth. "Emma's a wise lady. No doubt she'll realize this is the way of a recently married couple."

"Oh." The word seemed woefully inadequate.

"Newlyweds, I've been told, need an uncommon amount of privacy."

Juliana's cheeks stung with a sudden rush of color. "You're making me blush."

"It becomes you. You were much too pale when we first met. Now you have what poets describe as a peaches-and-cream complexion."

Juliana swallowed. She supposed she should take command of the situation, inform him she cared little for his opinions, but somehow the rebuke failed to materialize.

Fascinated by its satiny sheen, Drew held up a lock of hair for his perusal. His eyes glazed with a faraway look; his expression grew wistful. "When I was a lad in Glasgow, we had no coin for bread, much less for sweets. I used to stand in front of the confectioner's window, my nose pressed against the glass, and stare at jars of butterscotch and caramel until my mouth watered." He wound the curl around his index finger, bringing Juliana closer with each slow twist.

The image of Drew as a small boy, ragged, hungry, and cold, looking longingly through a candy store window, started a swell of sympathy within Juliana. He had always struck her as invincible, not needing anyone or anything to survive. How wrong her assessment of him had been.

"Ah, lass, your hair is the rich golden color of the candy I used to covet."

His voice mesmerized her. Juliana leaned toward him, her lips parting. This time it was she who initiated the kiss.

Would he think her bold? The question raced through her mind as their mouths met. All doubts fled at his ardent response.

His arms locked around her, flattening her against him. "God, how I love your mouth. It's sweeter than any candy. I can't seem to get my fill." His lips feasted on hers, greedily tasting, savoring, devouring.

When his tongue dipped into her mouth, her body tensed, then relaxed as she was consumed with a need as great as his. Her tongue tangled with his in innocent but intuitive love-play. He rolled on top of her, buried his hands in the glory of her hair, his weight pinning her to the mattress.

What sounded at first like the tapping of a distant woodpecker became more persistent. Drew rolled away from Juliana with a frustrated groan. "What is it?" he called out.

"Mr. VanDorn sent me to remind you that you and your wife have a bicycle outing planned," a servant answered from the hallway. "Would you like me to bring you some hot water?"

Damn Lawrence VanDorn's sense of timing. Drew ran an impatient hand through his hair. "Yes, bring it up."

Drew lay on his back, staring up at the ceiling, waiting for desire to ebb. If the servant hadn't interrupted, Drew would have made love to Juliana. Soft and yielding, she had all but melted in his embrace. Dammit! He had wanted her then, and still did now.

She made him feel twenty again, when love was a wonderful, exciting adventure. But he was no longer twenty, and love was no longer new. He had given his heart and soul to Victoria. Love like that happened once in a lifetime. The fact that their love affair failed to endure hadn't been Victoria's fault but her father's.

Why was he thinking of love? Drew wondered angrily. Juliana was nothing like Victoria. Nothing! The women were complete opposites. Victoria, dark and petite, was a purring kitten, completely helpless. Juliana was a tawny tigress, strong-willed and independent. Strange, he could hardly remember the color of Victoria's eyes.

Juliana propped herself up on an elbow. "Drew?" She placed her hand gently along his jaw and turned his face to her. "Is anything wrong? Did I do something to make you angry?"

Drew needed a target for his frustration. "It's high time you learned to exercise more prudence."

She snatched her hand away as though burned. "I-I don't know what you're talking about."

"You're much too gullible where men are concerned. Don't you have any idea where a kiss can lead?" Throwing back the covers, he swung his legs out of bed. "I'd advise you to exercise greater caution. Most men would have taken advantage of the situation." Myself included, he added silently.

Hurt by his attack, she countered, "That's peculiar advice, coming from you."

They glared at each other. The servant's arrival with a pitcher of steaming water forestalled the argument. However, it resumed the minute the door closed behind him.

"As your husband, it's my duty to protect you."

"I can protect myself."

"Ha!" he snorted. "If you had done such a fine job of taking care of yourself, we wouldn't be in this predicament."

His logic silenced her. With a final glowering look, Drew disappeared behind the dressing screen. He poured water into a bowl and lathered his face with soap. He was furious with himself and with Juliana, but most of all with Nick.

Good thing his younger brother was far away, or Drew would have throttled him. He winced as his razor drew blood.

Maybe he should have done so years ago. He had spoiled the lad rotten. And still did. He cut himself again and cursed soundly.

Because of Nick's deplorable lack of discipline, Drew had volunteered to suffer the consequences—Juliana. In his brother's stead, Drew had willingly accepted a lifetime sentence of slow, painful torture. He had married a beautiful, desirable woman, but by his own pledge, he was forbidden to touch her. And fool that he was, he had provided the lock for her door.

Juliana had allowed him a few kisses, but making love was another matter entirely. How could he press the matter unless she initiated the act? Her conviction that he had raped her made that possibility unlikely.

Drew managed to finish shaving without further mishap. When he came out from behind the screen, he noted that Juliana regarded him warily. No doubt she considered him a raving lunatic, he thought grimly.

"Your chin is bleeding," Juliana observed, her tone matter-of-fact.

"I'll meet you downstairs." Dabbing his chin with a handkerchief, he stormed from the room.

After lunch the guests congregated at the rear of the house where several tandem bicycles, designed for two riders, were propped against the fence.

"I'd love to go for a ride," Emma exclaimed.

"If you want to attend the ball tonight, you need to take an afternoon nap," her brother pointed out.

"Oh, Bertie, you're no fun at all."

"Besides, I'm no longer sure that cycling is good for one's health," Bertie expounded. "I read in the paper where a physician claimed it can cause the teeth to loosen and fall out."

Roger Morton nodded his head in vigorous accord. "I read the same article myself. Called the condition bicycle gums. Doctor said it occurred during rapid pedaling when the rider drew cold air over heated gums."

"Daddy, really." Suzanne giggled.

"At any rate, bicycle riding is a sport for young people," Lydia spoke up.

"Well, let's get a move on." Lawrence consulted his watch. "Suzanne and I want to be back in time for a carriage ride to Lake Saratoga."

"Are you sure you want to risk bicycle gums?" Drew asked Juliana. The twinkle in his eyes belied his serious expression.

"I'm willing to gamble." She laughed. "Cycling doesn't look that difficult."

"All you have to do is keep your feet on the pedals and maintain your balance. I'll do the rest."

Drew and Lawrence selected bicycles and wheeled them toward their wives. Suzanne, well accustomed to the sport, hopped on, wiggling her hips to adjust her skirt and bustle to the seat. With a wave of her hand, she and Lawrence pedaled down the drive and turned into the street.

While Drew held the bicycle, Juliana imitated Suzanne's moves, grateful for her Langtree bustle with its flexible stays. She held fast to the handlebars as Drew pushed off amid shouts of advice from their older friends.

"Hold tight, dear."

"Don't let too much ankle show."

"Careful your skirt doesn't catch in the spokes."

Juliana was too busy concentrating on the instructions to hazard either a wave or a backward glance.

Turning, Drew grinned at her worried expression. "Just keep your balance and pedal in a steady rhythm. Let me do the steering."

"I don't mean to criticize, but wouldn't it be easier to steer if you watched where we're going?"

"Point well taken." Drew chuckled, directing his attention to navigating their way out of town.

"Pedal and balance, pedal and balance," Juliana muttered under her breath. "Watch your skirts, don't show your ankles." Once they reached the village limits, she began to relax and enjoy the ride.

Lawrence and Suzanne had widened the gap between them, preferring to pedal at a brisker speed. Drew, in deference to Juliana's inexperience, kept a more leisurely pace. Juliana lifted her face and felt the wind fanning her cheeks. Feeling more confident, she looked about. All around, the foothills of the Adirondacks stretched out to meet them. The countryside rolled gently to form a pleasing panorama. Fields of white-blossomed buckwheat and green stalks of corn waved in a breeze that smelled of new-mown hay. Farther down the road was a wood thick with fir, pine, and other evergreens. Above, gray rain clouds gathered to blot out the sun.

As they approached a crossroad, they found Lawrence and Suzanne waiting for them. "It looks as if we might get a shower." Suzanne pointed at the sky.

"We're turning back," Lawrence said. "How about you?"

Drew pulled to a stop alongside them, then turned to Juliana. "Had enough?"

"I'm just getting the knack. Couldn't we go just a little farther?"

Lawrence wheeled the bicycle around. "Suit yourself."

"See you at the Lattimers'," Suzanne called as they headed back toward town.

"If I remember from my last visit, this road circles back toward Saratoga in another mile or so." Drew started down a dirt road.

Juliana was enjoying herself. It was wonderful to exchange the crowds for the simple pleasure of an excursion in the country. For a short time there were no greater hurdles than knowing how to pedal and balance. But no sooner had the winding road made a northward loop then it started to sprinkle.

"There's an abandoned farmhouse just ahead. Let's head for it." Drew hunched forward and pedaled faster. Juliana followed suit.

A quarter mile down the road a small stone building, the front door ajar, came into view. Sprinkles of rain became giant drops. Drew turned the handlebars sharply, and the bicycle bumped over the rutted drive. He hopped off and steadied the bike while Juliana dismounted.

"Hurry inside before you get soaked," he ordered. He wheeled the bike close to the side of the house where it was partially protected by the overhang of the roof, then followed her into the building.

The floor creaked underfoot, and field mice scurried to hide. The musty odor made Juliana sneeze. A stone fireplace stood at one end of the room, flanked by crude pine cabinets. Except for a broken chair draped with cobwebs and a few pieces of chipped pottery, the one-room house was unfurnished. The slate shingles kept out the rain that now fell in a heavy torrent.

Juliana stood in the doorway looking out at the driving rain. Absently, she wrapped her arms around herself, rubbing them to erase the damp chill that seeped into her bones.

"Here." Drew shrugged out of his jacket and draped it over her shoulders.

She looked up to thank him, but was unable to speak. The force of her emotions kept her silent. This man had become the center of her world, the most important person in her life. Everything she did, everything she felt, revolved around him. He could be arrogant, intimidating, domineering, and yet he had a gentle side. An almost noble part of his character bound her to him with invisible fetters.

She loved him.

The realization staggered her.

When had loathing changed into love? Was it possible to love someone you didn't trust? How had this happened? Why? One question chased another. Then the confusion settled, leaving her filled with a deep, abiding certainty that she loved Drew MacAllister, loved him now and would continue to love him all the days of her life.

"Warm enough?"

Juliana nodded and pulled her thoughts back to the present. "You always seem to come to my rescue."

Drew jammed his hands into his pockets. "Not always."

She wrapped his jacket more securely around her. Drew believed her an innocent victim of circumstance. How would he respond to Adele Westhaven's accusations? Who would he believe?

"Why the sigh?" Drew asked.

Juliana wasn't aware she had uttered a sound. "I was thinking of the ball tonight."

"Are you sure it isn't something else?"

She glanced at him fearfully. If he learned about her past, would he, too, think her a tramp and turn her out? Would he want a divorce or an annulment? "What do you mean?"

"You've been acting strange ever since last night. Who was that man you were talking to at the casino?"

"I already told you I didn't know him."

"Who was he, Juliana?" His gaze drilled into hers. "And don't lie to me."

She raised her chin. His manner put her on the defensive. "Why are you treating me like this? I'm not on trial."

"Then why not answer my question?" he asked reasonably.

"Stop badgering me," she flung back, frightened and irritated by his relentless questioning. "I don't like being cross-examined."

"What are you trying to hide? What are you afraid of?"

"All right, I lied," she admitted, feeling ashamed of her deceit. "That man you saw, Freddie Westhaven, is just someone I met once, very briefly, while at the convent."

"And that's all?"

"Yes." She shifted her gaze to stare unseeingly at the falling rain. "That's all."

His hands closed over her shoulders, and he forced her to face him. "After everything that's happened, you may find this hard to believe, but you *can* trust me. You're not alone anymore."

His words were consoling. Juliana desperately wanted to to trust him. But could she? She was so confused. Running her tongue nervously over her lower lip, she said, "The rain's stopped. It's time to go."

Before she could draw away, Drew cupped her face in his hands. His thumbs lightly feathered her cheekbones. "Don't be afraid. Trust." As though sensing her indecision, he released her and stepped back. "If you need me, I'll be there."

Juliana remembered little about the return ride to Saratoga

Springs. Her mind spun back into the past. She had been alone since her father left to explore the Rockies in his quest for silver. Except for Sister Margaret Ann, no one had cared a fig about her. In time, Juliana had grown from a quiet, gangly young girl into an independent woman.

Now she had someone who asked for her trust, someone who promised to protect her, someone to love. She should have felt wonderful. Instead, she was filled with fear. Would Drew abandon her after Adele Westhaven told him how she had tried to seduce her husband?

CHAPTER
15

THE NIGHT SHIMMERED. CRYSTAL CHANDELIERS DANGLED from the ceiling of the Grand Union's main ballroom. The dancers wore diamonds as badges of distinction—the bigger and bolder the gem, the more prominent the wearer. The sheen of silks and satins reflected glittering lights. Juliana was awed by the lavish display.

Her gloved hand tightened on Drew's sleeve. He smiled down at her, his eyes alight with admiration. "Don't feel intimidated. There isn't a woman here who can match your beauty."

"Thank you." Juliana returned the smile, happy she had taken her friend's advice. Emma and Maura had both insisted that she purchase the dress of peach-colored silk, with its small train adorned with clusters of roses in shades of peach and cream. A deep flounce of ecru lace crossed the low-cut bodice.

She waved her painted fan, scanning the crush of people. "There are hundreds here tonight. How will we ever find Suzanne and Lawrence?"

"We probably won't." Drew seemed unconcerned.

If a prearranged meeting with friends was unlikely, then

a chance encounter with the Westhavens was even more so, Juliana reasoned. Perhaps her worry had been for naught. How wonderful it would be to relax and enjoy her first cotillion.

Drew nodded at a passing acquaintance. "Daniel sent word he'd be here tonight, though I doubt our paths will cross."

"You never mentioned that Assemblyman Tennant might be here."

"His plans were still uncertain when last we spoke." Drew frowned slightly at her tone. "Daniel is shrewd. Saratoga Springs is the place to be. He knows million-dollar deals are made each afternoon on the north piazza of the United States Hotel. Besides, the mineral waters are good for his ailing health. At any rate, he's invited us for lunch tomorrow."

The information was met with dread. Juliana's first impression of Daniel Tennant hadn't been favorable. She had found him condescending and arrogant, a man intent on playing god with other people's lives.

Drew guessed her train of thought. "I know Daniel can be high-handed. But he's been very good to me—and to my career. All I ask is that you make an effort not to annoy him."

Juliana met his look. Drew asked little of her. It was not in her to refuse his simple request. "I'll do my best," she promised, summoning a smile.

"That's a good lass." He squeezed her hand. "May I have this dance, Mrs. MacAllister?"

"I'd be delighted, Mr. MacAllister," Juliana replied. She was proud to be the one he led onto the dance floor. Evening clothes seemed to have been designed with him in mind. He wore them with an air of casual elegance that many men envied but few could imitate.

The orchestra struck up a waltz. Recalling the instructions of her dance master, Juliana rested her left hand lightly on Drew's shoulder, then placed her right one in his outstretched palm. Mentally she heard the dance master count one-two-three, one-two-three, as they merged with the other dancing couples. At first her concentration was intense, her movements stiff and rehearsed.

"Relax, Juliana."

She obeyed her husband's soft command and found herself drowning in uncharted waters. How could she ever have thought his blue-gray eyes cold?

"Let the music be your guide."

Slowly her tension dissolved. With Drew's arm securely at her waist, Juliana succumbed to the exhilarating experience of her first waltz. She felt as though she were floating, her slippered feet barely skimming the floor.

She was sorry when the dance ended and Bertie Lattimer claimed her for the next waltz. After Bertie, there was a succession of partners. She caught glimpses of Drew dancing with one beautiful woman after another and felt a twinge of jealousy. She wanted to be the only one he smiled at, the only one to gaze into those silver-blue depths.

Drew reappeared at Juliana's side when the orchestra took an intermission. "I've located the Lattimers and the Mortons. They asked us to join them at their table. Emma's anxious to know if you're enjoying yourself." Taking Juliana's arm, he led her toward a row of tables that lined an entire wall.

Lydia Morton beckoned them with a wave. "Juliana dear, you look positively radiant in that dress. You'll have to give Suzanne the name of your dressmaker."

Emma beamed fondly. "It's Juliana who makes the dress, not the reverse."

"Isn't that Diamond Jim Brady and Lillian Russell?" Suzanne asked in a loud whisper as she and Lawrence joined them.

"Why, I do believe it is," Lydia said, inspecting the couple in question through her lorgnette.

Juliana couldn't resist staring at the flamboyant pair. The curvaceous, golden-haired darling of the New York stage was in her twenties. Her companion was a dark, corpulent man. Diamonds flashed from his shirt studs, cuff links, and even his watch chain.

Roger Morton dropped his voice confidentially. "Heard Diamond Jim has a stomach six times normal size."

"He never touches hard liquor, but has a weakness for freshly squeezed orange juice," Lawrence VanDorn added. "Friend of mine swears he saw Diamond Jim drink four gallons at a single sitting."

"Oh, my!" Emma exclaimed. "Imagine that."

"Saratoga boasts many famous visitors, doesn't it, Emma dear?" Bertram gave his twin an indulgent smile. "Two summers ago just before his death, Ulysses S. Grant finished his *Personal Memoirs* at Mount McGregor, not far from here."

"Mark Twain, his publisher, visited Grant often," Emma added. "Mr. Twain, as I recall, is quite fond of a friendly game of billiards."

Lydia's eyes moved restlessly over the crowded ballroom. Her expression brightened as a couple passed their table. "Yoo-hoo, Adele," she hailed the woman.

Juliana sucked in her breath. Her greatest fear was standing directly in front of her. The color drained from her face, leaving it ashen.

Lydia made the introductions, coming to Juliana and Drew last. "This is Drew MacAllister, an attorney and special friend of Assemblyman Tennant, and his bride, Juliana."

Adele's gaze slid over Juliana to fasten on Drew. "So pleased to meet you, Mr. MacAllister." She extended a gloved hand. "I don't believe we've met. Are you a regular visitor to Saratoga?"

"An occasional visitor only, Mrs. Westhaven," Drew returned easily.

As nervous as Juliana was, the woman's simpering manner grated. The voice she remembered as vitriolic was now syrupy with false sweetness.

Freddie stepped forward. "Juliana, we meet again. I can hardly believe my good fortune."

Adele's head turned sharply at her husband's comment. "Freddie, love, you're mistaken." She inspected Juliana closely for the first time. "Juliana? Where have I heard that name before?" Her jaw slackened as recognition dawned. "You." Her voice lost its sugary coating.

"Mrs. Westhaven," Juliana said with a polite nod.

The woman's eyes narrowed to slits; an unbecoming flush spread across her face. "I hoped I'd seen the last of you," she hissed.

Her comment elicited whispers from the small group who watched the enfolding scene with avid curiosity.

Adele's gaze swung to Drew, then back to Juliana. "You didn't waste much time finding yourself a rich husband, did you? You're a mercenary bit of baggage. At least you've found a more suitable profession."

Emma stepped to Juliana's side. "Those remarks are quite uncalled for, Mrs. Westhaven. You have no need to be insulting."

"Don't I?" Adele glowered. "I could tell you a thing or two about your precious Juliana—"

"Now, dumpling . . . " Freddie placed a placating hand on his wife's arm, but she shook it off.

Drew stepped forward. "Since you're intent on defaming my wife's character, perhaps I should be the first person you talk to. The music's starting. You can enlighten me during the next waltz." Drew took Adele's arm and led her toward the dance floor.

Casting uneasy glances at Juliana, the others paired off and merged with the dancers. Juliana and Freddie were left alone. "Shall we dance?" Freddie offered, seeming more amused than perturbed by the turn of events.

"How can you even think of dancing at a time like this?" Juliana tried to spot Drew and Adele among the throng of dancers.

"Come, just one waltz," Freddie coaxed. "You'll be able to keep a better eye on your husband from the dance floor." Freddie gave her the smile she had once found charming. This time it left her unmoved.

Reluctantly she acquiesced. Natural grace more than conscious effort guided her steps as she was swept onto the floor. "Smile," Freddie advised. "For the life of me I can't comprehend why you're so worried."

Exasperated beyond belief, Juliana could only stare at him. "Your wife must be filling Drew's ears at this very moment. I admit the incident that took place between us looked compromising, but we both know nothing happened."

"So what's the worst your husband can do? Divorce you?"

Juliana missed a step. It was one thing to entertain that thought privately, but to hear someone voice it aloud was an entirely different matter.

"Never fear, my pretty. Your husband doesn't want to

tarnish his sterling reputation. He won't divorce you any more than Adele will divorce me."

For a moment Juliana caught sight of Drew's tall figure, his head bent attentively. Would he believe everything Adele told him, just as Mother Superior had? Would he, too, send her away?

Ignoring her distraction, Freddie kept up a steady stream of small talk. "I visit New York City quite often. My friend James has a flat there. Perhaps we could meet and renew our friendship. James stocks your favorite wine." He chuckled when her eyes widened at the mention of wine. "I see you remember."

"Well enough to avoid it in the future."

"Ah, Juliana." He clucked his tongue. "Life is too short to spend it shut away from the world. It's meant to be lived to the fullest. My friend and I were doing you a favor actually."

"What are you talking about?" She nervously peered over his shoulder, hoping for another sight of Drew.

"You were much too lovely to be a nun. For a lark, we decided to put your vocation to the test. I claimed I could seduce you. My friend said I couldn't." Smiling confidently, Freddie whirled her across the floor. "We even had a small wager riding on the outcome. To tip the scale in my favor, I added a dram of insurance to the wine. An old potion known for its . . . aphrodisiac qualities. Pity Adele arrived when she did."

Blood hummed in Juliana's ears; she felt light-headed. Dancers spun around them in a kaleidoscope of color and motion. For a moment she thought she might faint. Then anger revived her.

Juliana stopped dancing and stalked off the floor. Dumbfounded, Freddie stared after her, then followed. He caught up with her as she passed through the French doors leading to the piazza. She whirled on him. "A lark? You nearly ruined my life to win a meaningless wager?"

"Don't be such a poor sport." Reaching out, he grabbed her left hand and raised it so her yellow diamond caught and refracted light. "Judging from the size of this rock, you got the best of the bargain."

She jerked her hand free. "I hope I never see you again."

"If you change your mind about visiting my friend's flat . . . " Grinning, he returned to the ballroom.

Juliana shook her head. How could she ever have thought that pale, insipid man attractive? How naive she had been. Until tonight she had only suspected his appalling lack of character. Now she knew beyond a doubt. He was a spineless worm, totally the opposite of Drew. *Drew*. Oh, dear, Lord. She began to pace the long porch. What must he be thinking? Would he give her a chance to explain? And if so, would he believe her? She was not blameless, Juliana admitted. Somehow she should have taken control of the situation before it had gotten out of hand.

"Westhaven told me I'd find you out here."

Juliana started at the sound of Drew's voice behind her. Hands tightly clasped, she turned, hoping to find compassion, fearing she wouldn't. Shadows obscured his expression.

She looked guilty as sin, Drew thought. A prosecutor's dream. One glance at her face and the jury would vote for a hanging.

Adele Westhaven claimed she had discovered her husband and Juliana, her hair in wild disarray, sprawled on the parlor sofa in her Philadelphia home. Juliana had looked like anything but the meek, subservient novice she claimed to be.

Drew could understand Freddie's attraction, even admire his discernment of beauty. The real difficulty lay in accepting Juliana's willing participation. The idea of her, pliant and eager in another's arms, aroused feelings he hadn't had time to sort out. Anger and jealousy, however, warred for priority.

"Adele Westhaven has made some very serious allegations." He advanced toward her. "She threatened to destroy your reputation, but I persuaded her that it would be advantageous to all concerned if this didn't go any further. Now I'd like to hear your version."

This was what she wanted, wasn't it? Juliana asked herself. A chance to explain. Why, then, the flash of resentment at having to prove her innocence? Her chin came up a notch; all traces of fear vanished. "Very well. Let's talk in the garden." Without waiting to see if Drew would follow, she walked down the shallow steps of the piazza.

Most guests were inside enjoying the cotillion. Only a few stragglers strolled along the landscaped paths of a garden the size of a city park. "I won't dispute the fact that Mrs. Westhaven discovered her husband and me in a very embarrassing situation. In her place, I would have come to the same conclusion."

"Are you saying that you tried to seduce him?"

Juliana stopped dead and swung around. "Is that what you think?"

He shrugged. "I'm merely restating what Adele told me."

Juliana started walking again, her quickened pace revealing her agitation. "It was just the opposite, although I didn't learn the details until tonight."

Drew caught her shoulders and turned her to face him. "Don't mince words, Juliana. I want you to tell me everything." His hands biting into her flesh, he pressed her against the rough bark of a tree bordering the path.

Juliana drew a deep breath, moistened her lips, then spared no details of the aborted seduction. She told how she was sent to the Westhaven estate to pick up some books for the convent school from Adele, a wealthy benefactress. Discovering that Mrs. Westhaven was out for the afternoon, but would return shortly, Juliana was invited to wait in the parlor. Her fatal mistake was accepting refreshment in the form of a sweet, fruity wine from Adele's apologetic husband.

The beverage had dulled her wits and made her slow to repulse Freddie's amorous advances. Before she could gather her wits, he had tugged the novice's veil off her head and the pins from her hair. At that point, Adele had burst into the room. Juliana ended her recital by berating herself for allowing herself to be duped by Freddie's flowery compliments.

"There," she said, glad all her dark secrets were exposed at last. "That's the truth, though I don't expect you to believe me."

Drew studied her upturned face. He saw defiance; he saw pride; he found no duplicity. "I believe you."

The unexpected admission brought a sting of tears to her eyes. "You do?" A smile trembled on her lips.

His hold gentled. His fingers kneaded her shoulders in a soothing, circular motion. "Aye, lass."

Juliana's relief was so immense she wanted to bury her head against Drew's chest, wrap her arms around him, and hold tight. She had been so afraid she might lose him. So afraid he wouldn't believe her. Afraid he wouldn't trust her. "Thank you," she whispered.

He crooked a finger under her chin and raised her face for a kiss. "My pleasure."

*   *   *

Once again, sleep entwined them in an intimacy both struggled to ignore in waking hours. Drew woke early to find Juliana's head resting on his shoulder, her leg casually thrown across his, his left arm curved protectively around her shoulders.

Sharing a bed with Juliana was creating havoc within him. All he seemed to think about these days was making love to her. If this continued, he would cast good intentions aside. Then he remembered his vow. He had given his word not to touch her. And she had believed him.

Drew eased from the bed, careful not to wake her, dressed quickly, and left the room. If he didn't keep a safe distance, he was afraid he would take her any way he could, whether she was willing or not.

Juliana was disappointed when she woke an hour later and found herself alone. Lightly she traced the depression in the pillow on Drew's side of the bed. Why did she crave his touch when the thought of it should repel her? She hungered for the exquisite sensations that washed over her each time they kissed. Unnamed yearnings roiled through her, leaving her dissatisfied and restless.

Temptations of Lucifer, Mother Superior would call them. But if this was temptation, Juliana could understand why so many people sinned. With a sigh, she kicked off the covers and climbed out of bed.

Promptly at midday Juliana and Drew arrived at the Grand Union Hotel. After being announced by calling card, they were ushered to Daniel Tennant's suite. The legislator greeted them at the door. He accorded Juliana a slight inclination of his head, then promptly forgot her. The aging politician pumped Drew's hand. "Saratoga is the place to be, boy. More deals take place on the piazza than on Wall Street."

"Have you sampled the waters yet?"

Daniel nodded, obviously pleased with his protégé's solicitous concern for his health. "Drank two tumblers of water from Congress Spring this morning. Plan to visit Hathorn Spring this afternoon. A colleague claims it possesses a greater abundance of minerals than any other Saratoga water."

They were shown into a parlor and seated at a table set with fine linens and silver. While the men talked of business deals, Juliana studied the decor. Elaborately carved black walnut furniture rested on flower-patterned carpets. Swags of heavy Brussels lace draped the tall windows overlooking a courtyard. Near a window was a coil of knotted rope, one end stapled to the floor, to be used as an escape ladder in case of fire, a requisite in all Saratoga hotels.

The assemblyman was seized by a bout of dry, racking coughs. When it subsided, he regarded Juliana through watery eyes. "Drew tells me you're becoming quite close with Emma Lattimer."

"I consider myself fortunate to number among her friends. She's been very kind to me."

"Hope you're more sensible than she. Her darn fool causes keep getting her into trouble."

"Do you mean her involvement in woman suffrage?"

"Precisely." He dabbed his eyes with a handkerchief. "What will you silly women think of next?"

"The movement has merit. Women face many injustices because of their sex."

With a flick of his hand, Daniel signaled the hovering servant to pour him a scotch. "New York has already been liberal where women are concerned. The Married Woman's Property Act passed in 1848 granted married women full control over their own real estate and personal property." He sat back with a smug look, silently daring her to debate.

But Juliana had done her homework. "The act benefits the women of the middle and upper classes, but it gives no protection to working women. Husbands can collect their wives' and children's wages and spend them in any way they please."

"Harrumph!" Daniel scowled into his scotch.

Juliana glanced at Drew, half expecting him to be angry. Instead, he winked.

Daniel's brows beetled. "Women should be content with their lot and leave politics to those more capable. Enough on the subject." He downed the liquor and slammed the glass on the table. Rudely dismissing Juliana, he addressed Drew. "How long will you be staying in Saratoga?"

"I'm afraid it's necessary to cut our visit short. We'll be leaving tomorrow."

Daniel Tennant slumped in his seat and ran a skeletal hand across pale lips before resting his gaze on Juliana. "Yes," he said with a nod. "Leaving early might be a good idea."

Juliana felt betrayed. This was the first Drew had said about leaving Saratoga early. Had he just reached that decision this moment? Or was he afraid the animosity between her and Daniel Tennant might reflect unfavorably on him? He was every bit as narrow-minded as the wizened old man across from her. But what hurt most was her suspicion that Drew viewed her as an embarrassment.

CHAPTER
16

NOTHING HAD CHANGED. NOW THAT THEY HAD RETURNED to New York City, she and Drew had once again reverted to being polite strangers. Juliana paced the length of Drew's study. Stopping before a tall bookcase, she randomly selected a book and leafed through the pages. She missed the intimacy of waking up next to him, the casual touches that left her skin tingling, the kisses that made her heart sink to her toes. She missed watching his blue-gray eyes sparkle with amusement. She missed his smile. She snapped the volume shut. This tension between them had to end.

Juliana heard the front door open and close, followed by the low hum of male voices.

"Mrs. MacAllister is waiting in the study, sir." Even with the door partially closed, she could hear the tacit disapproval in Gilbert's tone. "I tried to explain it would be late when you arrived and that most likely you would bring work with you. But she wouldn't listen."

Juliana sighed. The elderly servant was reluctant to accept her presence in Drew's life. He made no secret of the fact that he considered her an outsider, a nuisance. With a sad shake of her head, she replaced the book on the shelf, then turned as Drew entered.

Wearing navy blue trousers and jacket and pristine white shirt, he looked formidable and aloof. His somber expression heightened the effect. "Gilbert said you wanted to see me. Is there a problem?"

Juliana was tempted to invent a phony excuse, then upbraided herself for cowardice. If the tension between them was to cease, one of them had to make the first move. That someone, it seemed, was to be her. She straightened her shoulders. "You've been behaving differently toward me ever since we returned from Saratoga Springs. Have I done something to anger you?"

"That's highly unlikely, since we've seen very little of each other." He tossed a bulging leather folder on the desk.

"And that's precisely why I've been worried."

"I should think you'd be happy that we didn't have to spend much time together. I thought you understood that after our marriage we'd go our separate ways."

Juliana pretended an interest in a brass paperweight, picking it up, then setting it down. "I hoped Saratoga Springs had changed things. That we could declare a truce, perhaps even be friends."

"You're such an innocent. Haven't you guessed it isn't friendship I want from you? That should be obvious every time we touch."

Transfixed, Juliana watched as he came closer. When he was near, friendship wasn't foremost in her mind either. Unfamiliar stirrings began in secret places, forbidden sensations that she tried to banish.

"Don't deny it," he said softly. "You feel it, too, this attraction drawing us together. Unless we exercise restraint, it's going to get out of control." He ran his finger down her cheek. "Or is that what you want?"

He looked at her strangely, a look that made her feel hot all over. Juliana jerked away from his touch. "Of course not."

"Be careful, lass," he warned softly. "Don't start something you're afraid to finish."

"I don't know what you're talking about." But she did. She heard her words ring with falseness. It would take very little coaxing on Drew's part to make her forget her lofty ideals. She wanted him to make love to her, wanted to be his wife in more than name only. Dear Lord, she thought, pressing her fingertips to her temples, she must be depraved to have such feelings toward a man who had raped her. Suddenly the walls seemed to be closing in around her, making her feel trapped. Walking to the window, she stared into the night.

Drew had read the conflict on Juliana's face before she turned from him. He, too, felt enmeshed in a web, unable to extricate himself without exposing Nick. Juliana was a beautiful, desirable woman. And he wanted her. She was a constant distraction, haunting his dreams, taunting his waking moments.

What was wrong with him? He was experienced in the ways of women. Why not simply seduce her and cease this torment? Wearily he raked a hand through his hair. He already knew the answer. He wanted more from her than physical appeasement. Along with wanting, another need had been born. He needed her unconditional trust, wanted her to give herself freely and without reservation. He couldn't make love to her knowing she thought him guilty of a brutal carnal act.

He crossed the room. "Juliana?" he said, reaching out to her.

She shrunk away. His touch undermined logic. Pride kept her chin high, her back straight. "I just wanted us to be friends. I don't understand you, Drew; perhaps I never will. One moment you're kind and gentle, but I can never completely erase the memory of the night you attacked me."

"Then don't tempt the devil with sweet kisses or you may have hell to pay. I'm no saint."

Indeed, towering over her, his eyes a glacial blue, his mouth a cruel line, he looked like evil incarnate. Swallowing, Juliana edged away. "You must have papers to go over. I won't disturb you any longer." Inexplicably on the brink of tears, she quickly exited the room.

"Keep your door bolted, lass."

The admonition mocked her as she fled up the stairs.

The next morning Juliana found a note from Drew propped against the flowered teapot. She picked it up gingerly, tapping the edge against the wicker breakfast tray. She had lain awake for hours the previous night. For the first time, she had willed herself to recall the details of Drew's attack on her. She remembered rough hands squeezing her breasts and sloppy kisses landing haphazardly. She recalled her feelings of rage, frustration, and helplessness. But a piece was missing. There was something else, something hovering on the fringes of memory. She frowned, trying to remember.

"Go ahead," Mary Bridget urged. "Aren't you going to open it?"

The elusive fragment vanished like a puff of smoke. With a shake of her head, Juliana brought herself back to the present. Tearing open the envelope, she quickly read the message.

Mary Bridget felt Juliana's forehead with the back of her hand. "You look a mite peaked. Is it bad news?"

Juliana forced a smile as she poured a cup of tea. "No, not at all. It seems that Mr. MacAllister has decided I need a watchdog. He's given Jack orders to take me to the dog pound to select a pet."

"A puppy!" Mary Bridget squealed with delight.

Juliana wished she could share the girl's enthusiasm. But Mary Bridget had no idea of the motive behind the gift. Drew requested she bring home a guard dog, a ferocious animal to sleep in her room and protect her from unwanted late night callers. Though the note was brief, Juliana read between the lines. Without meaning to, she had hurt him. "I'm not sure if I should," she demurred. "A pet will only upset Gilbert's routine."

Mary Bridget contemplated Juliana's wardrobe, trying to select a dress suitable for the morning's task. "That old codger could stand to be shaken up a bit. He's too set in his ways."

Juliana hid her smile behind a raised teacup. "That he is, Mary Bridget."

Promptly at ten o'clock, Jack Burrows pulled up to the front door of the brownstone. Juliana, accompanied by Mary Bridget, descended the stoop, climbed into the carriage, and set off for the dog pound. The single-story wood structure located near Battery Park was situated between two larger buildings that flanked it like bookends.

Jack looked about, then shifted his pipe stem to the corner of his mouth. "This ain't the best part of town, miss. If you need me, holler."

Juliana smiled her appreciation. "Thank you, Jack, but I'm sure we'll be fine."

When they were out of earshot, Mary Bridget whispered, "My mum's hatpin would pack a bigger punch than that old geezer."

"Don't let Jack hear you say that. He'll tell you about the time in Liverpool when he took on the entire Royal Navy single-handed."

Mary Bridget rolled her eyes. "He already has—twice."

They were still laughing when they pushed open the door of the pound. The odor that greeted them was overwhelming, the result of too many animals in a poorly ventilated space. Mary Bridget pulled out a dainty handkerchief and held it over her nose. A ruddy-cheeked man with a shock of white hair and bushy sideburns came up to greet them.

"We're here to adopt a dog." Juliana shouted to make herself heard above the loud yipping.

"You're in the right place." He held out his hand. "Name's Hector Jones. I run this place."

Juliana accepted his outstretched hand. "Pleased to meet you, Mr. Jones. I'm told this place has been a favorite project of a dear friend of mine, Emma Lattimer."

"Friend of Miss Lattimer's, eh?" Hector Jones hitched a thumb in his suspenders. "She and her club ladies raised enough money to keep this place going. You might call this her pet project." Chortling at his own pun, he motioned for them to follow him.

Dogs of every description were chained in stalls that lined the length of the room. Juliana studied, then rejected each one they passed.

Mary Bridget caught Juliana's sleeve. "What about this one?" She indicated a large, strongly built dog with a thick coat and bright, intelligent gaze.

Juliana shook her head and slowly continued down the row. She stopped before a cage containing a small puppy with shaggy brown fur. The animal cowered at the back of its stall. At Juliana's coaxing, it timidly ventured closer. "I like this one."

"But, Juliana"—Mary Bridget sounded horrified—"Mr. MacAllister said you were to buy a watchdog."

Juliana knelt on the dusty floor and petted the small animal. The little dog responded by licking her fingers with its moist, rough tongue. "See, she likes me," Juliana exclaimed.

"That one's the runt of the litter." Hector Jones shuffled his feet. "Maybe you should listen to your friend, miss. You wouldn't want to get your husband riled."

Mary Bridget gestured impatiently. "What kind of protection would she be? Looks like she's afraid of her own shadow."

The pup cocked her head, one ear perked up, the other flopped down. Juliana took another look and felt her heart soften. "She's all the protection I need."

Hector Jones and Mary Bridget looked at each other and shook their heads.

Drew inspected the puppy curled in his wife's lap. "That dog couldn't protect itself against a flea."

"She's all the protection I need." Juliana repeated the claim she had made earlier.

Their eyes met. Juliana's clear gaze was eloquent. Drew felt as though he were drowning in a whirlpool of molten gold. Hope surged through him. Juliana's fear of him was ebbing. Someday, perhaps soon, she would give him her unconditional trust. There would be no need for locked doors. In the meantime he could be patient.

When Drew looked at her that way, Juliana's mind emptied and emotion ruled. The past ceased to exist; the future was of little consequence; all that mattered was the present. The world faded away, leaving only the two of them. She loved this man and wanted to show him how much, but an invisible bond restrained her.

Confused by her feelings, she scooped up the puppy and rose to her feet. "It's late," she murmured. "Good night, Drew."

He followed her into the hall and watched her ascend the stairs. Feeling the force of his gaze, Juliana paused and glanced over her shoulder. She found him standing at the foot of the steps, one hand on the newel post, staring up at her. His expression was dark, brooding, and a little frightening.

Juliana opened her mouth to speak, then closed it. What could she say? That she loved him but didn't trust him? Or that perhaps, deep down, she did trust him but couldn't understand him? That she wanted to close the gulf between them but didn't know how? More confused than ever, she sought the sanctuary of her bedroom and, more from habit than intent, locked the door. The metallic click sounded loud in the still house.

Two hours later Juliana slammed the cover shut on her newest novel and added it to the stack beside her bed. Another link in a chain of sleepless nights was being forged. Even the puppy was sound asleep on her braided rug at the foot of the bed. Deciding to try Mary Bridget's remedy for insomnia, she climbed out of bed, slipped on a robe, and went downstairs to fix herself a glass of hot milk.

The tiles were cool beneath her bare feet as she crossed the kitchen. A full moon supplied enough illumination to make turning on the electrical lamp unnecessary. The kitchen was strictly Gilbert's domain, one she rarely ventured into. She half expected the servant to appear at any moment and order her to leave. Rising on tiptoe, she searched through the cupboards for a glass.

"Looking for something?" Drew asked from the doorway.

The tumbler slipped from Juliana's fingers and smashed on the floor. She spun toward the voice, reflexively taking a half-step forward. A fragment of broken glass pierced her foot. "Oh," she gasped in a mixture of pain and surprise.

"Stay where you are," Drew commanded. "Don't move." He crossed the width of the kitchen in long strides, oblivious of the crunch of glass beneath the leather soles of his shoes.

Juliana stood rooted to the floor. She couldn't have budged if she had tried. Drew wore a ruby brocade dressing gown tied with a sash at the waist. A warm flush spread up her neck. There wasn't a shred of doubt in her mind that that was all he wore.

"Are you hurt? Did you cut yourself?"

Balancing on one leg, Juliana drew her other leg up to inspect her foot. A tiny splinter of glass protruded from her heel. "It's only a small cut. But if you have a tweezers and some iodine—"

Not waiting to hear more, Drew picked her up, carried her across the room, and deposited her on a chair. Kneeling on the floor, he took her foot in his hand. His brows knit as he inspected her injury. "I'll be right back."

He disappeared to return moments later, carrying the necessary supplies. After flicking on a light, he came over and, dropping to one knee, raised her foot. "This will hurt," he warned.

Juliana was touched by the concern in his voice. "Do whatever you have to."

In a single deft move, Drew removed the shard of glass

from her foot, then pressed a cloth to the site to stem the bleeding. "I'm sorry I startled you." His thumb caressed the arch of her foot.

Pleasure rippled along her nerve endings to form a warm pool of desire. Dazed by the heady sensation, Juliana stared down at him. The neckline of his dressing gown gaped in a deep V, revealing a thick mat of black curls. How would it feel? she wondered. Downy soft or crisp and springy?

Drew released her foot abruptly. "After I apply some iodine," he said, his tone businesslike, "I'll bandage it." Unscrewing the cap from a bottle, he poured the pungent antiseptic over the small puncture.

"Ahh . . . " she gasped as the iodine bit like a viper. When the stinging subsided, Drew wrapped a strip of white cotton around her foot. "Thank you," she managed, gingerly rising to her feet.

"Oh, no, you don't." He scooped Juliana up as though she were weightless, and strode out of the kitchen. "It could start bleeding again."

"I'm not a baby," she protested halfheartedly, looping her arms around his neck.

"No." He shook his head emphatically. "You're definitely not a baby."

Resting her head against his shoulder, Juliana stifled a sigh of contentment and enjoyed being pampered. Outside her bedroom door, Drew carefully set her on her feet. He made no move to leave. Juliana held her breath and waited, hoping he would kiss her again, the way he had in Saratoga Springs.

Instead, he reached out to fondle a thick strand of her hair. "I love the color of your hair," he confessed. "Its the exact shade of butterscotch."

Juliana nervously ran her tongue over her lips, the

action all the more provocative for its innocence. "Do you like butterscotch?" The question sounded inane, her voice thready.

A small smile played over his lips. "Yes, lass. It's my favorite." He pressed a chaste kiss to her forehead and then, releasing the curl to spiral down her breast, stepped away. "Be sure to lock your door tonight—before either of us does something rash."

He left her standing in the hallway still trying to compose a reply.

Wider awake than ever, Juliana, ignoring the pain in her foot, hobbled the length of her room. Her jade silk peignoir billowed with each movement. Something was drastically wrong. Things just didn't make sense. With a little persuasion from Drew, she would have invited him to her bed tonight. Yet he had exercised admirable restraint. She had been a prime target for seduction. And he had behaved like a gentleman. Could a person possess two distinct personalities, one brutal, the other kind and considerate?

Juliana stopped her restless prowling and stared at the bed—the same bed she had occupied on the night of the attack. Closing her eyes, she forced herself to recall the details. A sloppy kiss had awakened her out of a sound sleep. Chuckling, her tormentor had roughly stroked her breasts. Juliana had fought him. She dimly remembered ramming an elbow into his side and raking her nails down his smooth, hairless chest. Her eyes flew wide open.

Her attacker had possessed a smooth, hairless chest.

Her husband's chest was covered with a thick mat of dark curls. It hadn't been Drew after all. She blinked as another thought struck her. Then who had it been? And why was Drew protecting the man? Her injured foot forgotten, she sped from her room, determined to learn the truth.

The door crashed against the wall as she burst into Drew's bedroom. Instantly awake, he flung back the covers and swung his legs out of bed. "Juliana, what is it?"

"You lied to me. All this time, you let me think it was you who raped me. Why, Drew?" she cried in anguish. "Why did you let me believe that lie all these months?"

Shrugging into his robe, Drew approached cautiously. Here he was, an experienced attorney, skilled at using the English language to sway even the most unreceptive listener. But at this crucial moment, his tongue felt tied, his arsenal of words depleted.

God, but she was glorious in her agitation, like a beautiful tawny lioness, wild and untamed. He cupped her face in his hands, his eyes beseeching her for understanding and ultimately forgiveness. "Hush, lass," he pleaded. "Later will be time enough for explanations. But for now"—his mouth hovered above hers—"let me love you the way I've wanted to for so long."

A half sob ripped through her, the sound smothered by his lips as they slanted over hers. Juliana wrapped her arms around his neck. For long, tantalizing moments, they clung to each other. She felt no fear, no doubts, no reservations, only the need to be one with the man who shared her heart.

"I don't think I'll ever get enough of you. I've craved your sweetness all my life." His hands tangled in her hair, holding her willing captive while he plundered her mouth.

Through her thin silk peignoir Juliana could feel his heart pumping as frantically as hers. She reveled in the knowledge that Drew wanted her as she wanted him. Desperately. Greedily. Completely. Magic and madness. It was impossible to tell where one ended, the other began. She moved slightly, adjusting the contours of her body to fit his.

"Ah, Juliana," he murmured. He covered her eyelids, her

cheeks, her throat, with quick, fervent kisses.

Dizzy under the barrage of sensations, Juliana held on to Drew to keep from falling. The palm of his hand curved around her breast, and his thumb circled the nipple until it was hard and erect. She closed her eyes as the world spun faster. He made her feel beautiful, desirable. As though this were the moment she had been created for.

He fumbled with the tiny satin-covered buttons at her throat. Finally, when they were free, Juliana shrugged and the silken garment shimmered downward to pool around her ankles. The nightgown followed. "So lovely, so very lovely," he murmured, sweeping her off her feet and laying her on the bed.

"Kiss me again," Juliana sighed. Extending her arms, she welcomed him. Her mouth parted eagerly to receive his kiss. But kisses didn't satisfy the needs coursing through her. She wanted to touch him as he was touching her, to feel his skin next to hers.

Her hands groped for and found the sash of his robe. With an impatient tug, she pulled it free. Her touch conveyed a sense of urgency as she worked the robe down his shoulders. Taut muscle and smooth skin, broad shoulders and narrow waist. Her fingers sifted through the dark curls covering his chest. Crisp and springy, she marveled, her earlier question answered. She gloried in the feel of his flesh. Strange, never would she have believed a man's body could arouse such fierce stirrings within her.

Juliana felt Drew's muscles tense under her questing fingers. Lowering his head, he let his lips trace hungry forays over her body before suckling her breast. Arching against him, she cried out at the exquisite thrill that quivered through her. Sensations, until now foreign and forbidden, curled around the edges of her consciousness.

Then thought evaporated under the onslaught of desire. Juliana's nails dug into the slick skin of his back, and she held tight. She felt as if she were on a bobsled, careening down a mountainside, out of control. "Love me, Drew, love me," she whispered, heedless of her frenzied entreaty.

"Ah, my sweet Juliana. Come with me." Spreading her legs, he thrust his manhood inside her.

Hot pain seared her loins. Sharply she drew in a breath, squeezing her eyes shut and twisting her hands in the bed-clothes. The pain gradually eased, and her eyes fluttered open to find Drew staring at her in mute surprise.

"I didn't want to hurt you," he said in a low voice. "I never imagined . . . "

Boldly she fastened her arms around his waist and held tight. "Don't leave me," she begged. "Take me with you." She pressed her hips upward in invitation.

Drew shuddered. Then, burying his face in her hair, resumed the ancient tempo. They moved in unison to a timeless rhythm, racing toward a soul-shattering crescendo.

Nothing in her life had prepared Juliana for the devastating bliss she experienced while locked in Drew's embrace. She felt so close to heaven she could touch the stars.

CHAPTER
17

DREW HAD NEVER CONSIDERED HIMSELF A LUCKY MAN—until now. Juliana could be sweet, or she could be sultry; she could be enchanting, or enticing. She was all these and more. A constant source of fascination and delight.

The amazing discovery that she had still been a virgin was an additional bonus. He was tremendously relieved to know Nick hadn't been guilty of rape. And knowing he had been Juliana's first lover gave Drew inordinate pleasure. She had been his exclusively.

Tenderly he smoothed a long strand of honey-colored hair from her face. "Did I hurt you?" he asked. "The pain, so I'm told, only occurs the first time. After tonight you'll feel nothing but pleasure when we make love."

"The first time?" Juliana braced herself on an elbow and stared at him. The good sisters having neglected that part of her education, she was ignorant in the ways of a woman's body. She frowned, trying to comprehend what Drew was telling her. "Are you saying I was still a virgin?"

"Yes, lass, I was the first."

"But how can that be?" Juliana shook her head in disbelief. "I remember that night so well."

"What was the last event you recall?"

Juliana's face took on a thoughtful expression. "I remember struggling with a man I assumed was you. Then he flipped me over on my back, and my head struck the bed."

"And nothing else?"

"Not until Gilbert informed me you were waiting to talk to me. I remember I had a horrible headache as well as a gash on my head."

"That gash probably accounts for the bloodstain Gilbert found on the sheet. Poor man, you gave him quite a jolt. He was beside himself at the discovery."

"How did I manage that?" Juliana had difficulty imagining the unflappable Gilbert with ruffled feathers.

"After finding an empty liquor flask and money on the dresser, Gilbert assumed you were a trollop." Drew pulled her down for a kiss. "But he reversed his opinion rather abruptly when he found blood on the sheet. When he related his findings, we both came to the conclusion that you had been raped."

"All this time"—Juliana shook her head, overwhelmed by the far-reaching consequences of that eventful night—"I was so certain I had been attacked. It never once occurred to me that I might still be untouched."

Drew placed a hand beneath her chin and tipped her head so she was forced to meet his gaze. "Do you regret what just happened between us?"

Regret? she mused with a trace of sadness. How ironic Drew should feel the need to ask. Even after their bodies had shared intimate secrets, their minds remained strangers.

"No." Her gaze didn't waver. "I felt many emotions this evening, most of which were alien to me, but regret wasn't among them."

"Thank you."

He smiled, and the sight of it warmed her heart. "What about you, Drew?" She traced the curve of his lips with a fingertip. "Are you suffering pangs of remorse?"

He nipped the pad of her finger with his teeth. "How could I be when I find myself married to such a delightful blend of lady and minx?"

His glib retort didn't appease her. "If you hadn't believed I lost my virginity in your guest room, would you have offered matrimony?"

"That wouldn't have altered my decision. The scandal fostered by the newspapers would have been cause enough to offer you my name. Besides, I needed a wife, and"— he rolled over, taking her with him—"you'll do as well as any."

Juliana's outraged cry changed into a purr. Further thoughts fled as Drew's lips nuzzled the sensitive hollow at the base of her throat.

"In fact," he teased, "your qualifications are perfect for the job."

Juliana laughed, the sound full and rich. She staved off further distraction with a protesting hand against his chest. "You're avoiding the issue still. If you weren't responsible for the assault, who was?"

With a heavy sigh, Drew pulled away. Hands behind his head, he lay on his back, staring up at the ceiling.

She watched as his playful inclinations disappeared and his mood turned more serious.

"Too bad there's not a demand for women attorneys. Your persistence would win points before a seasoned judge."

Though his tone was heavy with reproach, Juliana needed to hear the truth. "Who are you protecting?"

A lengthy pause followed, then another sigh. "Nick."

"Your brother?" Juliana was stunned.

"Nick's a good lad, Juliana. He never meant you harm." Drew turned his head to gauge her reaction. "On the night in question, he and his friends were in the city celebrating, and Nick had too much to drink. The boys planned to visit a brothel after dinner. In his drunken state, Nick thought that's where his friends had taken him. I had just recently purchased this house, so Nick had never been here. When he found you asleep in an upstairs bedroom, he mistook you for a prostitute."

Juliana lay perfectly still, but her mind was busy. Drew's explanation sounded logical and convincing. But it was the concern in his voice when he spoke of his young brother that touched her deeply. It showed him for the sensitive, caring man she had suspected existed beneath the hard exterior. "You must love Nick very much to risk everything to spare him," she said quietly.

"I do, perhaps too much for his own good. Daniel calls me a mother hen. But I'm the only family Nick has. I've been responsible for him ever since he was an infant. I'd go to any lengths to avoid jeopardizing his future."

"Even at the cost of your own?"

He shrugged. "If that's the price I have to pay."

"Every time I think I understand you, you surprise me. You're a complicated man, Andrew MacAllister, but a good one."

Shifting position, he rolled to one side. "Funny, I think of myself as a simple man with simple needs." He burrowed a hand through her luxuriant dark gold curls. "And right now, my need is for you," he said, lowering his mouth to hers.

The urgency was gone, but none of the passion. If anything, anticipation heightened their senses. They made love again, this time at a leisurely pace, giving each other time to explore, to taste, to savor. Fingertips wandered over planes, mapped gentle curves, and memorized textures. Mouths and tongues sampled and cataloged unique flavors.

Ripples of sensation spread in an ever widening circle, gaining energy as they were swept across a sea of longing. Juliana felt as though she were caught on the crest of a tidal wave. She clung to Drew. Locked together, they hurtled toward a distant shore. Shuddering and calling out incoherent truths, they crashed on a mystical beach, the force devastating. When the floodwaters of desire receded, they lay sated and content in each other's embrace.

"I love you," Juliana whispered.

Drew pulled her closer, but didn't echo the sentiment. He had heard that pledge before. It had proved no more than hollow syllables uttered to fill a vacant silence. He had learned that to some women, after lovemaking, these words came as naturally as breathing. He had also learned a more painful lesson: giving one's heart left one vulnerable. Drew had decided years ago never again to be left defenseless. He wasn't ready to explore his feelings for Juliana, wasn't prepared to relax his guard.

Glancing downward, he found Juliana asleep. Her sable lashes curved beguilingly on cheeks the color of sun-ripened apricots, concealing tawny gold orbs that mesmerized him. Her slender curves molded themselves to his muscular frame perfectly. He had been amazed, then overjoyed at her passion. She said she loved him.

Juliana gave herself freely and asked nothing in return. Was she different from Victoria?

Drew wasn't expected home until late. Juliana decided that this would be the perfect opportunity to invite the O'Tooles for dinner in a small attempt to repay their kindness. She had debated whether or not to include Drew in her plans, but in the end had decided against it. If he didn't approve, he could very well forbid her to extend the invitation. Drew was wealthy, educated, and powerful, while the O'Tooles were poor Irish immigrants who lived in a tenement. The two were worlds apart. Best, Juliana reassured herself, not to force an unlikely friendship.

Mary Bridget had reported that her family was delighted at the prospect. The entire clan, Dennis among them, would arrive promptly at seven. At precisely six forty-five, Juliana went downstairs to supervise the final preparations. She found Gilbert in the dining room, lips pursed, counting the silverware.

"Gilbert!" she admonished, caught between exasperation and amusement. "Do you really expect our guests to abscond with their pockets full of knives and soup spoons?"

"With an unruly bunch of hooligans, madam, one never knows. And papists at that!" He shook his head in disgust.

"The O'Tooles are honest, hardworking people." All traces of humor vanished from Juliana's expression. "And you're forgetting, Gilbert, that until my marriage to Mr. MacAllister, I, too, was a 'papist'. By insulting my friends, you also insult me."

Gilbert's pale countenance grew even paler. "My profound apologies. I never meant—"

"In the future, weigh your words more carefully."

"Yes, madam." Relief spread across the servant's face as the doorbell pealed. "That must be your guests. I'll show them in."

A babble of voices preceded the O'Tooles into the parlor where Juliana stood ready to greet them. The entire group seemed to be talking at once. Juliana was immersed in an exuberant display of affection, making her feel like one of the family. Mrs. O'Toole and Maura hugged her breathless.

Maura whispered in Juliana's ear. "I think Jamie Flynn is going to pop the question."

Juliana hugged her friend even tighter. "Jamie won himself a prize. I hope he knows how lucky he is."

"Oh, Juliana, I'm the one who's lucky." Happiness radiated from Maura's face.

"Ahem." Mr. O'Toole cleared his throat. "I brung you a wee bit of Ireland to liven up your home." He handed Juliana a bottle of Irish whiskey. "Sorry I judged you so harshly, girl. What with them stories in the newspaper and all, I didn't know what to think."

Juliana accepted his gift. "Your hospitality made me feel welcome when I needed it most. I'll always be grateful."

The plaintive whimper of a newborn diverted Juliana's attention. Katie and Dennis, less sure of their welcome than the others, stood just inside the room looking awkward and ill at ease. Dennis held a wicker basket mounded with a pink baby blanket. A curly-haired toddler sucking his thumb held fast to his mother's skirt.

Juliana was shocked by the change in Katie's appearance. The last time she had seen her, Katie's body was swollen by pregnancy. Now, only a month after the birth of her child, she was almost gaunt. Despair dulled her blue eyes. Mary Bridget had confided that Katie still grieved over her husband's desertion and that the family was deeply concerned about her health. Sympathy for the young woman tore at Juliana's heart. She crossed the parlor with a welcoming smile. "Katie, I'm so happy you're here."

"I wasn't sure I should be, what with the children and all," Katie said hesitantly.

"Nonsense," Juliana contradicted. "I was eager to see

them. Mary Bridget talks about them constantly."

"Mary Bridget talks constantly," Dennis observed dryly.

"Dennis! Stop sounding like a big brother," Mary Bridget scolded, taking the infant from him. "You promised to be nice."

"Dinner is served," Gilbert droned from the doorway. His spine ramrod stiff, he led the way into the dining room.

Dennis held out Juliana's chair at the head of the table. Under the cover of scraping chairs, he said, "Mum insisted I come tonight. Are you sorry to see me?"

"Not at all. I'm glad you came."

Dennis studied her for a moment, then nodded. "I behaved like a bloody fool. Haven't met too many real ladies in my life. Guess you're my first." His face broke into an engaging grin. "Shall we let bygones be bygones?"

Juliana returned his smile. "Consider the matter closed."

"My, isn't this grand!" Mrs. O'Toole exclaimed, taking in the lace tablecloth and linen napkins, the crystal stemware and fine china, the ornate silver cutlery. "Puts my table to shame, it does."

"Never," Juliana refuted quickly. "Your table is surrounded by love and laughter and sharing. Those are much more important than fancy dishes and expensive glassware."

"Well spoken," Mr. O'Toole agreed, patting his wife's hand. "Shall we say grace?" They all bowed their heads while he asked the Lord's blessing on the meal.

Out of the corner of her eye, Juliana saw Mrs. O'Toole swat young Mickey's hand as he was about to swipe a roll from the bread tray. No sooner was the prayer concluded than Gilbert carried in a roast of beef on a platter. Murmurs of approval went up as he carved generous slices of the succulent meat.

Throughout the meal, the ever watchful Gilbert hovered close by. Katie's little boy, Liam, who sat on a chair bolstered with Drew's law books, was his prime cause of concern. Near the end of dinner, the child set his glass of milk near the table edge and reached for a spoon. His elbow sent the milk spewing in one direction, the glass toppling in another. Gilbert dived for the glass, catching it inches from the floor.

"Bravo!" Mr. O'Toole applauded. "Good catch, man, good catch. The Dublin Dragons could use a first-rate chap like you in the outfield. Ever play baseball?"

"I played a bit of rugby in my younger days." Gilbert straightened and replaced the glass out of Liam's reach, his thin chest puffing out with pride. "Quite good at it, too, if I do say so. Wiry and fast."

Juliana looked at him in surprise. It was difficult to imagine the prim and proper Gilbert engaged in a rowdy sport.

He returned her speculative look with one of equanimity. "Shall I serve coffee in the parlor, madam?"

"Yes, please," she returned, finding her voice.

Once the group gathered in the parlor, Mr. O'Toole broke open the whiskey, poured a small measure for each of the women and a more generous one for himself and Dennis. Mrs. O'Toole spied the spinet that had belonged to Drew's uncle.

"Do you play?" Juliana asked, intercepting her longing glances.

"I used to."

"Back in Dublin, Mary was the best organist Saint Cecilia's ever had," her husband bragged. "Played like an angel, my Mary."

"Patrick!" Mrs. O'Toole protested, though a blush of pleasure rouged her cheeks.

"Please play for us," Juliana urged. The others were quick to add their encouragement.

Trying not to appear overeager, Mary O'Toole spread her skirts on the piano bench and ran her hands experimentally over the keyboard.

Maura grinned. "See, Mum, you haven't lost your touch."

With her family grouped around her, she launched into a medley of Irish tunes. Gifted with fine voices, her children joined in. Dennis, in particular, possessed a lilting tenor voice that lent special feeling to the ballads. Katie kept somewhat apart from the others, holding the infant. Juliana went over and sat beside her.

Katie kissed the crown of the baby's head. "I named her Megan . . . after Sean's mother."

"A pretty name for a pretty girl." Juliana gently touched the baby's hand and was rewarded when the tiny fingers curled around hers. Babies were so fragile, she marveled, so very precious. What would it be like to be a mother? She smiled wistfully at the small bundle swathed in pink. "May I hold her?"

Katie frowned worriedly at Juliana's silk dress. "She might spit up."

"Please."

With utmost care, Katie transferred the sleeping infant to Juliana's arms and then, assured that Juliana was comfortable with the wee Megan, wandered over to the piano.

Juliana gazed at the tiny baby. Warm. Sweet. Cuddly. Totally dependent. To some a burden, to others a blessing. How would Drew react to fatherhood? She ran her fingertip over the fine black curls, nearly the shade of Drew's hair. What would a child of theirs look like? As though compelled by an unseen force, Juliana's gaze was drawn toward the door.

Drew stood, tall and silent, unnoticed except by her, his thoughts veiled. Was he angry? she wondered nervously. Would he be rude to her guests? Make them feel unwelcome? Juliana rose from the sofa, the baby snuggled against her shoulder, and went to him.

Wordlessly, Drew lifted a hand and brushed the baby's petal-soft cheek. The action, unexpected and tender, caused a lump to lodge in Juliana's throat.

Over the baby's downy head, Juliana and Drew locked gazes. The music dimmed; the room faded. The guests vanished. Their look spoke volumes. In the space of a heartbeat, complex emotions were made simple. Then, just as quickly, the simple became complicated. Hurt and unable to understand the reversal, Juliana saw the warmth in his silver-blue eyes harden into ice.

Belatedly Juliana became aware that the parlor was cloaked in uncomfortable silence. The singing ceased while the O'Tooles observed their hosts with unease.

Drew stepped toward Patrick O'Toole, hand extended. "Sorry I wasn't able to join you for dinner, but I had a prior engagement."

Juliana watched with awe as Drew played the genial host for the remainder of the evening. He shed his jacket, loosened his tie, and rolled up his sleeves. Exuding charm that enchanted the women and disarmed the men, he won them over. The O'Tooles departed amid promises to get together again in the near future.

The instant the door closed, however, tension resumed. Angrily, Drew turned to Juliana. "Why didn't you inform me you had invited guests for dinner?"

"I thought you might object."

"What kind of an ogre do you think I am? Did you expect me to toss your friends out like yesterday's newspaper?"

Juliana squirmed. "I didn't know how you'd react."

Drew picked his jacket off the back of a chair. "If you don't want me present when you entertain, kindly inform me ahead of time so I don't barge in and spoil the fun." Slinging his jacket over his shoulder, he started for the stairs.

Beneath the anger, Juliana sensed his hurt at being excluded. Contrite, she followed him. "I'm glad you came home early. The O'Tooles thought you were wonderful."

He didn't look back. "Don't make too much of it. I want to run for the state assembly, and the Irish vote is important in my district."

She stumbled to a halt midway up the stairs. Had his geniality been a ploy, a guise calculated to win votes? Then, slowly, her brain began to sort through the last two hours. She had seen Drew woo the shy Liam with a peppermint stick, watched him listen intently to Mickey's detailed description of a baseball game. His behavior hadn't been an act; children didn't cast ballots.

"I'm sorry, Drew," she said, her voice choked.

The apology came too late. The upstairs hall was deserted.

Using a back entrance reserved for late night callers, Willie the Mole slipped into the study of a Fifth Avenue mansion. "Well, boss, here I am."

His employer tapped his cigar ash in a crystal ashtray. "So far our plan hasn't worked. But MacAllister's luck is about to run out."

Willie scratched his head. "Don't know about that. The public is clamoring for news of him and his bride. Treat 'em like royalty."

"The public is nothing but a herd of fickle fools. They can be led as easily as sheep." His boss picked up an envelope and tapped it against his desk. "This will change things.

MacAllister and his wife will be the laughingstock of New York. Cartoonists will have a circus. When the hoopla dies down, no one—and I mean no one—will take that clown for a serious political contender."

"Not even Daniel Tennant?"

"Especially not Tennant." The other man puffed on his cigar. "The old man's days are numbered. He won't want to waste them on a born loser."

"You seem awfully sure of yourself, boss."

His boss smashed his fist against his desk, making Willie jump. "Is a slimy little gutter rat like you doubting me?"

Willie shuffled his feet. "No offense, boss. You know I'd do anything for you. Weren't for you I'd be rotting in jail."

Mollified, the other man leaned forward in his leather chair, took another puff of his expensive cigar, and blew the smoke in Willie's face. "I want you to make a delivery for me. See to it personally that Mrs. Andrew MacAllister gets my little invitation." He gave a bark of laughter. "I took the liberty of signing your name."

"Sure thing, boss." Willie snatched the envelope. "I'll see she gets it."

His employer propped his feet on the corner of the desk and crossed his ankles. Sticking his cigar in the corner of his mouth, he regarded Willie through the smoky haze. The onyx signet ring on his pudgy hand glimmered in the lamplight. "And in the unlikely event that MacAllister's luck holds, I have a few more tricks up my sleeve." He smiled cunningly. "I haven't played my ace yet."

CHAPTER
18

"JULIANA, DO CHANGE YOUR MIND," MARY BRIDGET PLEAD-ed. "I feel as if someone is walking on my grave, as Mum would say."

Juliana sighed. "I wish you'd stop that kind of talk. I'm nervous enough as it is. If only I had more time to prepare my speech . . . "

"Did Mr. MacAllister approve of you speaking to a bunch of ladies on woman suffrage?" Mary Bridget questioned.

"Not exactly," Juliana hedged.

"You did ask him, didn't you?"

"I mentioned I might attend a lecture on the subject."

"And . . . "

"He forbade me to go."

"Forbade you? And you're going anyway?"

"I have to. I'm the speaker."

"Let them find someone else."

"They already did, and I'm that person. Their speaker from the National Woman Suffrage Association canceled at the last minute. I'm flattered Emma recommended me as a replacement."

"Why didn't they ask her?"

"Because Emma is out of town visiting her cousin Lydia." Juliana's patience was tried to the limits. "I don't have time to argue. How do I look?"

Mary Bridget scanned the sage-green foulard silk dress and hat with its saucy plume. "You look as if you should be going to a tea, not some meeting of the Cyprian Society. Never heard of such a group. What's more, it's in a part of town respectable ladies avoid."

Juliana picked up her purse and her notes and left the house with Mary Bridget's warning sounding in her ears. Ignoring Drew's admonition not to attend bothered her conscience. But she had given her word, and people were relying on her. She couldn't renege.

Jack Burrows clucked his tongue in disapproval when she gave him the address, and the carriage rattled off. "If you want my opinion, ma'am, go to Ladies' Mile instead. Why borrow trouble?"

"Thank you for the advice, Jack, but my mind is made up." Juliana sat back against the cushions, her hands resting on the handle of her parasol, and resolutely stared straight ahead.

The carriage moved forward. After a time it left the nicer homes and shops for a seedier section of town. As they neared the waterfront, Juliana smelled the tang of saltwater. Tall masts of ships crisscrossed the horizon. Stevedores and burly seamen populated the cobbled streets.

Jack stopped the carriage before a small dilapidated building with grimy windows. "Sure this is the place, ma'am?"

Juliana pulled out her instructions and frowned at the address. "This is it." She tried to inject confidence into her tone. "You needn't wait. Just be back in an hour."

He assisted her down. "I'll be close by. Holler if you need me."

Juliana could see by the feisty set of his jaw that Jack's mind was made up. Secretly she was glad to know he'd be near. Notes in one hand, purse in the other, she entered the meeting place. Benches were arranged in a semicircle around a table she assumed was for the speaker. Though she knew she was early, she thought it odd that no one was present to greet her. She had hoped the person responsible for inviting her to speak would have the courtesy to be there.

A man, wearing a checked jacket and a bored expression, sauntered in. "Howard Batchelor from the *Town Crier*," he said by way of an introduction. He parked his thin frame on a seat in the rear.

The name of the paper sounded an alarm bell inside Juliana's head. It was the same scandal sheet that had printed the malicious lies about her relationship with Drew, the stories that had precipitated his proposal, threatened his career, and almost ruined her reputation. Why had they sent a reporter? Why their sudden interest in woman suffrage?

Spreading her notes on the speaker's table, Juliana shuffled through them. She had never addressed a group of people before. On those occasions when Juliana had accompanied her, Emma had always made it appear deceptively simple. But Juliana was so nervous that her palms were damp.

As the designated hour approached, a strange assortment of people began to drift in and fill the benches. To Juliana's surprise, the men outnumbered the women two to one. Soon the small room reeked unpleasantly of cheap perfume and unwashed bodies.

She studied the women in the audience. They appeared to be a sorry lot, bringing to mind an old bouquet of once bright flowers that were beginning to brown at the edges and wilt. The men, too, were a motley corps, for the greater part shabby and dissolute. Ignoring her, the men and women talked among themselves. Juliana wished fervently she had never agreed to this undertaking. How tempting it would be to disappear out the door without a backward glance.

"Ladies and gentlemen of the Cyprian Society," she began. The private conversations did not cease. For people with a professed interest in woman suffrage, they seemed totally uninterested in what she had to say. "Ladies and gentlemen, if you'll kindly give me your attention," she said in a louder voice.

The noise died down, and faces turned toward her. Now that she had their attention, Juliana was almost sorry she did. There wasn't a friendly face in the entire audience. She snagged the glance of the reporter in the back row. *Now what are you going to do?* his look seemed to say.

Juliana raised her head defiantly, the motion making the plume on her hat dance. "First of all, I want to thank you for inviting me to speak to you on behalf of a concern we all share—equality for women.

"While we may be free, we're not equal." She paused, trying to find a sympathetic face among her listeners. She found one in the second row and directed her next remarks to her. "If that's to change, then it's up to us to take the initiative."

"Only thing women should be changin' is diapers," said a beefy-faced man in the front of the room. Loud guffaws greeted his remark.

"Women got it too easy. Leeches, all of them, living off men," another sneered.

Juliana tried not to let the insults unnerve her. "If we hope to win our freedom, we must join the crusade for woman suffrage."

"Why do I need to vote? What do I care who's President?" a red-haired woman in the second row asked.

"Until we win the privilege of casting our ballots, we have no control over laws that affect our welfare. Tell me honestly, madam, are you happy with your life?"

"Sure, all these gals are happy," the man next to her answered. "What could be easier than earnin' a livin' flat on your back?"

The men laughed while the women looked to one another for support. "Shut yer trap, Charlie," the woman snapped. "It puts bread in my belly and a roof over my head."

Juliana needed a moment to recover from the shock. She should have realized from their dress and manner that the women in her audience were prostitutes. The reporter, she noted, was busy jotting notes. Dear Lord, what had she gotten herself into? Was this all a calculated trick? Was someone attempting to discredit Drew by making her look like a fool? However, woman suffrage wasn't meant to affect only the wealthy, but the poorer classes as well.

"Women—all women—need to have a voice in matters that influence our well-being. The time has come for us to stop accepting our role as second-rate citizens and demand our rights."

"You tell 'em, girlie!"

"Is it wrong to want to better our lot?" Juliana rested her hands on the table and leaned forward. "Is it wrong to want jobs that will pay equal wages, to assume guardianship of our children, and to control our own money?"

"What gives women like you the right to tell a wife to leave her husband?" a man in the back row called out, his words slurred. He climbed to his feet unsteadily.

Not sure how to respond, Juliana decided to ignore his outburst. "We must band together if we want our opinions heard. In January, the Senate voted—"

"My Alice started goin' to meetings like this, and some dried-up old prune told her she'd be better off gettin' a divorce."

"I'm not here to advocate divorce, sir, merely a woman's right to vote. If you'll kindly be seated . . . " She glanced down at her notes, nervously trying to recapture her train of thought.

"Who the hell do you think you are?" The man whipped out a pistol.

"Sir, please—"

"Try ignorin' me now."

Several women screamed in terror while the male members of the audience exchanged looks as though asking one another if the gunman was a plant or serious threat. Juliana's mouth went dry.

"Alice had no call to leave me." The gunman gestured with his weapon. "Ain't no crime for a man to stop for a nickel slug now and again. When I got home all I heard was her whinin'. Man's got a right to smack a woman once in a while to keep her in line."

Juliana's gaze was riveted to the gun. "If you'll put away your gun, sir, we can talk."

"Talkin's what started my problem." He raised his arm toward Juliana and took aim. "I'm here to end it. Save some poor bastard the hell you put me through."

Juliana, paralyzed by fear, watched as he pulled the trigger. The bullet whizzed just above her head.

The audience dived for cover. Frightened shrieks and the crash of overturned benches shattered the spell that held Juliana immobile. She ducked for shelter as the second shot rang out. Cowering under the speaker's table, she pressed her hands to her ears and squeezed her eyes shut, hoping, praying she wouldn't be the target of a madman's bullet.

When no shots followed, she opened her eyes, screwed up her courage, and peeked out from her hiding spot. Her eyes widened in disbelief. In the midst of chaos, Drew was grappling with the deranged gunman, trying to wrest the gun from the man's upraised arm. It went off, blasting a hole in the ceiling and sending down a shower of plaster.

Drew brought his knee up, connecting with the man's groin. The movement elicited a grunt of pain, and the pistol clattered to the floor. The gunman lunged for it, but Drew caught him by the coat collar and spun him around. Both men went down amid flailing arms and the sound of flesh striking flesh. The pistol lay on the floor inches from where the men battled. To her horror, Juliana saw the madman grope for the gun.

Not pausing to consider the consequences, she darted out and snatched up the weapon. Her hands shook so that she had to use both of them to hold on to the heavy firearm.

Drew's balled fist connected with the man's jaw, knocking him unconscious. Drew got to his feet. His eyes inventoried Juliana, raw concern clearly readable in his expression. He opened his arms, and, dropping the gun, she flew into them. They held each other tightly, both needing the reassurance that the other was unharmed.

One by one people scrambled out from under benches and formed a loose circle around the embracing couple. The red-haired woman began to clap; then the rest joined in the applause, calling out comments.

"Some punch you landed."

"Thought fer sure my days were numbered."

"He coulda killed us all."

"Man's crazy. Oughta be sent to Bellevue."

"Good thing fer us you happened by."

Jack Burrows arrived with two policemen in tow. "Heard

the shooting, guv," Jack said to Drew. "Thought you might need help." A throng of curious passersby crowded the doorway behind them.

One of the policemen handcuffed the gunman who was just beginning to come to. The other took out a notepad and pen. "All right, folks, I need some questions answered." Everyone started talking at once.

Drew spoke in a low voice to the policeman and then, keeping his arm firmly around Juliana's shoulders, hustled her out a back door. "I explained who we were and told him I'd come down to headquarters later to give a statement."

The door opened into a deserted alley. No sooner had it closed behind them than Drew crushed her in his arms, holding her so tightly she could barely breathe. But Juliana didn't care. The only thing that mattered was being in his embrace, feeling the strong beat of his heart against hers.

His mouth swooped down to claim hers. There was nothing gentle or tender in his kiss, only a fierce desperate need to possess. Juliana returned the kiss in full measure, holding nothing back.

When at last it ended, Drew continued to hold her as though he were afraid she'd vanish. "Ah, lass, you gave me a fright. Are you sure you're not hurt?"

"I'm fine." She managed a weak smile. "But I didn't finish my speech."

He hugged her, sighing deeply. "Why can't you be like other women and shop all day?"

"Do you want me to change?"

"No," he replied with amused resignation. "I love you just the way you are."

Juliana could hardly believe what she was hearing. She pulled away slightly so she could see his face. "You love me?" the words trembled on her lips.

"Yes, lass. So much so that my heart stopped when I saw that man point a gun at you." His gaze traveled over the alley, seeing the overflowing trash barrels and heaps of litter. The fishy odor of the docks pervaded the air. "Let's go home. I want to show you how much you mean to me."

Arm in arm, they made their way to the carriage waiting at the front. The milling crowd was too intent on watching the police lead off a man in handcuffs to give much notice to the well-dressed couple.

The reporter, Howard Batchelor, separated himself from the group and walked over to them. "I was all set to do a piece on Mrs. MacAllister speaking to a bunch of doxies, but what happened instead will sell more papers. Made a hero out of you, MacAllister. The mayor will probably give you a commendation after he reads my story." Tipping his derby, he strolled down the street.

"How did you know where to find me?" Juliana asked as the carriage moved homeward.

"I needed some papers from my study. When I quizzed Mary Bridget about your whereabouts, she confided you were speaking to a group called the Cyprian Society. Immediately I knew you were in trouble."

"I'm afraid I don't see the connection."

"Years in the convent have left you charmingly naive." He gave her an indulgent smile. "Have you heard of Aphrodite?"

Juliana frowned. "If memory serves, she was the Greek goddess of love."

"You may also recall she was born on the island of Cyprus. In some circles the word 'cyprian' is synonymous with 'prostitute.' How did you get involved with such a group?"

"An invitation came in the mail from a Mr. William Smith."

"Did you meet the man?"

"Well, no . . . " She felt foolish.

"Probably a fictitious name," Drew said, taking her hand. "But I'm convinced this whole affair was no coincidence. Someone went to a great deal of trouble to arrange all this."

They lapsed into silence for the remainder of the ride home.

The puppy announced their arrival with excited yips. As soon as they set foot inside the entryway, Mary Bridget stopped pacing and rushed to them. "I'm sorry, Juliana— Mrs. MacAllister." She wrung her hands. "I've been scared silly ever since you left. Please don't be angry with me for telling Mr. MacAllister."

Juliana hugged the girl. "On the contrary, I'm happy you did. I owe you my everlasting gratitude." Taking Drew by the hand, she led him toward the stairs. "Please see to it that we're not disturbed. I'll tell you about our harrowing experience later, but right now"—she gave Drew a radiant smile—"we need to rest."

In the privacy of the bedroom, she turned to him. "Being shot at is a small price to pay for hearing you admit you love me." She brushed plaster dust off his jacket. "I seem to recall that you said something about showing me how you feel."

Drew removed her hat, its once saucy plum askew. Next he removed the pins from her hair until it swirled around her face and spilled down her shoulders in a glorious mass. With an urgency underlying their deliberate movements, they undressed each other. Naked, they came together. Late afternoon sunlight filled the room with diffused light that added to the dreamlike quality of their lovemaking.

The pleasure was excruciating, each caress, each endearment, an affirmation of their love. Nerve endings quivered and blood hummed as hands stroked heated flesh. Hearts glided in a realm reserved exclusively for those in love. And the climax, when it came, was an explosion full of stars and music and joy.

Later, brimming with happiness, Juliana rested her head on Drew's shoulder. Drew loved her. The knowledge made her want to laugh and dance, it made her want to sing, it moved her to tears.

A single teardrop rolled down her cheek to dampen his chest. Drew looked down in concern. "What's wrong, lass? Is it something I've done?"

Juliana shook her head. "I never thought it was possible to love someone as much as I love you."

"You may not love me quite so much after you hear the entire truth about me." Bitterness edged his tone.

"Then tell me your secrets, Andrew MacAllister," Juliana challenged softly, "and learn that my love will withstand the test." She shifted so that she could see the suffering in his silver-blue eyes. "My love for you is strong. It won't falter."

"I'm a bastard, Juliana. I never knew my father. When he discovered my mother was pregnant with me, he abandoned her. Her family disowned her, leaving her to fare as she might with her child in the streets of Glasgow. Her life didn't improve until years later when Jamie Kincaid offered to marry her."

"And because of this, you think I would love you less?"

"Many would. Illegitimacy is a stigma, a disgrace. It makes one a social outcast. It's not the type of background that young women of good families marry into."

"It doesn't alter the way I feel about you. If anything, I admire you even more for the person you've become."

He searched her face for a long moment. Her eyes mirrored what was in her heart. At last he was able to accept her avowal as truth. "Juliana, lass, you make a man believe in miracles." Slipping his hand behind her neck, he drew her to him. "What about your parents? You never mention them?"

"There's not much to tell. My mother died when I was five. When I was ten, my father left me at the Queen of Angels Convent School for Girls while he went west to seek his fortune. I never saw him again. After a while his letters stopped, and I knew he was dead."

Drew kissed her troubled brow. "Does his death still bother you?"

"I'd rest easier knowing the details of his fate. I'm haunted by thoughts of what might have happened to him. Of not knowing whether or not he suffered and where he died. I'll never be truly at peace until I can put a cross on his grave."

Drew silently came to a conclusion. Her peace of mind could be purchased for a price. Tomorrow he would hire a Pinkerton man.

The uproar started as soon as the *Town Crier* hit the newsstands. Boys hawking newspapers on street corners watched their piles being rapidly depleted. True to Howard Batchelor's prediction, Drew was a hero. According to the reporter's account, Drew had single-handedly saved an entire roomful of people from a crazed killer. Juliana's name, too, was mentioned in glowing terms. She was cited for bravely snatching a loaded pistol away from a madman's grasp. No mention was made of the fact that the audience she had addressed was composed mostly of women who plied their trade in the streets.

The next day Drew made headlines for the *Times* and *Tribune* when Daniel Tennant publicly endorsed him as his successor.

In a mansion on Fifth Avenue, a man wearing an onyx signet ring hurled the newspaper into the fireplace. "Lucky son of a bitch." He watched the paper as the edges scorched, then burst into flame. "It's time to play my trump card."

CHAPTER 19

A CRUSH OF PEOPLE CONGREGATED IN THE LOBBY OF THE
Metropolitan Opera House, waiting for the performance to
begin. Juliana and Drew stood among a group of laughing,
chattering couples, the gentlemen garbed in evening dress,
the ladies bedecked in jewels. Seeing her husband smile
and nod while he listened attentively to the comments of a
man with a pencil-thin mustache, Juliana wondered if her
imagination was being overstimulated of late.

Recently Drew seemed withdrawn. When she had asked
him about it, he dismissed her worries with a kiss, then
made love to her so ardently that even now the memory of
it brought a blush to her cheeks.

"Have you turned a new leaf?" Drew asked Juliana with
an indulgent smile. "Since when do you tolerate such inflam-
matory remarks?"

Juliana recalled herself to the present, happy no one had
access to her innermost thoughts. "Forgive me," she said
with a smile. "My mind wandered."

The man speaking with Drew stroked his mustache. "I've
heard, Mrs. MacAllister, that you're an advocate of woman suffrage. I merely commented that you're hardly the

type depicted in the papers as a mummified and fossilated female."

"A common fallacy, sir." Juliana smiled, taking no offense at the man's remark. "Because of such portrayals, Susan Anthony did a report on the marital status of the movement's leaders. She was the only one who had never married, while the sixteen who did marry had a total of sixty-six children among them. Hardly a bunch of dried-up old maids."

"Sixty-six children? You don't say."

Drew placed his hand at the small of Juliana's back. "It's time for us to take our seats. Enjoy the performance, Edgar." With a final nod at his acquaintance, he guided Juliana through the crowd toward the theater entrance.

"You're not angry with me, are you?" Juliana asked.

"Angry? Whatever for?"

"For making my sentiments clear to your friend. Daniel Tennant fears such liberal views will harm your chances for election."

Drew shrugged. "Daniel's very conservative in his outlook. He's entitled to his opinion, as I am to mine."

"And what, pray tell, is your opinion?"

"Let's just say I'm less opposed to the idea of women gaining the right to vote than I was previously."

"You mean less opposed than you were before we met?" Juliana asked, jubilant at the notion that she could influence her husband.

His mouth curved wryly as he looked into her glowing face. "I'll admit some of your arguments have merit."

Juliana was still floating on his praise as they waited to be ushered to their box. This was her first visit to the much touted Metropolitan Opera House which had opened four years previously. Its splendor, quite simply, left her speechless. Tiers of box seats encircled the U-shaped house. Smaller loges, festooned with velvet draperies, flanked either side of the wide stage. The interior was lavishly embellished with gilt and crimson velvet.

Bending his head, Drew spoke in a low voice, "Like it?"

"Like it? It's magnificent."

"So are you. That gold dress makes you look like a pagan goddess."

Once again Maura's fashion expertise had paid dividends. Though reluctant to spend such an extravagant sum on a single garment, Juliana was glad she had heeded her friend's advice. The bronze satin gown with its heavily beaded low-cut bodice was a perfect foil for her tawny coloring.

A uniformed usher escorted them to a box where Emma and Bertie were already seated. Bertie kissed Juliana's cheek and pumped Drew's hand. "So glad you could tear yourself away, Drew. I know you've been abominably busy, what with Tennant's endorsement and all."

"Too busy," Drew confessed. "I promised myself some time ago I'd bring Juliana to the Met."

Emma indicated that Juliana should sit next to her. "To-night marks the American premiere of *Siegfried*. Lilli Lehmann, who sings the role of Brunhilde, is supposed to be superb."

Juliana felt like royalty. How fortunate she was to be in the midst of all this grandeur, to have friends like Emma and Bertie, but most of all, to have Drew. He had brought her so much happiness, so much joy, so much love. She sighed contentedly. With him, her life was perfect.

Juliana glanced up as a beautiful woman dressed in scarlet silk, accompanied by a balding, heavyset man, created a stir as she took her seat in the adjoining box minutes before curtain time.

"Isn't she striking?" Emma whispered.

Juliana turned to examine the doll-like beauty more closely. The woman was probably nearer to Drew's age than her own, she estimated, though only a single streak of gray in the raven hair betrayed the fact. While the brunette was petite, her voluptuous bosom threatened to spill out of its silken confines. Rubies and diamonds adorned her neck and earlobes. The woman's face, however, totally captured Juliana's interest. It was the sort that drew a man's attention and a woman's envy. The features had the delicate precision of a bisque figurine, her skin the ivory purity of a white camellia. "Yes," Juliana agreed at last. "Quite striking."

Emma's brow puckered thoughtfully. "I don't believe I've seen her before. Who do you suppose she is?"

"Her name is Victoria Dumouchelle. She's the daughter of Herbert Masters," Drew supplied, his tone void of emotion. Seemingly oblivious to the others around him, he stared unabashedly.

"Daughter, eh?" Bertie tugged at his ear. "Didn't know the old reprobate had one."

"She's been living abroad—in France, I believe," Drew said.

Just then the woman turned her head. Her soulful dark eyes flashed with recognition when they encountered Drew. Juliana's contentment evaporated.

The houselights dimmed; the curtain rose. Throughout the performance, Juliana sensed Drew's inattention. She was keenly aware each time his glance strayed to the lovely woman in the adjoining box. How well did he know Victoria Dumouchelle? The question repeated itself in her mind, deafening her to the music. She was almost afraid to learn the answer.

The German opera was concluded to thunderous

applause. As the lights came on after the last curtain call, the audience started toward the exits.

"On to Delmonico's," Bertie announced enthusiastically. "I'm in the mood for a juicy steak."

The woman in red, the lovely and mysterious Victoria Dumouchelle, seemed to have vanished without a trace. Juliana couldn't help but notice the way Drew's eyes scanned the throng as though hungry for one last look.

They joined the noisy group waiting for carriages on the corner of Thirty-ninth and Broadway. By the time the foursome reached Delmonico's, the popular restaurant was teeming with an after-theater crowd.

"Lucky for us you made reservations." Emma smiled fondly at her twin before turning to Juliana. "Bertie's so dependable. I don't know what I'd do without him."

Bertie beamed. "It's a man's job to look out for you womenfolk."

The maître d'hôtel approached and, after a stiff bow, led them past tall potted palms toward a corner table.

"André!"

A lilting French accent stopped their progress. Victoria Dumouchelle rose from a banquette and stepped into their path. Placing her small hand on Drew's arm, she smiled into his eyes. "*Chéri*, we meet again. I can't believe my good fortune."

"Victoria." The name seemed wrung from him.

Jealousy, heretofore unknown to her, swamped Juliana. She wanted to squeeze between them, to proclaim her rights, to tell the woman to go away and leave her husband alone. Drew was hers. Only hers.

"Drew," Emma said to fill the awkward breach, "please introduce us to your lovely acquaintance."

"Forgive my lapse of manners," Drew apologized, then

proceeded to make the necessary introductions, leaving Juliana for last.

"Your wife, *chéri?*" Victoria's lower lip jutted out in a pout. "How cruel of fate. After all these years, we are reunited, only to find that I am recently widowed and you, *mon amour,* newly wed."

"Victoria! Dinner is getting cold." The woman's heavyset companion stubbed out his cigar. The gold crest on his onyx signet ring winked in the candlelight.

"Coming, Father," she said, then turned back to Drew. "*Au revoir, cheri.*"

As far as Juliana was concerned, the meal was tasteless. She only picked at her food. Drew managed to eat only a small portion of his before pushing his plate aside. Emma and Bertie exchanged troubled looks, then gave up trying to engage their guests in conversation. All were glad when the strained evening wound to an end.

Gilbert had left a single lamp burning in the entranceway. Juliana started for the stairs, but Drew made no move to follow. "Go ahead," he said. "I'm going to have a brandy before coming up."

"I'll join you," she replied. "Perhaps brandy will help me sleep."

For a minute Juliana thought he was about to refuse her unusual request. Instead, he turned and went into his study, leaving her to trail behind him. Not bothering to switch on a light, he went directly to the sideboard, poured two snifters of brandy, and handed her one.

"I'm sorry if the evening was a disappointment." He quickly drained his glass, then poured another.

Juliana stared at him. In the meager light, his face was all planes and angles, his expression shadowed. She wanted to reach out, to touch his cheek, but did nothing. Drawing a shaky breath, she asked, "Who is Victoria Dumouchelle?"

"Someone I used to know . . . a long time ago."

"I see." Juliana's fingers tightened on the glass. "You were close friends?"

"No." Drew avoided her eyes.

"You were lovers, weren't you?" she asked, her voice a whisper in the quiet room.

An eloquent silence followed.

Carefully Juliana set her untasted brandy on the sideboard. Her heart leaden, she left the study.

Norman Wilcox poked his head around the door of Drew's private office. "Sorry to interrupt, sir, but there's a lady here to see you. I explained that your appointment book was filled, but she's insistent."

Drew looked up from his notes. "Did she give her name?"

The secretary bobbed his head. "Yes, sir. Madame Victoria Dumouchelle."

"Send her in, Wilcox. And see that we're not disturbed." Drew set his papers aside, rose, and rounded his desk just as Victoria swept into his office.

"André! I knew you would see me."

"Victoria." He took the hand she offered. "The years have been kind to you. You're more beautiful than ever."

"And the handsome boy I loved has become an even more attractive man." Her doelike brown eyes shone with moisture. "I never thought I'd see you again. Then last night . . . If only . . ."

"Don't." Drew squeezed her hand gently. "What happened between us was a lifetime ago."

"I should have been stronger. I never should have listened to Father."

"You were only seventeen—just a girl, hardly in a position to defy your father." Drew realized he was still holding her hand and released it.

"How different our lives might have been." Taking out a perfumed handkerchief, she dabbed at her eyes. "Father tells me you are a very successful attorney and businessman. That you plan to run for the state assembly next fall."

"Yes, Daniel Tennant has endorsed me to run as his successor. But you didn't come here to discuss my political aspirations. What can I do for you?"

"I came here seeking your legal counsel. My late husband left everything to me in his will. Now his daughter from his first marriage is claiming half of his estate." Victoria took a document from her purse and presented it to Drew. "Is this possible?"

He skimmed it briefly. "I'll need time to go through this more carefully."

"*Certainement.*" She flashed him a brilliant smile. "I knew I could depend on you."

He escorted her across the room, stopping at the door separating the inner and outer offices. She rose on tiptoe and kissed both of his cheeks before he could protest. "You'll learn, *chéri,* that I've adopted many French customs." With a gay laugh, she waved and left the office.

Juliana looked up from her seat in Drew's outer office where she waited for his secretary to announce her. Shock that the beautiful Victoria Dumouchelle had been closeted with Drew gave way to slow, simmering rage. Her knuckles whitened as she gripped her purse. The woman hadn't wasted time renewing an old *friendship.* She headed for the door to Drew's private office.

"Mrs. MacAllister. Please stop." Norman Wilcox jumped up from his desk. "I have to announce you first. You can't simply barge in."

"Can't I? Just watch!"

The determined gleam in her golden eyes gave the young man cause to reconsider.

"How do you expect me to get anything done with constant interruptions?" Drew demanded irritably without looking up from his work.

Juliana froze, one hand on the doorknob. Paying her husband a surprise visit suddenly didn't seem prudent.

Scowling, Drew glanced up from the contracts he was studying. The irritation on his face changed to surprise, then to genuine pleasure. He quickly got to his feet and came to greet her. "Juliana, this is an unexpected treat. What brings you here this morning?"

She came forward with a tentative smile. "I'm meeting Emma for lunch and thought I'd stop in and say hello. I arrived just as Victoria Dumouchelle was leaving."

Drew's expression hardened. "Victoria was here on business. Her late husband's will is being contested. She asked my advice."

Juliana thought she detected a certain defensiveness in his tone. "You're busy. Perhaps this wasn't a good idea."

"It was a wonderful idea." He smiled at last and lightly ran his hands up and down her arms. "No matter how busy I am, I'll always make time for you."

Those were the words she wanted to hear. She desperately needed to know she mattered to him. Juliana's eyes searched his. The warmth radiating back dissolved her earlier anxieties. When he looked at her that way, she felt invincible. "I love you, Drew. For some reason, it seemed important I tell you that."

"My sweet Juliana." His arms came around her. "Always strong and generous."

She shook her head in denial. "Where you're concerned,

I'm not strong at all. You're my weakness." Juliana felt a shudder ripple through him the instant before his lips slanted across hers for a hard, possessive kiss. Her world reeling violently, she clutched his shoulders, seeking stability from the very source responsible for the upheaval.

Reality filtered back slowly as the kiss ended. Juliana's cheeks were flushed. Her lips had the pink softness of a woman who's been thoroughly kissed. Drew smiled at her tenderly. "You should come by more often. This type of diversion could easily become a habit."

"And then you'd bark at poor Mr. Wilcox and complain that your work wasn't getting done."

Drew laughed and led her to the door where he gave her another light kiss. "Give Emma my love."

Later, over dessert, Emma brought up the topic of Victoria Dumouchelle. "Juliana dear, I don't want to distress you, but I think you should be warned."

Her fork poised in midair, Juliana looked up. Worry was plainly evident on her elderly friend's usually cheerful countenance. "It isn't your heart again, is it, Emma?"

"Bless you, child, no. My health is fine." Emma patted her hand and managed a faint smile. "It's that Dumouchelle woman. I don't trust her, and neither should you."

Juliana laid down her fork. The rich chocolate dessert had lost its appeal. "I don't, but I trust Drew."

"And rightly so. Forgive me for speaking out, but don't underestimate that woman. Has Drew told you much about her?"

Juliana's fears returned in a rush. "Very little, actually."

"I once asked Drew if he had ever been in love." Emma rested her folded hands on the tablecloth and leaned forward. "He confessed that once, long ago, he lost his heart to a beautiful young woman. Her father was enraged when he discovered their youthful affair and sent his daughter abroad. Drew said she was the love of his life. I think Victoria Dumouchelle is that woman."

Try as she might, Juliana couldn't dispute the probable validity of Emma's assumption. At the Met she had witnessed Drew's dazed reaction upon seeing Victoria again. Later she had heard Victoria's affectionate greeting. She had felt the tension.

"Fortunately for you,"—Emma sat back and took a sip of her cooling tea—"she has little reason to come into contact with Drew."

"Oh, but she has." Juliana recalled Victoria's satisfied smile as she left Drew's office. "Victoria has requested Drew's advice concerning her late husband's will."

"According to Bertie, Herbert Masters is a man without scruples. His daughter may be of the same caliber. I fear she wants Drew back. If so, she'll stop at nothing." Signaling the waiter for the bill, Emma tugged on her gloves. "Be careful, dear."

She would be careful, she decided silently. But how could she hope to compete with Victoria Dumouchelle? The woman was everything Juliana was not.

CHAPTER
20

THE GRAY AND GLOOMY NOVEMBER AFTERNOON PRESAGED winter. Wind whipped down from Canada, stripping the last leaves from the trees. Dark clouds scudded across a dark sky. Looking out the window, Juliana watched people with their collars turned up against the cold hurry homeward. Letting the curtain drop into place, Juliana crossed the parlor to turn on a light.

The click of the front door, followed by the sound of male voices, drifted in to her. She glanced up as Drew and a second man, a stranger, came into the room. An uneasy flicker in Drew's blue-gray eyes alerted her that something was amiss.

"Juliana, this is John Summers."

Juliana smiled and took the man's hand, musing that Summers was a misnomer for a man who more closely resembled autumn. Except for a white shirt, he man was dressed completely in brown. He was of average height and build with brown hair and eyes. Like a chameleon, this man would be able to blend into the environment and never be noticed.

"Mr. Summers works for the Pinkerton Agency. I hired his company to investigate your father's disappearance."

Though Juliana paled, she maintained her outward composure. "And were you able to trace him?"

"Yes, ma'am. Your husband wasn't able to supply us with very much information, but sometimes we get lucky. We checked all the assay offices in Nevada, and sure enough, he filed a claim."

"Then he's . . . dead?" Juliana's mouth went dry and she could barely form the words. She had known her father was dead since she was a girl, since the letters stopped coming. What she hadn't known, though, until this very moment, was that buried deep in her heart was the hope that she was wrong. That he might still be alive.

Drew stepped to her side and put his arm around her shoulders.

The Pinkerton man shifted uncomfortably. "I'm afraid so, ma'am."

Drew led Juliana to a sofa and urged her to sit. Going to the sideboard, he poured a snifter of brandy and, holding it to her lips, told her to swallow. While the liquor made her eyes sting, it ate like acid through the numbness that held her in a paralyzing grip. She squeezed Drew's hand to show her appreciation and then, in command of her emotions once more, turned to John Summers.

"My manners have been lax. Please sit down and tell me what you've learned."

"Yes, ma'am." He sat down gingerly.

Drew stood next to Juliana, one hand resting on her shoulder.

"Your father struck a rich vein of silver. But there was an explosion shortly after he filed his claim, and he was trapped in a shaft. It was two days before he could be rescued. He was still alive but in pretty bad shape when the men got to him."

Juliana blinked back tears.

"If you'd rather not hear this . . . " Drew's fingers on her shoulder tightened.

"No." She shook her head. "As much as it hurts, I have to know what happened. Go ahead, Mr. Summers. I want to hear everything."

The detective crossed, then recrossed his legs. "For the next week, your father drifted in and out of consciousness. On one of those occasions, he insisted they call a lawyer. When the lawyer came, your father dictated a will, naming you, his only child, as beneficiary. Unfortunately, he lapsed into a coma and died before telling the lawyer where to locate you."

"Then Father did find silver. His dream came true . . . and ultimately killed him." Juliana seemed to be speaking to herself.

"You're a very wealthy young woman, Mrs. MacAllister. All the money from the mine has been sitting in a bank all these years collecting interest." John Summers reached into the pocket of his jacket, pulled out an envelope, and handed it to her. "Here's the name of your father's lawyer and the name of the banker. They're waiting to hear from you." He rose to his feet.

Juliana stood on unsteady legs. "Thank you for the fine job you did, Mr. Summers."

"Sorry I had to be the one to inform you about your father."

"You mustn't say that. I'll rest easier knowing the truth."

"If you have any further questions, your husband can contact our agency." With a brief nod, he turned to go. "No need to see me out. Good afternoon."

Juliana remained motionless, her skin so pale it was almost translucent. Grief darkened her eyes to a deep, glittering topaz. She looked so fragile that Drew was afraid to touch her for fear she'd shatter. He felt her agony. He cursed himself for hiring the Pinkerton Agency, for despite her brave words, it would have been less painful to let the past lie undisturbed. "Juliana, love," he said, his voice husky, "forgive me for making you suffer."

"It was I who wanted to know. Remember?" A small laugh escaped that bordered on the hysterical. With an effort she brought her emotions under control. "I've developed a fierce headache. Please tell Gilbert I won't be down for dinner." Her movements wooden, she left the parlor.

He had wanted only to grant her peace of mind. But he didn't feel like a hero. Helplessly, Drew watched Juliana leave. She had told Summers she would rest easier knowing the truth. But would she? Would knowing the details make the cruel facts easier to bear? Or would it cause more pain? He loved her with a passion that overshadowed everything else. Dammit! Balling his fist, he slammed it against the door frame.

"Did something fall, sir?" Gilbert appeared in the doorway and glanced around the parlor. "I thought I heard a crash."

Drew struggled to collect himself. "No, nothing fell."

Frown lines creased the elderly servant's brow. "I hope Mrs. MacAllister isn't ill. She looked quite peaked when I passed her in the hall."

"My wife has had some rather upsetting news. She won't be down for dinner. Send Mary Bridget up to her."

"Mrs. MacAllister gave her the night off. Said it was young Mickey's birthday."

Absently massaging stiff muscles at the back of his neck, Drew pondered his choices. Did Juliana prefer to grieve in private? Or would she accept comfort from him? After all, he was responsible for her distress. Another thought brought him up short. His own guilt was preventing him from being at her side. Leaving a startled Gilbert staring after him, he raced from the parlor and bounded up the stairs.

Muted weeping from behind the bedroom door wrenched Drew's heart. Noiselessly he pushed the door open. Juliana lay sprawled across the bed, her face buried in a pillow to muffle her sobs. Letting instinct guide him, he went to her and, gathering her in his arms, rocked her gently. "There, there, lass," he murmured, "I dinna mean you harm."

The remorse in the rough Scots burr penetrated Juliana's grief. Her face wet with tears, she gazed up at him. "You'll never know how grateful I am."

"You have an odd way of showing gratitude, lass."

"Don't you see? Now I know without a doubt that my father really would have come back for me—he didn't abandon me. In my heart I knew he didn't, but I had to know for sure." She smiled through her tears. "He really did love me."

"Who could resist you, love?" Drew smoothed damp strands of hair away from her face, then rested his cheek on her head. "I couldn't."

The gallery of Old Masters at the Metropolitan Museum of Art was filled with a large crowd, most of whom were listed in the Social Register. The occasion was a reception inaugurating the fall season.

"I'm so glad you changed your mind about coming," Juliana said, taking Drew's arm.

"I didn't want to be accused of neglecting you. I know we haven't spent much time together recently, and suddenly I found myself missing you."

Juliana and Drew stopped to admire a large painting centered on the far wall. "That's *The Horse Fair* by Rosa

Bonheur, which was given to the museum by Cornelius Vanderbilt."

Drew smiled down at her. "Your knowledge puts me to shame. I confess this is my first visit."

Juliana returned his smile. "You work far too hard while I look for ways to fill empty hours."

"Wives are meant to be cosseted, and husbands to provide for them."

"I envy you sometimes. It must be very rewarding to have a profession you are so involved with. That would undoubtedly be preferable to manufacturing ways to spend one's time."

"You'd be much more content if you learned to accept the situation as it exists. You can't change the ways of the world, Juliana."

"I don't believe that." She shook her head stubbornly. "Once women achieve the right to vote, they will no longer be forced meekly to accept the choices of others. We'll no longer be powerless."

"It sounds as though you're rehearsing one of your speeches, but I'm a lot harder to convince than a roomful of dissatisfied women. Now"—he patted her arm—"let's not spoil our time together debating improbabilities."

Juliana opened her mouth to object, but changed her mind when she spotted Victoria Dumouchelle and her father coming toward them. Victoria looked exceptionally lovely in a gown of sapphire blue tulle.

"André!" Victoria exclaimed. "What a pleasant surprise. When I mentioned coming to the reception, you never said you would be here, too."

Juliana's expression froze. Happiness at Drew's companionship fled, leaving her sick with suspicion. Was Victoria, and not she, the reason Drew had changed his mind about attending this function? Was Drew grasping any excuse to be near his former love?

She felt someone staring. Glancing over, she found Victoria's father, Herbert Masters, watching her. When their eyes met, his mouth curled in a sardonic smirk. The parody of a smile sent a chill chasing down her spine.

Victoria's dark eyes swept over Juliana's gown of chocolate-colored velvet designed by Worth. "Julia, how charming you look in spite of such a drab color. Me, I never wear brown."

"My wife's name is Juliana," Drew corrected. "And she has a very sharp instinct for what looks good on her."

Herbert Masters scowled irritably and changed the subject. "Heard your friend Tennant is talking about organizing a subcommittee to discuss government contracts."

"So far it's only talk." Drew's expression was schooled not to reveal any emotion. "Daniel believes far too much money is being awarded to companies with vested interests."

"Harrumph!" Masters snorted. "His proposal would mean an even bigger waste of time and money."

"The figures he's compiling show differently."

"If you get elected, are you going to follow in the old boy's footsteps or be man enough to think for yourself?"

"If I'm elected, I'll not only be proud to serve on the committee, I'll hope to head it."

Hatred gleamed in the older man's eyes for a moment, then was hooded. Instinctively Juliana moved closer to Drew. Intense dislike along with an element of fear raced through her. Herbert Masters had the dangerous look of a cobra preparing to strike.

Victoria pouted, a coquettish expression that seemed inappropriate in a woman her age. "Oh, Father, you promised not to talk business. Naturally," she went on, addressing Drew, "this museum can't compare with the Louvre in Paris, but it's the best New York offers."

"Sorry, my dear. Let's look at the rest of the pictures." With a curt nod, Masters led Victoria away.

Drew and Juliana slowly circulated around the gallery, stopping to admire the works of Franz Hals, Tiepolo, and Poussin. "This *is* a young collection"—Juliana felt compelled to defend the artwork after Victoria's snide remark—"but someday it will grow to be one of the finest in the world." They were deciding what to view next when intercepted by Emma and Bertie Lattimer. Emma's usually rosy cheeks were pale, the lines around her mouth more pronounced.

"Glad to find you two," Bertie greeted them. "Perhaps Juliana can persuade my sister to rest while Drew and I find refreshments. I fear Emma has overtaxed herself."

"Don't fuss so, Bertie." Emma brushed aside his brotherly concern. "I'm a little tired, that's all."

"So am I." Linking her arm in Emma's, Juliana steered her toward a rectangular banquette in the middle of the gallery while the men went in the opposite direction.

Emma sank down with a grateful sigh. "Don't look so worried, dear. With a little rest I'll be fine. Now tell me, have you learned any more about your inheritance?"

"Drew arranged for me to speak with a banker on Wall Street this morning," Juliana explained, sitting next to her. "The money will be put in a special account. Drew insists it should be for my use exclusively. He wants nothing to do with it."

Emma nodded sagely. "For a man who opposes woman suffrage, your husband has some advanced ideas. Mark my word, he'll come around. Keep after him, Juliana. He could do our cause a lot of good."

"Sometimes I wish Drew wasn't running for the assembly. I know I'm being selfish, but I'd give up my fortune in a minute if he'd spend as much time with me. After he's elected, it'll surely be worse."

"A fine way for a wife to talk." Daniel Tennant, leaning heavily on his walking stick, rose from the banquette to glare at her.

Dismayed, Juliana realized the aged legislator had been seated at a right angle to her. Apparently he had been privy to her entire conversation with Emma. "Assemblyman Tennant," Juliana said lamely, "I didn't know you were here this evening."

"A man in your husband's position needs his wife's total support. You"—he angrily jabbed the floor with his stick—"you're nothing but an albatross. I rue the day I encouraged Drew to marry you." His usually sallow face an alarming shade of red, he stormed off.

Shaken by his tirade, Juliana caught her lower lip between her bottom teeth.

"There, there, dear." Emma gave Juliana a quick hug. "Don't let him upset you. Daniel has always had a temper, and now that he's ill, I'm afraid it's worse than ever."

She needed to compose herself before Drew returned. Her gaze strayed toward the gallery entrance. What she spotted there did little to calm her. Victoria and Drew were engrossed in conversation. Her hand rested on his arm; his dark head was bent toward hers while he gave her his undivided attention. Suddenly all of Juliana's shortcomings crystallized. She wanted to bury her head in her hands and weep. Her expression mirrored her despair.

When Juliana failed to respond to a question, Emma followed the direction of her gaze. "Victoria Dumouchelle is a shameless hussy. No decent woman would carry on like her."

"I wish I were more like her."

Emma clucked her tongue. "I don't want to hear you talk like that."

"We're complete opposites. She's beautiful, sophisticated, and well traveled. I doubt if she ever says the wrong thing. She'd make Drew a perfect wife."

"He already has the perfect wife, dear." Emma's staunch support brought forth a reluctant smile from Juliana.

Juliana's smile lingered as Drew completed his conversation with Victoria and rejoined her. Bertie came a minute later carrying a tray of dainty iced cakes and cups of fruit punch.

At first they were too busy talking among themselves to notice that their foursome had become the object of speculation. It wasn't until Emma chanced to see an ill-mannered person point a finger in their direction that it came to their notice. "I daresay, people seem to be unduly interested in us," she commented.

Juliana looked around in time to see a small cluster of people break apart guiltily. "I wonder what we've done to draw so much attention."

"Perhaps they're admiring my new jacket," Bertie quipped.

Thomas and Clarice Wentworth, longtime acquaintances of Drew's, walked in their direction. Drew stepped forward to say hello, but the couple continued on their way, pretending not to see him. Drew appeared more puzzled than hurt by the rebuff. "I can't imagine what's come over Thomas. We've known each other for years."

From the corner of her eye, Juliana watched as a gentleman sporting a handlebar mustache nudged another man, then whipped a newspaper from his pocket and pointed to it. In turn, both men turned to stare at Drew. Juliana could no longer ignore the premonition that something was terribly wrong.

The reception drew to a close, and people were starting to leave. Except for Bertie and Emma, no one spoke to Juliana or Drew. Indeed they seemed to be single-mindedly avoiding them.

Drew had gone to retrieve Juliana's wrap when she noticed a neatly folded newspaper on the banquette. She picked it up. It was the *Town Crier,* the same scandal sheet that months ago had printed her picture and made allegations about her relationship with Drew. Once again Drew's image was prominently displayed on the front page. It was the lurid headline, however, that jumped out at her: "Glasgow Guttersnipe Fools Public."

"What is it, dear?" Emma inquired anxiously. "You look as though you might swoon."

Her friend's voice sounded like an echo in an empty room. Ignoring Emma, Juliana quickly read the paper. The article revealed Drew's illegitimacy. His jealously guarded secret was now public knowledge.

"Juliana?" Drew's voice penetrated her fog. "Are you all right?"

Silently, her face ashen, she gazed at him.

Drew plucked the newspaper from her trembling hands. His expression darkened ominously as he read the banner headline. Wadding the paper into a ball, he hurled it to the floor. "I could kill whoever's responsible for this with my bare hands."

Emma and Bertie exchanged nervous glances.

Gripping Juliana's elbow, Drew hustled her out of the museum. Outside on Fifth Avenue, they waited for their carriage, a part of, but segregated from, the crowd.

A man Juliana guessed was Daniel Tennant's personal secretary shoved his way toward them. "Assemblyman Tennant wants to see you, Mr. MacAllister—immediately. He'll be waiting in his office."

"Tell him I'll be there."

Juliana shivered at the look on Drew's face. Daniel Tennant had overheard her say she wished that Drew wasn't running for office, that she'd give her fortune in exchange for more of Drew's time. Did Daniel believe her responsible for this duplicity? Would he persuade Drew that she had betrayed his confidence?

CHAPTER
21

"DREW, HOW DID THIS SLEAZY RAG GET WIND OF THIS?" Daniel slapped the newspaper on his desk so forcefully papers scattered from the breeze.

"I've asked myself the same question a dozen times."

"Who knew you were born out of wedlock?"

Drew sprang from his chair and paced the length of the office. "Besides you, only Gilbert and Nick and, of course, Juliana."

"So the secret of your past was safe all these years with your brother and servant? Then you told a woman, and the story immediately made headlines."

"Coincidence."

"Bah! Coincidence, my foot!"

"You're overlooking the fact that Juliana isn't just any woman. She's my wife."

"Dammit!" Daniel pounded his fist. "That doesn't mean she's trustworthy."

Drew stopped before a window and stared into the gloomy darkness. "Juliana would never betray me."

"Don't be so sure."

Drew turned to face his mentor. "What makes you say

that, Daniel? Do you know something I don't?"

Daniel leaned forward, his black eyes fever-bright, his voice raspy. "I heard her tell the Lattimer woman she'd do anything to keep you out of politics. She wants you all to herself."

"I refuse to believe Juliana is responsible for this story."

"Stop acting the besotted fool," Daniel sneered. "Use your brain! Who else knows about your illegitimacy?

"No one."

"No one, eh? What about your natural father? Could he be responsible? What do you know about him?" Daniel asked the questions rapid-fire.

Drew's blue-gray eyes looked as hard as flint. "Other than the fact that my father wanted nothing to do with Mother or me, almost nothing. Mother said he was from a prominent family, hinted that he was titled. It's my guess he was also married."

"I figured you were from good stock in spite of being born on the wrong side of the blanket." Daniel slumped back in his chair, his anger having taken its toll on his energy. "That leaves your wife as the prime suspect. Wouldn't be the first time a woman had resorted to spite and vindictiveness to achieve an end."

"Not Juliana." Drew walked to the cabinet, poured two tumblers of scotch, then handed one to Daniel and kept the other for himself.

"What you need is a wife who's content to stay in your shadow, wearing a smile and keeping her damn mouth shut. One who keeps her opinions to herself. I thought a girl fresh out of the convent would be more biddable."

Drew's mouth curved wryly. "So did I, Daniel, so did I."

"I'm not sure you realize the seriousness of this matter. People make a great show of pretending they're liberals, but when it comes right down to it, they're every bit as prudish as their Puritan ancestors."

Drew stared into his scotch, its amber color conjuring up a mental picture of Juliana with her dark gold curls and golden eyes. With an effort, he pulled himself back to the present and concentrated on what Daniel was saying.

"Most of the people who count in this town can trace their lineage back to the *Mayflower*. Do you suppose for a minute they'll want to associate with someone with a tainted bloodline? They're afraid such an association might contaminate them." Raising his glass, Daniel took a long swallow of scotch. "After tonight, forget any hope of being listed in the Social Register."

"That's not important."

"Like hell it isn't!" Daniel set his glass down with a thud. "Who are you trying to fool? I know this has you worried. A scandal like this could snuff out your bright future, politically and financially."

Drew sipped his scotch, welcoming its smoky bite. "Does this mean you're going to withdraw your endorsement?"

The question hung in the air.

"You've got the makings of a damn good statesman," Daniel said at last. He rubbed a frail, blue-veined hand across his mouth. "I've been grooming you to be my successor for years. But time's running short. It's too late to find and train another. Let's hope the ruckus dies a quick death. Given time, folks will find something new to gossip about. Provided, of course, that you do nothing more to cause even a whisper of scandal."

Drew nodded glumly. "I'll speak with you tomorrow." Setting down his glass, he left his mentor's office.

Outside, Drew tugged the collar of his overcoat up against the cold. He was glad he had instructed Jack not to wait. The long walk home would give him time to think. Anger at the night's revelation still churned within him. Too bad the gym wasn't open at this hour. He'd don a pair of boxing gloves and go a few rounds with a canvas punching bag. That always helped vent his temper.

He rammed his fists into his pockets. The vicious newspaper stories were dogging him again, just as they had months ago when Juliana had been spotted leaving his home. Someone was conspiring against him, plotting to destroy his reputation and his career. But who? Until recently, no one except Nick, Gilbert, and Daniel knew of his illegitimacy. Juliana might resent his ambition, but he could never bring himself to believe she would deliberately sabotage his dreams.

Hot air from a baker's oven wafted through an iron grate in the street. Drew was about to step around what appeared to be bundles of rags piled on the gratings when one of the bundles stirred. Street arabs, he realized, poor homeless children. Every city had them—Glasgow included. As a lad, he, too, had sought warmth in such places on cold nights. Pulling out his wallet, he withdrew several bills. "Here, son, buy yourself and your friends a blanket and a decent meal."

The urchin's eyes grew round at his unexpected good fortune. "Thanks, mister." He snatched the money with a grubby hand.

Head bent, Drew continued on his way, his footsteps hollow in the nearly deserted streets. If elected to the assembly, he had so many plans. Ideas kept secret even from Daniel. Children belonged in schools, not in factories. They needed protection from the cold, and food in their bellies. In most families, at least one child died before its fifth birthday. Better medical care could make a difference. But none of his plans would see fruition if scandal interfered. . . .

The pup greeted Drew in the entryway, barking and wagging its tail. "Hush, Cocoa, you'll wake your mistress," Drew scolded, stooping down to pet the little dog.

Juliana emerged from the study, still wearing the brown velvet gown she had worn at the reception. "I was waiting for you. How was your meeting with Daniel? Is he going to withdraw his endorsement?"

Shrugging out of his overcoat, Drew hung it on the coat tree. "Daniel is willing to wait it out, providing I supply no more grist for the scandal mills."

Juliana locked her fingers together. "He blames me, doesn't he?"

Drew avoided her gaze. "I think I'll have a drink before retiring. Why don't you go on up to bed?" He went into the study where a single lamp burned.

Juliana followed him. "Do you blame me, too?"

Drew paused in the act of pouring scotch. Juliana interpreted the slight hesitation as an admission of doubt. The realization sliced her heart, the wound deep and excruciatingly painful. "I swear"—her voice caught—"I never told a soul."

"I never thought you did, lass." His gaze held hers from across the room, steady and unwavering. "I don't know who's responsible, but I know it isn't you."

His words soothed her fears. She went to him and imploringly placed her hand on his arm. "I'm so terribly sorry about all this. I know how much being an assemblyman means to you."

"Do you?" He smiled humorlessly. "I rather doubt it."

"Is it power you seek? Prestige? Help me understand

why this is so important to you," she begged. "Don't shut me out of your life."

A lengthy silence ensued as Drew swirled the golden liquid in his glass. Shadows flickered; the mantel clock ticked. Juliana waited patiently.

"Most of my life I've been treated like an outcast, never quite as good as the rest. Even Uncle Angus, when he discovered my brother and me on his doorstep, was willing to take in Nick but wanted to send me back into the streets." There was a wealth of hurt and bitterness in Drew's confession. He took a sip of scotch, then continued. "To this day I don't know what caused him to change his mind. From the beginning I was determined to make him proud of me. I studied hard to make up for my lack of schooling, and finally, when I was admitted to Harvard, I think I earned the old man's respect."

Compassion stirred in Juliana, making her want to offer solace to the man who was outwardly strong but inwardly vulnerable. "This is why you want to run for public office? To prove that you're worthy?"

"Don't you see that if I'm elected it'll mean I've finally become a respectable member of society? No longer will I be the bastard child who had to fight and steal in order to survive."

"All of that matters not at all to me, Andrew MacAllister. I love you regardless of your background." Going to him, she rose on tiptoe and pulled his head down to hers.

He took what he offered and demanded more. Fueled by a need he didn't stop to examine, his mouth ravaged hers. Hot and moist, his lips moved over hers, smothering her startled outcry.

There was nothing gentle, tender, or even civilized in his touch. Yet his naked desire excited Juliana beyond belief.

Her mind spun to adjust to this strange but familiar lover.

Drew tipped her head back, arching the slender white column of her throat. He caught the sensitive skin at the juncture of her shoulder between his teeth and nibbled gently. An exquisite wave of pleasure shot through her. Final remnants of rational thought scattering, Juliana strained against him, surrendering to sensation.

Roughly Drew stripped off her velvet gown and her underthings and discarded them in untidy piles. With hands just as frantic in their haste as his, Juliana removed his clothing. Breathless, they tumbled to the carpet.

In the soft lamplight, Juliana's skin glowed with a creamy patina. Her eyes closed as his mouth made hungry forays across her bare flesh. A broken moan escaped her when his lips closed around a hardened nipple. In a frenzy of desire, she let her hands play over his superbly muscled body, already damp with sweat.

Drew uttered a groan of pleasure when her questing hand enclosed his male staff. Goaded toward delirium, he spread her thighs. His name formed on her lips as he drove himself into her. Juliana wrapped her legs around his hips and matched his rhythm. Fast and furiously, they raced headlong toward an invisible finish line. Simultaneously they reached the goal and attained the coveted prize.

The dining room table was slowly being covered with neat stacks of envelopes. The three women worked diligently. Mary Bridget folded the pamphlets, Emma stuffed each into an envelope, and Juliana addressed them. Gilbert brought in a tea service and a plate of shortbread, then left unobtrusively. A clock chimed five.

"Gracious!" Emma exclaimed. "I had no idea it was so late. We'll have to finish this another time. I must get ready for Alice Kent's dinner party, and so must you, dear." She smiled at Juliana.

Juliana concentrated on the envelope she was addressing. "Drew and I weren't invited to the Kents'."

"Oh, dear." Emma sounded distressed. "This is so embarrassing. I never would have mentioned the party if I had even dreamed you weren't included."

"Don't let it upset you. Since Drew's illegitimacy became public knowledge, we've been cut from a number of guest lists." Juliana added another envelope to the pile. "Besides, Drew has been working late each evening. I doubt if he has time for social events."

"I'm worried about Drew. First the story about his being a natural child, and now his business venture failing." Emma reached across the table and patted Juliana's hand. "I'm sure he'll find a way to resolve his financial problems."

Her pen poised in midstroke, Juliana stared at Emma blankly. "Financial problems?"

Emma and Mary Bridget glanced at each other, guilt and embarrassment on their faces.

"Pa was saying just the other night that it isn't likely a man as smart as Mr. MacAllister will go bankrupt," Mary Bridget piped up.

Juliana's stomach lurched. "What are you talking about?"

"It's in all the papers." Mary Bridget got up abruptly and began collecting empty teacups.

Juliana hadn't seen a newspaper around the house for days. Whenever she had inquired about them, she received a lame excuse. Apparently, Drew, with Gilbert's able assistance, had conspired to leave her ignorant of this latest catastrophe. A financial crisis would also explain Drew's extended hours at work. He left for his office before daybreak and didn't return until late at night.

"You mustn't think for a moment, dear, that my brother is like the others," Emma said as she prepared to leave. "Bertie is loyal. He won't withdraw his funds, as the other investors did. He has the utmost faith in Drew."

Long after Emma had left for home and Mary Bridget had departed to visit her parents, Juliana remained seated at the dining room table. Twilight crowded the room. The ticking of the clock marked passing time. She needed to talk with Drew. It seemed everyone in the city knew more about his business than she. Why was he keeping it from her? Did he think she wouldn't stand by him in his time of need? But above all, it pained her to think he was excluding her from his life.

Gilbert entered the room and cleared his throat. "What time would you like dinner served, madam?"

"I'm not very hungry, Gilbert." Juliana decided to test her theory. "But there is one thing you can do for me."

"Of course, madam. Whatever you wish."

"I'd like to see today's newspaper."

Gilbert's Adam's apple bobbed above his starched collar. "That's, ah . . . quite impossible."

"Why do you say that? Surely it's a simple request."

The servant glanced around nervously as though seeking an escape route. "I . . . ah . . . used it to wrap up the garbage."

"Well, then, perhaps you'd be good enough to go down to the newsstand and purchase one for me?"

"I can't," Gilbert confessed, his gaze settling on the Oriental carpet.

"And why not?" Juliana inquired, rising and going over to him. "Why can't you, Gilbert?"

"Mr. MacAllister's orders. He said absolutely no newspapers in the house."

"Look at me, Gilbert," she ordered softly. Reluctantly the elderly retainer raised his faded blue eyes to meet hers. "I only wish to learn the true extent of my husband's financial difficulties so I might be of help. I happen to love him very much. Do you believe my character so weak that a problem—no matter how big it might seem—might alter that love?"

"Weak, madam? Hardly." Gilbert looked appalled by the notion. "If anything, I've observed you to be a strong-minded but sensible young woman. Mr. MacAllister made a good match when he married you."

Juliana was touched by the unexpected tribute. "Thank you, Gilbert," she said, her voice husky with emotion.

Gilbert appeared a trifle disconcerted by his outburst. "If you still want a newspaper, madam, I'll gladly go down to the tobacconist's and get one for you."

"No, thank you, Gilbert. It wasn't fair of me to ask you to go against Mr. MacAllister's orders." She started past him toward the entryway. "I'll go myself."

"I won't hear of it." Gilbert assumed his haughtiest demeanor. "It isn't safe for a young woman to wander the streets at night. Mr. MacAllister would never forgive me if I let anything happen to you. I'll return shortly." He marched out of the dining room.

When Gilbert returned a half hour later, he carried a small bundle of newspapers. After thanking him, Juliana spread them across the table. She found the first article on the third page of the *Tribune,* the second in the financial section of the *Times,* another in the *Herald.*

Upon reading through them carefully, Juliana discovered Drew was the power behind AMAC Enterprises, a land development firm that was purchasing large tracts of property in Manhattan. Drew had just signed the biggest deal in his company's history, but now several silent partners had withdrawn their backing, leaving Drew to come up with the rest of the money—or declare bankruptcy.

Juliana rested her head in her hands and tried to think clearly. No wonder Drew looked tense and drawn. Everything he had labored for all these years was crumbling around him. She had once charged that he put too much emphasis on wealth. But now she understood why he was driven to accumulate material possessions. It wasn't the money itself he wanted, but the security it represented. As long as he had plenty of money, he would never again be cold, hungry, or defenseless.

Hearing the front door open and close, Juliana quickly got up and went to greet her husband. His stern but handsome face looked infinitely dear to her. He smiled when he saw her. Juliana's heart seemed to swell with love until it felt so heavy her chest ached. She took a hesitant step forward. His arms opened, and she rushed forward, hurtling herself into their welcoming circle.

He held her fast as though afraid she'd disappear. He smelled of fresh air and the faint scent of sandalwood. She rubbed her cheek against the nubby wool of his jacket and trembled as his lips brushed her brow.

"Why such a warm welcome, lass? I haven't been at sea." The Scots burr she had grown so fond of deepened his voice.

"I missed you," she whispered.

He drew back to study her. "Are you sure nothing's wrong?"

The naked concern in his expression unnerved her. Yet there were matters to discuss that could no longer be ignored. She steeled herself for the inevitable conversation. "It appears there is a great deal wrong." Taking him by the hand, she led him into the dining room where the newspapers still lay spread across the mahogany table.

Drew's encompassing glance took in the condemning facts. With an angry swipe of his arm, he knocked the papers to the floor. "How did you find out?" he demanded.

Refusing to let his temper intimidate her, she held her ground. "It doesn't matter. Is the situation as bad as the papers say?"

"Worse," he ground out through clenched teeth.

"Tell me about it."

"There's not much to add." He jammed his hands into his pockets. "I recently signed papers for the purchase of a large parcel of land. I put up sixty percent of the money, and my silent partners had agreed to supply the remaining forty percent. That's the way we've done business in the past. I thought they were honorable men." Contempt twisted his features. "Now they're refusing to back me, which leaves me responsible for their share. If I don't come up with the cash, the deal will be forfeited—and I'll be forced to declare bankruptcy."

"Drew, let me help." Juliana placed her hand on his arm. The muscles beneath her touch felt taut as steel. "I have the money Father left me—"

"Keep your money." He shook off her hand. "This is my problem. I'll handle it."

"But . . ."

He stalked from the room.

CHAPTER
22

SHE COULDN'T STAND BY AND DO NOTHING. JULIANA HAD been awake half the night wrestling with the problem of what to do. At first she had thought of asking Bertie Lattimer's advice, but after further consideration had changed her mind. Bertie might not know the true extent of Drew's problem. As a silent partner, should he learn all the facts he might feel his investment was in even greater jeopardy. That left only Daniel Tennant.

Happy that gloves covered her sweaty palms, Juliana glanced anxiously around the assemblyman's outer office. Except for a collection of framed photographs of himself and other prominent politicians, she observed that Daniel's office was as Spartan as Drew's.

"Assemblyman Tennant will see you now."

Juliana started at the secretary's voice. Gathering her handbag and her courage, she followed him into Daniel Tennant's inner sanctum.

The aged politician didn't bother to rise from his leather chair. Nor did he look up from the papers he was signing in a spidery handwriting.

Juliana tried to quell the nervous flutter in her stomach. "I appreciate your seeing me."

"State your case and be quick about it. I haven't got all day."

"Very well, I'll get to the point. Is Drew's financial situation really as grim as it appears?"

"Why not ask him?"

"I did."

"And what did he tell you?"

"That this was his problem and he'd handle it."

"Then why not follow his advice?"

"Because I happen to disagree. What affects Drew affects me as well."

"Afraid you're going to find yourself out in the street?" He flicked her a contemptuous glance.

Juliana struggled to contain her anger. Storming out of his office would accomplish nothing. "Then it's true that Drew might go bankrupt."

Daniel thrust his pen into its holder. "Drew's so-called friends are like a pack of rats leaving a sinking ship. They promised to put up a percentage of the money for this real estate acquisition, but now that the papers are signed, they're reneging on their part of the bargain. If Drew doesn't come up with their share of the cash, he stands to lose everything."

"I want to help."

"Then go home like a good little wife and stay out of trouble."

"Drew's a proud man. He would be furious with me if he knew I was here. Believe me, Assemblyman Tennant, I wouldn't interfere if there was any other way. But I can't sit back while he watches everything he's worked for be destroyed. I just can't."

"Just what do *you* propose to do about the situation?" His tone was heavy with sarcasm.

"My father left me a sizable inheritance," she began.

At the mention of money, Daniel's interest sparked. He seemed to notice for the first time that his visitor was still standing. He motioned impatiently. "Sit down, sit down. Tell me what you have in mind."

Juliana sat in the chair opposite the desk, her hands folded demurely in her lap. Only she was aware of their trembling. "I want to invest my inheritance in Drew's company, AMAC Enterprises, but I don't know how to go about it."

Drumming his fingers on the desktop, the assemblyman contemplated her. "Am I to understand that your husband isn't to know about this? That any arrangements we make will be our secret?"

Guilt flooded through Juliana, then quickly receded. She found deceit abhorrent, but knew of no alternative. "I offered him my help last night, but Drew refused to accept it." Her chin jutted out stubbornly.

Daniel chuckled, the sound like the crackling of dry leaves. "Drew met his match when he married you. You're every bit as feisty as he is. You'll never be an easy one to train."

"Women aren't pets in need of training. I fear coming to you was a mistake." She started to rise.

"Don't get riled." His piercing coal-black gaze pinned her to her seat. "Before I agree to help, you need to realize that by investing in Drew's company you stand to lose your entire fortune. Are you willing to accept the risk?"

"I am." She met his stare unflinchingly.

He nodded, then reached for the phone. Juliana listened attentively as he spoke to someone she assumed was a Wall Street broker.

"It's settled." Daniel replaced the receiver in the cradle. Brusquely he outlined the steps necessary to transfer funds and purchase shares in AMAC Enterprises. "Winston will contact your banker and have the papers drawn up for you to sign by this afternoon. Here's the address," he said, scribbling on a sheet of paper and shoving it across the desk.

"Drew's a proud man and extremely independent," she explained, surrendering to the urge to justify her motives. She tucked the address into her handbag. "For the present, I think it best that my investment remain anonymous."

"A silent partner in the strictest sense of the word, eh?" Daniel came out from behind his desk and walked Juliana to the door. "Can't say I approve of your outspoken ways, but you've proved your mettle today, girl." He extended his hand. "Good luck to you."

Weary but at peace with her decision, Juliana trudged up the front steps of the brownstone. She had signed the papers; the wheels were set in motion. Now all she could do was wait and pray that Drew could use her inheritance to avert disaster. Mary Bridget opened the door as she reached the top step.

"Oh, Juliana, I'm so glad you're here. Wait until you see him. He's been waiting over an hour."

"Calm yourself, Mary Bridget," Juliana said, stepping past her into the entryway. She couldn't contain a smile. In her excitement, the young Irishwoman's cheeks bloomed like roses and her blue eyes shone like sapphires.

"He's *so* handsome." Mary Bridget dramatically held a hand to her heart. "I think I'm in love."

"I can hardly wait to meet this person who stole your heart in a single afternoon." Juliana unfastened her fur-trimmed redingote, then untied her bonnet. "Who is he?"

"How silly of me." Mary Bridget giggled, taking Juliana's things. "Why, Nicholas Kincaid—Mr. MacAllister's brother."

"Nick?" Juliana grew pale.

"Oh, Juliana, he goes to college. Harvard or Yale. I can't remember which—I was so excited. I've never met a college man before." Hugging Juliana's redingote, she twirled around. "I think he likes me."

The profound shock of finding Nicholas Kincaid in her home was beginning to wear off. It was inevitable they meet again. Juliana was grateful the encounter had been delayed this long. "Where is he?" she asked, smoothing her hair.

"Gilbert told him to wait in Mr. MacAllister's study."

Juliana slowly walked toward the study. She opened the door and quietly stepped inside, oblivious of Mary Bridget craning her neck for another look before the door clicked shut.

Nick stood, his back partially turned, staring out at the street. It struck Juliana that in spite of having had different fathers, the two brothers bore an uncanny resemblance to each other. As though sensing her presence, Nick looked over his shoulder. They observed each other in a silence measured by lengthening shadows.

Viewing Nick was like seeing Drew as a young man. Both were dark-haired and of similar height and build. Their features, too, were much alike, but with subtle differences. Nick's face was that of a boy yet to become a man, unmarked by adversity or maturity. It conveyed an openness that Juliana found appealing. In contrast, cynicism had hardened Drew's features. While Nick grew up pampered and secure, Drew had scavenged alleyways for bare essentials. He had survived, but not without paying his dues.

"If you'd rather I go . . . " Nick's voice sounded strained.

"You're Drew's brother. I couldn't ask you to leave."

"You must hate me after what I did."

Embarrassment set Juliana's cheeks ablaze with color. Vignettes of that eventful night played through her mind. Then she thought of Drew, of the joy he brought her, and the final remnants of fear and anger dissipated. "No, I don't hate you," she said quietly.

"You don't know how happy I am to hear that." He smiled, the effect boyish and disarming. "Truth is, I don't remember a single thing about that night. First I recall is Drew hauling me out of bed and threatening to beat me to a pulp. I knew his reputation as a boxer, so it wasn't a threat I took lightly."

Relief left Juliana's knees weak. How awkward a relationship with Nick would be if he had a clear recollection of his amorous escapade. "I'm glad you're here. I gather you and Drew are very close. I've often wondered why you stayed away so long."

"Drew insisted. He said it was up to you to decide whether or not I'd be welcome." Shoving his hands in the pockets of his trousers, he dropped his gaze. "I wouldn't have come today if it wasn't urgent."

A tentative knock on the door was followed by a more authoritative one. Not waiting for a reply, Gilbert entered the study, carrying a heavily laden tray. He sent Nick, who stood at the far end of the room, a stern look, then turned to Juliana. "I took the liberty of bringing tea. If you need assistance, just ring."

"Thank you, Gilbert, that's very thoughtful of you."

The servant set the tea tray on a small table next to Drew's favorite Turkish tufted chair and ottoman. Lowering his voice, he addressed Juliana: "Should Master Nick exhibit any dastardly behavior, I'll be close at hand."

Juliana was both touched and amused by his offer. It was impossible to imagine the spindly old man defending her honor against a robust young male, and yet she knew the intent was sincere. "You're a kind man, Gilbert. Mr. MacAllister is fortunate to have you as a friend."

Gilbert rapidly blinked his faded blue eyes. "Thank you, madam," he replied gravely and then, recalling his composure, straightened. "Ring if you need me," he said again.

Juliana waited until the door clicked shut behind Gilbert before motioning Nick to join her. She sat in the tufted chair and spread a dainty linen napkin across her lap. Nick pulled up another chair for himself. "Tell me, Nick," she said, after pouring a cup of tea and handing it to him, "what urgent business brought you here this afternoon?"

"By all means, Nick," Drew drawled, entering the study in time to overhear Juliana's question, "do tell us what brought you here when I specifically ordered you to stay away unless invited."

The teacup Nick held rattled on its saucer. He stood abruptly, his napkin falling unheeded from his lap.

"What sort of trouble are you in this time?" Drew crossed the study, tossed down a leather portfolio, then rounded his desk and sank into the leather chair behind it.

Juliana glanced uneasily from brother to brother. Drew's expression was cold and formidable, one she was familiar with from earlier times. In comparison, Nick looked nervous, pale, and frightfully young. She couldn't help but feel a wave of pity for the young man. "Perhaps it would be best if I leave you two alone." She rose and moved toward the door. Her hand was on the knob when Drew stopped her.

"Stay, Juliana, please. Somehow I have a suspicion that

what my brother has to say will interest you also."

Juliana sat back down.

Swallowing hard, Nick wiped a bead of perspiration from his upper lip. "I have a confession to make, after which you may very well wish never to see me again."

"Let me be the judge of that." Drew leveled a steely blue gaze at his half brother that looked as lethal as the barrel of a dueling pistol. "Get on with it."

"It's my fault that the story about your illegitimacy got into the newspapers," he said in a low voice. He looked down at the carpet. "I wasn't even sure it would get into print. The chap who interviewed me said he'd have to sell the idea to his editor first. Promised he'd send me a copy of the finished article. At first I thought he'd forgotten about it. Then, later, I was busy studying for midterms, and it slipped my mind altogether. It wasn't until my friend Clarence asked me if I'd heard about AMAC Enterprises going bankrupt that I remembered. Clarence showed me the article. That's when I saw a reference to your being a . . . "

"Bastard," Drew completed the sentence.

Nick squirmed. "I swear I never meant you any harm. I was only trying to help."

"You have a strange way of going about it."

"I probably never told you this, but I'm so damn proud of you." Nick's words came out haltingly. "You've always been my idol. You started with nothing and accomplished so much. So when I finally had a chance to brag about you, I did."

Juliana went over to stand behind Drew. Placing a hand on his shoulder, she felt the tension his body transmitted. "We believe you, Nick," she said, hoping she spoke for both of them.

"Someone is deliberately trying to ruin my chances for

election." Drew slammed his open palm against the desk, the sharp crack making Nick jump. "It started months ago with the lies about my relationship with Juliana. Now this. I can't believe it's coincidence."

A frisson of fear swept over Juliana, chilling her. Hearing Drew speak the words out loud confirmed her own suspicions. There had been times during her stay at the O'Tooles' flat when she had sensed that she was being followed. Then there were the relentless scandals that plagued Drew. She shivered. Was some mysterious person plotting the demise of Drew's fondest dreams? "Who would do such a thing?" she asked.

Drew shrugged, his features grim. "Someone with a great deal to lose if I assume Daniel's assembly seat. But right now I haven't a clue."

Nick plopped onto a chair. "And I, like an idiot, supplied the ammunition."

"It might help if you told us precisely what happened," Juliana said.

Nick seemed eager to unburden himself and, without further encouragement, launched into his account. "This chap claiming to be a reporter came to the campus and looked me up. Said he wanted to do a feature story on Drew MacAllister and thought I might be able to give him a fresh angle. He treated me to dinner and drinks, all the while asking a bunch of questions. Seemed awfully interested in your background, where you grew up, what you were like as a boy. He was curious as to why we had different surnames and wanted to know about your parents. Every time my glass would get half empty, he'd fill it up."

"Go on."

"You know, Drew, how whiskey loosens my tongue.

Before I knew it, the whole story just slipped out. I told him you were a bastard without any idea who your father was and"—he gulped—"how back in Scotland you had to beg and steal in order to survive. Once I realized what I'd said, I tried to take it back, but he told me not to worry. He said when the public knew your whole story they'd admire you even more. That you'd probably win by a landslide."

"What did this reporter look like?" Drew asked. "Did he give a name?"

"He was a mousy little guy with brown hair and a mustache. He called himself Willie Smith. Funny thing," Nick said with a frown. "The whole time I thought he was taking notes, he was really sketching me. He gave the drawing to me when he left. Damn good artist." Nick reached into his jacket pocket and produced a folded sheet of paper. "See for yourself." Carefully he opened it for Drew and Juliana's inspection.

Juliana let out a gasp, unconsciously tightening her grip on Drew's shoulder. The picture of Nick was startlingly lifelike, yet captured his youthful innocence. Her questioning gaze met Drew's.

As though reading her thoughts, Drew opened a desk drawer and pulled out the newspaper sketches of Juliana that had appeared months before. The three of them studied the pictures. Though the subjects were different, the style was identical.

"Good God!" Nick exclaimed in disbelief. "They were all done by the same artist."

"So it would seem," Drew agreed dryly. Going to the sideboard, he picked up the decanter of scotch. "Nick? Juliana? Either of you care to join me?"

"Not me." Nick shook his head emphatically. "I've sworn off alcohol for life. I'll never touch another drop as long as

I live." He glanced at his watch. "If I hurry, I can catch the last train to Boston."

"Come back soon. Perhaps the Christmas holidays will give us time to become better acquainted." Juliana went over to him. At close range, she noticed his eyes were less blue and more silver than Drew's. And more troubled.

"You're sure? I don't want to impose. If my visit causes any problems . . . "

Juliana smiled. "It will distress me more if you don't come."

Nick returned her smile, then sobered as he turned to take leave of his brother. "Drew, I'm horribly sorry for the trouble I caused. I'd do anything if I could change things. You've been more father to me than brother, and this is how I repay you." His posture signaled dejection.

Drew draped an arm over Nick's shoulders and walked him to the door. "Stop worrying. I've weathered worse storms in my lifetime. Besides, I have you to thank for Juliana."

Juliana waited patiently for Drew's return, sensing the two brothers needed a few minutes' privacy. When Drew came back into the study, her heart wrenched with sympathy at his look of weariness. Though he did his best to hide it, the strain of the last week weighed heavily upon him. He sat in his favorite chair next to the forgotten tea tray, leaned his head against the cushion, and closed his eyes. She quickly crossed the room and sank down on the ottoman.

"Poor Nick." Drew sighed tiredly. "Since he was a bairn, I've shielded him from every unpleasantness. Covered up his mistakes. Made excuses for his shortcomings. By doing so, I did the lad a disservice. I realize that now. For the first time in his life, Nick must face the consequences alone."

Juliana rested her head against his knee. "Nick has the

makings of a fine man. You've instilled in him a solid sense of values. Now it's time to stand aside and let him learn how to apply them."

"How did you get so wise?" he asked, stroking her hair.

"I'm not wise at all, my darling. Where you're concerned, my heart governs my head. I'm only relieved that at last the truth is out. It hurt to think you suspected me of broadcasting your secret."

Bending down, he pulled her into his lap. "I never doubted you for a second," he murmured. "You're much too loving, much too loyal . . . " His lips nuzzled the sensitive spot behind her ear.

Twining her arms around his neck, Juliana decided further discussion could wait.

CHAPTER
23

A MUFFLED SOUND CAUGHT JULIANA'S ATTENTION AS SHE came down the stairs. The small dog who followed close behind pricked her ears and cocked her head in a listening attitude. Then nosing past her, the pup scampered down the stairs to the closed door of Drew's study, where she went into a frenzy, alternately barking and scratching the sill.

"Cocoa!" Juliana scolded. "Gilbert is going to be very unhappy if you mark up the wood. It was bad enough when he found you chewing Mr. MacAllister's favorite slippers."

Her reprimand had no effect. If anything, the pup continued her antics with renewed vigor. "Mr. MacAllister isn't in there. See for yourself," she said, opening the door.

Cocoa ran in and stood in the center of the room, her shaggy body tense. Even her one floppy ear seemed perked attentively. Puzzled by her pet's strange behavior, Juliana stepped into the study.

Shadows blanketed the room. The hair at the nape of Juliana's neck prickled. An unpleasant sensation similar to those she experienced on occasion during her stay with the O'Tooles crept over her. Frightened, she glanced about, half expecting to find someone watching her.

But except for the puppy, she was alone. The house was quiet: Gilbert was off seeing to dinner preparations; Mary Bridget hadn't yet returned from an errand to the dressmaker's.

"Silly goose," Juliana muttered, referring more to herself than to the pup. Bolstered by the sound of her own voice, she switched on a lamp.

While the dog sniffed about, Juliana conducted her own inspection. Neat piles of mail and papers rested undisturbed on the desk. Rows of leather-bound books were meticulously aligned on shelves. The table holding several crystal decanters of liquor looked as it always did. She made a mental note to remind Gilbert that Drew's supply of scotch was getting low. Her heart resumed a slower rhythm. Nothing was amiss.

But the pup, it soon became apparent, wasn't so easily appeased. Stopping in front of a small closet, the dog growled and pawed at the wooden door. Juliana reached out to open it just as Drew's voice rang out.

"Anyone home?"

Her intention forgotten, Juliana scooped her pet up into her arms, turned off the light, and hurried out of the study, closing the door behind her. She found Drew hanging his heavy wool overcoat on the coat tree in the entryway.

His face lit up with a smile. "I'm glad I decided to come home for dinner."

"Not as happy as I." Time together had become a treasured commodity, doled out in pittances. She understood why long hours at the office were required, but a continual desire to be near him made all separation painful.

"Show me how glad," he urged.

No further encouragement was necessary. Juliana was in his arms. Her lips opened under his. Driven by a primal urgency, she kissed him with wild abandon. His tongue, sleek and eager, delved into her mouth. With maddening thoroughness, it circled the orifice, the wet velvet rasp tantalizing the smooth inner surface of her cheeks and rippled palate until she purred deep in her throat.

Sandwiched between their bodies, Cocoa yipped in discomfort. Juliana and Drew broke apart. With a self-conscious laugh, Juliana set the dog on the floor. She went immediately to the study door. "Poor Cocoa. She's been acting strangely this evening," Juliana explained in response to Drew's puzzled expression.

"Perhaps she thinks she's found a mouse," Drew offered, draping his arm around her shoulders.

Gilbert arrived to announce dinner. "Mice, sir? In this house?" He seemed horrified by the suggestion. "I'll set some traps immediately."

Juliana suppressed a smile at the thought of the fastidious Gilbert waging an all-out war against a tiny mouse. "In the meantime, Gilbert, would you please take the dog to the kitchen? Perhaps a bone would distract her."

"Certainly, madam." Bending, Gilbert picked up the squirming pup and, holding it at arm's length, marched off.

Drew chuckled. "Between Cocoa and Gilbert, I believe we'll be well protected against an invasion of pesky rodents."

Throughout the meal, Juliana surreptitiously studied her husband. He ate so quickly that Juliana doubted he even tasted the succulent roast chicken, buttered carrots, and potatoes with parsley. While he still seemed tense, she was encouraged by the subtle changes she detected. He smiled more frequently, and his eyes gleamed with challenge rather than dimmed with defeat.

"You seem to be in better spirits." She kept her tone casual. "Does that mean your business affairs are improving?"

"It's still too soon to be sure, but I have reason to be optimistic." He put down his napkin and rose from the table. "I know it's terribly ill-mannered of me to leave you sitting here alone, but I have a stack of papers to review. Can you overlook my rudeness just this once?"

She tried to keep the disappointment from her voice. "Of course. I understand."

Crooking a finger beneath her chin, he forced her to meet his gaze. "I swear I'll make this up to you. If all goes well, we'll have cause to celebrate."

Later Juliana carried these words to a lonely bed. Hoping that Drew might complete his work and join her, she chose a negligee of shimmering mocha satin and rosepoint lace tied with satin ribbons. But when the hands of the ormolu clock met at midnight, she realized the futility of her wish. Putting aside her novel, she extinguished the light.

Willie the Mole furtively opened the closet door and peeked out into Drew's study. Except for that damn mutt, his plan was working perfectly. The sleeping powder he had slipped into MacAllister's liquor had taken hold. Sleeping like the dead he was. Willie chuckled. All that remained was to remove the safety cap from the gas jet, turn on the valve, and take his leave. The gas would do the rest.

His eyes on MacAllister's slumbering form, Willie crept out of his hiding place. He yelped in surprise as a mousetrap, carefully placed next to the closet door, latched on to his foot. He hopped on one leg, trying to free the other, only to succeed in having the mousetrap snap on to his finger.

"Goddammit!" Forgetting the need for quiet, Willie pulled off the trap and flung it across the room. He stuck his bleeding finger into his mouth. A quick nervous glance assured him his victim slept undisturbed by the ruckus. Taking an envelope from his pocket, Willie placed it on Drew's desk, then quickly crossed the study and turned on the gas. The hiss of escaping gas immediately greeted his ears. Nursing his injured finger, Willie took his leave. Boss would be proud of him, he thought.

Juliana wakened with the premonition that something was dreadfully wrong. Her body rigid with an unnamed worry, she drew a calming breath and tried to relax. The space beside her was still empty. The clock now read the hour of one. She stared at the ceiling, trying to recall what had awakened her. Then it came to her. For the second time that day she had been disturbed by a muffled noise coming from downstairs.

Tossing aside the bedclothes, she slipped into her peignoir and went downstairs. She halted before the door of Drew's study. She raised her hand to knock, but changed her mind. Would Drew think her crazed for bursting in on him? Would he be annoyed at the interruption? Should she simply go back to bed? She gnawed her lower lip in indecision.

This is nonsense, she concluded with an impatient toss of her head. What mattered was knowing whether or not he was safe. With this in mind, she flung open the door.

"Drew . . . " His name died on her lips.

He sat slumped over his desk. Scotch pooled on the mahogany surface from an overturned glass and dripped over the edge onto the carpet. Dear Lord, she wondered, had he drunk himself into a stupor?

"Drew!" she called again, louder this time. Still no response. She stepped further inside the study and noticed an envelope propped against an inkwell. A faint but distinctly unpleasant odor pervaded the air. A sibilant hiss whistled ominously. She whirled about. Her eyes darted around the room, seeking the source of the sound. They rested on a brass wall sconce that before the advent of the incandescent lamp had illuminated the room with gaslight. The safety cap lay on the carpet. Deadly gas was escaping into the room.

A half-sob tore from her throat. Then Juliana quickly gathered her wits. Holding the skirt of her negligee over her nose and mouth, she ran over to the wall sconce and closed the gas valve, then raced to the window and pried up the sash. Fresh air. She had to get him fresh air. "Drew, Drew, can you hear me?" she cried, returning and shaking his shoulders. She tugged and pulled at him to no avail. There was no way she could move him by herself. She had to get help.

Holy Mother, please don't let him die, she silently prayed as she sped toward Gilbert's quarters. Frantically she pounded on his door. "Gilbert, wake up! Help me! Please help me!"

The door opened a crack, and Gilbert's sleep-dazed face peered at her. "What is it?" He smothered a yawn.

"A gas leak. Drew's unconscious. We've got to help him." Panic made Juliana almost incoherent. She spun on her heel and raced back to the study, Gilbert close behind.

Between the two of them, they half-lifted, half-pulled, Drew from his chair and then, one on either side, dragged him into the entryway.

Juliana sank to the floor and lovingly cradled Drew's head in her lap. "Please, please, be all right. I love you so much," she crooned. "I couldn't bear to lose you."

His head rolled to one side; his eyelids flickered. Tears

streamed down her cheeks to fall on his face. He opened his eyes, and her heart leapt with relief and joy.

Gilbert peered down at them anxiously. "Madam, shall I ring for a doctor?"

"No," Drew whispered hoarsely. "No doctor."

Juliana was frightened. Had the gas fumes affected his mind? Was he lucid? "But, Drew, you could have died!"

"No doctor." His voice was stronger this time.

Juliana looked at Drew questioningly. The steely resolve in the blue-gray eyes staring back at her removed any shred of doubt. He was not only lucid but in full command of his faculties.

"Help me upstairs." Drew struggled awkwardly to his feet.

"Here, sir, lean on me." Slinging Drew's arm over his shoulder, Gilbert wrapped his own arm about Drew's waist and led him toward the staircase.

Gilbert's thin frame bowed under Drew's heavy weight. Juliana went to Drew's other side and assumed her share of the burden. Laboriously, they climbed the stairs. Once inside the bedroom, Drew collapsed onto the mattress, eyes closed, his face ashen.

"Should I ring the doctor after all, madam?" Gilbert asked nervously.

Without opening his eyes, Drew reached up and caught his wife's hand. "Juliana is the only one I need. She'll look after me."

Gilbert looked at Juliana for guidance. With a small smile of reassurance, she told him she'd call him if need be. After the elderly servant reluctantly departed, Juliana tugged a chair closer to the bed.

"Don't leave me," Drew muttered, renewing his grip on her hand.

Giving his fingers a gentle squeeze, Juliana leaned over to brush a lock of dark hair from his brow. "Never fear, love, I won't leave you. Hush, now," she soothed.

In the long hours preceding dawn, Juliana, her thoughts turbulent, watched her husband sleep. Drew had almost died this night. But why? Had he tried to take his own life, as it appeared? The harder she searched for answers, the more elusive they became. True, he had cause to be despondent. Scandals threatened his political success, then precipitated a financial crisis. Both of these exacted a heavy toll from a proud man. But probably the most painful blow of all was Nick's betrayal. Could these events have combined to drive a man as strong as Drew to a point where life was no longer worth living?

No, she couldn't convince herself of this. Drew was much too brave to seek a cowardly solution.

Cramped from sitting too long in one position, Juliana shifted her weight. Something sharp jabbed into her side. Reaching down, she pulled an envelope from the pocket of her peignoir. She held it for a long time, staring down at her name typed across the front. It was the envelope she had seen propped up on Drew's desk. Funny, in all the confusion, she didn't even recall picking it up.

Finally she found the courage to open it. Two sentences were typed across plain white stationery. She read, then reread, the message: "I am in trouble. Suicide is the only way out—Andrew MacAlister."

Her initial reaction was one of enormous relief. Her belief in Drew was vindicated. He hadn't attempted to take his own life. The missive itself contained the clue.

A second reaction followed in swift succession. Fear dug icy talons into her very soul. A faceless madman had invaded their home and tried to murder her husband.

The sky above Manhattan was streaked with a mélange of rosy hues when Drew awoke. His eyes immediately sought Juliana, who was curled in a chair next to the bed. A tumble of curls the color of wild honey framed her face, which even in repose was both innocent and seductive. A hint of a smile softened his mouth. He remembered that, earlier, teardrops had fallen on his face. Upon opening his eyes, he had found her holding him as tenderly as a newborn. She had looked like an angel then; she looked like an angel now.

Juliana stirred slightly, and a single sheet of paper slipped from her lap. Drew caught it before it touched the floor. Curious, he quickly scanned the contents. Disbelief, then outrage, contorted his features. He crushed the note in his fist.

Frowning, he concentrated on recalling last night's sequence of events. Heartened after reviewing the latest reports on AMAC Enterprises, he had poured himself a scotch. Suddenly he had become groggy. The next thing he recalled was waking on the floor in the entryway with Juliana and Gilbert hovering over him. After reading this note, did Juliana think he had tried to kill himself? Was that why she guarded his bedside? Did she feel she had to protect him from himself?

Drew got up from the bed and paced the length of the bedroom. He had to know her feelings. "Juliana." He spoke so sharply she woke with a start. "I need to hear the truth." He thrust the crumpled note at her. "Do you believe this garbage?"

"Of course not," she replied, stretching and yawning. "Read the note again. Go ahead," she urged when he appeared confused by her request.

He did as she asked, then looked to her for verification.

"We MacAllisters," she said with a smile, "always spell our name with two *l*'s."

Drew's recovery was rapid. Overruling Juliana's objections, he returned to work the following day. Another, more pressing, argument ensued that morning over the breakfast table.

"I wish you'd reconsider," Juliana beseeched. "The police ought to be notified of the attempt on your life."

"For the final time, I don't want them involved. Another whiff of scandal would prove more lethal than a leaking gaslight." He set down his coffee cup and picked up the morning paper. Minutes later he threw it down in disgust.

"More bad news?" Juliana asked worriedly.

"There's an item in the gossip column about my having had lunch at Delmonico's with Victoria. It seems every time she and I meet, word manages to get into print."

Juliana carefully spread marmalade on a slice of toast and refrained from comment.

"There's no truth to the rumors, of course." Drew drained his coffee cup. "But best you hear about them from me rather than another source."

"Can't someone else handle her legal affairs?" Juliana asked, knowing she must sound like a jealous wife.

"Victoria's been out of the country so long she doesn't know another attorney. Think of it as a favor to an old friend."

"Some old friend," Juliana grumbled after he had left for the office. "Why can't he have old friends who are fat and ugly?"

"Were you speaking to me, madam?" Gilbert inquired as he entered the dining room.

Juliana shook her head, embarrassed to be caught talking to herself. "Who was at the door?"

"This message just arrived for Mr. MacAllister." He indicated the pale lavender envelope he carried on a silver tray. "Shall I instruct Jack to deliver it to his office?"

Juliana picked it up. The scented note addressed in a flowing script was obviously from a woman. Victoria Dumouchelle would be her first guess. "I'll see that he gets it."

"Very good, madam. Would you care for more coffee?"

"No, thank you, Gilbert." Juliana retired to the privacy of her bedroom. After telling Mary Bridget she had a headache and didn't wish to be disturbed, Juliana sank down on the bed, envelope in hand.

For fifteen minutes she waged a losing battle with her conscience. Then, despising herself even as she did it, she carefully opened the envelope. As she had suspected, it was from Victoria. What she wasn't prepared for was the message inside. In her note, Victoria reminded Drew of their prearranged assignation for that afternoon at her hotel suite.

Juliana hated herself even more when at the appointed hour she walked down the corridor leading to Victoria's suite. She had no definite plan in mind and wasn't sure what she was going to say or do. Her brain was numbed by the thought of Drew secretly meeting his former lover. All she knew with any degree of certainty was that she would not give her husband up without a struggle.

She was about to knock at the door of suite 1013 when she became aware of voices from inside drifting out through the open transom. She immediately recognized those of Drew and Victoria Dumouchelle. It took her a moment longer to register the fact that what she was overhearing wasn't a lovers' tryst but a quarrel.

"You can't rekindle a spark that died years ago. It's no use, Victoria. Give it up."

"Drew, you don't mean that. You said I spoiled you for other women."

"Find yourself another attorney. Consider me off the case."

"How dare you!" Victoria screeched. "Go back to that slut you picked off the streets. You have so much in common."

"Now you sound like your father's daughter."

Juliana stood rooted to the spot. Drew didn't love Victoria; he loved her! The realization strummed through her veins like a symphony. Victoria meant nothing more to him than a bittersweet memory of a bygone day. How foolish her imaginings had been.

Bemused by the conversation she had just listened to, Juliana was slow to react when the door opened. Drew stood on the threshold. He looked as stunned as she on coming face to face.

Juliana dropped her gaze. Her face burned with shame at being caught eavesdropping. Turning, she began to walk away.

"Wait!" Drew's voice crackled with authority.

Juliana stumbled to a halt. She wanted desperately to disappear, to fade into the woodwork, to be anywhere but where she was. Drew's fingers dug into her arm as he roughly whirled her around. "What are you doing here?"

She flinched at the fury in his expression. "I . . . ah . . . a note came after you left this morning."

"And you opened it?"

She nodded miserably.

"You didn't have faith in me, did you? You didn't believe our love would stand the test?"

Juliana was frightened. She felt Drew slipping away and didn't know how to hold on. "I do have faith in you." She clutched her handbag to keep her hands from trembling. "I didn't trust her. I didn't have enough confidence in myself."

But her painful admission came too late. Drew was gone.

CHAPTER 24

CHRISTMAS WAS ONLY A WEEK AWAY, BUT EVEN VIEWING the spectacularly decorated windows at Macy's that afternoon had failed to lift Juliana's spirits. The entire time she had found herself wishing Drew were there to admire them with her. With a sigh, she carefully placed the black leather gloves she had purchased for Nick in a box and began to wrap them in bright red tissue paper.

Nick planned to spend the holidays with them. Mary Bridget was beside herself at the prospect. During his visit, it would be difficult to pretend there was nothing wrong, when she and Drew were barely speaking.

Juliana found their estrangement intolerable. She knew she had been wrong to go to Victoria's suite, wrong to eavesdrop on their private conversation. She had acted on impulse. If only Drew would give her a chance, she could make him understand. But he was avoiding her. It was almost as though she had ceased to exist, she thought sadly. Almost like the early days of their marriage. When Nick's gift was wrapped, Juliana added it to a small pile beneath the Christmas tree in the parlor.

"Juliana!" The front door burst open.

Drew was home. There was an excitement in his voice that had been absent of late. Hurriedly leaving the parlor, Juliana found him in the entryway. Snowflakes glistened in his dark hair and dusted the shoulders of his overcoat. In one hand he clutched an enormous bouquet of hothouse roses, in the other a bottle of champagne. His expression shifted from contrition to jubilation, then back again.

Juliana stood perfectly still, not daring to move. For one precarious moment, the world stopped spinning on its axis and hung suspended. She sensed that the course of her entire life would be determined by what happened next.

"Can you forgive me, lass, for behaving like a fool?"

Juliana blinked back tears. "I'd forgive you anything." Then, half laughing, half crying, she was where she longed to be—in his arms. "I was afraid I had lost you."

"I was hurt and angry at what I thought was your lack of trust. But I was wrong." He held her tight. "Daniel finally confessed that you invested your entire inheritance in my company. You had faith in me when no one else did."

"I know how much your company means to you. Regardless of what happens, we'll manage. Maybe I can learn to use a typewriter."

Drew picked her off her feet and whirled her around. "I'll buy you a typewriter, two if you like. Anything, just name it. Thanks to you, AMAC Enterprises is solvent."

"Is it really true?" Juliana pulled back so she could see his face. "Do you mean it?"

He kissed her soundly. "Already one of my former partners came by to say he'd like to reinvest. Only this time," he added with a grin, "he promised to provide the money before the contracts were signed."

"Drew, I'm so happy for you."

"We did it, Juliana. Together." He carried her toward

the stairs. A long-stemmed rose dropped unnoticed from the bouquet.

"I'm sorry I behaved like such an idiot where Victoria was concerned."

"Had the situation been reversed, I would have acted the same way," he admitted. "A long time ago I thought Victoria was the love of my life. But when her father discovered our affair, her belief in our future together faltered." He began to climb the stairs. Another rose fell unheeded.

"Victoria's everything I'm not. I kept thinking how she'd make you the perfect wife."

"Seeing you outside her hotel suite, I was suddenly sucked into the past. All I could think of was how Victoria had failed to trust me. Your actions seemed to reflect that same lack of trust. In the heat of anger, I failed to recognize the dissimilarities between the two of you." He paused at the top of the stairs. His lips touched hers in a soft, lingering kiss. "I failed to distinguish gold from glitter."

Using his foot, he pushed open the bedroom door and carried her inside, leaving the door ajar. Two more blooms drifted to the hall carpet. Outdoors, the first winter storm of the season gained momentum, causing the windows to rattle. But inside, the bedroom was warm and cozy, a lovers' bower. A fire crackled in the hearth, and the lamp on the dressing table cast a mellow light. Mary Bridget had thoughtfully turned back the bedcovers.

"For once I'm glad there's a lock on the door. I don't want any interruptions tonight."

Juliana giggled. "There's no need for a lock. Our privacy is ensured. Gilbert's nursing a cold. He's sound asleep with a mustard plaster on his chest and his ears filled with oil of camphor and wads of cotton."

"Poor Gilbert." Drew's wicked smile showed no hint of

sympathy. "How did you get rid of Mary Bridget?"

"She's helping her family decorate their Christmas tree and won't be back till morning. She even took the dog with her as a treat for young Liam." Juliana began to undo his tie.

Drew lowered her feet to the floor. Juliana shifted so that she slid against the length of him. As her body caressed his, it brought the awareness that his manhood was already hard and swollen with desire. The knowledge pleased her. Laughing low in her throat, she pulled off his tie, then held it out and watched it fall.

"Playful, eh?" Drew chuckled. "Most games are more fun with two." He slipped his fingers into her thick amber tresses. His movements deliberate, he searched for the pins and combs securing the sleek coil at the back of her head.

When the last pin had been removed, Juliana arched her neck and slowly swung her head from side to side. Dark gold hair rippled down her back like a bolt of burnished satin. Drew caught a handful of it and, wrapping it around and around his fist, pulled her closer. Juliana bestowed a flirtatious kiss on his lips, one that promised more than it fulfilled. "My turn," she murmured against his lips.

Mimicking the manner of a servant, she relieved him of his overcoat as well as his jacket. Then all traces of servility vanished. She unfastened the buttons of his shirt and slid it off. He wore nothing underneath. His powerful body could have been that of an ancient gladiator. His splendidly mus-cled torso gleamed bronze in the firelight. To Juliana, he was the quintessential male—primitive and exciting. She combed her fingers through the mat of black curly hair that covered his chest. Daringly, she circled one flat dun-colored nipple with the tip of her finger.

He inhaled sharply and jerked away. "That's cheating, lass. Careful or you'll forfeit the game." He turned her around and began unfastening the long row of tiny fabric-covered buttons at the back of her dress. Bending his head, he traced his progress down the curve of her spine with the tip of his tongue.

Juliana's eyelids drifted shut at the tantalizing wet rasp. Reality spun away in a whirlwind of sensation. Her dress fell to her feet with a soft rustle.

With maddening slowness, Drew removed her petticoats, bustle, and corset until she stood wearing only a lace-trimmed chemise and drawers.

Her impatience grew.

One hand splayed across her midriff, Drew pulled her hard against him so that her body fit his, snugly, perfectly.

Her head lolled to one side. He nipped at her neck with his teeth, and she moaned. Like a hot wind blowing across the Mojave, his breath swept her overheated flesh. And like a desert breeze, it only intensified the heat.

Just as Juliana turned within the circle of his arms, the lamp on the dresser blinked once, then went out.

"The storm must have downed a power line." Passion deepened the timbre of his voice. He kissed her, a long drugging kiss that had her clinging to his shoulders for support. "We'll make love by firelight. All night long . . . "

"Not quite," a strange male voice intruded.

A startled cry escaped Juliana. Drew's arm tightened around her protectively. "Who's there? What do you want?" he demanded from the faceless figure lurking in the hallway outside the room.

Disembodied laughter rang through the darkened house. At its sound, Juliana felt an icy chill of fear. Shivering violently, she huddled even closer to Drew.

Drew's gaze darted around the room, seeking a weapon of some sort. A pistol waited in the bottom drawer of his desk—but his desk was downstairs in the study. His eyes rested on the iron poker propped against the fireplace. If he could reach it . . . He sidestepped in that direction.

"Stay where you are," the voice ordered. "You'll move when I tell you to and not a minute sooner."

Drew stalled for time. "If it's money you're after . . . "

"Rest easy. It's not your money that's in jeopardy; it's mine." Herbert Masters pushed the door wide open and sauntered into sight. In his left hand he held four long-stemmed red roses, in his right a long-barreled steel-gray revolver.

"Masters! What the devil?"

Herbert Masters? Juliana's befuddled brain was trying to make sense out of the bizarre turn of events. Why was Victoria Dumouchelle's father here in their bedroom? And why was he carrying a gun?

"You left an easy path for me to follow." Masters casually tossed the flowers toward the bed. "Hope you don't mind me letting myself in. Any second-rate burglar could have picked the lock on the basement door."

"What are you planning to do?" Juliana forced the question past the lump in her throat.

Masters's gaze was riveted to her scantily clad body. The firelight behind her made her fine batiste undergarments nearly transparent. His tongue passed over his lips in a lascivious fashion. "As good as they were, Willie's pictures didn't do you justice, my girl."

"Damn you, Masters." Drew's voice held a cutting edge. "You'll rue the day you dared look at my wife that way."

"Brave words for a dead man."

Juliana gasped at the implication. "You can't mean that."

"Can't I?" A cold smile twisted Masters's mouth. "I tried everything else, but nothing worked. This is a last resort. I hired Willie to follow you and report anything unusual. Then I enlisted the help of the press in my scandal campaign, but to no avail. MacAllister, you bastard, you always managed to turn things to your own advantage." He advanced farther into the room, his heavyset body blocking their escape. "Thought I'd make you look bad by tricking your wife into making a suffrage speech to a bunch of whores, but that backfired, too."

"I thought I smelled a rat in that affair," Drew snarled.

"You came off looking like a hero, and your wife didn't fare badly either. Figured I had you beat when Willie found out you're a bastard. The news almost forced you into bankruptcy. Almost! Damned if I know how you pulled that one out of the fire."

"Why do you hate me so?" Drew asked. "Is it because of Victoria?"

"I ought to have killed you then. It sickened me to know someone of Victoria's background would cheapen herself for a guttersnipe. No way was I going to allow you to marry my daughter. Sent her packing to France the minute I learned what was going on."

"That was years ago, Masters. Why persist in your campaign to destroy me?"

"Because money is even more important to me than my daughter's honor. I stand to lose everything I've worked for—millions—once you're elected to fill Tennant's shoes. You could ruin me."

Drew frowned. "How could I possibly do that?"

"You signed your own death warrant when you told me you wanted to head a committee to investigate government contracts. With you nosing around, it wouldn't take long to discover I've been receiving substantial remuneration on contracts for years. You might even discover certain bribes

I paid out for winning no-bid government contracts. By the time you finished, not only would I be penniless, but I'd spend my last years rotting in jail."

"You're the one responsible for the attempt on Drew's life?" Juliana ventured.

"No, dear girl, that bungled affair was Willie's doing, not mine. The incompetent fool! Thought he was being clever getting the job done without bloodshed."

Drew's hand balled into a fist at his side. "You'll never get away with this, Masters."

Herbert Masters threw back his head and laughed. "Oh, but you're wrong, MacAllister. Dead wrong!" He laughed. "It'll look like a domestic quarrel that ended in murder and suicide. After all those rumors circulating about you and my daughter, no one will think it strange you and your bride argued."

The man's calm was frightening, far more so than any nervousness or agitation would have been. Juliana instinctively pressed closer to Drew, but he moved away slightly as though wanting distance.

Masters leveled the gun barrel first at Drew, then at Juliana. "Now which of you wants to die first?"

A low hum commenced in Juliana's ears, making her light-headed. Herbert Masters wasn't simply crazed, he was truly evil. He meant to cold-bloodedly murder both her and Drew.

Drew took a half-step forward. "You can shoot me first."

"How noble," Masters sneered, aiming the revolver at Drew's head.

In mute horror, Juliana watched Herbert Masters's finger tighten on the trigger. The instant before the shot exploded Drew shoved her to the floor and took a rolling dive toward the fireplace.

Masters cursed. Assuming a wide-legged stance, he aimed again, both hands gripping the weapon. Juliana screamed just as Drew sent the poker slashing upward. Masters saw the blow coming and turned his shoulder to deflect it. The gun went off a second time, the bullet smashing into the mantel.

Drew sprang to his feet, reached down, caught Juliana's arm, and half led, half dragged her from the bedroom. They ran down the hallway toward the stairs, familiarity guiding their footsteps in the dark. Herbert Masters's footfalls pounded after them.

An orange fireball blazed down the stairwell, followed by a thunderous explosion. The bullet struck Drew. He buckled beneath the blow, the impact sending him tumbling down the stairs with Juliana in his wake to land in a heap.

"Bastard!" Masters yelled. "No sense in running. I took the precaution of locking the doors. The keys are in my pocket."

Recovering first, Juliana untangled herself. She had no idea where Masters was at the moment. "Drew," she whispered frantically, nudging him when he was slow to stir. Her fingers came away sticky. "Oh, dear Lord, you're hurt."

"Forget me," Drew panted. "There's a gun . . . bottom drawer . . . desk."

Masters disappeared into the bedroom, then returned using a splinter of kindling as a torch. He confidently advanced down the hall. Juliana scrambled to her feet. She fled into the study, tripping over the ottoman in the dark.

"One down, one to go," Herbert Masters crowed, spying Drew's crumpled form. "We'll see whether you're dead or just playing 'possum."

The heavy thud of a boot striking flesh brought bile

to Juliana's throat. She placed a hand over her mouth to keep from retching. There was no answering response from Drew, not even a groan.

Tears streamed down her cheeks. Juliana picked herself up off the floor, scrambled across the study, and hunched behind Drew's desk. She blocked out the thought of Drew lying at the foot of the stairs. He wasn't dead. He wasn't. She refused to acknowledge the possibility. It was up to her to save them both.

She heard Masters search the dining room, parlor, and finally move toward the study. She peered out cautiously, then ducked back. The torchlight cast grotesque shadows on the walls. She waited in growing panic as the room grew brighter and brighter from the advancing flare of light.

"I know you're in here," Herbert called from the doorway. "Why not give up gracefully?"

Juliana very carefully eased open the bottom drawer of the desk. Inside, just where Drew had said it would be, was a pearl-handled revolver. She picked it up. The gun felt small, heavy, and cold. She had never fired a weapon before. But all one had to do, she had observed, was point the barrel, cock the hammer, and pull the trigger.

"Get out from behind the desk," Masters ordered. "It would be a pity to ruin a fine piece of furniture with bullet holes."

Juliana stuck her head out. Masters stood limned in the light of the burning stick of kindling, squinting into the shadowy recesses of the study. Her slight movement drew his attention. Grinning, he raised his arm and fired.

Juliana squeezed her eyes shut and fired back. She opened them again at the sound of scuffling. In the dim light, she saw Drew wrestling with Masters for possession of the gun. The torch smoldered on the floor nearby. Juliana rushed forward and scooped it up before it could do any damage. Herbert Masters and Drew were locked together, partners in a macabre dance. The men were evenly matched in weight, but because of Drew's injury, Masters held the advantage. Not daring to breathe, Juliana watched Drew grasp Master's wrist and force it down. His face was pale and streaked with perspiration. Blood trickled from a wound in his side.

The gun went off. Each second that followed seemed an aeon. No one moved. They could have been three figurines immortalized by a photographer's flash. Then, slowly, Herbert Masters sagged to the floor. His lifeblood pumped from a gaping hole in his chest.

Drew slumped against the door frame. He held an arm up invitingly. Juliana needed no coaxing. She hurried to him and was enfolded in his loving embrace. She buried her head in his chest, her body quivering with the aftershocks of terror. He held her gently, tenderly, his cheek resting against her hair.

"I was afraid he had killed you," she said, shuddering. "To lose you would be to lose my heart."

"Just as I lost mine months ago."

Juliana tilted her face up to his. Tears clouded her vision, their crystal haze making her eyes sparkle more brilliantly than the yellow diamond on her finger.

"Goodness gracious!" Gilbert bustled forward, cotton batting dangling from his ears, a lighted candle in one hand. "I thought I heard a sound."

Just then the lights went on. Gilbert's eyes grew round in astonishment as he took in Juliana's dishabille, Drew's bloody torso, and Herbert Masters's lifeless body. "Goodness gracious," he repeated. "May I be of assistance, sir?"

"Your appearance is timely." Drew's mouth twitched in wry amusement. "Please ring the police and inform them that Mr. Masters has met with an unfortunate accident. Ask them to come immediately."

Gilbert started to do as bidden, his plaid flannel robe flapping about his ankles.

"And, Gilbert," Juliana called after him, "ring for a doctor. Mr. MacAllister's been injured." The look she gave Drew told him that although she had been overruled once, this time she was in charge. Placing her arm around Drew's waist, she helped him up the stairs.

It was nearing midnight when the police finished their investigation and left. After examining Drew, the doctor declared that except for a broken rib Drew's injuries were minor. The gunshot wound was superficial.

The storm's fury was spent, though snow continued to drift downward, cloaking the city in a pristine beauty. Peace and tranquillity reigned within the brownstone as well. Juliana turned out the light and slipped beneath the sheets to snuggle next to Drew, her head nestled in the hollow of his shoulder.

For a long while both drew comfort in knowing they were out of harm's reach. Uppermost in their minds was the knowledge that their lives had nearly been sacrificed to satisfy an evil man's greed. Along with this came a vast sense of gratitude that they had been spared.

"Masters taught me a lesson," Drew said reflectively. "Like him, I placed too much value on material wealth. Then you entered my life." A smile played upon his lips. "It wasn't until I encountered a beautiful maid asleep in a sylvan glen that I recognized my true heart's desire. I love you, lass, and always will."

Brimming with love, Juliana returned the smile. *Always*. The word sang throughout her being. Always meant forever.

CHAPTER
25

January 1888

THREE WEEKS SEEMED LIKE THREE YEARS. THAT WAS HOW long it had been since Drew had left on an extended business trip. But tonight the waiting would be over.

Juliana dressed with care in the new gown Drew had sent her. It had arrived just that morning with a card that read, "For a special occasion. Wear it tonight—for me. All my love, Drew." The dress was a masterpiece of pale apricot silk adorned with delicate lace and cinched at the waist with satin rosebuds. It was lovely enough to be a wedding gown.

At precisely seven o'clock, she was to meet Drew at an undisclosed location. She had no inkling of his plans.

"Jack's waiting out front with the carriage," Mary Bridget announced, poking her head around the bedroom door. "No fair asking him a bunch of questions."

Juliana sighed in exasperation. Drew had apparently enlisted the aid of the entire household staff in carrying out his surprise. "I promise not to pry." After giving her reflection a final inspection, she picked up the fur-lined cape Drew had given her for Christmas and hurried out.

Mary Bridget smothered a nervous giggle as she

handed Juliana her muff. "Mr. Drew's meeting you this way is so romantic."

"Don't bother waiting up," Juliana said as she left.

Everyone was acting strangely this evening, Juliana mused as she sank into the carriage's velvet cushions. As if the entire world, with the exclusion of her, were privy to a secret.

Her thoughts drifted as the carriage slowly wound through traffic-clogged streets. It was a new month, a new year. She wondered what changes it would bring. Would Drew be elected assemblyman? The scandals had undoubtedly hurt him, but oddly enough Herbert Masters' attempt on their lives had won them an outpouring of public sympathy. November was still many months away. Drew's determination and charm would place him in good stead at the polls. Pity women didn't have the right to vote. She'd love nothing more than to be able to cast her ballot for her husband. In the meantime, however, she would continue to speak out on her behalf of woman suffrage. Someday perhaps . . .

"We're here, miss," Jack sang out.

Juliana peered out the carriage window, astonished to find that the new Saint Patrick's Cathedral was their final destination. "Are you sure this is the correct address?"

"Quite sure, ma'am," Jack replied cheerfully.

Her mouth opened, but before questions formed, Bertie Lattimer, his face wreathed in a cherubic smile, swung open the carriage door. "Bertie! You're in on this, too?"

"I wouldn't have missed the opportunity for the world." Bertie assisted her from the carriage and, placing her hand in the crook of his arm, escorted her up the front steps of the cathedral.

A young priest met them in the vestibule. "The

archbishop sent me to hear your confession. If you'll follow me. . . "

Totally confused, Juliana looked to Bertie for an explanation. He merely smiled and shrugged his shoulders. She quickened her pace to catch up with the priest. "My confession, Father? Whatever for?"

The priest appeared surprised by the question. "Why, it's customary, of course, before a wedding."

"Whose wedding?"

"Yours." He stepped into one of the confessionals in the transept of the cathedral.

More confused than ever, Juliana stepped inside and knelt down. "Bless me, Father . . . " Crossing herself, she easily recalled the Catholic prayers she had said since childhood.

"Go, my child, and sin no more."

With the priest's absolution still in her ears, she left the confessional. She looked around and noticed a group of people congregated in a side chapel near the front of the vast cathedral. An organ played softly; flames danced atop a host of candles. The sweet scent of roses perfumed the air. Bertie waited for her with his ever-present smile.

"Bertie, I don't understand what's going on. Who's getting married?"

"Drew arranged for the two of you to be remarried." Bertie patted her arm affectionately. "He knows how much your faith means to you, and doesn't want to keep you from it."

"Drew arranged all this?" Juliana still couldn't comprehend what was about to take place.

"Yes, my dear. Right down to seeing that the banns were published. The archbishop himself will perform the ceremony." Bertie gently drew the dazed young woman toward the chapel. "We wouldn't want to keep the archbishop waiting, now, would we?"

Mary Bridget came up to take Juliana's cape and muff. She quickly pinned a wispy veil of Valenciennes lace in her hair, then handed her a bouquet of yellow roses, the same flowers that had composed her bridal bouquet once before.

Juliana felt herself under scrutiny. Looking around, she saw the pews filled with friends. The entire O'Toole family was present, including Katie who looked much happier now that Sean was coming home. According to Mary Bridget, Sean had written begging Katie's forgiveness and vowing to end his errant ways. When Maura caught Juliana's eye, she excitedly pointed to her engagement ring, then at the young man next to her. Jamie Flynn, Juliana assumed with a smile. Emma was there, of course, and even Judge Spears, who had performed the first ceremony. Nick was present, too, along with Jack Burrows and Gilbert and Daniel Tennant.

At a given signal, the music changed. Juliana glanced toward the altar, her golden gaze captured by silver-blue. Drew, appearing as arrogant and handsome as he had the first time she saw him, stood tall and straight next to the archbishop. But Juliana had divined the true character behind the arrogance—and in so doing had lost her heart.

Her head high, her gaze never wavering, she went to him, eagerly and joyously. The ceremony began; the vows were repeated.

"Now, lass, we're truly wed," Drew said softly in a voice no one could overhear, "before God and man." The statement was reminiscent of one spoken on a sunny afternoon in July.

"Before God and man," she repeated. Love shone from

her like a beacon; it illuminated her smile, glowed in her eyes.

Arm in arm, they turned away from the altar and began to walk up the aisle. Drew had gifted her with candlelight and roses, music and dear friends. But Juliana's smile grew misty as she thought of his greatest gift of all. The child growing within her.